krishna fluting

KRISHNA FLUTING

JOHN BERRY

The Macmillan Company
New York   1959

w

The Macmillan Company, New York
Brett-Macmillan Ltd., Galt, Ontario

Printed in the United States of America

Library of Congress catalog card number: 59-13780

to my mother

In this book everything has been invented except the truth. If there is no truth, there is no book. If there is no invention, there is no book. Who can be offended by the truth? Who can be offended by invention?

contents

Contents

krishna fluting

◇⊙ "I was born to rule over principalities; instead I suffer privation. Somewhere along
the line the papers proving my right to rule were
lost. They would have made my inheritance so
easy! Instead of suffering as I do now, I should be
served and treated with magnanimity. I am so
piqued at the loss of the papers that I am unable
to show the infallible signs of noble birth which
are also rightfully mine, namely, magnanimity and
service."

—*The Pious Puzzles of Ananda Mahadev*

one

"'Fools and desperate men shall come to me.'" The young holy man from the plains stood before seven Tibetan women, begging bowl outstretched, an invitation, not clamorous. A topknot of long hair, bleached and reddened by exposure to sun and rain, was all he wore; but, being conscious only of the great Self, he was not self-conscious. Priestly markings of sandalwood paste gleamed on his forehead, giving him a roguish look. The enormous dark eyes of the forest philosopher, wide set like those of some other forest creatures, smiled at the woman who had called him a fool. He quoted further from holy writ: "'Even dogs and women shall come to me.'"

"I come, Sannyasi!" One of them ducked her head, whinnying, showing long, betel-stained teeth.

The others laughed at this sally. "Which of your gods says that, Sannyasi?"

"Lord Krishna, of whom thy gods, too, are a slight emanation, my mothers."

Several small coins dropped into the bowl by way of insurance. "For thy Lord Krishna, then—a slight emanation of our Lord Buddha."

As he blessed them and passed on down the mountain, one of the women whispered to the others. Squatting there, hugging their knees, they rocked with naughty laughter. "But he has taken the vow of chastity!" "How do you know?" "They always do, like the Yellow Lamas." "What a waste!" "Not like our Purple Lamas!" "If Liliu gets hold of him—" "Oh, ho! Ah, ha! She will make a Purple Lama of him." "No, no, she is a Bon Po, a devil worshiper. She will take him

3

down to Hell with her." There was a moment of awkward silence during which they clicked their Buddhist rosaries.

They were waiting by the roadside, as always, in the middle of Tashiling—"the place of blessing"—a town that falls like an arrested avalanche down the face of a mountain in the eastern Himalayas. Although they were sitting on the bottom step of the local bank building, they carried their entire family wealth on their persons, in the form of magnificent gold earrings. Shaped like small chandeliers, these were heavy enough to pull the lobes of the ears down—a Buddhist beauty mark and wishful sign of longevity. Their broad, robust faces were weather-beaten. Deep laughter wrinkles stood ready about their bright, crinkly eyes. Over her high-collared wraparound dress each one wore an apron from waist to ankles, with horizontal rainbow stripes, and heavy necklaces, and an amulet—a brass and pewter box containing charms and prayers and a horoscope cast by the priest on the day of her birth.

Sometimes hilarious, sometimes secretive, they watched and commented as delicate Nepalese women passed by, small-boned Lepchas, Bhutias, Eurasians, Marwaris, talkative Bengalis, a few turbaned Sikhs; and once they fell silent as a tall, blanched skeleton of an Englishman with snow-white hair drifted by like a wraith of the past.

Suddenly they leaned forward to listen. In the distance they heard the sound of a motor laboring up the mountain road; growing louder and louder as it came into town, the noise began to splay out in a familiar pattern of directions, volumes and pitches, along alleys, between buildings. They were ready for it as it came charging around a bend in the road, downhill by the post office. A desperate-looking station wagon, steam pouring from its radiator, gasped, backfired and collapsed, exhausted, just below the Bank of India. It had chinned itself into the Himalayas, nine thousand feet in fifty miles, from Dwaraka, where the plains of Bengal end.

The tough little Gurkha driver, looking tired but chipper, jumped out and began to untie the baggage, which was lashed to the rear of the car. A tall sahib without a hat, in khaki shorts and sandals, disentangled himself from the Indian passengers, climbed out, leaned against the baggage to relieve the strain on the ropes.

"Upper Mazumdar Lane?"

"That side, Sahib." The driver waved at a flight of wooden stairs that sliced through the embankment and continued on up the mountainside.

Two iron boxes and a canvas bedroll emerged from the heap of luggage, tumbled into the road. The Tibetan women seized them and began to scuffle among themselves, laughing but arguing fiercely. Each woman wanted to take all three objects. Three women succeeded in getting one each. Quickly throwing a loop of rags around their burdens, they hoisted them up on their backs and cinched them there with cloth bands passed around the top of their foreheads. Yelling happily, they started off.

"Put that down!" the sahib shouted at one of them in Hindi. "It's too heavy for a woman!"

"Not this woman, Sahib! Climb on top! What are women for?" As she twisted her neck to grin at him, her headband slipped and the iron box thudded down in the middle of the road. A British Land-Rover coming down the mountain stopped while the coolie woman retrieved her burden, the sahib helping her, scowling however.

"Sorry!" He looked up at the Land-Rover. An Indian girl at the wheel stared at him unsmilingly, clutched the blue-and-gold border of her sari and drew it across her face. As he smiled at the incongruity—and because he knew her—her eyes flashed, inhumanly big, and the Land-Rover leaped at him. He stepped aside, received a faltering look from her as she passed. Perhaps her foot had slipped off the clutch. . . .

The three coolie women, with his luggage, bounded up the stairs like mountain goats, turning off in the wrong direction at the first crosspath. The sahib took the stairs three at a time, shouting at the women. They disappeared up a path along a row of houses with flower gardens in front. He stopped and lit a cigarette. "God damn their leathery necks to hell," he said, reflectively, with a kind of admiration.

A thin, dark-haired woman in European dress edged toward him through a garden. "Lost your coolies?" It was an odd, singsong voice. As he nodded, she turned and barked an order at a Nepali youth who was working among her flowers. Dropping his hoe, he raced up the path after the Tibetan women.

"He'll bring 'em back," she said. "These natives, you can't trust 'em. No moral fibers, no brains. A lot of junglies, that's what we British call 'em. Junglies." Peering stealthily at him out of her mynah-bird eyes, she pretended to pick an insect off a little rose tree. "American, eh? Same as we British. Would you be Mr. Peter Bruff?"

"Yes." He did not ask how she knew.

"How do." She moistened her lips, pushed her dark, wavy hair back. "I'm Mrs. Dutton. Monica Dutton . . . I say, it must be beastly hot on the plains."

"It is. Beastly hot."

"I can always tell when it's beastly hot down there, because all we Europeans come up here. I live here. I own all these houses—and those—and those—" She gestured vaguely, first at the pretty cottages along the path, then farther down the mountain, over corrugated iron roofs, ugly but practical where there is heavy rainfall. Everything was up and down—bicycles would be impossible. No two houses stood at the same level. "That is, I manage them."

"Where do you suppose my baggage is by now?" Peter Bruff asked.

"It's coming." She glanced obliquely at him. "Over there I have a lovely bungalow, quite secluded—just for you."

"Thanks; my friends are expecting me."

"You won't like it up there with Mr. Scott. He's going to have an Indian in the same house with him, and you know how they are—noisy, nasty, thieving creatures—"

"Don't worry," he said in a low voice, and there was real commiseration in it; "I'm part Indian, too."

Monica Dutton concentrated on a pink rose which had suddenly become infested with insects too small to be seen. Her hand shook. "Don't ever say such a thing, Mr. Bruff," she said in a stricken voice. "Ever!"

The Nepali boy came into view with the Tibetans in tow. All four were chatting animatedly, sweating and panting.

"If I could get a good price for my property, I'd sell out and go home—to U.K.," Monica Dutton was saying. "After all, I'm English. I had a Spanish grandmother."

"Fine people, the Spanish," Peter Bruff murmured, bracing himself for the Tibetans.

"Everything's ruined since we British left. The communists are

going to take over. The Indians—everything's going to hell! You
Americans could rule India. Why don't you?"

"No time."

"This bungalow—it's yours for nothing. It's all ready for you.
There's a cook—"

"Thank Liliu Acquileia for me."

The three coolie women approached, giggling and dragging their
bare feet with embarrassment, but watching Monica Dutton as if
for a sign. Peter Bruff dropped his cigarette and firmly wrested the
heaviest box from one of them. Ignoring her squalls of protest, he
hoisted it onto his shoulder. Sedately, balancing the box, he led the
procession on up the mountain.

Monica Dutton widened her finely flaring South Indian nostrils in
disapproval. "Daft," she muttered. "Fair daft!" She began to caw at
the gardener in Nepali. When Peter Bruff had disappeared, she
walked swiftly up the lane the Tibetan women had taken, but turned
off on a narrow trail that zigzagged steeply down the mountain.
Without pausing, almost running at times, she descended farther
and farther, down narrow lanes where vehicles were impossible.
Few Indians lived here, no Eurasians, but Chinese and Tibetans.
Beyond the lower Chowrasta, the market place, was a warren of
wooden houses, long shanties, roofs joined together, alleys and by-
paths a few feet wide running between them, garbage in the gutters,
mangy dogs slinking away, and many, many children, dirty, ragged,
and jolly: beautiful children, and each of them with little twin
serpents from nostril to lip.

Monica trotted swiftly down a long, narrow passageway with
doors opening into apartments and connected houses on either side.
There were smells of cooking, of spices, curry and rancid butter,
grease and smoke and meat, rotting and cooking; and, above all, the
proud, magnificent odor of packed Tibetan humanity—*foetor tibeti-
cus*—the never bathing. At the end of this passageway was a heavy
door. Here Monica stopped. She did not knock, Western fashion,
but scratched on the door with her fingernails. A sullen half-caste
boy let her in. He had near-red hair and green eyes that slanted
rather, and high cheekbones; the mouth had a bruised look, but
there were no external scars.

The room, in semiobscurity, lighted by a glaring electric bulb that hung from the ceiling, was furnished in an expensive confusion of tastes, Tibetan and Chinese, Indian and European. Monica stood uncertainly, looking about her; then she half bowed, her body remaining in a kind of crouch; a servile, fawning expression crept across her face, as an inner door opened.

two

Balu, the servant, looked out of a window on Upper Mazumdar Lane, rolled his exaggerating eyes around on their whites, and shot through the house on short, sturdy bowlegs. "Sahib!" he shouted. "He is here—*right now!*"

The auburn-haired man, crouched over Whitney's *Sanskrit Grammar*, straightened up and took off his reading glasses, grimacing as the noise of banging and howling reached his ears. Opening the door that led out on the veranda, he found Peter Bruff settling with the Tibetan women. They were demanding triple pay, not only because they had got lost owing to his insufficient directions, but because he had hurt the feelings of one of them by taking the box away from her. Presently they laughed, accepted the money he offered, and backed away, giggling and whispering; for they had just participated, as it were, in a warm greeting: instead of the curious ritual of the handshake, the sahibs had embraced like ordinary people: first on the right side, then on the left side.

Already Balu was dragging a big brass kettle of boiling water from the kitchen into the bathroom. While Peter Bruff got out of his traveling clothes, Tino poured whisky, set Peter's glass within reach, by the soap, and began stalking restlessly through the house, drinking and humming. From time to time he looked in. Dipping a brass mug first into hot water, then into cold, Peter sluiced it over himself, soaped and rubbed with a fiber sponge, sluiced some more, Indian fashion. The water drained off through a hole in the wall, the floor being set at an angle for this purpose. Balu held his whisky for him— with averted eyes, for in post-British India the sight of a truly naked adult tends to be either sacred, as in the case of holy men, or insult-

9

ing, but it is seldom to be taken lightly. Furtively Balu noted that the sahib wore a short, heavy black cord around his neck, and suspended from it was a tiny square of gold, with the sacred Sanskrit syllable OM—Peace—on it. A blasphemy indeed! Sanskrit and Peace were reserved for born Brahmans only, and this sahib was not even wearing a sacred thread over his shoulder. Well, at least—Balu checked swiftly—he was not a miserably foreshortened Muslim! Krishna had been more than generous.

"How long do you anticipate that it will take you to bathe?" Tino asked through a cigarette.

Peter Bruff's scalp, forehead, and ears moved back, accessory to his grin—his teeth very white in the swarthy face. At the moment, he looked to be about fifteen, around the face. "Ten minutes," he said.

"Seems rather a long time." Tino resumed his pacing, drinking and smoking. Under his breath he hummed the *Dies Irae*. With a few changes he might have been a cardinal. "I expected a corpse," he said almost reprovingly. "I thought you were finished last year, after Tibet. It's unseemly."

"What is?"

"Oh, that you should do such things with impunity. . . . Don't!" he winced half-humorously as Peter yawned, stretching his very handsome and capable physique in all directions. "If you want to please me, don't remind me of how I am."

"How are you?"

"Let's just leave it at that. I live the life of the mind." Then he told Peter about his work. It was summer vacation at Bharat University down on the plains, where he taught, and it got hot there, and he came to Tashiling which he disliked. Why didn't he go to Kalimpong or Darjeeling? Because—he faltered for only a second, then went on smoothly—Tashiling was cooler, and he could concentrate more easily on the book he was writing: "Varieties of Social Concern in the *Bhagavad-Gita* and the *Divina Commedia*, a Comparative Study." This would be followed by a book comparing the theologies, then by one on the aesthetics of the two great metaphysical poems. He hoped Peter, as a poet, would help him out from time to time.

Peter sat on a stool, and Balu hurled water on him and scrubbed his back, making him totter. "There was a French lady," Peter said delicately, "a teacher at the Ashram—Mlle. de—"

"Rosière. That was a mistake," Tino said. "I shouldn't have told you. It never would have worked out. She's a Buddhist. I'm a Catholic."

"Whisky." Peter's arm reached out blindly, supplicating, found the glass. It was the first time he had heard Tino make an issue of his religion. "I take it, she's still in Tashiling?"

"You can take it, and—it makes me uncomfortable to talk about her with a—naked person!" Tino took their glasses and went out. Bringing them back refilled, he said, "You'll be going down to the Ashram right away, I suppose?"

"*Nischoi*—I must."

"Your dharma, no doubt—to look for the python that got Lady Edith's cook and those two villagers? They call it Kaliya, by the way."

"They always do," said Peter. "He's the Serpent-King. Lady Edith wrote that she's feeling 'rather pipped' or she'd shoot it herself. That means she's dying."

"It's inevitable," Tino said with veiled sarcasm, "that she should summon you from Kashmir to do the job. You see, there were no men here—only man-eaters and women."

"I suppose I'd better see Aunt Mary tonight." Peter sounded grim.

"Yes, better to get it over with. She'll expect you to do the right thing by the woman you brought back from Tibet, Liliu—"

"What the hell do you expect me to do?" Peter snapped. "I got her into India, didn't I? I got her kid brother into the Ashram, didn't I?"

"I don't expect you to do anything"—Tino was suave now—"but the general opinion is that you've come back to acknowledge the boy as your son and to marry this Liliu—or Pema—that's her real name, isn't it?"

"That would be why Indira snubbed me. Lady Edith's assistant. Just now, down on the road. I have business with her, too."

"Her, *too?*" Tino laughed incredulously.

"Her brother was my friend. I need her help with some manuscripts he left me. Don't look so ironical—it isn't becoming. I'm surprised you swallowed the story, Tino. The boy's name is Gori

Govinda, and he's Liliu Acquileia's half-brother, not her son, and he's half Russian—they had to change their names, can't you see?"

"Acquileia! Sounds Catholic. Ought to be a law. . . . The story goes that she nursed you back to health, and that, in gratitude—"

"The story is wrong." He glanced keenly at Tino. "She's a witch, and she poisoned me on the way back from Tarok Dzong. . . . If she ever comes near me again, I—shall tell her that she has done me a grave disservice." He began toweling himself furiously, as if to efface the memory his skin might have of her.

Again Tino began to pace about, more quickly now, as if he were stronger for having shaken his friend's poise.

Standing before the mirror in his room, brushing his short, thick black hair, Peter was for a moment intensely aware of his own features, because Tino, behind him and to one side, seemed to be studying him rather piercingly. Was he looking for the conflict of races in him? If so, he had better not get in the line of fire. Peter glowered at himself: brown, sunburned face with broad forehead, not very high; the mouth wide, tense, mulberry-colored, lips full; chin cleft a little off center; jaw irregular but strong, lean; wide blue-gray eyes, much too light, with the eyelashes of a horse, black; heavy eyebrows meeting over a blunt, handsomely crumpled, broken nose; a small white scar, partially interfering with one eyebrow, gave him, at the moment, a slightly fiendish look of concentration.

"You have a touchingly ugly nose."

Peter exhaled, smiled slowly, acknowledged the insult as the caress for which it was intended. Delicately he curried the wings of the black fell that spread across his chest like the shadow of a big bird; then he laid the brush down. They drank. "I am an ugly man," he said.

"Your aunt is ugly too," Tino said cheerfully, to improve the moment.

"No, there I disagree. You have to be able to appreciate granite."

"That's probably it. I'm indifferent to nature. But I admire your Aunt Mary. I admire Philadelphia Quakers. They're the extreme left, as Catholics are the extreme right. We understand each other."

"I'm not a Quaker; you're not a Catholic."

Tino shrugged, relativistic, took a turn around the room, and drifted out, leaving Peter to dress. In his own room Tino stood for some time with his back to the mirror. Suddenly he whirled around and glared at himself. Opening his eyes as wide as he could, he drew his lips back, making as many wrinkles and exposing as many of his teeth as possible, until he felt that he was sufficiently repulsive. However, he had fine teeth, and he was soon inspecting them for cavities. Locking the door, he put on his glasses and carefully plucked two bristles from the end of his nose, brushed his eyebrows, then worked for a long time on his hair, encouraging those unscholarly auburn waves which, according to an unforgettable confession of Mlle. de Rosière's, ravished her. Snatching off his glasses, he glowered magnetically into his own dark eyes. Then he put on a pair of tight greenish trousers without pockets, which he had bought in Rome. He had never dared wear them before. He did not wear them now—in fact, he could not quite button them all the way. Sadly he peeled off the Roman trousers and got into some decent tweeds.

three

Mary Nayler was a gaunt, big-boned old woman with gray-brown hair drawn back severely into a knot. Without make-up or ornament of any kind, wearing a plain brown woolen dress, her very simplicity, her negation of style, was so consistent, so deliberate, that it affirmed her personality more effectively than "vain attire" could have done. There was something vaguely alarming about her: an air of primitive vitality and purpose, of a nature to implicate one morally, like martial music. A tremor which caused her head—massive, noble, pioneer—to shake continuously, though slightly, added to the impression of energy held in leash only with difficulty. The smile, incapable of nepotism, with which she greeted her nephew was like the smile of a benign principle summoning him back to his true dharma.

"Aunt Mary," he said, and involuntarily he reverted to the "plain speech" of the Society of Friends, "I thought thee was going back to Philadelphia."

"Now, thee knows that would have been wasteful, Peter." She spoke with a deliberate and special kind of drawl, *bouche carrée,* the mouth squared, as it were, for the origination of words. "As long as I was here on private business—which thee ought to remember —I thought I might as well turn a hand at something useful." The intonation of "useful" was at once ironical and ambiguous—it could be construed as minimizing the usefulness of the action, or her own usefulness, or questioning that of Peter, or as a reference to the vanity of all human enterprise that was not guided by the Inner Light which was, moreover, unpredictable in its consequences. It was well calculated to goad Peter without giving him grounds for

15

argument. Merely a Query for the Conscience. "I've been with the Friends Service Unit, down at the Village Project in Bihar."

"Thee looks peaked," he said, noting that the tremor was a trifle more decided than it had been the previous year.

"It's just malaria. It reduces one's efficiency. Bihar Friends"—her gray eyes gleamed and her mouth got squarer than ever, her delivery more ritualistic—"Bihar Friends had a concern for my flagging strength, and so sent me here for a month or two. I expect Irene to arrive tomorrow—she got a touch of sun, as they call it here. So now they're short-handed. . . ."

Peter felt himself go weak. He badly wanted a drink, although he had considered himself fortified as much as practicable before coming. "I didn't know she was in India."

"That's because thee has been sojourning in remote and lofty climes," Mary Nayler drawled, her clichés double-edged, invulnerable because they were possibly self-directed. The slight, involuntary shaking of her head seemed at times a kind of negation of Peter or of anyone else given to self-seeking, at times a disqualifying of herself as a judge. A mere nervous affliction, it continually intensified her meanings and enriched their ambiguities, although she did not at all need such an advantage. "When thee feels strong enough thee might come down to Bihar. Thee doesn't look quite so drink-ravaged as thee did last year, Friend."

"Tosh!" he said, a little seduced by her cantankerous charm and wickedness. "Thee knows good and well I had dysentery."

"Swear not," she murmured; then, with unexpected gallantry: "Thee is a pretty boy, Peter. I hope thee doesn't have to marry out of Meeting."

"I don't have to marry at all," he said shortly, coloring however.

"Good. Irene and I never doubted thee. Thee can meet her at the train tomorrow, if thee doesn't mind." Abandoning Peter and the plain speech, she turned to her other guests. Before Jim Chen, the young Chinese-American from Honolulu, her manner altered, became simple, kind, almost deferential. She half-slumped as if in apology for the discrepancy in their sizes, families, and religious histories.

Mary Nayler's platonic contempt for music—including hymns—

as irrational, amoral, and heterodox, had never prevented her from
patronizing it as "a bond of fellowship," if used medicinally. This
time (Peter swore at her with silent respect as he watched her work
along the Main Line he knew so well) Jim Chen would benefit—if
she had understood him correctly, he was bitter at being Chinese.
Tactfully she persuaded him to take up his guitar and sing some
of the American folk songs he had sung during his recent visit to
the Bihar Project. In a deep, intense voice not loud but passionate,
the broad-shouldered little man sang "Come, O my love, and fare
you well, You slighted me, but I wish you well." Curved lips barely
parted, face masklike, only his eyes, behind half-closed lids, moved
with the grief and irony of the song. And he sang about Unfortunate
Miss Bailey, whose ghost "then vanished gaily"; but the magic was
missing, the risky leers of his eyes and the intonations that should
have been funny were eerily wrong, ruined by some humorless
ghost of his own. Someday, Peter thought, he would tell Jim Chen
that he sang sad songs best.

It was raining now, and sufficiently cold at this altitude for a fire.
Peter sat by the fireplace, feeding little sticks of beechwood into
the flames—discreetly between songs, for he knew how touchy Jim
Chen could be. On the other side of the fireplace, resting her gaze
sometimes on the fire, sometimes on the singer, sat Mlle. de Rosière.
She and Tino were not looking at each other, and for a moment it
was hard for Peter to bear; he felt as if those two were holding on
to something to keep from being drawn into a vacuum between
them. Mlle. de Rosière had dark hair, quick dark eyes, a classic
profile with the nose thin and high-bridged, pure white throat, mo-
bile features, rouged mouth a little tired. Peter had heard once
that she came to India *pour mourir*, to die—but that in itself was
not alarming. Nowadays it would be strange to meet a foreigner in
these far corners who was not driven here by a demon. . . . He
hoped that Mademoiselle would not will to die literally, although,
as a Buddhist, she was certainly entitled to die in the mystical sense;
that is, "to die to the world." She did not look as if she had even
incipient tuberculosis. Doubtless she was too thin by American
standards, but he could see how a delicate man—and he himself,
so nearly chaste, was easily embarrassed by bodies—might feel

reassured by the timidity of her breasts. Even her pessimism could
be attractive, provided it had no rationale. In Peter's opinion, a
woman should not protrude too much. . . . Suicide, teaching school,
asceticism, whatever it was they intended, he hoped she and Tino
would foil each other's plans.

On the mantelpiece was the little gray lamp he had brought back
last year from Tibet, where at last he had tracked down his cousin
William, Mary's son, Irene's husband. The lamp, which had belonged to William, was saucer-shaped, pinched up on one side for
the wick. Tarok Dzong was the name of the monastery where Peter
had found it—where William had died. . . . And there Peter had
joined forces with Liliu Acquileia, who had no sense of proportion. . . .

A cat with long silken fur glided into the room, ignored the song,
the singer, the listeners, and came straight up to Peter. It pressed
against his legs, staring up at him with pale, plantlike eyes. Then
it sat down, laid one ear back slightly, tail urbane, with the expression of one pretending distractedness, and was completely self-
contained. After a moment it went out of the room as if it were walking invitingly along the edge of a precipice. No one had made a
move toward it, perhaps because they did not wish to disconcert
the singer, perhaps because they had not really noticed it, absorbed as they were with one another or with the music or with
themselves.

Gradually Peter felt himself becoming remote. He had the sensation that the center of his consciousness was now actually located
about four feet behind him and about eight feet above his head.
This phenomenon had occurred to him before, usually during con-
versations in which he took no part, and he associated it with eye-
strain, which waiting always produced in him. The voice of Jim
Chen came to him like sound heard under water. Rain was falling
heavily on the roof. Peter thrust a stick into the fire, smiling just
a little.

Irene Clifford—Irene Nayler—was coming, was she? With a touch
of the sun for an additional weapon—the strength of weakness.
Even if she were mad, it would make no difference to him, for he
was not about to demolish his fortifications. There would be de-

fense in depth: he would withdraw—farther up, farther down, farther back—nearer his own sources, away from hers, into Asia. Liliu Acquileia was waiting. . . .

The Naylers, the Cliffords, and the Bruffs had intermarried for the past two centuries in the Philadelphia area. They looked alike, they thought alike, they were alike. As a result Peter had not very much missed his father, who had died on one of his trips to India, while doing famine-relief work with the Quakers. But he did miss his Kashmiri mother, whom he had never known. His father had married her on principle, because he as a pacifist believed in intermarriage as the solution to the problem of war. She had named the boy Arjuna, a Kshatriya name, since she was a member of the warrior caste; and then she had died. After weighty deliberation, his father had compromised, in the Quaker tradition, by allowing the warlike name to stand, but in the middle, between Peter and Bruff, so that it could be designated by an initial. But Peter, from the time he learned to write, always wrote out his name in full. And for his warrior name—his schoolfellows said Arjuna sounded like a girl's name—and for his dark pride, he had fought many a battle with the Anglo-Saxons. He had also fought, on occasion, for Cousin William, who was extremely shy. And for Irene Clifford he had broken more than his nose, because instead of marrying him she had married Cousin William. But that was later. First the nose, then the heart. And last year he had nearly broken his neck looking for her runaway husband. . . .

The folk songs had stopped, but Peter was still listening, gently swinging his foot to the vanished rhythm, when he became aware of speech, and that he was staring into Jim Chen's face. Quickly he developed a decent grin, self-mocking, an echo of his aunt. Jim had been gazing back at him with curious, glistening eyes—like petrified tears, Peter thought. Now he came and sat down by Peter, fingering a few faint chords on the guitar.

"Everybody was singing but me," Jim mumbled so softly that Peter was not sure he had heard aright. He had known Jim for several years, off and on, but only according to the simple formula by which Jim wanted to be known: as a physically strong person with an ethical view of life, who was in India rather than in America

—he seldom mentioned Hawaii—because his fellow countrymen discriminated against him on grounds of race. True, Jim had once confessed to him, in India he still had to explain sometimes that he was human; but it was easier in India. Here discrimination was universal, formal, impersonal, and a foreigner, carrying with him the prestige of mobility and the exotic splendor of the West, could wade through it with impunity because he had no caste to lose, but only such secondary things as life or sanity. Like Mlle. de Rosière, he was a teacher down at the Ashram, the orphanage-school for half-caste children, which Peter had helped to found.

"I've been wanting to talk to you," Jim said. "You know that manuscript you brought back with you from Tibet?"

Peter nodded. He had brought back for Mary Nayler to take home to Irene, if she wished, the only three possessions William had left when he died at Tarok Dzong: besides the gray lamp on the mantelpiece, there was a small Quaker book called *A Guide to True Peace*, and part of a Tibetan manuscript. Although he knew some Tibetan, he could not read the characters properly. The abbot of the monastery, who had already copied the manuscript for his library, told him that it concerned the adventures of a mythical hero of Tibet, one Maudgalyayana.

"Mrs. Nayler let me borrow it last month when I was visiting the Bihar Project. I've been translating it."

"I didn't know you knew Tibetan."

"I don't. I'm studying it. The best way to learn a language is to translate it—or speak it with people. Some day I'll go to Tibet," Jim said dreamily. "I want to ask you about it—but not now. Maybe after I've finished the translation, I'll ask you."

As Tino and Mlle. de Rosière were rather silent, Mary Nayler had overheard some of Jim's remarks. "Have you deciphered it yet?" she asked, maneuvering the chairs so that they sat in an uneven semicircle before the fire.

"Part of it," Jim said. "It's called 'The Book of Maudgalyayana's Descent into the Underworld in Search of His Mother.' The local lamas tell me it's a different version from the one they know." The story, he said, dealt with the wanderings of Maudgalyayana, his attempts to find his mother in the world of the dead, and to rescue her. Sometimes her ghost approached, but her words were mostly unintelligible. Maudgalyayana's questions were ill chosen, equivocal as in a dream, and the answers of his mother's ghost consisted of foreboding hints. She could not rid herself of hatred for the living world—of which her son was a part—the world of Illusion which had been her downfall; indeed, her hatred and her love were indistinguishable from each other, so that the hero found it necessary to guard against the fitful and ambiguous plottings of the ghost. A bird from the upper world told him that he could accomplish his purpose only by the magical utterance of Truth. However, Jim had not yet got to the Truth. Instead he had come upon a disquisition on Mahayana doctrine, undoubtedly inserted by a later generation of lamas.

Mlle. de Rosière, hobbling a little over the English syllables, spoke in her musical, throaty voice: "The bird, was it not a goldfinch? In Europe of the *moyen âge* the goldfinch transported in his bill one drop of water each day, down into Hell, to moisten the lips of the damned."

Unconsciously Peter moved his tongue forward to touch his lower lip, then nearly burst out laughing as he glimpsed the merest flick of tongue in the corner of Jim Chen's mouth. Quickly he glanced about, but saw no other admissions.

"I don't know—it doesn't say." Jim shifted uncomfortably and was silent.

"The Buddhist Hells are more complicated than those of Christianity," said Mlle. de Rosière, "but perhaps the quality of Hell is the same everywhere, is it not?"

"The temperature varies a lot," Peter said. "Actually, the dry heat isn't too bad. But one drop of water, and the humidity goes up. Then you should hear." He was barely able to check the flow of triviality with which he desired to annoy his aunt.

"Some Quakers," said Mary Nayler, "have been rather famous bird watchers. Down at the Bihar Project Friends often get up quite early in order to watch birds. Irene never missed a morning —until lately. Unfortunately we are troubled by rats in that area. The rats eat the birds. We fear an epidemic because of these unusually large creatures, and so we have planned a rodent-extermination campaign—reluctantly, because we respect the Hindu belief that one ought not to take life. We need someone to talk to the villagers, someone who understands them better than we do." She glanced mildly at Peter, but the slight agitation of her head warned him of a whole world of activity that knew well how to involve him, to bind him with his own help, to wrap him up like a mummy in a life that was not his own.

"Bandicoots we call 'em," Peter said with a happy little shiver as he felt the alcohol coming to his aid, at last. "The British didn't like 'em either. I remember once down in Andhrapur, they organized a big parade as part of an educational campaign against 'em. They had somebody make a great enormous bandicoot, as big as a bull elephant, out of papier-mâché. Bigger, in fact. It was a float, you see, and a good one. This bandicoot had fleas hanging on him as big as hot-water bags, and the fleas had germs as big as your fist. Well, they assembled on the other side of the hill—you know how the town's laid out?—and they started to march through the railway tunnel into Andhrapur. The whole population was waiting. Everything went off smoothly till the procession had got into the tunnel—people pushing and pulling the bandicoot float. Then they remembered that they had forgotten to check the timetable. What reminded them was this: the Delhi Express came along, annihilated the marchers in exactly one second—they felt no pain—and plowed into the back end of the float, which fitted down over the engine. Whistling horribly, this great whacking bandicoot burst out of the hole in the mountain and went raging down on the population of Andhrapur. You can imagine what effect that would have on an impressionable people—I know, because I'm half impressionable myself."

"No, no!" cried Mlle. de Rosière. "It is not true!"

"They went mad," Peter assured her. "Some temporarily, some permanently. Andhrapur now has a famous Temple of Ganesha, sacred to the bandicoot, Ganesha's vehicle—you know the statues, the tradition—"

"No, no!" Refugees from the plague must not talk about tumbrils.

"It is true. Thousands and thousands of bandicoots are fed there every day. . . ."

Mary Nayler had gone to the door in response to a knocking
which Peter had not heard. Breathless from his defense against his
father's people, he sank back into his Aesthetic Continuum, to gaze
out dully into the face of Dr. Bhattacharya, a teacher at the Ashram.
He was one of those rare, regal Bengalis, quite big, yet fine of fea-
ture, who have always the quality of a host about them, as if they
were inviting the world to an unlimited supply of tea and sweets—
shundesh—on the good Bengali earth. Leaving his umbrella by the
door—it was streaming water that would run down to the Ganges
—he entered and made a graceful *namaskar*, bowing. Mlle. de
Rosière and Mr. Jim Chen were his colleagues at the Ashram, he
said in his somewhat rotund Oxford accent—and Mr. Bruff—what
a privilege! The founder of an Ashram, and a poet—just like Tagore!
With what avidity he had read Mr. Bruff's poetry! There was also
Mr. Bruff's fame as a destroyer of those of God's creatures whose
karma it was to prey upon human beings. . . .

"Lady Edith was resolved that you should come." The black, unfathomable eyes glittered at Peter from behind gold-rimmed glasses
—they were neither friendly nor unfriendly, in spite of the Mother
India smile, the ritual warmth which he probably felt to some extent. "We were desolated that we could not put you up at the
Ashram, after inviting you—but it was important that you should
come. How fortunate that Professor Scott was already here! I trust
that you have not suffered inconvenience?" Turning to Mary Nayler,
he discussed the Ashram for a while—through her he had joined
the Wider Quaker Fellowship; through him she had become interested in the Ashram. Then he spoke to Peter again: "We are close
to Nature at our School of the Future—too close, it now appears.
The animals are coming back, now that the British have gone."

"Pythons aren't usually man-eaters," Peter said.

"This one is not usual, as Lady Edith will tell you. She is not
well enough to shoot it, although she is an excellent riflewoman.
She does not wish to ask help of the local constabulary, because it
might be the beginning of interference by Government in the affairs
of our Ashram. I myself am prevented by religious scruples from taking life, but neither can I stand in the way if you wish to do so."

"Dr. Bhattacharya," said Mary Nayler, "was unable to attend the

Tercentenary Meeting of Friends in England. The passport regulations require one to be vaccinated. He refused at the last moment —at great inconvenience to himself—because it would mean taking the lives of germs. I doubt if Friends ever thought of that."

"I'll see Lady Edith tomorrow," Peter said. "I hope she's not seriously ill."

Dr. Bhattacharya hesitated for a moment, then, in a tone of sorrow and self-deprecation: "I believe it to be the result of nonvegetarian diet, causing a poisoning of the vital force. Repeatedly I have desired her to go to a specialist in England, but she will not leave our Ashram. Perhaps she will go when you have killed the python." He added, as if embarrassed: "If you knew her better, you would understand how the unfortunate deaths in the valley have caused her such needless anxiety for the school."

After a leisurely cup of tea and a refill, Dr. Bhattacharya said that he would be delighted to take Mlle. de Rosière and Dr. Chen back to "our Ashram" whenever they were ready. There was an abundance of room in the Land-Rover, as there would be only five passengers. Miss Dattatreya—Indira—was waiting down on the road with a new inmate for the school. No, no, she did not mind and she would not get wet. The top was up.

In guilty confusion, Jim Chen and Mlle. de Rosière began looking for their coats and umbrellas. By the time they were ready, Peter was down on the road, trying to see into a completely inscrutable Land-Rover, the same one that had attempted to run over him that morning: It crouched there in the rain with a look of blind alertness, regretting nothing. The doors were locked from the inside, the heavy side curtains were up, windows and windshield were steamed over with the breath of the occupants. Peter called out and listened. The rain replied, loud as a volley of drums on the taut canvas top of the Land-Rover.

"Indira!" he called out, rapping on the side curtain. Slack, disorderly bunches of rain tugged at the umbrella he had prudently brought. "I came here to see you!" It sounded like a thundering threat. He certainly had not intended to say that, nor in that tone. The corner of one of the side curtains moved, and he lifted it up and looked in. The girl stared at him out of the darkness, furious but controlled, unafraid. This time she did not conceal her face with the border of her sari, and Peter saw that she was beautiful. Although he had seen her face before, he had not quite known this, for she was mistress of the strange but useful art of seeming plain. In her arms, a fold of the sari about him, was a child of six or seven years, blond, thin, nearly naked. Clinging to Indira, he stared at Peter with wild green, oblique eyes. On the other side of them was a double-barreled rifle and two boxes of ammunition.

"You are seeing me," she said in Kashmiri, her voice quivering, "and I am seeing you."

"I am seeing you, but you do not see me."

There was a pause—she had not expected him to understand or to reply in Kashmiri. "You have frightened the child with your shouting," she said. "Kindly excuse us now." She meant, Go away!

Peter smiled at her. He could hear Dr. Bhattacharya and the others talking in the distance as they started down the wooden stairs. "Indira, when Gori Govinda was born, I was a schoolboy in America."

"Your affairs do not concern me," she said in English, icily.

"The truth concerns you," he persisted in Kashmiri, and all at once, carried away by a sudden emotion, he made to her a strange vow: "By the memory of your brother Ananda Mahadev, who was my best friend, I swear that I will never speak anything to you that is not the truth."

For a moment the veil of Maya parted between them, and they looked at each other like very young children.

She said: "The boy is not yours, but he and you belong to the woman, Liliu Acquileia. The time has not come to speak of my brother."

"You, who know me so little—"

"I speak what I feel, and what Ananda Mahadev would feel."

"Ananda Mahadev and I did not judge each other harshly."

"That is true," she said thoughtfully. "I am very severe because of what I have seen. This child in my lap"—she pulled the sari around him reassuringly—"was roving in the jungle like a wild animal, cast out by his mother's tribe, abandoned by his white father. No, I am not tolerant, I have taken sides."

"You are militant." He glanced at the rifle beside her.

"That is for the python. Lady Edith has taught me to shoot—so you need not come to our rescue."

"But you are a Brahman—and a woman!"

"So I am told." Her irony came down like a curtain between them, perhaps because Dr. Bhattacharya and the others were nearly there. "You have placed yourself at a great disadvantage, Mr. Bruff. Already you have told a lie: you have said that you would speak only the truth to me. Only God can truthfully say that."

"It sometimes happens," Peter admitted, "that those who claim to be God are impostors. Is it so certain that those who deny them are not also impostors?"

A solid torrent of water rushed down the mountain, under the stairs, under his feet, and he wanted to go with it. Up and up the interminable stairs of rain, in darkness, he toiled. For thirty-six hours now he had not slept, but he could not sleep yet. A phrase of stately irony—"exceedingly disconsolate"—built itself like trick stairs for his disorderly thoughts. It occurred to him that he had always had a hard time giving official labels to his states of being. Lust, for instance, was not a simple thing for him, for he was both lustful and inherently shy. Two traditions of chastity, Christian and Hindu, had always joined forces to help or stifle their unbelieving but informed and respectful heir. Never had the battle so gone against those ancient disciplines as it did now. He had lain with Liliu Acquileia, or rather she had possessed him as he lay ill during the journey from Tibet, and although a year had passed since then, he had not exorcised her yet. It had been a fatal mistake to bring her to Tashiling, but he had done it, unable to take her farther, both because he had not the strength, and because she refused to leave this place. Somehow she had known that he must always come back here. So he had gone, to be free of her, leaving unfulfilled his promise to work with Lady Edith at the Ashram. With or without Liliu Acquileia he was not free; but he was resolved not to go to her again. In a special way that he could not fathom, in his inexperience, she was too pure for him—not with the purity of Irene, but with the integrity of a monad, of the cat that makes use of man, that lurks in the doorway and neither comes nor goes, and the door is neither open nor shut. . . . What he wanted right now was a woman in his arms—not Liliu Acquileia, nor Irene, but one for whose spirit he would have a direct, central response, and who would have that for him, *billah!* And she must be good to look upon and good to— well, such as Indira.

"What lofty thoughts are you having?" It was Tino coming down the stairs, his pale features Italianate, framed in his black umbrella. "You have the wrong face for Dante. Anyway, I'm Dante. You're Renaissance. . . . You ran out fast. Are you climbing back to say good night to your aunt?"

"Not tonight. I'm too tired to be alone with her. One of us might win." They turned off where their path intersected the stairs, and walked slowly toward Tino's house. There, instead of going to bed, they began to drink hot rum—Peter in the hope of numbing his sensibilities so that he might sleep, Tino because he wanted to put off going to bed. Meanwhile Peter talked freely from the surface of his mind, in any direction Tino liked, and Tino liked the subject of the Maudgalyayana manuscript, so he told him all he knew about it and perhaps a little more. The rum was pleasant, although he soon reached a plateau of stupefaction beyond which he could not seem to climb. . . . What was Jim Chen's interest in the manuscript? Peter didn't know—a *billet-doux* from Aunt Mary, perhaps. . . . Once again he became trivial, but without relief.

"Why did you tell that rat story tonight?" Tino wanted to know. "It wasn't true, was it?"

"What do you think?"

"What should I think? Are you a myth maker?"

"If I know something is true," Peter said, "I'll lie like hell to prove it."

"That's not what I meant, but never mind—I meant something that's none of my business. Isn't it your bedtime?"

"Not yet," Peter said. "Tell me all you know about pythons."

"What I know is confined to classical antiquity." Tino tried a caricature of himself, with pinched lips, as a desiccated scholar.

"I can tell you the origin of the word. As for snakes in general, I fear and envy—I mean, I despise them. Did you know"—he hurried on, his cheeks flushed with embarrassment—"that the brass serpent which Moses hung on his staff is a symbol of Christ?"

"No. . . . Pythons are the only snakes that incubate their eggs. The female loops herself around them and then her temperature goes up exactly six degrees, as in a fever patient. They also have vestigial claws and hips."

"Hips," Tino muttered. "You sound so affectionate."

"Pythons are wonderful," Peter said. "They really are. Forty feet long, four hundred pounds—one I shot in Assam. A Naga tribe had been giving him people to eat. He was beautiful, all iridescent—blue-green, opal, different jewels—then all the color went away after I'd killed him—the way colors leave a seashell when you take it away from the water."

"They were giving him people to eat?"

"Oh, yes, certainly. Themselves. Nagas are snake-people. They liked having him around, because he was a god and he made them feel important. They called him Kaliya, too. They had to ask him first if I could kill him, and he said yes. There was always something very impressive about his decisions."

"It isn't that I don't value the truth of the imagination," Tino began, "but it's the confusion—"

"No, really. Pythons *choose*. It's as if they had always known it would be this way. They know who the victim is to be, and they'll choose him out of a series or out of a crowd. They'll often pass up the most likely ones—the ones you think you'd take if you were a python—and very calmly and swiftly and gently they take the one they've decided on. There's no question of escape. It's like Divine Grace, arbitrary and inscrutable—"

"*Basta!*" Tino shuddered and got to his feet, weaving a little. "Whose side are you on? Good night!" Just before going to bed, Tino tried on the Roman trousers once again, struggling manfully with the buttons. If he could take five inches off his waist. . . . He picked up a beautiful shaggy turtle-neck sweater, mottled light gray and dark gray, and held it up to his chest. A Tibetan woman had made it according to his specifications. Unfortunately, as it was of yak hair, it would not stretch enough to go over his head. "How beautiful!" he murmured, not at what he saw in the mirror, but at an inner vision of himself in the hair sweater and the Roman trousers. "*Allumeur!* What if she called your bluff!"

four

For half an hour Peter had sat in darkness, cross-legged on the floor, in the last of his yoga postures, without moving; but his gaze did not presume inward toward the awakening of Kundalini, the life force, with whose traditional serpent form he was not reconciled. Defeated in the "posture of victory," he gazed through the big open window of his room, across the mountains and valleys of Sikkim, to Kinchinjunga of the Eternal Snows, Lord of the Five Treasures of Krishna, third highest and most inaccessible mountain in the world. It was only a glimpse, repeated from time to time. The same wind that poured into his room, chilling his nakedness but not his heat, sent torrents of monsoon clouds across the sky. . . . The python of the Vedic nature hymns—Old Holdfast—had coiled himself around Rain Mountain—thus said the ancient Aryans, thus said the people still—around the sources of the water, until the land was parched and there was evil everywhere; then the god went up the mountain and asked a question, and Old Holdfast said, "Yes, now it is time," and the god drew his sword and cut through the great coils, and the water tumbled down over the perishing world so that it might live again; then the hero in his season became the oppressor, to be slain in his turn, though respectfully, since each of us contains the other; and all was repeated every year at the breaking of the monsoon. . . . The moon struggled through tides of darkness, a swimmer fighting to breathe, lost in the flood. So had Peter's friend, Indira's brother, once fought and lost in Ganga Mata, River of Life.

Beyond those clouds, beyond Kinchinjunga and the Great Barrier in that dimension, lay Tibet and the monastery of Tarok Dzong, the bones of William Nayler, and the old abbot who had spoken

31

of the unity of death and life. And there he had met Liliu Acquileia who was such a unity. Since meeting her, the abnegation of the senses—of Maya, for his purposes—toward which he had secretly reached had become impossible. Not once had he succeeded in thinking of Nothing.

Peter believed in no world but this, but he did not wish to reduce this world further except in the special sense of concentrating it into an epic poem, and his life into the discipline of writing it. He had seen men—like the saint, Lama Tendar—filled with joy and peace because they rejected this world, and—to him the most acceptable of ironies—this world was theirs, in joy and peace, because they rejected it. Their reasons—belief in an infinite life beyond—were unimportant. They were free to do what they liked, usually nothing visible, because of a core of nurtured indifference which attracts life to it, according to a kind of Carmen principle of flirtation: Who loves me I love not; who loves me not I love. Peter did not wish to love any more. He wished to write the *Krishnayana*.

Now it was raining again; torrents were joining other torrents, rushing down innumerable mountains on their way to Ganga Mata. The swimming moon was drowned, yet it persisted somewhere, and moved the tides from its invisible redoubt. Peter stood up, closed the window, rain splashing in on him—it felt warm to his chilled body, soft and warm as fingertips. . . . Standing with one knee resting on the edge of his bed, he felt his heart pounding, pounding, as if a beautiful woman were lying there. With shaking fingers he reached for a box of matches, with the idea of burning himself. On second thought he lit a cigarette.

A scratching of fingernails at the door which led out into the garden brought him bounding noiselessly across the room. Seizing a *gamcha*—a "sweat cloth" or flimsy red towel of sorts—he knotted it around his middle, turned on the light, opened the door. It was Monica Dutton, leering crazily, her black eyes aglow, holding a black umbrella over her head. Neither of them spoke. Standing inside, she bowed half-mockingly—drugged, she was a lemur—and presented him with the first of three packages she had clutched under her arm. It was a fine white sash of silk, a ceremonial gift such as Tibetans make to distinguished guests. The second package

was long, thin, cylindrical. He unwrapped it: cloth, wound on a
wooden rod, which unrolled like a scroll. It was an old, particularly
fine, Tibetan painting on silk, framed in brocade: the Adi-Buddha,
as a young Indian prince, sat upright in orgiastic embrace with his
shakti—his female emanation—Tibet's most characteristic represen-
tation of God, explained as the union of infinite compassion (the
male principle) with perfect knowledge (the female principle).
The third package contained the top of a human skull, carved and
inlaid with gold tracery and incrustations of jewels: a begging bowl,
but one which only the Dalai Lama might use. To Liliu Acquileia,
of the ancient Bon Po religion, these objects perhaps would not
have the usual meanings.

Monica's thin, crooked fingers trailed admiringly over his back,
and her wildness communicated itself to him. Grinning and arching, moving constantly, she was around him, then in back of him,
holding his raincoat for him. He slipped it on over the *gamcha*, then
his boots, and went out bareheaded into the rain. At first Monica
tried to walk with him, but he pushed her ahead of him. She capered
before him under her umbrella, looking back and grinning like
some demon of the place. Down the zigzag trail she guided him,
through the glistening darkness of the town, down to the lower
Chowrasta, almost running, a shadowy form, through rat alley and
jungle warren, down the long corridor to the heavy door; then she
disappeared.

Dressed in his new Tibetan clothes—white trousers, a red and
gold jacket trimmed in fur, and green felt boots—the boy Gori
Govinda moved about silently in the outer room. It was illuminated
by three small guttering oil lamps before a Bon Po demon in one
corner. There was no door into the dimly lighted inner room where
Liliu Acquileia and Peter were, only heavy curtains, and the boy,
his reddish hair troubled by fitful attempts at sleep, watched to
see if anything were needed.

The first time he went in, he lit incense and there was a feast of
sweetmeats and liquor—steaming *chang*, made of millet, in big
carved sections of black bamboo bound in silver. And Gori Govinda
served them, handing everything to Liliu Acquileia, who first sam-

pled it, then passed it on to Peter, using only the thumb and fore-finger of the right hand. From time to time, affecting to be displeased with some dainty, she would throw it over her shoulder, into a corner—the boy would sweep it out in the morning. Once she caught Gori Govinda tasting the *chang* before giving it to her to taste be-fore giving it to Peter—it involved putting into his mouth the same thin bamboo tube through which she, then Peter, would suck up the liquor from beneath the fermented seeds. With a Chinese it would not have mattered, but now they were in India where even Jim Chen required special treatment, besides, Liliu must always make a show of knowing distinctions, especially with this man, for whom her horoscope had destined her at birth. Liliu snatched the tube away from the boy, and he did not know if she would poke out his eye with it, or merely whip him across the face. She was about to do one or the other, when Peter cuffed her vigorously on the temple. With a cry she fell over and lay on her belly, whimpering. They were sitting on a kind of bed or dais, with sausage-shaped bolsters around them, and Peter mashed her down into them by sitting on her legs and leaning back on her as if she were a mat. Surely the world would come to an end now, thought Gori Govinda. But it did not. Through the black tangle of her hair he could see her thick red mouth and the glint of her white teeth—she was smiling! Moreover, holding her there, Peter made Gori drink some *chang*, the two of them sharing Liliu Acquileia's bamboo straw, and eat some sweets. And Peter, his face russet and swarthy, for he was drunk at last, let Liliu Acquileia up and she kissed his hand to apologize for having bruised it with her head. From this man she would endure anything, thought Gori, but from another she might exact the most frightful payment—he, Gori, knew. Peter said several saintly things, then looked furious and dangerous, and the boy went out.

The second time, he brought a silver urn of tea and jade teacups with chased silver around them, and fantastic little pagoda covers on them, of silver and turquoise, and a bowl of lichi fruit and small violet-tinged golden mangoes from Goa-side. Peter drank the tea but ate nothing. With the red *gamcha* tied loosely around him, he sat cross-legged, remote, withdrawn as if to some deep center within him, indifferent to the outer marches; indeed, he had an ascetic look—lust and spirituality, tranquillity and petrifaction being often so similar in their effect upon one's appearance. . . . Paler than buffalo butter, thought Gori Govinda admiringly. This god seemed to change color and shape with the thoughts that passed through his marvelous head and with the gestures of his glorious body—never the same, alternating, lama-lofty, or like a demon over the altar, or a fighting horse.

The third time, they did not awaken when he came in. Soon it would be dawn, and Peter had said that he would leave before it was light outside. Quietly Gori put a vase of rosebuds near the bed. Raindrops hung perilously from the crimson buds. A crimson drop stood out on his thumb, and he licked it off to avoid staining his new clothes, for he was immaculate. Not only had she herself bathed, she had made Gori bathe, as if he were at the Ashram. Standing over the sleepers, superior because he was awake and clothed and they were asleep and naked, yet he began to tremble with a dim commiseration as if he were in the presence of two victims of a terrible accident, to whom he must minister. Without a sound the fox-eyed boy sank down to his hands and knees, as if impelled toward the more concentrated shape of a former birth, made real and operative by his faith.

For an hour, two hours, Peter lay withdrawn in solemn sleep, at the very core of the mountain of sleep, and having touched the dark source, needed no more; yet for a while some drug held him there. Somewhere in the walls of the silent room a timber cracked between two seconds, the nerve ends seized their daggers, and the man began to emerge from the mountain, door after door, closing each behind him. Gravely he opened the last door, and as he looked out there was a kind of vanishing as of some shy noctule. Gravely, by the little light, he acquainted himself with his estranged and rediscovered flesh. For a moment he had an impression of translucency, of seeing the forms within, the subcutaneous textures and all the rhythms of the various structures, strong and delicate, each with its special dignity and its cry. They were like a jungle—no, a garden—of symbiotic organisms, fruit and trees and flowering vines, with beasts and a man and woman and brooks and a dawn sky, and towering over all but the sky, watched and watchful as a regent with his own will and purpose, a serpent.

It was not yet dawn. . . . He put out his hand—her breasts were firm and high, cuspate, with large, dark aureoles and nipples like little pegs; her body rounded, durable and crisp; a deep, curving drop from the hips into the waist. Under his gaze, under his hand, she opened her eyes and looked at him steadily. The upper eyelids were like archers' bows, taut, the corners next to the small, retroussé nose slightly crossing the lower lid there in the epicanthic fold, forming a sharp, downward-pointing angle in which the tear ducts were not visible. The skin of the eyelids was of a perfectly smooth, waxlike texture and appeared tightly stretched from corner to corner, narrowing and immobilizing the horizontal apertures so that they did not move when the eyes moved. The irises, full of shadowy convolutions, were opaque, cinnamon-brown with tiny particles of green and gold. When the whites appeared, as they did in the kiss, they had a startling effect. Her skin, which she kept pale, had undercolorings tawny and apricot, intensified by cosmetics over the high, broad cheekbones. There were still traces of the saffron, henna, and rouge which she had cunningly applied to different parts of her body.

Words and half-words had tumbled from him, English, Nepalese, Tibetan, and sounds he did not care to consider in cold blood. Liliu Acquileia had not forgotten. A massive shadow against the predawn light that came in through the window, she rose to her knees, sank back on her ankles, regarded him out of darkness as he sprawled there regally tolerant. Now she would be delicate; for she had been indelicate during the night—or delicate, rather, in ways that had appalled him. And yet he was there.

"You have praised me with compassion," she said in a low voice. "I praise you with knowledge, Lord."

Peter closed his eyes, smiling vacuously. His last words with Indira had embarrassed him by referring, perhaps by accident, to this convention, that for a time God must be regarded as incarnate in the man, and be worshiped by the woman. It was a Hindu ritual to which Liliu Acquileia was not entitled, yet she made use of it, as she made use of Buddhism. For purposes of profanation, the assertion of individuated subjectivity, of rebellion, it would be at least as acceptable as, say, a Black Mass, provided he could remain inert. Inertia, the refusal to participate, was the greatest sin. It was that by which Satan tried to usurp the role of God.

"No," he said, turning away his head and lifting his knee, almost maidenly.

"Lord, it is time," she said. "A year passes, more than a *kalpa* of time for me waiting. . . . A woman is sobbing long in the next room. I think I hear beloved footsteps. I am wrong. It is some inconsequential person. . . ." This way she wept, till, seeing him acquiesce: "Timeless one, beautiful and benign," she began, intoning the words as if she were lost in some remote, dark consciousness of hordes, infinitely ancient, "I praise you, therefore I exist. You are the sea of light. Before you was nothing; there is no after. Swimming in you, I was born, I live, I shall die and be absorbed forever." Bending forward so that her hair covered his feet like a great cat, she kissed them and exclaimed, her voice breaking, a crone's, artful or genuine, it was the same! "Your feet arch and curve like wings, immeasurably complicated"—gesture of haruspices, her words faltered—"with bones slender and succulent—as the framework of a panoply—made out of the skeleton of an azure bird!"

"What kind of bird have you there?" God demanded, suddenly austere amid His jostling images.

"A white hawk, a white sea hawk."

"White or blue?"

"Widow-white and Krishna-blue, Lord! Bones of azure, panoply of white wings." Gently she swayed to and fro, chanting, rather as she had done last year when he had been about to leave her, and had felt himself dying: from poison if not from an esoteric science of nomenclature—he respected her sources too much to simplify—there being more than one way of gaining power over the unknown. Now the incantation went: "Your legs are powerful rivers, Divine One!" These she worshiped. "Whoever dies therein shall be merged with you, forever free from *Samsara,* the round of rebirth."

"Come to the hirsute river, paler than grass. . . ."

"Your thighs are the karma and dharma of the builders of temples."

"What kind of temples, Liliu Acquileia?"

"The turning spires of Lhasa the Most Holy, sacred to Dorje the Great Thunderbolt." Thus, groveling: *"Om mani padme hum—* Jewel in the Heart of the Lotus—all things come to you, all things proceed from you. Around you the universe revolves. You are the lawgiver, adorned by the skulls of the envious, the small, the impotent. . . ." She checked herself. In this particular and most gifted body, God did not like to be reminded of his horrible aspects, so dear to Tibetans. "This world, from here to here"—she indicated a span above the navel to a span above the knees—"this world, Creator, is a stretch of nebulae, a constellation of stars, very pure, full of portent."

"You read my body as if it were my hand!"

"It is your hand, Lord! You who created the world with it, at your pleasure you punish the world, crushing it in your grip as if it were no more than a heart!"

As the dark form bowed over him, he sat up, feeling the drug work in him. The sun drilled through the window behind her, through coils of fog, blinding him; yet he continued to stare into it, as yogis do, fascinated by the illusion he was able to create: It was a huge eye, its heavy lids open wide. There were no eyelashes. Moving slightly, it focused unblinkingly upon Peter's gaze. The iris was dark, the pupil disproportionately large, and darker, containing a fire-colored glow in which a pale form appeared to be dancing. It held a look of satiety that was at the same time immensely seductive. Proud and melancholy, familiar as a relative, infinitely learned, gradually it became like Peter's eye. . . . Again the dark form came between them.

"Am I acceptable, Omnipotent One?"

The legs of the blind God snaked out, involved his kneeling worshiper, hauled her down into his horrible coils.

five

Smoke was coming out of the kitchen chimney, which meant that Balu was having his early morning cup of tea; but Tino's curtains were still drawn. Silently Peter entered his own room through the garden, removing his boots so that Tino would not hear him come in. It was the only kindness he could permit himself then, for his heaviness was something other than the *tristitia* of animals afterward. Rather it was as if he had been falling for a year—a year during which he had barely worked on the *Krishnayana*—and had finally hit bottom. One does not easily change directions in mid-air. There had been an outrageous intensification of his existence in one modality, which could not be added to, but would in spite of him supplant the modality he intended. Knowing this, he had fought against it for a year, and the fight had become a third way. Now he had lost the direction, "the straight way," his dharma, for which he believed that he willed to live.

The heavy iron box, still locked, lay near his bed. It contained his life work, the unfinished manuscript of the *Krishnayana*, and the Sanskrit notes of his dead friend Pandit Ananda Mahadev, the folk versions and priestly interpolations upon which it was based, though only in a formal sense. Peter started to open the box, but instead he sat on it, his head in his hands, and stared blackly into himself, found there, like St. Anthony, the familiar doubts and temptations. Yes, he was a fool, right enough! Having published one slim volume of poems—precocious, embarrassing to remember —here he was at twenty-five, involved in writing the Epic of the Age, and it was interminable. Not so his life. Perhaps not the age either. . . .

39

How long he sat there on the cold iron lid, he did not know, but he became aware that something had just solicited him. From the guava bush outside his window came a sound that touched some recess of his nature that had never before, perhaps, been wholly awake; and his mouth opened in the rustic, half-incredulous grimace with which a powerful organism greets the uncannily delicate and true. Again it came: the fluting song of a bird, pure and keen and formal, a limited utterance of five notes, like five symbols:

A reply came faintly in the distance—three notes, uncompleted. And the bird in the guava bush sang again, differently this time, but still in approximately the same pattern. And each time he sang, he varied the tune slightly, shortening, omitting, doubling the notes, trilling this one or that one, and at times he might have been singing more than one note at once, in mysterious tonal ambiguities. It was as if his life were devoted to the attempt to fulfill an ideal melody to which his songs all referred but could not state, and could not not state.

Peter crouched on his knees, uncouth, before the window, but the bird watcher was unable to locate the bird because of the heavy foliage of the bush. Like any other clown, he would have liked to demand of someone the "meaning" of this thing, even though as a poet he thought he knew the vanity of verbal parallels, translations that start from other motives and reach other goals. It was not artifice, but original, innate, compulsive, the signature of a race. Yet for this ten minutes—this ten months in the lifetime of a goldfinch—it stopped its courting and seeking food and whatever else it is that birds do—stopped its "practical-moral" existence to sing with its whole being. . . . Now it was gone.

In the next room Tino was making polite getting-up noises. Peter lay down on his bed and writhed, to muss up the covers. Then he lay still. Suddenly he rolled over the edge of the bed and landed with a thump on the floor, mostly on his side. He got up and went hastily into the bathroom, where he began to throw mugs of icy water over himself. This time he did not want Balu to attend him.

"I suspect Chanchal of practising brahmacharya—complete chastity," Tino said at breakfast—he looked harassed and preoccupied. "I hope you two will get along together."

"No reason why we shouldn't." Peter said cautiously. He was not looking for irony this morning, and perhaps Tino had not intended any.

"He's quite a patriot—touchy about India. Gets awfully rhetorical sometimes."

"It's tropical exuberance," Peter said. "I have a streak of it."

"You may have to make a little special effort, but he's a good friend."

"Sure." It seemed to him that Tino was being overly solicitous, if not naïve, but he did not say so. Let this fellow Chanchal come, and trust to circumstances. Neither of them would be riveted to this house, although he himself liked it here; besides, he preferred to share expenses with Tino rather than to take a room somewhere. With reasonable thrift he managed very well in India on the hundred dollars a month which he received from the investment of his inheritance.

"I especially wanted you here, with Chanchal coming—"

"A Bridge Between East and West?"

"Jesus!" Tino got up and went out, leaving Peter to finish breakfast by himself. After a moment he came back. "Sorry," he said. "Make a special effort with me too, will you?"

"Don't worry," Peter said with a certain tenderness such as one might feel for a convalescent or for someone who is grouchy because he has not long to live. Weightier matters exercised Peter's spirit.

"I am under what is known as a strain," Tino said wryly, sitting down again, but he looked as if he were less under a strain than before. "I got a letter from Chanchal this morning, special delivery. He'll be on the same train as the lady you're going to meet, so I'll go down with you, if you've no objection. . . . Chanchal is some sort of relative of Dr. Bhattacharya, and when Dr. Bhattacharya heard he was coming up to stay with me for a couple of weeks, he asked him to bring his gun—to shoot a python. I thought I'd better mention this. Maybe you can hunt together."

"Kaliya will be safe!"

"Kaliya—ah . . . I've never been hunting in my life. I'm near-sighted—can't see to shoot unless I have special glasses, which I'm too vain to wear. But I should think that the more hunters you have, the better your chances are. You can be beaters for each other —you know, *flush* the python?"

"Let's take a large view of the matter," Peter said. "I'll see Lady Edith this afternoon. Maybe there is no python."

"Balu!" Tino was furious. Jumping up abruptly, so that his chair fell over backward, he stood pointing a trembling finger at the bowl of porridge on the breakfast table. "You—you damned little bastard!"

Balu circled out of the kitchen, rocked over to him, his face agree-ably suicidal. "What is it, Sahib?"

"Look! Just look!" Out of the half-inch of sugary milk and juice remaining in the bottom of the bowl, Tino spooned the sediment. "There! There!" And he confronted Balu with several tiny black objects shaped like forked twigs.

Concentrating until his nose almost touched the spoon, Balu at first registered disbelief; then he clucked, and shook his head. "Oh, ho! I am very bad!" And he seized the bowl and started out with it.

"Take these with you." Tino swept a disgusted hand at Peter's bowl, which was less than half empty.

"But, Sahib, it is only the legs."

"Only—God!" Tino was paper white. "Only—"

"Only the legs, Sahib. I always pick out the rest, since you told me, but the legs always come off in the boiling; then they are hard to find." Rocking about with the wild precisions of a palsied barber, he collected the dishes; then he added philosophically, straightening up the fallen chair on his way out: "Cockroaches are *too* tender, Sahib. They even lose their legs in the sugar sack—*oh*, so easily!"

"Close the sack! Tie it up! How often must I tell you?"

"I do, Sahib, but they push their babies in through the sack so that the babies will grow up inside. . . . Sahib, if you would not scrape the bottom of the bowl with your spoon—the legs always sink to the bottom—"

"Get out! Go away! You're fired! *Jao! Jao!*" Weakly Tino sank into the chair, with shaking fingers accepted the cigarette Peter offered him. "I hate him," he said. "I hate India."

"Don't think about it," Peter said, taking a piece of toast and passing some to Tino. Tino shook his head and continued to sit morosely staring out the window at Kinchinjunga without seeing it.

"In Singapore I ate some on purpose," Peter said. "They were stewed. I couldn't go the baby mice, though."

"The—"

"Baby mice. Alive, of course. You hold 'em by the tail, dip 'em in lotus honey. That's what I went there for, but I changed my mind —I was sensitive then. Some toothless old mandarins loved 'em."

Tino opened his mouth—"Aaargh!"—then, unexpectedly, he laughed, as a man will when he reaches the precipice of moral indignation and finds that he has not jumped.

They met Monica Dutton as they went down the trail from Upper Mazumdar Lane to the railroad station. Leaning suddenly over a garden fence in front of one of her unrented houses, with a gay parasol—although a high mist obscured the sun—she looked fresh and optimistic, more British than ever. Surely it was another creature who had guided Peter down the mountain last night, leaping, feral, grinning back at him over her shoulder!

"It's beastly hot on the plains," she said with satisfaction. "I heard it on the wireless. There'll be a cholera epidemic."

"Don't count on it," Peter said, but among his sympathies flickered the desire to dance round a caldron with her in celebration of her warring worlds and his.

"Going to the station? The train's late. It's never on time—now. Landslides, you know. Tashiling's going down the mountain. Right down the mountain—into the river!"

"Hurry up, for Christsake!" Tino murmured out of the side of his mouth.

"We British built it, takes British to maintain it. These nasty Indians don't know how to hold back the mountain. It takes engineers —brains." She tapped her head knowingly. "*Responsibility* . . . You'll find the train's late!" she called after them. Much farther away, leaning down from the sky like a gargoyle, she screamed something else.

"Probably says she'll see us later," Tino muttered. "She will, too."

"No, she said something about a Persian gentleman."

"My God!" said Tino.

A locomotive, nearing the station, gave a little bright, breathless shriek as if it were straining itself to arrive on time. Its track, with a gauge of twenty-four inches, paralleled with precision the surfaced road up from the plains, sharing the same perilous ledges along the mountainsides. Actually there had been a series of mistakes in timing, due to anxiety, which had brought the miniature train in early. It was barely creeping along, in order to cut down this embarrassing advantage. Looking like an educational toy for rich children, the gorgeous little coaches, rose and mauve, pea-green, yellow and blue, pulled by one infant engine, pushed by another, bridled into the station. Huge people got carefully out. Then it was like a fair, with a string of gaily-painted booths. In front of them people were struggling with their loot, which stood between them and freedom. In India, no one with possessions travels light.

Peter and Tino waited on the side lines where they could command a view of all the coaches. There seemed to be an unusual degree of commotion on the platform by the last coach. A tiny pale man with jet-black hair and a magnificent wavy beard was shouting at a crew of coolies who were laying their wicked hands on his baggage—some eight or nine enormous trunks and an assortment of suitcases, baskets, and packages. "Oo-wait!" he barked, his lips hooting phonetically to form the W, then scissoring tightly downward at the corners, ravaging his face, showing dangerous white incisors. "Oo-wait!" and his fine big black eyes flashed, at bay, menacing. The coolies paused, but remained in motion, lawlessly yelling and jostling as if this one moment of delay would mean their ruin. The ferocious little man darted forward, one arm arching high in the air, as if to strike; but on reaching a point beside the door of the compartment he became motionless and very nearly beautiful, with his face lifted, like a Seraphic Father in ecstasy. A white hand rested for a moment on the rigidly offered arm, and a woman stepped down. Slumping a little, as if in apology, she thanked him. When she straightened up, she towered over him. She was dressed plainly in black, with no ornaments of any kind, no make-up. Her long blonde hair, under a black hat like a beret, was gathered in a knot at the back of her neck, quite low, as if the abundance of it required her back for additional support. Clear blue-gray eyes, set wide apart, gazed calmly out over the turmoil of people and things, searching.

Then Peter's aunt and Jim Chen were with her. Peter started forward, but reeled back momentarily from a thickness of coolies running with steamer trunks on their heads. A hand on his shoulder made him turn around. "I want you to meet Chanchal," Tino said. Very slim and trim and military, with a small mustache, khaki coat and trousers and British army boots, Chanchal offered his hand. At the same instant Peter bowed, hands clasped prayerfully before his face, in the correct Indian greeting: *"Namaskar."* Both recovered at once and switched roles, Chanchal making the *namaskar* just as Peter reached for his hand. They would almost certainly have come to a focus on each other in the next instant, had not Chanchal panicked. Coolies had seized his four iron boxes, his bedroll, and the guncase he had leaned against it in order to acknowledge the introduction. Now he turned on them with a screech, gesticulant, disintegrated, his big protuberant, almond-shaped eyes—he was East Bengal—promising blood, fire, and the Brahman's Curse. The coolies grinned appreciatively while he lacerated them to cover up his confusion. Only a moment before, he had looked like a dark Englishman.

The bearded little man, keeping his coolies behind him, conducted Irene and Mary Nayler through the crowd. It was Mr. Chehil Kashani, Tino's Persian colleague from Bharat University. Standing on tiptoe, he embraced Tino first on the right side, then on the left side, then stood back discreetly and moved the corner of a virgin handkerchief until it exactly coincided with the outside corner of his right eye.

They met only for a moment, for it would not do to have the

coolies simply standing there with the heavy boxes balanced on their heads. In the general rush and passion of the place, Peter saw his way clear not to go with Irene and Mary Nayler and Jim Chen in their taxi, but conveyed to them by gestures that he felt called upon to help with the many baggage-maddened coolies of Mr. Kashani and of Chanchal Bhattacharya. "Thee looks well, Peter Bruff," Irene had said, slurring the "plain speech" so that others might not hear and feel excluded. In her movements had been repose, in her direct gaze, though he knew it well, a steadfastness that had made him wince, as at a strong light unfiltered by earth's dusty atmosphere.

It was a slow trip up the trail this time, not only because of the tremendous quantity of baggage, but because Mr. Kashani insisted on going first, with the coolies last, according to his protocol, and he could not walk fast. A pair of pointed, highly polished shoes, with heels two inches high, compressed his feet into tiny ideals. After a short distance, he halted the entire caravan while he opened a trunk and took out an elegant silver-headed ebony cane. Leaning on this, he hobbled and minced, minced and hobbled up the trail, smiling wonderfully, with beads of agony bedewing his forehead. The coolies were sweating too and getting a bit wobbly under their burdens. Finally Peter persuaded Mr. Kashani to let them flee ahead, assuring him that they would stop at the right address, because the landlady would be waiting for them—and besides they would hardly have the strength now to go farther. Peter was in a mood to say more, but Tino murmured, "His toes are permanently crossed, the big ones under the little ones," and surreptitiously crossed his fingers to illustrate; and, as if that were not enough to arouse one's appreciation, he added lugubriously, "Absolutely trustworthy," which for some reason made Peter snicker.

Mr. Kashani's baggage lay piled high in front of the tiny bungalow where they had passed Monica Dutton. Here, patrolling her mountain kingdom, she awaited them. "How do," brightly she greeted her new tenant who, after all, was a European, wasn't he? Persia was the Sick Man of Europe, or so they said. And she studiously ignored Chanchal. They left Mr. Kashani and all his possessions with her.

"A monument to British immorality!" Chanchal's rhetoric rolled out, painfully distinct, for he was both intellectually committed and proud of his English elocution.

Squirming inside, Peter glanced back to see if Monica had heard the insult, but she was busy haggling with the coolies for Mr. Kashani. Peter wanted to object to the cliché, to say that it was one bigotry against another, on and on, and that he, Peter, was not disinterested. To his relief, he heard Tino tell Chanchal to try to act like Tagore. What did he mean? Oh, you know. Universal—that sort of thing. He did not want to be around when Tino would tell his Bengali friend that Peter did not have the inestimable advantage of pure stock. Peter did not wish to hate Chanchal; in fact, he rather looked forward to staying in the same house with him. He had always considered Bengalis to be nearly unknowable, and here was one made captive by a friendship. Probably something wrong with him, Peter reflected cynically—for which he would compensate by uncommon virtues—or he'd be at home in the bosom of his clan, instead of defiling his Brahmanhood by consorting with beefeaters.

Chanchal was having a lordly bath, attended, as was proper, by a Sudra, Balu, whom he had naturally commandeered with a thousand-year-old look that compelled him to his dharma. Waiting to take his own bath and to change his clothes, Peter absently dumped the contents of his pockets, including his wallet, on the table in the living room, and started to wander toward his room. Tino stopped him. "Where to?"

"Down to the Ashram," Peter said. "I want to see Lady Edith."

For a moment Tino dawdled as if he were trying to make up his mind about something; then, looking past Peter, not at him, he said brusquely, "Don't leave your money lying around."

Obediently Peter gathered up the wallet, cigarettes, keys. "You're right," he mumbled from the past. "It's sinful to leave temptation in people's way."

For a second Tino seemed confused, thrown off guard by the unexpected Quakerism; he lowered his head, smiled up out from under, Machiavelli: "Balu is a scoundrel. He'll extort money from you if you aren't careful—he has a way of holding you to promises you never made—quibbles over words when you object. Says your

Bengali was lacking in precision at the crucial point, that, in effect, you promised. . . ."

"Fire him," Peter suggested recklessly, testing; he felt that he was beginning to need confidences from Tino, whose disingenuousness made him anxious.

"Oh, I couldn't do that. He's got too much on me. Besides, he's a good flutist. Soulful as hell."

"You like him?"

Tino shrugged, relativist. "He's a complete bastard, pious, immoral, hypocritical—"

"How old is he—to be all those things?"

"I don't know. You don't have to be so old. . . . I think he's a dwarf. Once he told me he was eight, and I believed him. Another time he swore he was twenty-four. And he could be, you know. He just could be."

Darting out from his back-scrubbing dharma in the bathroom, to get some oil, Balu poised for a moment just outside the door, bounced noiselessly, from one foot to the other, swivel-eyed, grinned at the sahibs. They were talking about him! Had they noticed his charm at last? *Arre babal* If he played his cards right, he could still become a landlord!

Abruptly Tino's expression changed. "Balu doesn't steal. Not like that." And, as Peter glanced at him keenly and went into his room, Tino followed him. "Look," he said, "it's just possible someone might think *I* left the money there—for them."

"Fine view of Kinchinjunga from this room," Peter said, feeling suddenly both guilty and betrayed, as if someone were making a terrible sacrifice for him when all he had wanted was a friendly look.

"Chanchal is my friend."

"Enough, enough!" Peter started undressing wrong, caught his boot on the inside of his trouser leg, sat down on the bed to contemplate the folly of it. If he could just say something splendid, wise, and tolerant that had only to be heard to transport the hearer with the Inner Light!

"You think you understand, but you don't," Tino pursued coldly —he did not smile as Peter held up his trapped boot in a futile gesture. "I make loans to him. He's very poor. He has a wife and two kids—twins."

"I thought you said he practiced brahmacharya."

"He does. It was an accident. Her mother died, he was comforting her—but that's not important. The thing is, he couldn't afford to come here on his salary. He never tells me when he's broke. Too proud. I found him nearly starving once, and I gave him a bawling out. He'd never ask for money, even now. He's a Brahman, you know, and it's not good form to give money directly—"

"Right," said Peter, and some devil made him add, "So you leave it lying around and he takes it."

"Well, for Christsake, Bruff!" Tino shouted in a sudden rage. "After three years in this goddam country, you still don't understand? He's a Bengali—civilized, complicated—something a Quaker wouldn't understand, but an Italian might!"

"Or a Scotchman might and a Kashmiri might not. Why don't you come off it, Scott?"

"The trouble is, you're an idealist. You don't understand *people!*"

"What do you want me to understand?"

"Chanchal."

"You lack humility."

Tino turned abruptly, went to the window, and looked out. "You can respect a man without understanding him," he said.

"So now we have arranged friendships!" Peter grinned—he was beginning to enjoy the quarrel. "You're too impetuous, Tino. Your friend now irritates me, whereas before—"

"He annoys me too. That's not the point."

"What is the point?"

"The difference between you and me is, I don't identify a man with his words or his actions, or with his thoughts—or even with his feelings. He's always in back of them, always in reserve, never committed—not essentially. A Protestant can't admit this. That is"—Tino had cooled off at high altitude and was looking for a way down—"if you are one. Quakers claim they're not anything, don't they?" And, as Peter did not reply, but merely looked at him quizzically: "Look here," he burst out in sudden remorse, "I mixed it all up. I owe you an apology."

"Pish!" Peter said, unwilling to let him crawl back into his hole so easily. "Every man to his own stupidities."

Tino stared at him in silence. "Wait here," he said; then, on his way out, he called back over his shoulder, "Categories and hierarchies." In a moment he was back with a bottle and two glasses. "Hierarchies and categories," he muttered, pouring out whisky. "And the truth is like your goddam python that writhes through the whole jungle of 'em, changing colors, choosing people, devouring them—around and through and among—"

"And over," said Peter. "This is too early," but he drank. The splashing had stopped in the bathroom, and he was about to go in for his bath, when Tino refilled his glass.

"I want to tell you something." Tino looked pale, sunken in, yet somehow callow. "I went out last night. When you went out, I couldn't sleep. I went out, see? I walked. No," his hand, eloquent as a bodhisattva's, said it was not a matter of someone else's comings and goings, but something that was Tino's. "I walked in the rain. There was a Nepalese girl. She walked with me for a hundred yards, under my umbrella. Then she touched me. I paid her to go away." He drank and was silent for a moment. "You think that's not much?"

A dim loyalty made Peter launch out intuitively, although he did not know what much was. "If you say it is, it is."

"Everything in life surprises you, doesn't it?" Tino was looking at him from a frosty distance to show that he was not asking for contributions. "Everything surprises you, but nothing shocks you. Visualize somebody who is just the opposite: shocked by everything, surprised by nothing." The hand said, That is Aretino Scott. "If you are surprised, you advance. If you are shocked, you retreat. This"— he held up the glass of whisky—"is the closest I have ever come to going anywhere." The fingers designated a barricade between his brain and the rest of him. "Yes, I know the maps—I am an accomplished cartographer—but I have never been there. Perhaps that is why I have not gone. I am constitutionally incapable of going. I sit on the wharfs—one must sit somewhere—and I watch the voyagers. I envy you, Peter. I think that is the correct word, rather than 'jealous'—although I have known for some time that I do not know myself, and in fact my actions have made me deeply suspicious. Now you see why it is I froth at the mouth sometimes. A man standing in a bear trap of the spirit—should I say spirit?—may bite you if you come near, for all kinds of reasons, you understand. Or rather, you do not understand." He stood up as if to finish the conversation. "I attribute to other people a greater predisposition for suffering than they ordinarily possess. My passion to spare them from pain often makes me inflict the equivalent in preventives." And the accomplished cartographer winced at the eighteenth century flourish which he had just bitten out of his soul.

"Do you love Mlle. de Rosière?"

Tino smiled craftily. "As an example of envy," he said, "I envy your freedom in being able to ask such a direct question. I must learn. . . . Yes, I love her, as I have loved several times before—frequently, in fact," he said, as if to make sure Peter would know he was lying. "And as before, nothing can come of it."

"The fact that you envy me means that something will come of it." Peter was sitting cross-legged on the bed, a towel around him.

"You look as Indian as the Upanishads when you say that." Tino laughed but regarded him as it were with alarm. "You don't know me."

"Try everything and find out. We are concentric with each other— and with Chanchal Bhattacharya."

"Concentric? Where in Hell is our common center?"

"It is not that," Peter said in the ritual answer of the Upanishads, indicating an illusory presence with his right hand, and another with his left. "*Neti, neti.* Not this, not that." There was the sound of a door opening. "*Tat sat.* It is that."

six

Someone was behind him on the path, he knew, but he did not know how he knew. Perhaps it had been a distant footfall, the exclamation of a bird, or a stone dislodged, the sound of which had reached him but had not entered his mind until now; for he had been thinking of the venture to which he must persuade Indira when he reached the Ashram. Now he squatted down in the shade of a cliff, lit a cigarette and waited; but no one came. The heat rising up from the valley made him begin to sweat as he sat still, although he wore only Kabuli sandals, a pair of dark blue shorts, and a white bush shirt, open and loose, and a khaki bush hat. Peter continued on down the mountain, giving no sign that he was aware of being followed, for he had learned to treat indirection with respect, especially when it might affect him directly.

The trail dropped down four thousand feet, through forests of Himalayan oak and larch and black juniper. The lower the altitude, the more closely the trees were woven together by ropes of vines, until they were nearly a solid mass, humid and musky. Deep concentrations of bamboo, with separate stalks eight inches in diameter, shot skyward sixty feet in static explosions of green. Cryptomeria, toon, simal strove sunward to abnormal heights, fighting the welter of vegetation that followed them up. The creepers, like usurers, tied them together, giants and all, in a thorough cartel, preying upon the earth into which they were destined to subside. Doomed and proliferating, from the forks of these trees everywhere, rotting them, were parasitic orchids—gorgeous little vomits of color, cream and crimson, mauve bouquets, liver-lovely, all spickled and spackled.

Again he paused and listened in the uncool shade, amid leaves

53

virid and glassy, and flowers of the secondary colors of saris—where the sun is so male, all things else—even colors, even men- -veil themselves and are subtle. Even as he stood there, in the unmoving air, a tendril languished across his arm, inviting him to be absorbed. There was no sound from the unseen tracker; but the jungle was not silent. Peter heard and felt the unfathomable Sigh of the forest. It came of innumerable sounds emitted by plants: flowers opening, and pods, leaves falling, pushing up of sprouts, the slow rise and fall of trees, above all the endless dripping of moisture, leakage of experiential time, from leaves to leaves into the porous ground; flourishing, dying, replenishing, germinating, process of the planetary mold, effluvium of earth, *ennui mortel de l'immortalité*, it sighed even when Peter did not listen.

At one point the trail skirted a landslide caused by what had been a clear brook, but now, in monsoon season, was a savage brown torrent. Carrying boulders and trees with it, down to the river below, the spate had gashed through the watershed and exposed a huge half-oval of bedrock, the interior structure of the mountain. From this wound, Peter could see part of the valley: A mile to the left, on the near side of the river, terraces of a tea plantation, and some white buildings with red roofs—the Ashram. To the right, up the river, a deception of tributary valleys, shadowed by jungle; there a fiery splash of color—it would be a krishnachura tree—looked at him, and he started down the last slope.

The noise of the river, a harsh whisper in the distance, then a roar, grew louder, wilder, more confused, approached the intensity of a continuous crash, to which the ear must become gradually adjusted. At the bottom of the valley Peter came to a ragged edge where primeval violence had torn the jungle off. A strip of wasteland, where nothing grew, stretched the length of the valley and beyond. New-made sand, rocks, bleached and scarred and mutilated boulders lay strewn along it. Down the midst of this devastation the river force raged in spate. It hurled itself, cataclysmic, from side to side in the deep, narrow cage it had gouged for itself from the Himalayas to the Ganges, grinding boulders all along its depths, carrying on its crest a foam of fronds and trees and turf.

The path divided, the main part going to the Ashram on the left, the other, an unused track to the right, upstream. As Peter glanced covertly back at the landslide up the mountain, he thought he glimpsed a figure running across the exposed thread of the trail. Instead of continuing on to the Ashram he turned upstream toward the krishnachura tree. Near the river there was a stirring of air, but the trail soon reeled away from it. Sweat was streaming down his body. He removed his shirt and rolled it up as he walked, not because he would be any cooler that way, but merely because when he sweated he liked to sweat without impediment.

The trail skirted the jungle edge, growing fainter and fainter, finally disappeared altogether. A little farther on, a winding hundred yards from the river, stood the krishnachura tree. A small, clear brook, evidently from a spring nearby, flowed past it, down the slope into the river. Peter drank, then removed his sandals and waded up the stream.

The tree was about forty feet high, with a spread of fifty feet. Its trunk, smooth and perpendicular, might have been four feet in diameter. Magnificent, orchid-like blossoms, crimson, orange, deep yellow, a flaming circlet with a crest—"the Crest of Krishna"—covered the whole tree. Occasionally one of them dropped heavily to the ground or into the brook, floated down to the river, then out into other forms. This was a tree shrine, Peter saw, abandoned perhaps, for there was no sign of recent visitors. Still, with delicacy, he went out of his way to circle it because he was sweaty and in an unwashed mood; but he glanced at it as he passed.

Leaning against the trunk, between two massive roots, was a stone image of Krishna. Balanced on one foot, the opposite knee raised sideways, waist swaying outward, a flute pressed to his lips, the god was dancing to his own music. It was a weather-beaten, stumpy, almost comical little statue, less than three feet high, hacked out by some village workman of long ago; yet the grace of movement was implied, a magic fluency that continued on into the roots of the trees, into the rhythms of the dropping flowers, the rising land, the river passing, the beholder. The face, with its puckered yet smiling lips joined to the flute, the half-closed eyes greatly elongated and drooping in the middle, barely concealed a mysterious concentration of joy.

"What's Thee up to now?" Peter muttered to God in passing, as a man will when his Fates are queasy.

A few yards farther on, he heard the sound of a small waterfall. It came from a thicket of fern trees and plantains at the base of the escarpment in which the mountain ended. Here he found a deep pool into which the brook fell some ten feet from a wide ledge. Beyond that he could see no sign of the brook. Quickly Peter scrambled up on the ledge, with some obscure design of finding the source of the water. An oblique outcropping of rock concealed the mouth of a cave or grotto, out of which the brook flowed. Cautiously he looked in, then entered. As his eyes became accustomed to the gloom, he saw that the grotto had been used as a cell by hermits and holy men, Brahman householders in the Fourth Stage, perhaps, who had put their affairs in order and had retired to the Himalayas to contemplate Reality. A bed, hewn out of the rock wall, was worn smooth by centuries of use, like the floor. Walls and ceiling were covered with carvings, bas-relief, mostly of Krishna and his friends, out of the living rock. These varied in the degree of skill with which they had been executed, but nearly all were in the erotic convention of Hindu sacred sculpture. Successive generations of Krishna worshipers, some corrupt, some refined, some both, had striven to outdo their predecessors in piety. By practicing the most rigorous austerities, they had sought to diminish in themselves the power of this illusory and transitory existence. At the same time, they had glorified the Divine, representing it in terms of the most joyous human experiences of which they could conceive. For them, these experiences were exceedingly sensual and, to the lonely hermit, sociable, Krishna being both Eros and Agapé. For them, religion was a pleasure.

Peter shivered slightly, as if from a draft of air between his body and his soul. Out of a crevice, from its source deep within the mountain, the water flowed, crossing the floor of the cave. A small person might have wriggled through the narrow passageway, closer to the source. The air of the cave was almost cold, scarcely affected by the booming sun outside. Waiting beside the entrance to the outer world, Peter wiped the drying sweat from his body, but he did not put on his wet shirt. The clammy shorts flapping against his thighs annoyed him, so he took them off. The Indian G-string he wore under them, being of little consequence, remained.

He did not have long to wait. Down by the krishnachura tree, a sleek black head appeared, a flash of color—the rainbow apron—and Liliu Acquileia was treading in deliberate sacrilege across the shrine of Krishna. She came swiftly, warily, her head high in the air, sometimes stooping as if to inspect the ground for footprints, although he had left none. It was as if she were proceeding by the sense of smell, sniffing the air for his spoor—Peter felt suddenly weak at the thought—but then, perhaps she knew this place and was merely playing a hunch that he would go to the brook's source.

From the darkness of the cave he watched her circle the pool. There was something tigerish in the silent intensity of her movements. Now she was prowling to and fro in the ferns and plantains and in the lush growth of jungle that resumed close by. Then she had not known of the cave, unless, from a distance, she had seen him near this place. Coming back to the pool, she looked at the ledge, climbed up, stood uncertainly before the cave entrance, listening. Her eyes were dilated, showing the whites, and her red mouth was open as she folded her heavy breathing out and in noiselessly. Reaching into her sleeve, she drew out a curved, stiletto-like knife with a turquoise handle. As she entered the cave, Peter seized her. She fought powerfully, clawing and biting, but making no outcry. He squeezed her wrist until the tendons and muscles of her hand grew numb, relaxed, then he shook the knife out of it. Slowly he released her, but stood in the entrance, blocking her escape. With his bare toes he pawed the knife behind him, and heard it drop into the pool below.

Panting and sullen, she glowered at the floor, awaiting her fate, neither looking at him nor speaking. A dumb, glazed look settled over her face, outraging him worse than the knife, and he was swept by indignation, by rage, by the compulsion to follow her into the feral depths to which she had retreated and there, burning and blasting her with the vengeance of the Lord, change her identity. . . . The change was in him, not in her, it being but one backward step from wrath to lust, as she well knew. It was all the same to him, as she fell against him, whether the sob she gave was purely histrionic, or one of remorse, or relief, or triumph, or merely love. Trembling and pale, stiff as the figures in the bas-relief about him, he stood fallen. With her arms around him and her face pressed to him, she slid down, down to a posture of prayer. . . .

Savasana, the Pose of the Corpse, this Earthly Vessel, which once held fire and water, earth and air, and darkness, light and force, now lay shattered on the stone, a thing used by Kundalini the life force in its peregrinations, and flung aside. Into his body, from the stone bed, crept the ancient lunar cold of the Himalayas. Before his dull gaze and above him the same stone writhed, frigid, orgiastic—gods, humans, and demiourgoi battering at their limits—a nest of lovers caught eternally in the act, according to their heart's desire, a static ecstasy in frozen fire. And all was Krishna, the Predecessor, the Possessor, He Who Comes After. . . . The formal unity was this, which Peter had not seen until now: All these vignettes, carved through centuries by limited human beings to celebrate the illimitable joy of Krishna, were arranged between two parallel lines that ran without interruption around and around the cave, over and under and through and among and beyond, without apparent beginning or end; for one set of lines came out of the aperture in the mountain whence the brook issued, and another set went in. At first Peter assumed that these two parallel lines represented the River of Life, Ganga Mata; but it was too sinuous, and its source on sacred Mount Kailasa was not shown. These were the coils of Ananta, the Endless Serpent, called also Shesha, End, because he is formed of the Residue left over from the Creation of the Cosmos, which he encircles. He is guardian of the life energy which he replenishes and from which he is entitled to replenish himself with all elements that are compatible with his peculiar metabolism.

Uprooting himself from the stone, Peter stepped out into the hot sunlight, naked, shielding his eyes with his hand. Liliu Acquileia remained on the stone bed. "Come wash yourself," he said; and as she did not obey or answer him, he went back, raked up her clothes, and threw them down below into the ferns. She stood in the entrance, the oiled strands of her hair veiling her almost to the waist.

As he took her by the wrist to pull her out, the humid length of her body, arousing in its vertical unfamiliarity, swam against his bareness and he encircled her with his arm. Bracing herself against the sides of the cave mouth, she drew him in, pushing on the rock. He released her, backed out of the cave, appealing, commanding her with his eyes. She would not follow. Her voice, polite now, dispassionate, almost self-effacing, was at variance with what she said:

"If there had been another woman, I would have killed her, Lord. Nothing could save her."

"And if I came to meet Krishna?"

She withdrew farther into the cave. "Whatever has desire will die, Lord. Whatever will die, its death can be now as well as then, if that is suitable."

"If there is that in me which leads where you cannot follow—"

"You will never reach that place, Lord, without this emanation of you, myself."

"And if it is I myself?"

For a moment she paused, and the night of the cave looked through her eyes. Her voice arched up as if to sting itself: "I love you, Lord. I would die for you, but I would also kill you. That is only one proof of my love. Whatever imprisons your soul—whether it be a woman or a sacred scroll or a school—that prison will be destroyed!"

"Your mind is the prison, Liliu! Open it!"

"No!" she threw herself against him, crying. "You do not understand. Do not be offended. It is only karma, not a threat. Is that any way for a woman to talk to God? No, no, it is only that I am for you." With her mouth to his skin, she began to persuade him once more.

With an effort of the will he detached himself and, turning his back on her, again stepped out on the ledge. The sun dazzled him. For a moment he teetered there, peering to make sure of the pool —not for anything would he have dashed his brains out on a rock. A shout from below the krishnachura tree startled him—it was Tino and Chanchal and Jim Chen! Peter dived into the pool, swam around under water, found the knife and thrust it deeply into the sand on the bottom.

They had walked too fast, carrying guns, ammunition, and what looked like lunch baskets—an Oriental outing, with charades! Tino was regretting it. With disgust he plucked off his wet shirt. Sweat was flowing down his soft white torso, into his trousers, which clung darkly to him. These, too, he began to skin off, despite the shame he felt at his sedentary body. "I hate this sort of thing!" he snarled. "We saw you from up there—"

"You saw me?"

"From 'way up there." Tino jerked his head toward the landslide. "We were going down to the Ashram, and we saw something moving. Jim could tell it was you by your conspicuous features, and insisted—"

"Did I insist?" Jim sounded waspish, precarious. He started to remove the white shirt which he wore open down the front, and the half-boots into which the bottoms of his tight blue jeans were partly tucked. When he stooped, he did not allow his abdominal muscles to hang over the top of his jeans.

"Nasty stuff, sweat!" Tino threw his shirt, socks, and underwear at the little waterfall, and hobbled on soft white feet into the pool. "Look at these superior bastards!"—Chanchal and Jim—"They're not sweating; they just glisten. They have smaller sweat glands than we do, according to a Chinese doctor I know."

"It's not true!" Jim rasped. "They're as big as anybody's."

"He says, if you live in a tropical climate you've got to have small sweat glands," Tino quibbled, splashing himself—he was not badly formed, but flabby, with a little more stomach than chest. "It's logical. Otherwise you'll sweat to death, like me. Main idea is to remove impurities—it's like Purgatory—but who knows where it'll stop?"

"A typical remark," Jim muttered darkly.

"Jim, I *like* little sweat glands!"

"You called me a bastard, and you weren't smiling."

"Do I have to smile every time I— Listen, I only call two classes of people bastards: those who aren't and those who are. Now, don't be one for Christsake!"

"That," said Peter, "is a statement."

"Gentlemen," Chanchal said, "this is a sacred spot, 'as holy and enchanted as e'er beneath a waning moon was haunted by woman wailing for her demon lover.'"

Peter shuddered and cast a quick look at the place where he had thrown Liliu Acquileia's clothes. Fortunately the ferns concealed them. As soon as possible he would try to draw the men toward the Ashram, although he was no longer in the mood to go there himself.

"I was suffering," Tino said. "Don't hold me to account for what I say when I'm suffering."

"Why suffering, Tino?" Chanchal was full of solicitude.

"First, because I'm cutting down on my drinking. Second, panic. I get panicky when I sweat. Come into the water—friends."

"Why do you think I came to India?" Jim Chen's round, boyish face quivered with lacerated sensitivity. "Because I got sick and tired of Americans taking one look at me and saying—to me, an American: 'Well, well, a Chinaman! How did you ever learn to talk like an American, you little yellow bastard?'"

"They don't say that!"

"They do, they do! They think it, anyway. And I don't even know Chinese. If America isn't my country, then where *is* my country?" Two bitter tears stood in his eyes.

"Gentlemen, I will bawth in the river," Chanchal cried abruptly, turning away.

Tino called after him with alarm: "Don't go in that river—you can't even swim!"

"You'll wind up as silt in the Ganges!" Peter warned.

"In Ganga Mata there are no discussions of sweat glands." Chanchal did not go far, but looked around and with a sad smile allowed himself to be persuaded.

Jim Chen stood nonchalantly on an elevation by the pool, his stomach drawn in, ready to dive; but not just yet. Although he was quite small, his body was excessively developed. Chest, shoulders, arms, calves, and the rest, had the grotesque muscularity that is achieved by fanatical and sustained effort; yet his waist was so slim it might have been laced in by an invisible corset. As he waited there, half-poised for the dive, he looked perfect and self-sufficient. Only for a moment he stood thus, until Tino, peering at him myopically, said, "My God!" Then, smiling faintly, Jim leaned forward, bounced in the air, executed a perfect jackknife. Heron-like, Tino watched the pale yellow form sharking about under the surface, through lightings of blue-green, yellow, and ivory. After that, Tino held his own stomach in, but irregularly, for the effort fatigued him.

For a minute Peter observed Jim's rippling, changing form, and he thought of that part of the *Krishnayana* in which he retold the ancient and sinuous tale of the Sage Narada, the holy man who so far expanded his consciousness that Krishna appeared before him and offered to grant a wish. "I wish to know the secret of your Maya," said Narada. "No one can know that," replied the god; but the sage persisted, and Krishna said, pointing to a pool, "Dive in there, and you shall experience the secret of my Maya." Narada dived into the pool. When he emerged, it was as Sushila, the beautiful daughter of the King of Benares. In the course of time she married the prince of Vidarbha, a neighboring kingdom, who became king upon the death of his father. Queen Sushila was extraordinarily happy, experiencing all the delights of love and the fulfillment of dharma. Many children were born to her, and there were grandchildren, and all of them were gifted, some with beauty, some with intelligence, and there was not one of them who did not have fundamentally decent instincts. Then a war broke out between Benares and Vidarbha. In one terrible battle Queen Sushila's husband, father, and many of her sons and grandsons were killed. Beside herself with grief, she built a huge funeral pyre on the battlefield and laid their bodies on it. With her own hand she set fire to it. When the flames reached their height, she cried out, "My son! My son!" and cast herself into the pyre. It was cool and refreshing. Someone had her by the hand and was leading her out of a pool. "Did you not call for your son?" Krishna asked the Sage Narada gently. . . .

Jim surfaced, his hair plastered against his head, gave an equisnort, splashed water in Peter's face, dived down again, scissoring his curly legs after him like the two halves of a caudal fin. As Peter climbed out, Chanchal averted his eyes—the Brahman had kept on a pair of voluminous white drawers, and was splashing himself at a shallow margin of the pool. Peter noticed that he did not wear the sacred thread, prescribed for all men of his caste.

The water was cold; the sun was hot. Brushing the water from his skin, Peter began to shiver, his muscles bunching autonomously here and there like a horse pestered by flies. How to get the men away from here before somebody discovered the cave? Tino was busy wringing out his clothes, and could hardly be expected to put them on until they had dried somewhat. Meanwhile Jim Chen would almost certainly take it into his head to climb up on the ledge in order to look like a statue. He would find the cave. Peter would say, Pardon me, but there is a naked witch in that cave, who does not wish to be disturbed, because she is in the midst of a very special curse. . . . All at once Chanchal's drawers, Tino's testiness, Jim's physique, Liliu in the cave, himself here, caught him off guard; he began to shiver and snigger with spastic abandon. Again he looked at Chanchal, and laughed a deep, irrevocable sort of laugh.

He was sitting down now, still laughing, trying to drink from the bottle Tino had handed him, but he was shaking too hard. Whisky splashed everywhere except into his mouth, and he nearly dashed out a tooth with the neck of the bottle. Snatching the bottle, Jim Chen got a grip on Peter's head and poured a neckful of whisky down him. Peter subsided, with only occasional convulsions. "Malaria," he said. "It comes *back!*" The last word was a yell, and he was laughing again as if he intended to keep it up. All at once Jim Chen grinned and straightened up. Whatever it was had passed sympathetically into him: his muscles bunched and sank unpredictably along his gigantic little torso. "W-What's the m-matter with me?" he quaked. "N-N-Never hap-pened be-f-fore!" Tino began to rub him, but a paroxysm of shaking seized him. "N-No!" As the little man crouched there trying to control himself, his big pectorals stood out like the breasts of a woman. His belly muscles, contracted, looked like huge gloved fingers clasped around him. The bottle rattled against his teeth as he drank from it unaided. To ensure themselves against hysteria, Tino and Chanchal also drank.

Peter was precariously quiet as Tino pulled another bottle out of the basket he had brought. "To chills and fever!" Tino cried. "It

comes *back!*" Chanchal screamed, doubled up with laughter. Jim
Chen lay on his side, near the guns, his head propped up on one
hand, in classical repose, authoritative.

"It's not malaria," he said; "it's buck fever. You passed it on to
me before I realized what was wrong with you."

"What is this buck fever?" Chanchal was suddenly sober.

"A case of nerves," Jim replied. "You went off half-cocked this
morning when you made us join you in this snake shoot. What was
the big rush? Why didn't you wait for Peter? You knew he came
all the way from Kashmir, that he's an experienced hunter—"

"Buck fever is not Indian," Chanchal retorted haughtily. "Nor
is python fever. I believe it was Mr. Peter who began to shiver first?
Further, it was not I who requested assistance. Further, it was Tino
and yourself who insisted upon accompanying me. Am I a boor?
Could I say no?"

"You are not a boor at all," Tino tried his hand at peacemaking,
"but you've never been hunting in your life—confess it! It was lucky
Jim happened by and was kind enough to go along. You know I
wouldn't be of much help if you actually met the damned thing."

"Indians can take care of India," Chanchal muttered sullenly,
beginning to dry himself with an enormous flowery towel which
he took out of one of the baskets. "We know our duties."

The bottle went around again, Chanchal taking his share—against
all Brahman rules. Peter wondered about that, about the absence of
the sacred thread, about Chanchal's willingness to take life. Doubtless he considered himself a "liberal," if not "Westernized." Angrily
Peter noticed, all at once, that his own rifle was with the other two
guns; but he said nothing. Once he started to talk, he might arouse
their curiosity about his presence here, as he was not very good
at keeping secrets. If they discovered Liliu Acquileia, it would be
most unfortunate. Yet, to save him, he could think of no plausible
reason to give them if he asked them to leave.

"You say you know your duties," Jim said—it was as if he had
received Peter's thought about Brahmanism. "How is it you're so
eager to shoot a living creature? Don't you know it'll set you back
about ten million years in your journey to Nirvana?"

"Ha, ha! You think all Indians are yogis?" Chanchal's voice was theatrical; his big oblique eyes roving wildly, he paced about in his wet drawers as if preparing for some dashing action. "There is nothing I will not do! Nothing! Show me a piece of beeph—I will eat it!"

"It's true," Tino said. "He will eat beef if necessary—but don't give him the bottle again."

"I can drink rivers!"

"Rivers, but not liquor," Jim insisted with deliberate malice. "You're not supposed to, and you can't."

"Poppycock, sir! I have had thrice as much as you!" He took another drink and wiped his mustache, first one side, then the other; then his agile index finger became a symbol of oppression defied. "One thing, Mr. Chen! Tell me one thing I cannot do! Just one thing!"

Jim grinned maddeningly. "You can't take off your drawers."

With his head lowered as if he were about to charge, Chanchal glared at him in outraged silence.

"That's what I mean," Jim pursued with a slightly contemptuous gesture. "Indians are prudes."

Chanchal disintegrated. "A bloody lie!" He roared, and charged. Catlike, the Hawaiian rolled on his back, raised his feet, caught Chanchal in the stomach. For a moment Chanchal was suspended in air, draped over Jim Chen's small, prehensile feet.

"As I was saying," Jim remarked coolly, flexing his calves as Tino and Peter carefully lifted his attacker to safety, "India is one big taboo. Oh, they're lofty talkers—the world's greatest liberals—but they don't do a damn thing about it. Talk, talk, talk, from the *Rig-Veda* to the present, like the monsoon rains, and it all runs off into the Bay of Bengal! They're even worse than Americans about race. Worse about religion; worse about sex, too. Anal-compulsive Aryans all of 'em!"

"That," said Peter, beginning to chortle again, "is a very funny concept."

"I lost my balance," Chanchal panted, his speech thicker. "A guest of India is my guest. Unfortunately I fell toward him." Again he reached for the bottle. "So that's what you think," he said, swaying somewhat. "That's what you think?"

"That's what I think." Jim lay with his hands behind his head, knees drawn up and half-crossed, knotting his thick calf muscles by pointing his toes rather decoratively.

"You are wrong," said Chanchal. "It is the fault of British prudery. Before them, the people never thought of such trivial things as sex. We lived a healthy village life."

"The British have gone. You're on your own."

"It is a long history. The Muslims were exceedingly immoral—"

"The Muslims are in Pakistan now," Jim pursued relentlessly.

Peter began to dress. Perhaps he could lead them away from the place, then return. . . .

"In truth," Chanchal was saying, "we Hindus—we think it is *oh-so-bad* to expose the facilities. It is an insult of the worst."

"Even in bed?"

"Never!"

"Even in your most private bath?"

"*Never, sir!*"

"Tell me one thing," Jim said, looking more catlike than ever. "Why is the word for penis the same as the word for treasure—*dhan,* from the Sanskrit—"

"God damn it, if you please, sir!" Chanchal shrieked furiously.

"You must admit—"

"To quote the Western proverb," Chanchal said coldly, " 'When in Rome, do as the bloody Romans do!' " The white drawers dropped to his feet. He swayed defiantly. "Go to hell, all of you! You are insulted!"

Jim Chen leaped up and shook hands with him warmly. "Congratulations!" he cried. Tino shook hands with him. "Thank you very much, Chanchal," he said. "This is a great privilege." Dizzily Chanchal looked around for Peter, tottered over and shook hands with him. "Good show!" Peter said. Once more, grinning foolishly, Chanchal had to shake hands all around, faster this time. Suddenly he fell over the edge and disappeared into the pool.

Within a few seconds Jim and Tino had pulled him out, fighting like an octopus. Now he lay quietly on the rock. He was ashen in color. "I have been punished," he said. "Give me my drawers."

At Peter's desperate suggestion, they agreed to begin the python hunt "properly" at the Ashram with a cup of tea and some judicious queries about the habits of the quarry. Weighed down less by Chanchal's melancholy than by their part in his disgrace, Jim Chen and Tino had dressed in silence—Jim had become modest and courteous, having won some sort of victory. To cover his humiliation, Chanchal, with Peter's gun in his hand, pretended to stalk the jungle nearby, to Peter's discomfiture. Suddenly there was a strident shout, a yelping, a jabbering, the sound of blows. Chanchal emerged, electric with triumph, dragging a small, struggling man—a Lepcha —by the hair.

"Ha, you see? This wild bloke had been spying on us!" he howled, cuffing him. "A Peeping Tom!" And he continued to berate him, first in Bengali, pulling him about by the hair, then in English, boxing his ears, for the benefit of the others, to regain the dignity he had lost a short time before. "You are lucky, my good man, that I did not cook your goose with this gun!" He banged him with the barrel. "What is your game, you blackguard, you scoundrel, eh? Do you want the burra sahibs to know that we are all sneaking Indians, eh? Were you going to shoot a poisoned arrow into us, eh? Speak up, you blinking savage! You will end your days in Old Bailey!"

Quietly Peter took the man away from him. Holding him only in a formal way, Peter began to question him in Nepali and Tibetan, since he did not know the Lepcha language. The captive was less than five feet tall, but hard and wiry, with the bulging calves of a mountain dweller, toes fanning out, moving autonomously like fingers. His hair was cut close to the scalp all around, up to a flat, horizontal topknot that rocked like a fringed plate balanced on his head. The features were Mongolian, delicate, hairless, leather-colored, with a jawbone that persisted eerily beyond the other contours of the face in an involuntary semblance of arrogance. His clothing consisted of a leather vest that stopped short of the navel, a leather belt with a bit of a groin pocket, and some beads and amulets. When Peter let go of him, he stood looking the tall sahib straight in the eye, as hillmen do, and answered in about five words.

Chanchal leveled the rifle at him. "Let me deal with him! You don't know these blokes!" As if by accident, Peter lounged between them, his back to Chanchal. The Lepcha disappeared into the jungle, casting one last, glittering look at Peter, as if to emphasize whatever message it was that he had delivered.

"Let him go," Peter said. "He only wanted to warn us that we're on sacred ground. I told him we were just going."

"Sacred ground? He's not even a Hindu! He's only a—a junglie!" the Brahman exclaimed.

"Then you can be all the more grateful to him," said Peter.

The early afternoon sun did not penetrate the branches of the krishnachura tree as they circled past it. Between the roots, in the deeper shadow, the god appeared now to be merely a part of the tree, the unheard flute unseen. They proceeded down the trail to the river, and on to the place where the trail divided. Here Peter abandoned them under pretext of returning to Tashiling for an appointment. He would rejoin them "in ten minutes" at the Ashram.

As soon as they were out of sight, he returned swiftly to the krishnachura tree. Liliu Acquileia's clothes had disappeared, and so had she. The Krishna image lay face down in the dirt. Setting it back in its place between the roots, he dusted it with his handkerchief. Unconsciously as he did so he smiled in response to the ancient smile. A krishnachura bloom plopped to the ground near him. He placed it on Krishna's flute, and left.

The Lepcha was waiting for him by the river. Graceful as a fox, with perfect economy in his movements, he led Peter along the riverbank, upstream for a short distance, until they had passed the rock cliff; then he turned and started up the mountain. There was no trail at all that Peter could see. Although he had said that he would come, he hesitated, haunted by a sensation of familiarity, of design. Even Chanchal's discovery of the Lepcha had been like ritual, badly acted. . . . The Lepcha looked back at him questioningly and again he followed. It was almost straight up. Using their fingers and toes, grasping at branches and roots, they pulled themselves up about two hundred feet, to the top of the rock cliff. On this wide ledge the Lepcha left him, disappearing along the mountainside on some business of his own.

The sannyasi did not move or look up as Peter approached. Seated in the Lotus Posture, his eyes half closed, smiling a little, he was deeply withdrawn. Peter sat down near the man who had summoned him, and waited; but he did not quite face him, for several reasons. The sannyasi was very young, and Peter had come to share, more than he knew, in India's predilection for age, a cultural gerontophilia, which assumes that the young, born out of Old Night, have not lived long enough to have discovered anything new. To have composed himself then and there, opening his mind to an unknown holy man, would have been a little like opening his mouth to an unlicensed dentist. Added to this, and perhaps most important, was the fact that the sannyasi was difficult for Peter to look at directly, because he was beautiful, and men tend to regard that as unfair in another man, that is, as a potential threat to their own manhood, carefully nurtured as it must needs be, and simplified by a long and complicated process. Nor was the beauty of this sannyasi of the safely impersonal kind that is found in statues of gods representing principles, nor the generalized spiritual beauty of Agapé, both of which cause the life energy to center, with few exceptions, in the upper thorax. This was the beauty of Eros, which, fully looked upon, suggests nothing short of an embrace, as often as not in defiance of the law.

In the periphery of his vision—for thus, in his pudicity, he compelled himself to regard the sannyasi—Peter was aware of having seen him in many places, but always as adumbrations, intimations, as in the stone Krishna below, as in the song of that bird in the guava bush. Masks, all of them; for the Substance itself, being infinite, omnipresent, had no form of its own; yet men, unable to concentrate for long upon the invisible, had represented it as the Serpent-Shielded One: that state of fullness of being, the goal of desire, within a finite human individual, associated with the endless serpent, betokening the several ways men have of breaking through, extending or evading the limits of their individuality.

The sannyasi returned to the world of appearance, which was, for him, a way station between realms of reality—"returned" not in the sense that there had been even the slightest diminution of his presence "here," but only in the sense that he now chose to emphasize in his consciousness a particular time and place. Slowly the eyes opened in a very deep and smiling salutation, such as that with which God is said to contemplate his own beauty. "Yet how can we meet," he seemed to say, "who have never been parted since the beginningless Beginning, and how can we separate from each other, except for purposes of Maya, manifestation, playfully as it were, yet seriously, as befits the highest entertainment, to turn the Wheel of Life?" Upon this delightful recognition—for he was gazing directly into the eyes of the Serpent-Shielded One—Peter did what anyone else, especially an Indian, with his tropical exuberance, might have done under the circumstances of *darshan:* With an involuntary cry, he flung himself down in obeisance, *pranam,* before the sannyasi. For a moment the brown hand rested lightly on his head; then it was over. Without moving from the Lotus Posture, without speaking, the sannyasi had departed to business elsewhere in the Realms. Peter was free to go.

It was too late this time to ask his practical help, although it was possible that he was already well informed about Peter's concern with the python. Sannyasis sometimes had powers over wild creatures, and could cause them to come and go, to fawn and to attack, even to dance, in obedience to a flute or drum, sometimes to obey commands without any apparent signs from the holy man. Those who had no such powers either stayed away from dangerous animals, or were among them only for a short time, there being much deception in the forest, but no fraud.

seven

Children, scores of them, like a new race—blondly fresh, with long, oblique green eyes, Asian features rose and gold-tinted, ivory pallors out of Europe—were playing on the field at the Ashram. Classes were over for the day. Most of the boys, with Jim Chen coaching them, were involved in a soccer match. Wearing only shorts or girded-up *gamchas*—there were no uniforms here—they played with great abandon, kicking the ball with their bare toes. The girls, also barefoot, in saris and frocks of all colors (saris for the older girls, frocks for the younger ones), were playing volley ball and badminton. Mlle. de Rosière, in a yellow sari and sandals, sat under a mango tree, watching them. From time to time she glanced languidly at a book called *Friendly Anecdotes*, which Mary Nayler had given her. Neither Indira nor Lady Edith was in sight.

There were five principal buildings, all of them whitewashed, with corrugated iron roofs painted brick red: the girls' dormitory, the boys' dormitory, the large, rambling bungalow where Lady Edith and Indira lived, the schoolhouse where classes were held when it rained—otherwise one sat on mats under the mango trees— and, at a distance, where the tea bushes began, the factory where the tea was processed. A vegetable garden, fruit trees, and a model farm began at the jungle's edge and extended toward the factory. There were large Sindhi milch cows, some Danish goats, and Australian poultry. This complex school-plantation-community had only a few paid employees. All students and staff members were expected to work on an average of two hours every day to maintain the Ashram; and this they did with happy inefficiency.

Gori Govinda, who had been watching the soccer game from the

71

side lines, at first had hidden ineffectually behind a group of other
boys—perhaps because Peter had last seen him in his magnificent
Tibetan clothes, and now he was wearing only a green *gamcha*
which Jim Chen had given him. Seeing Peter look about uncertainly,
then start for the bungalow, he dashed over to greet him and to offer
his services. For the first time, Peter noticed that he had the look
of Liliu about him—the mouth not quite so thickly curved, different colorings, the features and bone structure not so compact; but
there were correspondences that made Peter vaguely uncomfortable.
The boy had emerged from childhood during the year since Peter
had first brought him here: emerged perhaps to an ordinary-enough
life in this land of early and arranged marriages, where boys who
are too pretty—and Gori Govinda was such a one—do not always
have time to find it out, and so may fare no worse than the next
fellow.

"I thought you had left the school," Peter said in English, the
lingua franca of the Ashram.

"No, no, no!" Good, he had learned that No's must come in
bunches or they are worth nothing in Indian currency—one No
meaning Yes, two No's meaning Maybe.

"But last night you were not here, were you?"

"In daytime I am here, at night save and except when *she* wants
me."

"You should stay here at night also," Peter said, avoiding his gaze.

Jim Chen came bounding up, panting from his exertions on the
field, supplanted Gori who stood uneasily by. "What happened to
you, Pete? I don't blame you for leaving. Those two! Imagine taking your gun! Mighty hunters—ha! They went on down the valley.
Come over to my room. I have to stay here, but I'm lending you my
rifle."

"Thanks just the same," Peter said with a sort of lazy self-mockery.
"I'll get my rifle back tonight. Anyway, I climbed a cliff and got
tired—and Kaliya won't be out for a while yet."

"Go on," Jim told Gori in a low voice, without looking at him, "get
into the game. We missed you." The boy ducked his head in sullen
embarrassment and sidled away—not to join the game, but to watch
from a distance.

"I was just telling him, he should stay in the dormitory with the other boys, especially at night."

"Don't worry," Jim said easily, "he's here most of the time. Some nights he stays in town with his half-sister—I think you know her? Not many of these kids have relatives who accept them, you know. Lady Edith thinks it's a good idea to encourage it when they do."

For just a second Peter hesitated—he was hardly in a position to insist—then he shrugged:

"I don't much agree, but it's your responsibility. I was just thinking of the python."

"Oh, we're not afraid of him any more," Jim said, "now that you're here."

"One year I did some hunting," Peter said levelly, ignoring the heavy irony. "Different kinds of man-eaters. I couldn't go on with it, though. I was very idealistic then."

"You are now."

"No, not very. . . . It's just that killing destroys me. I can't do it in cold blood, and hot blood—well, I can't always count on that. Try killing a hundred flies one after the other, and see how long it takes you to feel human again! All right, imagine larger animals— really large ones now that the British hunters have gone and they've had years and years in which to grow. And beautiful! Some of them are like prehistoric creatures."

"Chinamen know their dragons," Jim said quizzically. "Just bring in your Kaliya. Prehistoric, eh?"

"Sixty million years. The fossils show no difference between pythons then and now. Of course, humans are more plentiful nowadays. . . . Are you sure you won't keep Gori Govinda here? Or if he must go to Tashiling, don't let him go by the trail."

"I'll see that he goes in the jeep after this," Jim said hastily. "He can ride into town with Indira—or I'll take him myself. You might mention this to Lady Edith." As Peter gazed meditatively at the bungalow, Jim said: "She's out giving shooting lessons to Indira. You'll find them down there south of the farm, by the river. Better give them a few minutes to practice—Indira needs it. Come to my room, won't you? There's something I want to talk to you about."

Jim's room was in a wing of the boys' dormitory, separated from

the students' quarters by the rooms of Dr. Bhattacharya and the
Sanskrit teacher, a pundit from Benares. "Sorry I can't offer you a
drink. Rules of the Ashram." He held out a box of big black cheroots
—Peter shrank from them, lighting a cigarette instead.

"Don't leave the soccer game for me," Peter said. "I know my
way."

"I wish I did. . . . No, no, this is an occasion," Jim said. He
was lying back in a big chair, booted feet on another chair, a glint
of mockery in his eyes as he lit a cheroot. The afternoon light slanted
in through the window to an odd effect: the heavy blue smoke
clung closely to him in the still air, like a loose garment through
which he could see without being seen. "My pay here is nominal,
or didn't you know? That means I'm free to come or go as I like—
within reason, of course."

"Stick around," said Peter. "I have a feeling—you know, a money
feeling?"

" 'A great fortune is ordained for you, wait patiently'! You've
been eating too many Chinese fortune cookies." Jim laughed, then
frowned. "I wasn't hinting. All I need here is board and room. Lady
Edith wanted to pay me more, but she can't really afford it, and I
have some money. The tea plantation isn't doing so well just now
—not enough skilled workers. We want *you* here, Pete. You're the
Founding Father."

"One of the three," Peter corrected him, "and not really, and
I'm no good for it."

"Who is? Ananda's dead, Lady Edith—soon you'll be the only one
left of the original three. Or did you think one of *us* could manage
it? I don't want to be tied down. Bhattacharya is a windbag. Indira
is a woman—I mean, of course, Lady Edith—"

"Lady Edith will recover," Peter said, "and Kaliya won't be here
long, and neither will I."

Slowly, lazily, Jim's smoke shroud disintegrated and his amused
eyes appeared. "I also have a cottage in town," he said. "There I
can even offer you a drink."

On the walls were photographs of famous athletes, among them
the little man himself: Jim Chen grinning, with a baseball bat and
a ball; Jim Chen in swimming trunks, standing on a box, holding a

silver cup and flanked by two pretty blondes in bathing suits; Jim Chen holding over his head a bar bell with enormous weights on it —veins stood out on his forehead and neck, but his white teeth flashed for the camera.

"It isn't just vanity," Jim said modestly. "These pictures remind me to keep fit. This climate—if I don't watch myself I get soft. I was in good condition then." He brought out of his desk a large photograph of himself, nude—a regular fortress of a torso surmounted by the flower-like face of a four-year-old, hungering for protection, for the breast.

"Tremendous," Peter said in the respectful tone of one remarking upon a calamity; for there was something in that physical exuberance, that excessive shapeliness, that reminded him of the morbid swellings which afflict so many Indians. "How did it—how did you—"

"Weights," Jim said. "Try 'em—I'll show you how. You've got a splendid physique, but you need to develop it more. What do you say? I'll put four more inches on that chest, two on your biceps—"

"Not just at the moment." Unconsciously Peter used the phrase his father had habitually used at table when declining a dish forever. He glanced around him at trophies of prowess. Variously disposed about the room were a tiger skin, a rhinoceros horn, several guns, including a .45 Colt in a holster, a small knife collection, athletic equipment and, neatly stacked in a corner, a weight-lifting set.

"It isn't all here," Jim said, picking up a hundred-pound bar bell and tossing it speculatively in the air a couple of times, "but it's enough to keep in condition with. I just lent sixty pounds of it to Tino Scott, to start him off. Of course, he can't lift it yet," he chuckled. "I sent it up with a boy from the village. The trouble with Tino is, he's weak. If he follows my advice, I'll make a man of him."

"He's already a man," said Peter.

Jim smiled tolerantly and replaced the bar bell. "By definition, yes. Sure. Psychologically, then—something he said made me think he's never even made out with a girl. Can you imagine?" As Peter said nothing, Jim went on in a man-to-man tone, increasingly throaty, confidential: "I wouldn't touch a friend's girl—know what I mean? Tino especially. That would be a rotten trick, wouldn't it? You can't tell about others, though. If you have a lot of vitality, and then this climate, and the opportunity—women being what they are. . . . By the way, if you like these pictures, I have a larger collection up at the cottage. Care to see 'em?"

"If I'm up that way," Peter said, "sure." The atmosphere in the room had become very close, partly from the cigar smoke. Peter made a sort of lurching movement toward the door, although his feet remained planted where they were.

"I like you," said Jim, "I like you very much. Don't mind the things I say sometimes." He laughed heartily, made as if to maul Peter, thought better of it, and flung the door open to anticipate him; but instead of going out he picked up a rifle, sighted along it, then handed it to Peter. "How do you like it? Will it stop your Kaliya?"

Peter examined it swiftly—it was new, a .470 No. 2 double-barrel, with an electric torch for night shots, telescopic lens, and wide V express sights for easy snap shooting at short range. Leaning it carefully against the wall, he said in the curiously exalted monotone sometimes produced by tightened vocal cords:

"It is a good gun, as a gun. It will stop a python or any other living creature, if you hit him in the right place. In the case of a python—you undoubtedly know this—it should be either in the head or just in back of the head, to sever the spinal cord. The bigger he is, the more accurate you have to be, to keep from merely wounding him. As for your other question, no, I do not like it. I do not like those things on it. I do not like guns."

"I'll remove the 'things'! I wouldn't use them for game, but a pest —a *python!* Forgive me, I've never—"

"Leave them on," Peter said brusquely, "as long as thee can. I don't regard him as a pest, or as game either."

"Quakers don't believe in killing, do they?"

"No," Peter said, moving slowly out the door, into the hall, "they don't like it one bit." The plain "thee" had slipped out unexpectedly, to his annoyance.

"I wasn't sure—"

"I'm not a Friend, not a Hindu—or, yes, I am—also a cousin,

a son, a nephew, American vertebrate, Indian, a sort of man, or maybe you don't think so?" He glared down into the hurt face of a four-year-old, then suddenly melted and without thinking chucked him under the chin.

"Listen"—Jim made as if to beat the wicked hand away, but wisely missed—"listen—don't do that. . . . Listen, don't kill that python. Let me do it, won't you?"

"Do it," said Peter, "but don't try it alone. I have to go after him anyway."

The target was a chunk of wood roughly ten inches in diameter, swinging at the end of a rope which was tied to the branch of a tree. The muzzle of Indira's gun followed it, weaving slowly back and forth—it was a bolt-action rifle in .333 caliber. With every shot, her body, which probably did not exceed a hundred pounds in weight, jerked violently from the recoil. Her sari, colored like a sunset, was tucked up, revealing slim bare feet and the loveliest, the very loveliest of legs, braced apart. The two long, thick braids which usually hung down her back were wound around the top of her head, the way Lady Edith wore hers. A bit of saffron silk was knotted at her throat. In despair—for she had failed to hit the target—she turned to speak to Lady Edith. At that moment, seeing Peter standing at a distance, entranced, she sank to the ground at Lady Edith's feet and unhitched the sari to cover her legs and feet. There she remained for some time, in confusion, pale but with bright rosy cheeks and a suspicion of wetness in the eyes. With a sudden gesture she undid her hair and let it fall down on either side of her face like huge dark blinders, so that it would require only a very slight movement to conceal her face entirely.

Lady Edith sat in a high-backed wicker chair with her back to Peter, the gold border of her pale blue sari over her head. At Indira's whispered announcement of the visitor, she straightened up. "Go now," she said in an unfamiliar quavering voice. "It was not too bad—you're improving. Would you mind coming for me in the Land-Rover in about a half hour? I'll be quite all right."

As Indira passed him, with lowered eyes, she saluted him with clasped hands in the soft, formal greeting, *namaste*. Awkwardly he replied. To his surprise, she was wearing rouge and lipstick—risqué, to say the least, for an Indian woman. Kohl around the eyes, yes—with the excuse of improving the vision; but Western cosmetics! He had had a flash of inexcusable beauty.

"Stay there for a moment!" Lady Edith called out to Peter, without getting up, without turning around, and she fumbled in a bag she had in her lap, drawing out a small mirror and lipstick—he had never seen her use that before. And those hands, the handsome, capable hands he had liked so much: something was wrong with them.

"Edith?" Impulsively, full of foreboding, he circled around in front of her, but she concealed her face in a fold of the sari, like a Hindu woman. Was she playing tricks on him?

"Peter, my dear!" she croaked, and held out her hand—it was emaciated, clawlike. Kneeling beside her, where Indira had sat, he wept silently, embracing her. The dry, skinny hands rustled over his hair like dead leaves. The sari fell back, revealing a beautiful death's-head: the ash-blonde hair was now scanty, white, the forthright blue eyes dreadfully sunken, the fresh cheeks drawn and wrinkled; and the teeth, well formed but never very good—they were gone, and in their place a set of false ones that might once have been suitable; but now they were ludicrously too big, having failed to shrink with her face. She could not quite close her lips over them. On one of the dry front teeth was a hasty smear of lipstick. "Don't feel badly." She tried to laugh or to cry, but could do neither properly. "I seem to have eaten something. . . . How nice it is to have you here—so handsome—and crying, too!"

Caressing the head in her lap, she gazed tranquilly, as if quite satisfied, out into the valley, at the howling river passing; as if her eyes saw only wholeness now, not particulars, the wholeness that one sometimes feels in dreams, which one can take up or leave at any point with equal relevance. The dream was already in her voice. It was as if she were aware of many previous deaths in herself, yet could not but be moved by each anticlimactic occurrence, each reminder of that ironic continuity wherein seekers after oblivion, regardless of merit, regardless of belief, are too commonly rejected on the grounds of the incompleteness of their experience, their unreadiness, the presumption of undefined, beginningless creatures in expecting anything so definitive as a termination!

At that moment Peter remembered, with total recall, the words she had spoken to him on the death of Ananda Mahadev, his great friend, her lover. Like a true Oriental—and indeed the skeleton in her family closet was that of an Indian ancestress, whom Edith alone, at the cost of exile, had invited to the feast—Edith had avoided referring overtly to the tragedy of Ananda's drowning. "May I tell you of something I realized today?" she had said to Peter that day, on nearly this very spot—they had just received some young orange trees from her uncle's tea plantation, where she had grown up. "Often, when orange trees die they put forth, in their last year, a heavy bloom. Did you know that? The tree feels death nearby. It hastens to mature its fruit. The leaves fall, every leaf, so that the last strength will all go into the fruit—although it's really the seeds that are being prepared. For a few weeks the branches of the bare tree are hung with a multitude—very large, pale oranges, like ornaments. They are perfect in shape, in size, in texture; but they are not to be eaten. There is no taste in them. Pale as the winter sun in Essex, they gleam—a galaxy of them in that naked and skeletal tree. . . . Then the tree is dead, and all the fruit drops off— oh, light and eager as apostles! They run and bounce in all directions, carrying the seeds inside them. Some will take root . . . somewhere . . . you never know where. That's the way it has always been."

Now he was composed, but he continued to sit on the ground beside her chair, holding her bony hand like a prince who is not easily gulled by the transformation of a princess into a hag. Indeed, they might have been lovers once, had they not both loved Ananda Mahadev so well.

"That girl isn't a very good shot," he murmured, free at last as with an old mistress or priestess at the far edge of night.

" 'That girl' tries too hard—so little time to tell her, to show her. . . . Did you notice the make-up—hers, I mean? She saw me put it on—the better to greet you with my dear!—and she had to put it on, too, out of sympathy so there'd be two of us, in case of trouble. I told her that the future abbess of the Ashram has no right to look

like a harlot—at least, not to start with! She said she did. Wouldn't
that give you confidence in her?"

"No," said Peter, "she has no solidness. She tried to run over me
with the Land-Rover."

"It was a purposive accident—she was moved in several different ways when she saw you. She has since apologized to me."

"She hasn't apologized to me!"

"It isn't likely she will now, my dear. Diana doesn't like to be
surprised by Actaeon—with her sari up! Do you like her?" she asked
abruptly.

"I—I don't know. What a question!" he stammered.

"I'm more and more surprised that anyone has time for fibbing,"
said Lady Edith. "Now listen, before I forget—my mind plays
little coy tricks on my will, to get a wink of sleep now and then:
Indira nearly ran over you, because she's in love with you and
doesn't want to be."

"I think—you must be mistaken."

"Don't take it too seriously. She doesn't admit it to herself. Perhaps she never will. She will be no threat to you whatever. She
thinks you're not attending to your dharma, so she doesn't quite
approve of you; but she means to attend strictly to her own. This
python, for instance—"

"Her caste duty is to teach—to direct the Ashram—not to kill."
Hastily Peter sought to change the subject.

"You saw the saffron scarf? The priestly color. A Brahman can
also sacrifice, you know. She thinks the director should know how
to shoot—in case she gets no help from anybody else."

"I've come to help," said Peter.

"So be it." Lady Edith sank back in the chair and closed her eyes.
Almost like a third person with them was her desire that Peter make
the Ashram his life. No words of hers could bring it about—had
they not been through this matter many times before? No one
could impose it from without, or achieve it by an emotional trick.

At first Peter had thought himself unfitted for such a post, because his interests were too diffuse, his temperament too unstable,
and the one direction he himself willed consistently was the writing
of the *Krishnayana*, with which any other kind of steady work

would very likely be incompatible. Now he was not so sure; he would have been willing—in fact, he longed—to try, not just out of duty, out of loyalty to Edith and to Ananda Mahadev, but because the place was all at once more attractive to him than he had ever imagined it would be. The trouble was, he had too many commitments in this part of the Himalayas, and one of them made the others impossible of realization: If he understood his temperament in its present condition, it would be about as easy for him to stay away from Liliu Acquileia as it would be for him to stop falling once he had tripped.

When Indira came with the Land-Rover, he carried Lady Edith to it—she was remarkably light—and rode back with them. Some girls and boys were waiting for her at the bungalow with garlands of flowers. Peter started to carry her again, but she insisted on walking, leaning on him, with Indira supporting her on the other side. Slowly, with difficulty because of her infirmity, yet gracefully, like one encumbered by a rich and heavy robe, she bowed so that the children might garland her.

"The river's so noisy," she muttered as the children trooped sedately off, then broke into a run. "And that fluting—" At the steps in front of the veranda she stopped and frowned at the shrubbery. An enormous crimson bougainvillaea had flung itself passionately upon the south wall of the house, to run new April tendrils under the red iron sheeting of the roof. "I suppose that's been there all the time?" Her voice was tired and querulous now as she spoke to Indira.

"Yes, Lady Edith, for a long time," Indira replied softly.

"I've been too busy to notice. That big boy, Rajan—ask him to clear it away immediately." Then, standing on the veranda, she reflected: "No, he wouldn't like that. I wonder why I— Just have him pull it out of the roof. Have him train it away from the house and build a neat trellis for it. Or somebody . . . Let Gori Govinda paint the trellis white, if he wants to—he's always around the bungalow. Next October get somebody to remove the trellis and trim the vine into a bush—and be sure to keep it that way, or you'll soon need a new roof. Will you remember, Indira?"

"I shall remember."

Lady Edith looked at her searchingly for a moment, then she drew the border of her sari across her face so that Peter should not see the appalling grin to which her smile had fallen. "You will have many things to remember." For a moment the dying woman clutched his arm, then she went inside with Indira, who motioned for him to wait on the veranda.

After a while Indira came out, looking pale but composed; the make-up was gone from her face. She had put on a dark blue sari, but she did not cover her head with the border of it. Her hair was coiled around the top of her head again in that stately way, making her seem tall, an illusion that was strengthened by the grace and dignity of her movements. Gone was the air of self-consciousness with which she had been afflicted under his gaze a short time before. Now she was the acting director of the Ashram, depersonalized by the responsibilities of her office, fortified by a whole culture based on the principle of duty—her youth, her sex, and her beauty being now entirely beside the point, as far as she was concerned, whether one knew it or not, and Peter knew that he ought to know it.

"Lady Edith is sleeping now," she said—they were sitting near each other on low wicker stools. Dispassionately yet intently she studied his face for a moment. When she spoke, there was a note of wonder in her voice: "Because of me, she did not ask you to stay at the Ashram. Did you know that?"

"I knew it. . . ."

"Yet you came—because you are loyal. Had you been here, it would have been better for you."

"It might have been worse. I'm not the person for this place."

"Do not make the same mistake I made, Peter. I did not recognize who you were—or I forgot who you were. I forgot what my brother told me once when I was sitting in judgment on somebody. He said: 'Indira, you and I come of a narrow-minded family. Let us be exceptions. A person is a village, a city, a world. He who sees only one inhabitant per person is ill instructed.'" Seeing the wryness and the love in Peter's face as he recognized the acrid style of his dead friend, she leaned forward, appealing to him: "I have caused you enough harm—forgive me! Come here to live. Stay with us!"

Inwardly he tottered toward her—she was beautiful, and she had the old starriness in her dark eyes that were big enough to jump into—the same odd, luminous quality that Ananda had had. It was almost irresistible, but not quite, because there were considerations. Peter veiled his eyes. Constellations of ambiguities appeared. Lady Edith was both a romanticist and a fanatic, whose interests could best be served by mating Peter with Indira; and although her motives were undoubtedly of the highest, her judgment was impaired. Wishful thinking had led her to declare that Indira was "in love" with him; the next step obviously was for her to persuade— or instruct—Indira to overcome her dislike, to get him to stay here, on the grounds that his help was needed for the survival of the Ashram. Even had he come here to stay immediately upon his arrival at Tashiling, he would not have been free from Liliu Acquileia.

He said: "Don't worry, I'll come for a few days. I want to be close when the python appears again. After that—well, I'll come when you need me, but not to stay. It's not my life. . . . As for the other—there's nothing to forgive."

The slow, bowing, sideways motion of her head signified her acceptance; then unexpectedly she smiled, glancing at the little golden amulet he wore on a cord around his neck for sentiment and ornament.

"Do you never reverse it?" she asked.

"No—why?" He fingered it, looking down at it with difficulty, the cord being short, because its previous wearer had had a slenderer neck than Peter's.

"This side—the OM—protects the world from you. That is for everyday use. The other side has a mandala on it. It protects you from the world. You are right—it would be ignoble to wear it that way very often."

"You recognize it?"

"Of course. Ananda gave it to you. It has been in our family for a long time." As she stood up, Peter stripped off the amulet and handed it to her. Swiftly she reversed it and put it back over his head, scraping his ears with the cord, which she could have avoided had she been willing to touch him with her fingers. "Wear it," she said, "but with the mandala out, for the time being." Without a backward glance, she disappeared into the house, leaving him tingling and weak from the touch of a cord which he had worn twenty-four hours a day for many months. Protecting him now was a tiny metaphysical shield engraved with a labyrinth into which the forces of evil were meant to be irresistibly seduced through some fortunate hebetude in their natures, thereby diverting them from their legitimate goal, his heart. The fact was, that little gold amulet with the heavy black cord, against Peter's particular form and coloring, was more interesting than he knew.

As he started up the mountain trail to Tashiling, a warm, steady rain began to fall, and he stopped under some plantain trees to consider whether he should go back. In that vulnerable moment, panic and grief and dread seized on him in defiance of the mandala: the irrecoverable past, the intolerable present, the all-too-escapable future. Of the two persons who had befriended him when he came to India, had reconciled the dialectic of his two worlds, had strengthened him toward some kind of wholeness in his lonely way, Ananda Mahadev had died, Lady Edith was dying. And that incalculable lust with which he must contend now more than ever, which had been given its freedom almost inadvertently during his illness the year before, embraced him with arrogant confidence that it would never be subdued or "sublimated." There was no one to whom he could turn for help. The *Krishnayana*, like its author, would remain unresolved, unfinished. "Junglie!" he addressed himself; but he had no heart for tender exhortation. Below the daylight inventory lurked an equivocal desire to take council with Kaliya. Indistinguishable in that night were death and the womb and life. Staring into the plantains, with their scandalous clusters, he passed his hands over his rain-slick body in melancholy pride and protest. Abruptly reaching out, he wrenched off a plantain, peeled it without touching the fruit itself with his fingers, and ate it voraciously. It was not nearly ripe enough. Despair had always produced in him an obsessive craving for sweet things.

Naked and motionless, he lay under the sheet, which stretched tautly from his toes to his chest, formalizing his body like the tomb

effigy of an English king. Within that austere form the nerves in
their grooves, after one agitated pause, had resumed their feeding.
What kind of mysticism was this, that stripped off the individual
consciousness only to lay bare the unlimited aggressiveness of individual subjectivity? Only a subtle, absolute nuance, the difference,
as between being and not-being, as between God and Satan . . . In
his fantasy Peter had outraged the sister of Ananda Mahadev.

Dully, somberly, in the periphery of his senses, he was aware of
Liliu Acquileia stirring about, preparing more sweets with a dash
of this and a dash of that—opium or hashish or some drug that
would probably turn out to be equally habit-forming. It was belladonna that he resented, not so much because it was a poison of
doubtful legality, as because it was a lasting love potion which
made it much more difficult for him to reach decisions at all relevant
to his dharma. Not that he was always sure what Liliu Acquileia
had given him, or indeed if she had given him anything of the sort
at a particular time, unless she chose to tell him. For him, merely to
imagine that he had been given an aphrodisiac was almost the same
as if he had actually been given one, so that he was likely to co-
operate with unnecessary intensity in his own seduction. At these
times he did not recognize himself, because he did not believe that
he was free.

"Why are you dressing so soon, Lord?"

Even after she had repeated her question he did not reply, but
finished dressing, then stood with his back to her, looking out the
window where he had seen the eye of Ananta-Shesha-Kaliya. The
truth, as he saw it then, was too cruel to tell—that he neither loved
her nor liked her; that she reduced his humanity to the danger
point by fortifying that in him which was cruel, debased, and merely
sensual; that for her he had betrayed his dharma, without which
he was not whole; that he would never see her again. It was not
even as simple as that: He had brought her here, he was partly
responsible for her, he was in it as deeply as she was. By his weakness he had encouraged her to look upon him as belonging to her.
The worst difficulty in disengaging himself from her arose from the
fact that she loved him, and not—he was sure—for his erotic prowess,
because there was that in him which protested all the way and

would not be absorbed. Smoldering, he lacked tenderness. Without comfort, he could not comfort her. . . . The quality of her love he did not question. Although he was short on experience, he had learned to respect all sorts of love on principle, because he had found so little of it in the world. Luck, rather than a strongly developed sense of survival, had until now protected him from its more virulent manifestations, except in the case of Irene Nayler.

"Your eyes were turned in like a yogi's, though it was I who lay under you." Liliu stroked him with her fingernails, yet his body remained aloof, like that of the Buddha caressed by Mara's daughters, except for the most elementary of reflexes. As he replied, she bit him through his shirt; he did not flinch.

"I always show the whites of my eyes; it is a gallantry." The evasiveness was partly from compassion, partly from a feeling of danger, lest she somehow find out that in his most private fantasy he had been thinking not of her, but of Indira.

"Turning the eyes, turning the back, it is the same, Lord. I have not seen you today, because there is someone hiding in you."

" 'I am large—I contain multitudes.' " Devising the best way to tell her, the best way to attack, he found himself suddenly on the defensive, disingenuous and banal.

"If I rail at you, Lord, kill me with your hands but do not bruise yourself on me—I would never wish to cause you discomfort. I ask you to remember only what I said to you in the cave, so that you will not be grieved. . . . It would be better if she would go back to her country."

The quiet certainty of her voice involved him, convinced him of danger—whether to Indira or to Irene at the moment, he did not know; to one of this region, all other regions—Kashmir or America —were far countries. The pulse throbbed in his throat as he said: "Some of my friends are women, some are men. I need them all."

"Some are neither men nor women," she said mildly, as if she were quite disinterested, "but they too die. It is strange. They die of friendship. That one who came for you—a widow and a virgin —her husband was her friend. When he walked, he swayed from the waist, and he talked like a girl. That is why she has the face of one who guesses!" By degrees her voice had changed, rising in un-canny caricature of William Nayler's lisp.

"Liliu Acquileia—" Peter was about to tell her that she was in very bad taste indeed, when it occurred to him that she had just said—or rather done—something quite odd. Last year in Tibet, the story was that Cousin William had died at Tarok Dzong before her arrival there; yet she had just mimicked his voice! "A pious woman," the abbot had called her, "deserving of any help that you may give her," for that she had gathered up the bones of the venerable white holy man and sent them down to the monastery, there to be made into lamps, to burn on the altar, praising God day and night. And all this at her own expense, for a man she did not know. During the confusion brought about by his illness, Peter had given one of these lamps to William's mother, his Aunt Mary, along with William's more ordinary relics. "You cannot judge him by such superficial things," Peter said softly, cunningly, to goad her into further ad-mission.

With an expression of scorn she opened her mouth to speak; then her eyes grew wide, and she sank down to the floor, stroking him. "I know only what they said of him at Tarok Dzong—it is wrong of me to repeat such foolishness!" Smiling and complaisant, she teased him with her fingertips. "After all, he was a holy man, your cousin, but he was not like you!"

A lithe, sudden leap and Peter was out of her reach, his eyes glinting down on her from an immense distance. "You heard him speak, Liliu! You saw him! Did you nurse him as you nursed me —with a little of this and a little of that? He would not take you out of Tibet, would he?"

"Lord," she quavered with an injured air, "if I had harmed that poor holy man, would I have had the lamps made? Surely they would have prayed against me, and rightly so!"

Again Peter turned from her, strengthened in his resolve never to see her again, even though he could not bring himself to punish her in other ways. He had not loved his cousin, and he did not like vengeance. William had been at the end of his rope, and desired to die, according to the abbot; and Liliu had been determined to

live. As for the lamps, they would not pray against her, because
she had seen to it that William, after his deliverance from this world,
achieved Illumination; had she not had them made, on the other
hand, William's ghost, according to the politics of the occult, would
have been justified in working all sorts of evil against his murderess;
not that William would have done any such thing—on the contrary, he would have prayed *for* her, like a good Quaker. Not knowing that, however, she had done the conservative thing.

In his abrupt movement away from her, his foot collided with a
basket-like wicker stool, sending it spinning. With it went a pair
of Liliu's felt shoes which had been concealed under it. Bits of paper fluttered out of the shoes, along the floor. Liliu was on them like
a cat, snatching them up, but not before he had seen names written
on them. Brutally he flung her on the bed, knelt on her, pried open
her hand, finger by finger—she fought ferociously, then burst into
despairing sobs as he forced her to relinquish the scraps of paper.
The name of Lady Edith was soiled and worn, barely legible. Aretino
Scott's name had been recently inserted. The newest name was
that of Irene Nayler. Babbling incoherently, Liliu struggled to free
herself, but he continued to hold her down. Fearfully her eyes
roved over his face, found there anger, grief, disgust—he avoided
her gaze, as if to return it was to vomit. In Tibet she would have
been lynched, stoned, or beaten to death—for practicing the most
abominable kind of black magic: trampling steadily upon the names
of her enemies until they were dead, perhaps with the help of still
other means.

"What will you do, Lord? Speak to me! It is for love of you—it
harms no one—how can it? It is only spite, jealousy, not magic—
you do not believe in it—you yourself told me. You are magnani-
mous, Lord; forgive me for loving you too much! Lord, speak to
me!"

"You dirty bitch!"

"Yes, Lord, yes, yes! Say more! Make me a clean bitch! Spit on
me, beat me with your shoes—that will efface the magic—no harm
will come to your friends!"

One moment a clear policy of moral action; the next, a dark
jungle. Out of his mouth, opened to say "I never want to see you

again," burst a sob, a curse. He spat in her face; he snatched off his sandal and beat her with it—the most degrading form of punishment and, under the circumstances, the magic best calculated to nullify the effects of her crime. From head to foot he pounded her with the sandal, weeping at the violence he was doing to them both. She endured it better than he. Writhing and mewing, she offered herself to his blows, hiding only her face—then she offered it too, languishing, tear-stained, smiling a little. . . .

It was quite dark when he started for Tino's to get his rifle. He could not wait for Kaliya. Perhaps he could lure him out, have an accounting with him, and leave tomorrow. As for the risk, Peter more than half-welcomed it. Although his chagrin was not, and never had been, of suicidal proportions—in certain ways he was not very sensitive—he did have the inclination tonight not to play it safe. . . .

At the end of the alley he narrowly missed colliding with a bundle on legs that looked like Gori Govinda. The boy's head, face, and torso were swathed in a *chaddar*, a sort of blanket—a conventional way of avoiding recognition in all sorts of weather; but the pale, well-formed legs and feet were quite bare. Ducking past Peter, he flashed at top speed into the alley leading to his sister's apartment.

Farther up the mountain, on a cross-lane with which he was un-familiar, a second apparition flew out at him. Monica Dutton, her precarious poise shattered, gesticulated at him, chattering in a mixture of eerie English, Bengali, Nepali. Peter went with her on the trot. There was the "secluded cottage," all right, with the shades drawn as she had said.

"Go away," Peter told her, a tinge of disgust in his voice.

That rocked her into a queer, cockneyfied English. She stood still and grinned like a weasel. "Surely," she said. "I'll just go away. I don't want to be 'ere. . . . If you 'ave to break in, do it quiet, eh? We don't want no scandal. . . . Take care 'e don't shoot *you*, Peter dear!" The last phrase spiraled softly out of the darkness of some shrubbery nearby.

"Jim!" The door was locked. Peter knocked loudly and called again. "Jim, it's me—Peter Bruff!" No answer. He banged heavily on the door, beseeching. "Jim! Let me in—it's an *emergency!*" Still no answer. He gave the door a vigorous kick, loosening the bottom hinge.

"What do you want?" a voice replied from within, muffled and surly.

"Be quick about it, for Christ's sake!" Peter yowled, hammering away at the door.

As Jim was not very quick about it, Peter squared off to try conclusions with the door, when he heard the key turning in the lock. The door opened a few inches and Jim's face appeared, all gray and queasy. "What is it? What do you want?"

Peter's foot was in, then the rest of him, pushing before him the little man, singularly enfeebled.

"I've come for that drink you promised." Peter closed the door behind him. "The goddamn drink—I need it bad."

"Go away, please," Jim said in a broken voice—he had a brightly figured Kashmiri bed cover clutched around him. "Get it somewhere else, can't you? Come back later—some other time. I've—I've got a woman in here—can't you see?"

"Go ahead, I won't bother you." Crudely Peter waded through the precious bric-a-brac that littered the house, opening doors and cupboards. Under a Kashmiri pillow covered with fine needlework he found the loaded revolver. For a moment he regarded it with a fixed expression, then his mouth went over on one side in a sour smile. He left the gun where it was and began to search for the drink, for which he now had a felt need. Among a collection of too sweet liqueurs and brandies he found a bottle of good Scotch.

Jim was sitting on a sofa, weeping shrill, keening tears, his face buried in a fold of his bed cover—it had fallen open, exposing his mighty little knees, which banged together convulsively.

"Every time I try it—" Sobs made him start again, then again: "Every time—somebody stops me!"

Within ten minutes the near-suicide was bitterly cheerful. Monica peeped in from the outside, under a window shade which, she well knew, did not fit at the bottom. The two men sat with a bottle before them, like a pair of contented buddies, chatting and drinking, practically embracing—Peter at least had his arm thrown over the sofa back in a sheltering way. The position Monica was forced to assume was both exposed and awkward. She would have to come back later and take her chances—Liliu would want to know if anything untoward occurred. A lady had to keep her gentleman.

"If I'm not an American, what *am* I?" Jim was harping plaintively on the old theme.

"I dunno." Peter plucked at the label on the bottle of Scotch. "You've got more stickers than anybody I ever saw. . . . Stickers—labels—a big supply of 'em. Let me know when you find out which one is you."

"No emotional security." The words came dreamily out of Jim's mouth, as if they had been worn so smooth that an infinitesimal throb of his consciousness could set them in motion without further effort.

"Yeah!" Peter slapped his thigh and rocked back and forth, spilling part of his drink on Jim's bed cover. "That's *right!* No niche in life!"

"That's it." Jim fell into the trap.

"What are you, a virgin?" Peter was suddenly dignified. "Everything whirls in space—niches too. *Panta hrea.* Sooner or later you get a notch in your niche. Then where are you? You don't know. Or else you're not. . . . Pretend virginity and you suffer real rape."

"You don't understand—that's not what I meant at all." Jim smiled ruefully and got up for some soda. They had been drinking straight Scotch, and he was just beginning to notice it. When he came back—Peter had spied on him discreetly to see that he did not go near the revolver—he appeared to be more in control of himself. The bed cover was cleverly draped over his shoulders, not so much like a Roman toga as it was like a Greek chiton, leaving the legs unimpeded.

"What I meant to say," Jim resumed, "was that I don't really fit in anywhere, not with Chinese, not with Americans, not even with other Chinese-Americans. They're vulgar, the Chinese-Americans—"

"How many have you known?" Peter parried him with the same glibness, off the surface of his mind—had he thought about it, it would have taken him back at least ten years, to a time when he had believed it worth while to correct bigots.

"Plenty. They're just too damned American for words. They can't be themselves. I feel closer to Caucasians. They don't feel close to me, that's the trouble. Take your aunt, for instance. Sure, she's nice to me, but do you think I can't see through it? Old American stock —*noblesse oblige*. You think for one minute she'd let Irene marry me?"

"She just might," Peter said, taking an overdose of Scotch. The color drained from his face. Since his last interview with Irene Nayler, she had been through quite a lot. Jim had said he had a woman in here—

"Don't make me laugh! Irene's an unusual type, sensitive—don't worry, I respect her. She might marry a Chinaman to promote World Peace!"

"Come off it, Chen!"

"No barriers in bed—oh, no! But in the daylight, where everybody can see. . . . And Lady Edith—why do you think she got you here to kill that goddamn python? I was here, wasn't I? She knows I'm a good shot—she's seen my trophies. I'll tell you why: She didn't want to be indebted to me. She—"

"Jim," Peter interrupted quietly but persistently, "you know I'm part Indian. I assumed you knew that Lady Edith is also part Indian."

"Of course I know it," the perfectionist shrilled at him, "but she's a Westerner all the same."

"So are you."

"Indians are as bad as anybody," Jim muttered, ignoring the interruption. "You don't know what it's like."

"Come to think of it," said Peter, "your eyes really do slant to a fault. Then there's your complexion. Can't you do something to improve it?"

No one had ever said such a thing to Jim before. He stared at the perpetrator for a long moment, unable to speak. Peter's wicked grin was totally enigmatic to him, and he proceeded to misread it.

"She told you! She said she wouldn't—see what I mean?"

"Sure," said Peter, who did not, but merely wanted to be difficult.

"What she didn't know—never did know—was that I was sick when she asked me to shoot the python! She *chose* that time! You don't believe me?"

"Sure, I do." Peter's grin had vanished—he felt himself blushing a little.

"You don't! Neither does she! Everything I stand for—"

"Jim!"

"I'm washed up!"

"All the same," said Peter, "Lady Edith has never discussed you with me. I haven't the foggiest idea what you're talking about, but I have some very good medicine for bacillary dysentery. Of course, if it's amoebic—" As he laid his hand on Jim's arm, he dropped his gaze, wondering if it would help to confess that Kaliya had had a suspicious attraction for him just now. Jim had "saved" him from the impulse, at least; but it would not do to tell him so—not yet. . . .

Jim was looking at the same thing Peter's eyes had absently fixated on: a green *gamcha* imperfectly stuffed down between the cushions. It was only when Jim poked it out of sight that Peter became aware of what he had seen.

"It was everything at once," Jim said. "There was a girl—a Eurasian—just before you came. Tried to blackmail me—starting ugly rumors. When somebody betrays you—everything seems horrible, hopeless. . . . You know what I mean?"

"Yes," Peter uprooted himself slowly, painfully from the sofa. "Yes, I do."

Jim's face followed him up like a satellite moon, palely beaming. The short, mighty arms flowed out of the bed cover, supplicating. Again, that look of a four-year-old prisoner in a fortress.

"You know, when you save a Chinaman's life you become responsible for him—you know that, don't you? You don't mind having a Chinaman for a lifelong friend, do you?"

"Not a bit," said Peter, feeling old and weary; then, just before going out, he patted Jim on the head, labels and all, and pulled the bed cover shut over Jim's ventral surface. "Now be a good boy," he said. "Don't catch cold, get to bed early, and—try to conserve your vital forces. I'm counting on you to help me when Kaliya comes."

Someone had locked the outside door to Peter's room, so he had to come in the front way. Except for a light under Tino's door, the house was quite dark. As Peter stole cautiously by—he did not wish to encounter anyone just then—there was the resounding crash of a heavy object falling to the floor and rolling across it. Peter hesitated for just a moment, then softly turned the knob, looked in, and wished he had not. Professor Aretino Scott, wearing an athletic supporter, was developing his body with weights. Having recovered the one he had dropped, he now stood with his back to the door. Feet planted about thirty inches apart, he lowered his torso until it was at right angles to his legs. One, two, three, four, five—he was raising the heavy dumbbells from the floor to his shoulders and lowering them again, counting rapidly under his breath. Quietly Peter closed the door.

When he did sleep he had floating and flying dreams, then he settled down upon the Divine Lotus and was puissant, calm and infinitely balanced, because of the music of a flute. As long as the flute continued, all was well. The Lotus, upon which he was seated cross-legged, floated over the Abyss, or rather within the Abyss, near the top. Himalayan ice walls, blue-green, were all around, whereon appeared, as in the temple at Tarok Dzong, bones and death, demons gesticulant, and monstrous couplings of death and life, god and devil, man and beast, and other forms that were only seemingly incompatible. Liliu Acquileia worshiped him, her red mouth open to show white, in-slanting teeth, and her eyes were turned in, showing only the whites. Smiling the inward smile of compassionate wisdom, Peter the Buddha remained serenely detached. . . . The Lotus moves slowly upward to the sound of the fluate, bearing him out of the Abyss, toward a more likely place—Nirvana? Passing the last earthly pinnacle, he sees Irene standing on the treacherous edge of the Abyss, stretching out her hand to help him, although she herself is in danger of falling. Abstractly he knows that there was a time when he would have liked to warn her with a word or a gesture, but now he is too deeply rooted in the absolutely general to make a particular movement without ages of preparation. Besides, the help she needs is to help him, and he is beyond the need for help, even should he decide, at the last minute, to return to the world of sentient creatures as a bodhisattva. Tottering there, very pale, leaning out into space, she watches anxiously as he rises above her; then she

sees what it is that lifts him—that which he cannot see because of
the petals of the great Lotus that protrude beneath him. Soundlessly,
with a look of horror, she lets herself fall into the Abyss. Before he
can stop himself, he moves a little to look down at her fiery trail, and
his timeless balance begins to disintegrate. There is nothing to hold
on to, nothing on which he can get a good grip, for the Lotus is pure
Spirit, dominated by the flute. The tempo quickens, the Lotus sways
from side to side. "Stop!" Peter cries out to the flutist, who stands
there, gleaming a little in the darkness. The flutist plays on, imper-
turbable, smiling, his lips joined to the flute. . . . A woman like
Indira and like his mother looks through a window above him and
to the right. If only he could reach her! The Lotus is falling away.
He stands up to jump and fly and swim to the window, but at that
moment he sees what it is that has lifted the Lotus and him on it:
it is the head of Kaliya! Too late now to jump-fly-swim to the window
—he falls, slithers, slides down the great column of the serpent's
body, into the dark coils, into Hell. . . .

With a yelp Peter started out of his sleep, sat up in bed and tried
to recollect himself. After a few minutes he felt his way out of bed,
across the room, into the garden, where he stood until he was fully
awake. It was still very dark, but he did not want to go back to sleep
yet. . . . Using Peter as a focal point, retreating, passing, returning,
weaving him, now here, now there, echoing with some momentous
urgency through the darkness, was the voice of a strange bird, cluck-
ing like a castanet, as if it wanted to sing but was prevented by an
excess of feeling; as if, Peter thought, it were rebelling against its
present form and temperament which made it so difficult for it to
communicate with him. "What is it?" Peter whispered, but it was
raining and the unseen bird skittered off, its passionate message
delivered only in part, from dark to dark.

Back in his room, seated cross-legged on the bed, a blanket around
him, he opened at random a tiny seventeenth century copy of the
Theologia Germanica which Irene had given him on his seventeenth
birthday. For the past year—since meeting Liliu Acquileia—he had
not looked at it, although, with his preparation, it might have continued to have an antiseptic effect. Now it was as if he were briefing
himself on the resources of the enemy, to use them himself, if need

be, even as Moses used the brass serpent to ward off the serpents of the wilderness. For tomorrow—and tomorrow had already hatched —he would encounter Irene.

" 'Nothing burneth in Hell but self-will,' " he read, and lit a cigarette, and inwardly, like one who has been there more recently, he argued with the dusty monk, chucking heathen words at him out of the *Krishnayana:*

> " 'Here motions fail,' the Prince said, 'and the will
> Is silent, yet is frequently re-burned.
> Here even the weak are malcontent.' "

inordinate affections

eight

Perilously, one after the other, he hoisted the big brass water pots overhead and let the cold water wham down over his face, his torso, and his wriggling nethers—blind, gasping and drinking, a lower form of life, Matsya the fish, kissing its way without a thought through its medium. . . . Reconstituting himself, cutting across eons, he combed his hair for a long time, regarding himself quietly and somberly in the mirror. The hair was the same as before: short, thick, compactly modeled on the head and neck; but his face changed. Lowering his head, he combed away, head down, looking out from under heavy eyebrows, forehead furrowed; then gradually evolving, he combed his head back until his face was upturned, looking down at itself. Light and air entered his features, vulnerable expanses under the eyebrows, nose, chin, cheekbones. . . . The chin, firm enough, was imperfectly cleft; that is, the cleft was a little off center, so that the left side was rounder than the right; it was one element in the resemblance of the left side of his face to his mother's people, and of the right side to his father's people— a division of which he alone was aware.

The height of his cheekbones, especially the left one, was accentuated by the habit he had, on melancholy days, of leaving the jaws slightly open and the lips closed—a misleading habit of poets, which often means only that they are perhaps justifiably dying of love for their own beauty. For Peter modesty was almost a fetish, because it did not come naturally. The fact was, he found himself infinitely attractive. He was overcome with wonder at his bodily existence. In spite of its resourcefulness, it struck him as being unaccountably fragile and unsubstantial. Like an imagined landscape, it was

99

different every time he considered it, varying with mood, weather, surrounding colors, time of day. . . . The eyes themselves, from which one has a right to expect certain confidences, were ventriloquists of his identity. Only the teeth remained fairly constant; but as they were not properly a part of the face, to question them seriously before a mirror was an unnecessary provocation. They spoke for the skeleton, whose semipermanence was frivolous compared to the permanence he intended for the *Krishnayana!*

A moment of languorous indecision, then he took sides, braced himself against the self-contemplative, muliebrile aspect of himself —which Irene had always mysteriously brought out in him, through certain active traits she had, traits that exactly duplicated some of his own, so that, to complete her, as it were—or rather, to complete their accord—he became obligingly passive, not deliberately, but in spite of himself. Today would be different. Sober as a theologian contemplating the categories of evil, Narcissus took one last, steadying look in the pool, poured himself a tumbler of whisky and drank it neat, shuddering; then half a tumbler, not shuddering. When he was dressed and ready to go, he paused and checked his pocket flask to see if it was completely full. Staying at Tashiling could be expensive as well as fatal, he observed. As soon as Kaliya showed himself, Peter must have an accounting with him, then leave right away. In most places he could do without whisky very well, and did. Tobacco, *chang*, and betel nut, which were cheap, usually sufficed to distract him ever so little from his variegated tensions. . . .

Irene stood in the doorway, leaning out a little, her hand stretched toward him in greeting as he approached very sedately.

"I saw thee through the window," she said in her slow, clear voice, smiling gravely but not reprovingly, although the fragrance of his breath embalmed the air around him.

He had not remembered her eyes being quite so blue; but of course it was the blue dress she was wearing—he noticed it with some disapproval. It was simple enough, with sleeves and a high neck, no vain ribbands or other frippery, but it clung, and the ripened lineaments of her body seemed to him to be not in the central tradition of Quakerism. Black would be more seemly for a widow, he thought bitterly—or white, since she had come to haunt him. Well, he was not the same either!

"Thee looks pretty well, considering," she said, leading him to a sofa.

"So do you," he drew the line, refusing the gentle, exclusive familiarity of the plain speech, addressing her from ambassadorial distances.

"Mary's out," she said in a matter-of-fact tone, and complied for the moment with his formality. "I'll make you a pot of black coffee."

"Not at the moment, thanks." As he lit a cigarette, she looked about for an ashtray. Finding none, she took the little saucer-like gray lamp from the mantel and set it on the coffee table before him.

"I don't think Aunt Mary would want that to be used for an ashtray," he said, a bit shaken.

"She isn't sentimental," Irene said. "Anyway, she gave it to me, and I believe things ought to be used by the living, don't you?" She looked at him intently. "Thee might give me a cigarette—you might as well."

"I didn't know you smoked," he mumbled, and dropped the packet on the sofa, between his legs, groped it out ignominiously.

"I thought I might try it." Coolly she accepted the cigarette, then the light. "My Uncle Samuel Colley wrote a history against smoking," she said. "Originally people swallowed the smoke. Do you think that might be more effective?"

"I don't know," he said. "No, I don't think so. I think it would defeat the purpose."

"I see." She drew on the cigarette, without inhaling deeply. "People like to look at the smoke. The History says that people who can't see don't much like to smoke—isn't that interesting? Perhaps it's a sort of symbol of transitoriness. They hope their sorrows will go up in smoke. The joys go too, though, don't they, Peter? It makes one philosophical—like those skulls the medieval monks kept by their bedside as a reminder—but I don't mean to be morbid!" Smiling, she dabbled the ashes of her cigarette into the ashtray-lamp.

Feeling suddenly cramped, compressed into this room, Peter took a deep draught of smoke, exhaled all at once, and stood up as if he were going to plummet off through the roof. "I think we'd better walk," he said.

They climbed on up the mountain trail, above the town, neither of them saying a word, till they came to the upper trail that goes on a level course toward Gwalpara and beyond. Peter walked unevenly, but he carried himself with an arbitrary erectness which gave the impression of bodily control. The trail led through a forest of sal trees that stood like tall pines above the ferns. Only occasional orchids and creepers betrayed the tropical at this altitude.

At one point where the underbrush lay partway across the path, Peter's arm suddenly shot out and stopped Irene.

"Just stand quietly."

It moved, and she had a glimpse of bright, unblinking eyes, a flat, diamond-shaped head; and a long, shiny light brown body flowed like a stream of oil down a branch and disappeared into the underbrush.

"Thank you," she said calmly. "I wouldn't have seen it. I believe that was an Indian bronzeback. It would have a yellow stripe along its undersurface."

"They don't always like you to see their bellies." Peter smiled grimly as they went on.

"I saw Dr. Bhattacharya this morning," she said. "He says snakes killed fifty thousand people in India last year. Peter, that is a serious problem."

"Yes, it's pretty serious, but"—he made an oily little gesture, watching her out of the corner of his eye—"what to do?"

"I don't like snakes, Peter," she said in a moved voice. "I've always been ashamed to be at odds with any of God's creatures. I try to love everything—"

"It isn't respectful to love everything," he said shortly.

"Oh. I wonder. . . . When I was a little girl I saw you playing with a snake. I was frightened—you know, quite frightened. I'm so glad you didn't chase me with it."

"In those days I wouldn't have thought of it."

"Do you know what I did after that? I caught a snake, a very small one, in a glass jar. I kept him in my room for a whole month. I petted him; I let him twine around my arm, even around my

neck. Oh, he became quite fond of me! I never overcame my aver-
sion for him. I used to bring him carrots and things, but he wouldn't
eat—I thought he ought to, so I'd leave them out for him. He
wouldn't touch them. One day he died. It has weighed on my conscience ever since. . . . I wonder why he wouldn't eat?" For a moment she had the look of an old child, troubled, requiring explana-
tions of elementary things which, once explained, lost their meaning
or grew out of recognition.

"Some snakes prefer mammals," he said, lurching a bit to one
side. Good God, she *was* lost—'way out yonder! It gave her a kind
of depth. A good thing she was dressed in blue, after all. In black,
just now, she would be as irresistible as a slavey.

At a footbridge over a small waterfall, they stopped and leaned
on the wooden railing—Peter fixated momentarily on the rainbow
sheens that hovered over the turbulence below. . . . There was a
place in Pennsylvania, in Swarthmore Woods, that had looked
then as this looked now. It had been a pretty good place to swim,
until the fight; then it wasn't much fun any more. William wouldn't
go in, of course, and the other boys got nasty, tried to take his
clothes off—to see if he was a girl, they said. Oh, they were bastards!
And yet—well, Peter won the fight, in a manner of speaking, but
he lost his friends. And Cousin William . . . Turning his back on
the waterfall, Peter hung a buttock on the rail and swung one foot.

"This is as good a place as any," Irene said quietly. "I had a concern to see you, Peter. Thank you for going after William."

"He was my cousin."

"So he was."

"Aunt Mary paid me well for it."

"Thee went to the end of the world—for what?"

"A job's a job." He twisted his torso halfway around, unneces-
sarily, to hurl the cigarette butt into the waterfall. Involuntarily
she clutched at him to keep him from falling, but did not quite touch
him after all. They proceeded on down the path toward Gwalpara.

"Well," she lagged a little, forcing him to slow down, "thee tried
to do thy duty and I tried to do mine as I saw it. We failed, didn't
we, Peter? Both of us."

"We did, by God; we certainly did!"

Her eyes said gravely, "Swear not," but she smiled and went on: "Doubtless thee has been too busy to think very much—about things —concerning us. I haven't missed a Meeting since thee left—I don't say this in pride—such regular attendance could make one suspicious, couldn't it? But I mean, I have thought a good deal during the Silence—about what I did and why. Peter, I think I would do it again."

"I think you would," he said, "and I would, and William would. You would do your duty and I would survive and William would run away and die."

"Not if I did it really and truly in the spirit of Christ."

"He would run twice as fast."

"I think thee may be mistaken about that," she stammered, coloring. "It's—It's too complicated—embarrassing to talk about. . . . I mean, I'm not accustomed to talking about intimate matters. . . . William was weak, thee was strong. I had a clear leading to support and strengthen him—so I married him. My personal preferences did not come first. The first shall be last—and the last shall be first."

"I have deliberated somewhat"—he kept a stony profile to her —"on this willingness of yours to sell your soul and give the proceeds to the poor—"

"Thee's on shaky ground theologically, Friend," she said gently. "Thee may have had a bracer too many."

"No, Friend, I have had a bracer too few." In his effrontery, he offered her the flask.

Irene hesitated for a moment, then took it.

"Drink as long as thee can—I will go with thee." Gazing departingly into his eyes, she raised the flask and drank, not just a little but a lot. There was a long pause during which she stood motionless, looking serenely into space. All at once Peter realized that she was not breathing. He smacked her on the back, shook her. . . . Gasping, tearful and scarlet, she came up from the long dive. Swiftly he fed her handfuls of water from a rivulet that came out of a village up the mountain, and she breathed again.

"By God, thee did it!" he laughed, himself drinking, and capitulated to the plain speech. "Lest I think thee is not at one with all the Universe!"

"Lest thee think I set myself above thee!" she choked in a gravel voice. "Uncle Samuel Colley—also—" She could say no more.

Taking advantage of her un-Quakerly silence, Peter said:

"I have also considered the matter of thy personal preferences, and I think that first things always come first with thee—thee has always known which side thy unleavened bread is buttered on. Thee needs weakness—sickness if possible—so thee can be sure of being necessary to someone without having to yield thyself up really and all the way, because he might be the Devil—and in fact he would be. Thee wouldn't know what to do with a real man!"

Irene stopped and leaned against a tree, her head bowed as if in prayer. When she looked up, her face was flushed, and her mouth formed the little square of Bryn Mawr as she blasted him with un-Friendly fire:

"Has thee considered, by the bowels of Christ, that thee might be wrong?"

Over the trees a red-shafted flicker broke the scansion of its flight, uttered the piercing sob of its race, and dived down into some foliage where, from time to time, it repeated its distress. Peter staggered, opened and closed his mouth. Cromwell had him by the short hair. Irene turned and began to walk briskly down the path, the way they had come.

"Thee confuses me!" he protested, following her.

"I don't confuse thee, Friend. Thee is confused. Don't strain thy brains. Go thy way in peace, and God be with thee!"

Peter shambled in front of her, made her progress less certain, stopped her by degrees. One more step and she was in his arms, she or he having staggered. There commenced in him the desire for vengeance, and at the same time he felt compassion and the old melting sensation that was a token of his susceptibility, promising blind chivalry, gratuitous love for the girl who had inspired so many of his adolescent verses. They had embraced before, but as two idealistic virgins—not like this, and not after conflict. His fingers dug into her beautiful blue rump.

"In Christ, Peter, in Christ!"

The cross, the garlic, and the ash stake had been elevated against the werewolf. His talons dangled, the blood dropped to his feet, the center of urgency rose to his brain.

"Thee need not be ashamed if thee loves me in Christ—as I love thee," she said. And then, a bit anxiously: "Why does thee turn away, Peter?"

Unable to say a word, he stood looking out across the valley, wishing himself in those high mountains to the north, where there is always snow.

nine

Lunch would be a little late. A note informed them that Aunt Mary had been in and had gone out again for a few minutes. Standing by the window, Peter felt for his flask, pulled it out, asked Irene for a glass. Vaguely she pushed her hair back.

"We shall drink together," she said, laying her hand on his arm. "Whenever thee drinks, I drink."

"That's damn silly," he grumbled. "Be thyself!"

"Thee's damn sure of thyself, isn't thee?" She was pale, exalted by depravity.

Peter laughed uneasily and slipped the flask back in his pocket. "All right, thee wins." A kind of zany daring in the matter of Testimonies was in the Quaker tradition, but in Irene's character this element almost of abandon was unfamiliar to him. It struck him that that touch of sun she had got down in Bihar must have affected her more than a little. "Irene, I'm concerned for thee—"

"And I for thee." Softly she put her arms around him, under his jacket, one hand across from the flask, and pressed him to her in exactly the same way he had done to her up on the mountain. Wide-eyed, she raised her mouth, from which the color had fled, for him to kiss.

Unnerved by this sudden reversal of roles, he kissed her with something less than ardor; but his restraint did not communicate itself to her. If only he could say, "In Christ, Irene, in Christ!" But she would construe that as mockery, since she had already rejected his concern for the norm of her character. Intuitively he felt that either to reject her or fully to accept her while she was not quite herself would be to endanger her, to do her a graver disservice than she had

107

ever done him. With womanly tact and ambiguity, he caught her hands, kissed and held them, as if it were a precious liberty rather than a precaution.

They were released from each other by Mary Nayler clomping up the path, carrying a basket. Mr. Kashani was hopping along beside her, or a little behind her, vaulting from time to time on his ebony cane. Inside those wicked little boots his toes were continuously crucified. Mary had on a rusty-looking black dress—by Jesus, there was a real widow! Judging from the expression of grim optimism on her face, she was being rather impatiently patient—the old girl could spot a phony every time, but a hieratic conscience usually kept her silent. She had Mr. Kashani's number now, and she was trying hard not to recognize it. Peter had never seen her looking quite so out of sorts with a foreigner. But, then, she was getting awfully old; more than malaria had gripped her; for Mother India was cunning as a witch to search out and widen weaknesses, erode the strength, develop the defects of foreigners, working on them like a great caricaturist.

Mary did not pause, but tramped ponderously from the front door, through the house, into the kitchen, throwing off her black coat and hat on the way, and talking for relief. She had planned to have pork chops for lunch, in fact had already started cooking them with Mr. Kashani's help, when it had dawned on him that he was about to commit an abomination. She should have known —did know, in fact, but he had come unexpectedly and she had forgotten. The mere sight and smell of pork chops cooking meant that he would have to go through an elaborate Mohammedan ritual of purification—prayer and fasting, seven baths on each of seven consecutive days, and more hand-washing and face-washing, this-washing and that-washing, more sedulous than a raccoon, he being somewhat particular; not that he could ever get really clean again. As Mr. Kashani had allowed himself to be dissuaded from going away at once—since the purification ceremonies would be about equally severe in any case—Mary and he had gone out again and got some mutton which he thought he could eat.

There were only two pigs in all of Persia, Mr. Kashani explained, and they were kept isolated in a Christian laboratory for experimental purposes. Naturally he was desolated at having caused all this additional trouble and expense. The least he could do to make up for it was to sing them some Persian songs. This he did from the living room, casting glowing looks at Irene, whom he could see passing back and forth in the kitchen.

Feeling suddenly tired, Peter lay down on the sofa and soon drifted into a torpor. Had it not been for Mr. Kashani, he would have slept; but the elegant little bunch of whiskers sang one song after another in a passionate, piercing voice, without accompaniment and without pause—he said they were about a Circassian girl —a blonde—who wore fatal black trousers, and about a dervish who succeeded in uniting himself with God, about Paradise, about accepting the Universe without quibbling over details. . . . The little concert wailed on and on, over the kitchen noises, painful, absurdly sad, and rather beautiful. When necessary, Peter encouraged him with looks and gestures so that they would not have to talk.

Mr. Kashani was sitting in the same place where Jim Chen had sung his folk songs the other night. Odd resemblances, Peter reflected, not repetitions but approximations, variations, a hidden pattern of which one had only intimations from time to time: like the song of the bird he had heard the other morning. . . . With a hidden, seductive smile as he felt it coming, Peter allowed a wave of ecstasy, as of unlimited possession, to pass into him, held it or was held by it for a moment, shuddered, and let it go. It was only his norm, his point of reference, his self. All he needed was to touch it occasionally, something yoga had enabled him to do whenever he liked; but he was prevented from doing it very often by a kind of pudicity, a supraerotic self-effacement which made him unwilling to monopolize the role of Cosmic Lover for more than a moment at a time, and rarely. The retention of joy was a career for those who needed to be reminded constantly that they were the center of the universe. Peter needed few such reminders. What he really knew, he could take for granted and forget. His dharma, as center, was to go forth from himself in ignorance, want and risk, to create that which did not yet exist, at least not in this Kali Yuga of time and space. In a moment of time the wanderer oneself greeted the stay-at-home oneself, as Mr. Kashani's dervish perhaps greeted God, but then one went about one's business, or His business as the case might be, even if one had to deal with fatal black trousers. A mark of vulgarity to try to prolong a greeting, as if one did not know how to act. True, that dervish made the most of his opportunity in uniting himself with God; but there was much to be said for long engagements during which one acquired experience: that was not to be sneezed at. It would be appreciated by all, in the long run. . . .

It was his dharma to go forward even in darkness so deep that his excellent night vision was not always one hundred per cent effective. There was the matter of Kaliya. He must go scouting for him tomorrow, not that there was much hope of finding him—in fact, he wasn't due to come out again for another week—but simply because he had told Jim Chen that they would go together, tomorrow, forth. It would not be a total waste of energy either, because Peter had intended, within a day or so, to look over the ground that lay within Kaliya's sphere of interest. A close knowledge of the lay of the land was absolutely necessary, as it would not be in the case of a tiger, for instance, where a general knowledge of the terrain would suffice. A tiger killed frequently, was conspicuous, had never developed his faculties for concealment and the detection of danger, for the simple reason that he himself was the danger. The only real threat to his life was man. In tiger country, whenever a man seriously wanted to find a tiger, he could do it. A python presented altogether a different problem. The rare man-eating python fed punctually every two weeks, varying only by a day or so. After feeding he invariably withdrew to a hollow tree, a cave, or crevice in the rocks, where he would be safe from attack; for during the time required to digest his prey, he was torpid and defenseless. Nothing short of a forest fire could drive him out of his hiding place. To shoot a python, it was necessary to await him in the vicinity of his probable attack, starting preferably two or three days before he was expected. Mobility, alertness, exact knowledge of the area, and a warning system if feasible—these were the essentials. It would certainly be well to have a couple of other hunters about—provided they had cool heads and knew what was what. Jim *might* be all right, after all. Chanchal—no. To await a python and then to sustain his attack was more unnerving than any other external conflict

Peter had ever known, because of the eerie form, character, and habits of the creature, and one's knowledge of the singular way in which he extinguished the life of his prey.

Pythons lived forever, unless they got killed. This one could easily be the same python that had "founded" the Ashram, as it were. Lady Edith had not said so; he had not thought to ask—indeed, there was so little left of her, that one had to be most miserly, a pinchpenny, in conversation that required any response from her, but—

Once there was a python. . . . That was before Peter met Lady Edith. Peter was staying in Benares with Ananda Mahadev, working on the *Krishnayana*, when a letter came from her, asking Ananda to come to Tashiling. As Peter could do little with the Sanskrit material at that point without Ananda's help, he went with him. They found Lady Edith demoralized. When the British got out of India, she had elected to stay on. Her uncle had left her the tea plantation, his best wishes, and any number of dependents—family servants, several very old people, and some orphans, half-castes, some of whom were probably her cousins. Other children came from neighboring plantations whose British owners had sold out and gone elsewhere. For the first time in her life Lady Edith was in a state of panic. There were heavy taxes to be paid, a tea plantation to be run, and children everywhere. Finally, a python had taken one of the servants not far from the bungalow. Lady Edith was afraid for herself, afraid to go after the python for fear it or some other creature—she was now at the stage of exaggerating dangers —would come while she was gone and attack the children; afraid she would be killed and her orphans would perish in the jungle. That was when she had written to Ananda Mahadev, her loyal friend ever since they had gone to school together in England.

During the weeks Peter and Ananda stayed at the plantation, certain things indubitably happened. Ananda and Lady Edith decided to get married the following year, when he would have finished his work at Benares. One fervent afternoon Ananda, Lady Edith, and Peter stood on the riverbank and made the plan for the Ashram. The python didn't turn up again. If he did, Lady Edith said, she thought she could manage. Peter, too, in an access of idealism, swore to return the following year, with money if possible, to help make the enterprise a success. . . . But it was Lady Edith who managed it after all, up to a point, when Ananda was drowned that year in the Ganges.

Indira, who saw her brother once in Kashmir before his death, was similarly wanting in realism. She adopted as her own the plan he unfolded to her. When he died and all the family money came to her, she traveled from Kashmir to Tashiling and gave the money to Lady Edith—from Ananda; and herself also. The money was not enough. Two women were not enough either.

Peter did not learn of Ananda's death till a year later—he had isolated himself in a remote region of Ladakh, to work on the *Krishnayana*. At the end of that year he was due to present himself with Ananda at the Ashram. Then, learning of Ananda's death at Benares, Peter began drinking more than was good for him, had a blazing siege of dysentery; and it was just at this point that the past caught up with him: His aunt came to India, got in touch with him, and asked him to look for her son. . . . On returning from Tibet, he was too shattered emotionally by a succession of disasters—Irene, William, Ananda, and now especially Liliu Acquileia—to think of working with Lady Edith. It was all he could do to keep from expressing to her his bitter cynicism. Lady Edith did not reproach him or argue with him; perhaps she knew more than he told her. It was Indira who was fiery, intolerant, angry with him for breaking his promise. . . . Then again the python. Lady Edith had asked Jim Chen to help, had she? Well, anyway, Peter was here once more, in the middle of the recurrent past, trying to make of it an entirely unpredictable Now. . . .

A thin, quavering wail from Mr. Kashani made Peter's arm flop out on the coffee table by the sofa, not so much in protest as in sympathy. His fingers touched the little lamp from Tarok Dzong which contained the ashes of two cigarettes. William, too, had gone forth, but not from himself. Toward himself. That had been a long journey, as the abbot had said. . . .

Benares, the Holy City on the Ganges. Sacred cows, big and milky-white, with hills on their backs and massive horns that curved out like the arms of dancers in gestures eloquent and mysterious—and those eyes: enormous, elongated as if with kohl. The goddess Kali, bloodthirsty and benign, looked out of them. Their dung was very holy, and many were the seekers who smeared their bodies with it: seekers and holy men—sadhus from all over India—and, sometimes, strange, wind-struck Westerners, unrecognizable as such, naked, with sun-baked features, seeking to bury their botched lives in an orthodoxy beyond time and place.

William had been such a one. Emaciated, with matted hair and beard, this white sadhu who called himself Sambuddhananda, had prostrated himself before the great stone phallus, Shaivite emblem of the generative power of the universe, or God; had mortified his flesh by fasting, his spirit by begging, according to the rules of the sect to which he was currently attached. Day and night he meditated on the banks of the Holy River in which he made his ritual ablutions before dawn every morning.

Although he had known for some time that William had followed him to India—as he had always followed him everywhere, except in the case of Irene, where William had preceded him—Peter had avoided him in order not to be uncivil. At the very least, disregarding Irene, he was sure that William would never give up hope that their views on love would cease to be dissimilar. Now, in Benares, having just learned of the death of Ananda, Peter was in no mood to meet anyone—except Ananda, who was neither here nor there. . . . After a bad night Peter made his way from his room near the Hindu University, down through the tall rushes, to the Ganges. A swim in cold water, he felt, might revive him for his journey— he planned to catch the morning train at Mogulserai.

By the pale light that was beginning across the second great bend in the river, he could make out, here and there, the dim shapes of yogis and devotees performing their religious exercises on the riverbank. All at once he blundered into two men seated on some rushes, smoking hasheesh, a common device among sadhus for reaching a state of abstraction without the tiresome discipline of yoga. One of the men was his cousin. William was smiling slightly, but he did not move, nor did he seem to see Peter. The young Nepali priest beside him also appeared lost in a highly satisfactory inner condition—his flower-like face reminded Peter of a certain very subtle stone Buddha of the Late Gupta period.

At that moment Peter could not have spoken because of his grief. Nevertheless he sat down beside them on the riverbank and waited, "after the manner of Friends." For half an hour he sat there and meditated on the varieties of death, love, and karma, but in the end he was not very successful, for he was out of Quakerly practice and could not compose himself.

There was not even a pretense at dawn. The sun coughed itself up anyhow, looking bloated, then less bloated, and got about its business of frying the earth. Somewhere Peter found a little anger, and drawing strength from it, arose and walked some distance upstream for his bath, where William, on returning from Nirvana, would not see him. The water was the color of earth, and the sky was the color of water, and the fishermen's boats were floating downstream sideways, stern foremost, any way but the right way; and all was one with the day, and the day was one with the All, and all that was was wrong, *billah!* " 'The paths of their way are turned aside,' " he muttered; " 'they go to nothing, and perish.' *Job*, 6:18. . . ." He decided to slosh himself quickly at the well near his lodgings, and catch the next train for the mountains. . . .

"Death is not definitive," Mary Nayler had said calmly. "It's a kind of shirking. The less fuss made about it, the better. Thee might tell me what else thee found out about William." That was in Kalimpong, where she had come to meet Peter on his return from Tibet. Drug-ridden, sick, he had tottered up to the Himalayan Hotel from the caravanserai where he had left the pious woman Liliu Acquileia.

"The abbot of Tarok Dzong," he said, "was of opinion that William was of a pretty high spiritual attainment." He gave her the three earthly possessions William had left her. . . .

Dysentery, probably, rather than malaria, had caused Peter to lose consciousness at about nineteen thousand feet, and to fall gently forward on his mule. On coming to, he had found himself tied to the saddle. About four inches to his right, a bottomless abyss, full of swirling clouds. A sheer, bluish-white ice wall three inches to his left. And the mule heaved and swayed and waggled as if it had many lives to lose. There was not much traffic. The trail widened a little and he called out to his Tibetan guide, "Are you sure this is the best way?"

The guide laughed. "It is the worst way. It is no way."

Rage had been coming to Peter with increasing ease. Striving to control himself, "Why?" he rasped. "Why?"

"Chinese soldiers guard every way that exists. This way does not exist."

They descended to a dreadfully bleak and barren valley where boulders sprouted out of the ground. A river lay ahead of them, but the guide circled indirectly, so they did not come to it until after nightfall, far upstream. They forded this river, and another, and another. From now on they traveled at night and hid among boulders by day. . . .

The abbot of Tarok Dzong monastery was a big, robust old man who knew Hindi. "Do not be afraid of embarrassing us," he said when Peter apologized to him on arriving. "The Chinese authorities seldom come here now. We have no treasures left; besides, it is not a healthful place. They do not like it."

Peter did not wonder. There were few inhabitants in this landscape of sharp declivities and rocky, thin earth. The monastery stood on a mountainside above the village half a mile away. A few stone huts clustered about the square base of the monastery on the leeward side. Several grimy children were playing with human bones. Observing Peter's expression when a little girl held up a skull to let sand run out the eyeholes, the abbot smiled and said: "Here we live with death on terms of equality, my son. We believe in the unity of death and life. It would be a pleasure to talk with you of these things, for you are a fine, lively young man and you tempt me to discourse."

"The talking would indeed be a pleasure," Peter said, recalling the old Quaker graveyard by the Meeting House, back in Philadelphia, which Friends had had paved over for a parking lot, "but if I am to keep death and life separate until I can think of them as one, I must be on my way very quickly. I was told that a white holy man named Sambuddhananda came this way."

"He was here," the abbot said, leading Peter into the chapel. By the light of guttering oil lamps, fantastically painted gods and demons screamed and taught and philosophized and copulated on the walls. Among the religious objects were several begging bowls made of the tops of human skulls. Swaying with weariness, Peter waited impassively.

"First came the Nepali priest, from India," the abbot said. "The Chinese soldiers were in the village then, looking for a certain pious woman from Lhasa. They shot him, although he had not yet completed his pilgrimage to the cave of Milarepa. The villagers hacked up his body and threw it on the mountainside near some trees, just as we do with our own dead. The vultures had cleaned his bones so that they were suitably dry when Sambuddhananda came looking for him at the Place of Death. He sat down by the bones and never got up again, for he was very sick with fever. For three days he fasted and prayed, writing letters, but the wind blew them away, all but one which he wrote in a book. I myself brought him food and medicine every day, for he would not leave the spot where the bones lay. Then the snow came and covered him up."

Peter reflected for a moment, then he said: "Sambuddhananda was my cousin. Have you anything of his that I may take back to his family?"

The abbot went to a dark corner and rummaged in a basket covered with hides. Finally he pulled out a Tibetan manuscript and the little book *A Guide to True Peace*, "To William from Irene." Penciled shakily on the flyleaf of the *Guide* were words from the death-day of William Nayler: ". . . . The bush by Shiva's bones has snow frozen in crystals both over and under its thin twigs— six to one proportion—unevenly, and looks almost exactly like a wild plum in bloom. A bird came. . . ." Then the abbot took down from the altar a small gray lamp. After salvaging the wick and pouring the oil into another lamp, he wiped it dry and handed it to Peter. "He need not be reborn," he said. "He was already of very high attainment, or he would not have been so courteous to death. Now he is indeed free from the Wheel of Life." Peter must have looked doubtful, for, "It is our custom," the abbot explained, "to pound exalted persons' bones into a mortar to make these altar lamps. Day and night, as they burn, they continue to praise God. This fine one, at the expense of a pious woman from Lhasa, is made from the bones of Sambuddhananda. Take it; we have others."

"It would appear," Peter said, "that Sambuddhananda has achieved Illumination, thanks to the pious woman."

The abbot looked at him in great surprise. "My son," he said, "he died upon a very difficult pilgrimage."

Lunch went according to plan—the revised one. That is, it went more quickly than it would have, if Mary had not had to make that second trip to the market. Few days in her life were unscheduled. This afternoon she must call again on Lady Edith, and before that there would be a private talk with Peter, concerning whom a few fateful words had just been exchanged by the two women in the kitchen. Tactfully, but without much waste of time after lunch, she organized Irene and Mr. Kashani out of the house —they would take a leisurely drive to the Ashram, there to await Mary, who would follow them after her conference with Peter.

As she poured him a cup of coffee, the slight shaking of her head gave her a peculiarly foreboding air, as if her conscience were not entirely at ease because of something she was about to do to him. Perhaps she would speak of Irene's health. If she didn't, he would have to. Nervously he lit a cigarette, held the smoke in his lungs for a long moment, huffed it out the side of his mouth away from her, since smoking was one of the things she least approved of. Unobtrusively she set the little gray ashtray before him. It might have been a sacrificial gesture.

"Friends have a low opinion of human nature," she began with impenetrable ambiguity, "but the doctrine of Original Sin is not widely held among them. Neither is the doctrine of Predestination, for that matter. Thy life over the past three years has not shattered my hopes for thee, since they were never very high. On the other hand, thee has not given me undiluted satisfaction—not that that was ever thy primary ambition. It isn't so much the sins of the flesh, to which thee is prone, thee being not only of a nervous and sensuous disposition, but also of exotic and therefore incalculable antecedents, and, in a sense, outside the Discipline. It's the sins of the Spirit to which I refer. Thee has avoided me for the past year, Peter, as though thee feared I might attack the Devil. Thee labors under a misapprehension. I don't overestimate the body, as thee has come to do in thy youthful instability. On the other hand, I do not scorn it—as young people so often do. The body is needed for the reproduction of Friends."

"So thee found that out!" Peter laughed.

"I'm old." Her eyes were zealous for the Middle Way, her head of a primitive noble denied alike the solemn and the frivolous, denied whatever was too lofty, whatever was too vile, denied perhaps her own veiled absurdity. "I'm not so clear as I used to be about putting first things first. I was just thinking of the best way to broach the business."

"I suspect that thee has broached it," he said, flicking ashes into his saucer.

"I have reason to believe that I may be deteriorating. I'd be glad if thee would give me some advice."

"Thee needs no advice, Aunt Mary—all thee needs is information."

"Well, well," she sighed, "perhaps thee's right. We might consider that later." Dropping her voice and leaning forward, she looked not only keen but conspiratorial: "I have been interested in the Ashram for some time. I understand it is in financial difficulty, and that seems to me a pity. Doesn't it to thee?"

Controlling his impulse to reply instantly, Peter sank his chin in his hand and gazed fixedly at nothing for a long moment, then he replied: "It has occurred to me that thee might feel a concern."

"Does thee think fifty thousand might tide them over?"

"Dollars or rupees?"

"Dollars."

"I think it might," Peter said, and his eyes were so bright that his aunt would have smiled, only he might have thought it self-congratulatory. As a first installment of thanks, he tossed his cigarette into the fireplace—he would not grub it out in the lamp-ashtray—and sat with her in silence for a few minutes. It was the first time in years that he had been able to accept money from her without pain. This time it was not for himself, at least not directly. Several times, over the past three years, he had felt obscurely, perhaps erroneously, that she had tried to buy him back, as it were, with sumptuous gifts, into a life that was essentially one of self-denial. In the gift to the Ashram, there would be no strings attached. Yet it would enable him to keep his promise to Lady Edith and Ananda, at least the promise to bring money to the Ashram.

"Money will always be a problem for them," Mary resumed presently. "However, it has been my experience that subscribers can always be found to contribute to worthy enterprises whenever money is really the question. I think Friends at home will be interested when thee tells them about it."

"Thee is much more eloquent than I am," he said warily.

"The place appears to present special problems—the wild life, for instance, but I expect that with proper managing these problems can be pretty well solved. I have taken the liberty of offering a bounty for the python—privately, of course, in order not to draw the attention—"

"Thee did that?"

"Certainly; it's the sensible thing to do."

"Aunt Mary, that's my job!"

"A little healthy competition won't hurt, besides"—she looked at him tenderly—"serpents are traditionally said to be dangerous. Thy obligations lie elsewhere. Dr. Bhattacharya assured me that his nephew is an excellent hunter. Chanchal is here at my request. I also asked Mr. Kashani to come. Jim Chen has not yet made up his mind. . . . Thee knows, guns and killing are abhorrent to me as a pacifist, but this is a matter of protecting human life against a reptile. I have personally bought the ammunition in order to implicate myself to the full."

Peter leaned back in his chair, rummaged for a cigarette and lit it. Absently he put the match stub in the little lamp from Tarok Dzong. The wrath left him speedily, as if it were wrath against a rock or some other object slow to change. A kind of admiration took its place; but he did not soften except in his voice, which had got raspy a moment before.

"Does thee want to implicate thyself, Aunt Mary—or to extricate me? I have made certain commitments regarding the Ashram, and I don't want to be extricated yet."

"Not yet, but in time," she caught him up benignly. "It's not too early to make provision for the future. Don't begrudge me a little share in thy future, dear Peter! I have so little of my own. Thee and Irene are my future—my children. And, Peter, I am much comforted by thy new protestations toward her. . . ."

"My—My—" Peter stammered, reddening. Good God, what had Irene told her?

"Thy impulses are sound." Mary smiled a bit unevenly and took his hand in hers, then quickly let it go, lest it feel the need for liberty. "And blushes are both pleasant and seemly in a young man."

"Protestations!"

"Certainly, protestations. Let us be honest. There were probably protestations even before the Society of Friends. Thee is unduly pessimistic; but consider for a moment whether thee is entirely comfortable in thy present life. What does it hold out to thee but confusion? Is thee sure thee isn't following it out of pride, because thee lost Irene temporarily—"

"No! It isn't that—not any longer, Aunt Mary. I'm sunk in this life —here—I'm involved—"

" 'Sunk' is a good word. I always felt thee didn't fully appreciate the Testimony of Simplicity."

"It doesn't fit, not any longer. Thee doesn't understand. This is Mars. It isn't in thy experience."

"Indeed? How much are two and two on Mars?"

"One," said Peter, "always one."

"In the absence of comprehension," Mary said with a sigh, "I suppose it is best to wait for a clear leading. In the meantime, one can try to be helpful and hope for the best. . . . I have given some thought to the problems of the Ashram, and it has occurred to me that it needs a capable, experienced director. Isn't that so? Lady Edith seemed a bit listless when I mentioned it, but I think she will see the sense of it. Dr. Bhattacharya would be a good man

for the post—a rare, practical idealist. As a member of the Wider
Quaker Fellowship, he has been invaluable in organizing international seminars. . . ."

Peter got up, shaking his head in drastic rebuttal of her negating
head, subtled by usage in its arc and second nature. "Is thee trying
to make me unnecessary? To deprive me of every ground of confidence except—except the past?"

"No, Peter, only to give thee a wider choice. All I want to deprive
thee of is limitations! Thee was born to both worlds—take them!
What's holding thee up? It's only a question of a base of operations
—here or there." Massively she stood confronting him, the color
risen to her cheeks; then in a softer tone, seeing she had gone too
fast and too far: "I may be wanting in humility, but not in affec-
tion for thee. It's just that—when one gets old, one gets into an awful hurry to complete things—just a few things. . . . Forgive me.
Thee's young and patient."

Holding her hand for a moment, he thought of Liliu, of Indira, of
Irene, the three impossible worlds, and of the *Krishnayana* which
made for him the only possible one, the real, the essential world that
was neither one nor the other, but was parallel, abstraction, approx-
imation of "the apparent state of things," a new report on Maya,
the original artifact, but going back, beyond the older report, to
the same source, illuminating both afresh. Looking down at her
ancient hand, that was so like Irene's, he pretended to read it, drawing his finger along the lines of her palm: "The beloved entrusted
to the folds of the tent, Krishna makes secret promises of return to
the mountains of essence, accomplishment of forgotten works, building of cities in the wilderness!"

"That is exotic to me," said Mary, but she recognized a reference
to his epic—a two-dimensional pageant flashed across her mind,
of humans, deeds, movements, to be shifted and interrelated, as in
a picture game played by sleepy children, with the possibility of
some useful delineation of the compulsions of history, the framework
of effort, stern moral duty of the adult, inculcating at best the Testimonies of the Society of Friends, and, failing that, the scarcely less
helpful precepts of Hinduism; in either case, a little bridge between

East and West, because it was Peter who was writing it. In a personal sense, that is, as therapy for him, provided that he did not apply himself too steadily because of a possibly disproportionate view of its usefulness, it could be better than bird watching. *"Paradise Lost* is the only epic I can think of at the moment, but I'm sure there are many others. By the way, did thee know that Milton's secretary was a Friend? I intend to purchase all the epics when we return to Philadelphia, and thee may have them all, if thee will advise me. It has occurred to me that the little stone summerhouse in back of the main house would be a good place for reading epics— and for writing one. I'll have bookshelves put in it, and a desk. Nobody will disturb thee, and of course there will be no financial worry, because, in a few years, it will all belong to thee and Irene. . . ."

"I have a leading to write it here," Peter said quietly, sitting down again beside her. Elbows on knees, he glowered up as if out of a cave; then he leaned back, raised his face upward, and was vulnerable, trusting, all the while looking at her. The strange transition, due perhaps to the lighting and the angle, had its effect.

"A star is useful." Mary's eyes were seduced. "There was a time when I knew that, Peter. Perhaps it is more useful than any use anyone can put it to. Do thy work. If thee can come home and do it, it will be better—perhaps even better for thee." How ancient she looked now, sunk back in herself! "The seed cannot return to the fruit, nor the fruit to the flower, nor the flower to the tree; nor can the tree return to the seed from which it sprang."

"Neither can the child go back into his father's womb, though he be as capacious as a hammock," Peter said.

Sharply, unexpectedly she peered at him: "Thee's a zany! If there's an Indian or a Tibetan woman, consider well, Peter! Thee's an American—India's an afterthought for thee. Marriages between men and women of the same village are strange enough—because of the difference between men and women—but marriages between men and women of different worlds—it's like blind people coming together. Haven't I seen it?"

"I have night vision," said Peter. "I thought thee approved of intermarriage."

"For people who have nothing to lose but their prejudice!" she said forcibly. "Thee's a Bruff. Naylers, Cliffords, and Bruffs don't need intermarriage. They don't start wars!"

Peter chortled: "What's done is done: I *am* a war. I'll think about it, though; I certainly will think about it."

"Indians aren't the only ones who believe in arranged marriages. I do. . . . There's something I should have told thee when thee was twelve years old—I only hope it isn't too late. It's this: Sex is somewhat misleading."

"What?" He stared at her incredulously, transfixed with embarrassment—he had never heard her utter that word before.

"Don't make me repeat it." She was blushing furiously, avoiding his eyes, but there was on her face the adventitious leer of grief that he had seen several times in a mirror. "There is one item of business," she said heavily, and this time the habitual irony of her speech was unmistakably self-directed, "which I have not mentioned, through an oversight, because I assumed—it was self-evident. I am responsible for William, for the whole thing. It was for my sin that Christ died!"

"He died to give man a guilt complex!" Peter snapped, jumping up and roving around the room. Had she identified William with the other Illumined One? "Religion is somewhat misleading. Sure, it was thy fault, and it was my fault, and Irene's—and William's, too. It was the fault of Eve and Kaliya and of Adam the Apple. Only—" He came back and, finding her nearly weeping, softened down beside her and comforted her.

When she had composed herself she murmured hoarsely, with an air of bewilderment: "William and Irene were not in accord in the matter of personal relations. . . . Sometimes I think Friends ought to have children. Doesn't thee think so? I'd be grateful if thee would consider whether thee has a feeling of responsibility in this matter. . . . All my life I've had to fight against something in myself—a kind of impatience—it gets worse as I grow older. Forgive me. I don't really want to be highhanded—to put pressure on thee to act contrary to thy convictions, but—if thee can see thy way clear —Irene lies very heavily on my heart. She isn't well, but she will be, Peter, she will be, with thy forbearance and thy love! Don't answer now, but—I beg thee: Give it thy consideration."

"I will," he said.

"And if thee is minded to lay thy concern before the Lord, He will help thee in thy struggle. Thee will get atop it!"

"Would that be fair?"

"Then—open thy mind to the Silence!"

"That I will do."

ten

The long leaves of juniper and larch swam unanimously into the wind that came rushing down from the Mongolian steppes. In the filtered sunlight, houses, trees, creatures were blurred like water colors that had been swept with a broad water brush. Tea bushes swarmed in regiments up the mountainside below the town; above it, against the skyline, furious with the wind, pranced the tall fantastic cryptomerias—after monsoon and vernal equinox they would stand like theologians, Gothic and entranced, against the frost.

Peter sat on a bench in the upper town, facing the little square that had once been fashionable and European. It was the center of what had been first a squalid village, then a British military bastion, a resort, and all of these things together. The British had built up Tashiling as a military outpost against the unreconciled kings of Sikkim, Bhutan, Nepal, and Tibet—and perhaps China even then —at this most vulnerable approach to North India. Gradually it had become a hill station where British officials with their wives and children could escape the summer heat of the plains, and a resort where the masters of lonely tea plantations in the surrounding valleys could gather with their kind. Victorian buildings, quarried out of the Himalayan granite, stood as monuments of that particular vanished dynasty. Indian troops now manned the fortifications on the heights, to dissuade secessionists—"with blood and fire," as the vegetarian governor had said—and the Chinese. Indians had taken over the tea plantations. Women in bright saris and Tibetan aprons, not British frocks, paraded in the square. Nepalese, Bengalis, Sikhs, Marwaris . . .

Peter closed his eyes. During the past year erotic fantasies had

125

bedeviled him constantly as a result of his experience with Liliu, so that he had found it almost impossible to work on the *Krishnayana*. It would pass, he was sure it would pass—everything he had ever read assured him that it would; but would he be philosophical when it did? Within minutes he would go down the mountain to Liliu Acquileia because he would be unable not to go. In the meantime, his fiber stiffening, he would try to rebel. . . . He had sat down beside a decrepit old Parsee because he wanted reminders of mortality, sickness, and theology to quell the flesh. Now the gimlet-eyed ancient stood up, wearily affronted, his eyes sliding to one side in a lethargy of contempt, and made off. Folding his hands piously in his lap, Peter slouched down until his head rested on the back of the bench, and prepared to open his mind to the Silence, as he had promised Mary Nayler he would. The world flooded in. Without thinking, he smiled gaily at a Madrassi woman in a yellow and red sari that was pulled up in a special way between her legs. Instantly she veiled her face. "*Agnus Dei*"—he sat up to get a grip on himself—with Tino's strength, or anybody's—"*inflamma cor nostrum amore Tui.* . . ." *Inflamma!* The word inflamed him.

On his way down from the square, he came to that point where one path led to Liliu's and the other to the Ashram, where both Indira and Irene were. He had assumed that he was going to Liliu's, but he was not thinking—he seldom thought to any noticeable extent unless he was talking or writing. Mildly surprised, he found himself going on to the Ashram. At the bottom of the valley he felt another odd, but calmer, disinclination to go where he had supposed he was then going. Instead of turning left to the Ashram, he took the little-used trail upstream, along the riverbank, toward the krishnachura tree. Where the trail first wandered away from the river he encountered for a moment a niche of silence in the muffled roar of the water. The air was very still, very close; the scent of jasmine hung over him in a thick, invisible fog. Then the silence was shivered by the voices of birds, like the pealing of silver bells. They were a kind of killdeer like those he had known in Pennsylvania. They folded their long wings, unfolded their long legs, dancing, winnow-striding impartially over ground or air, haunting the river.

Mysteriously excited, single-minded, they marched down the trail in relays and greeted Peter out of liquid brown eyes with orange eyelids; then with squeals of melody they flung themselves headlong into the remotest angles of space.

It was a very hard climb indeed for him this time; he was sweating violently and even trembling a little when he reached the top of the cliff; for the center of his strength was dwelling alternately in the Three Citadels—the loins, the heart, the brain—instead of deploying itself appropriately through the limbs, as he knew would have been the case had he not been a backslider from yoga.

The sannyasi was waiting for him. With what grace, what lively intelligence and wit he bade Peter welcome—without opening his mouth, without lifting a finger! Like a polio victim in an iron lung, immeasurably privileged, universal because he could not be particular, the small brown naked man looked everything with his face —mostly his eyes. Words, he seemed to say—or not to say, to assume —not even to assume, for assumptions are such toys—words are Process, and we, here, in the Eternal Now, are result, end, *telos*. Sit down, then, between words, between the beginning and the end of words, in the middle, before and after experience, in Being, at one with me, where indeed you have always been, where you will always be, and let the dust of words, of existing, settle around the figure of yourself before your dharma carries you once again into equally lawful forgetfulness and the strife that motivates your Maya.

Uncouth and dripping, with his consciousness diffused, Peter swayed before the elegant little figure; then he sat down crosslegged, like the sannyasi, facing him. Perhaps truth comes more naturally to naked men, he thought. Here he would try again to open himself to the Silence, as he had promised. Afterward he would speak of Kaliya. . . . By degrees he composed himself; but he was not willing to go all the way, not willing to absorb and be absorbed. In this incarnation—for him the unique one—he had other work to do, and perhaps it was harder work than this; for there were some, he knew, to whom wisdom would always be premature, would always mean settling for too low a price, and it was their dharma to resist for as long as possible, then to go out fighting, furious and unreconciled. That would be a compliment to life, a mark of gallantry. . . .

The great, deep, liquid eyes, set wide apart under a broad forehead, gazed like those of a forest creature at the first perceived dawn of the world; not at Peter, but at the World as Spectacle; gazed with the innocence of a god, a bodhisattva, sophisticated beyond particulars by sympathetic births in all the illusory forms of life, and even now, through sympathy for all his sentient creatures, postponing indefinitely his return to the infinite subjectivity of the universe from which he had been moved to objectify himself. Before, he was Eros; now he was Agapé, aloof bestowal of Krishna's dawn light.

It was the Recurrent Face which appeared perhaps once or twice, perhaps not at all, during a moment of peculiar sensitivity out of all the slow, fluctuating eons of ancient civilizations. Peter had recognized it once in sculpture at Angkor Vat—not the hundreds of approximations, but the One that stood apart, revealed by an impossible accident of genius—perhaps once at Sarnath, and repeated half a dozen times—if the sun had not affected his cognitive powers—at Ajanta, in the face of the Illumined Buddha. Standing on the desert, in the shade of a boulder, not far from those caves, Peter had kicked up a piece of carved stone that spoke directly, poignantly, to something more than his understanding, surmounting barriers of time and idiom and the attritions of the Process. It was the merest fragment of the Face—part of the mouth and cheek; and yet it was all there, *in omnibus partibus relucet totum,* the Whole. It was one with the stone Buddhas in the cave farther up the hill. The setting sun shone into the cave mouth to reveal them, illumined as by an inner light, looking out—and in—on the world of mankind with ultimate wisdom, infinite compassion, and with a very subtle touch of irony suggesting close acquaintance with the discrepancy between Reality and Appearance.

Slowly the great elongated eyes moved and looked into the light eyes of the visitor, where they saw more than the visitor—all things as visiting emanations of the permanent. It was as if there had never been a time when these two lives had not been together. Almost immediately the tense face of Peter relaxed, and then it began, by imperceptible degrees, to mirror the inward, slight smile, at once abstract and personal, of the sannyasi. The brown eyes closed, as it were discreetly, and stayed closed, the heavy, coarse lashes forming a pattern of a shadow on the beardless cheeks.

The knot of his being was loosened, but from that ultimate withdrawal Peter was glad to be released, to paddle in a blue lotus-lake of thoughts, not far from the shore, formulations of mind retreating to the algae at the water's edge, forestalled by furtive mauve fishes and somnolent swans with bass-viol voices. Then—it was no fantasy of the moment—a dream came to him that he had had last night or last year, had forgotten on waking, had not known until now that he had dreamed. . . .

The waters grow bitter-lipped, gray-white and blue, gripping the bow, sending accusations of spray over the vessel. Through fog and mist, grasping the rail at the prow, Peter enters a sphere just emptied by someone, a valued, injured fugitive who conceals himself in the elements, for he does not want to be found. Peter has an important message for him, which he is sure will improve matters. Anxiously he peers ahead of him into the gloom, but he can see nothing in this chaos.

It is perhaps in the forenoon when his boat puts in at a glassy purple bay. It is cold. Twelve brown Brahman boys, not yet in puberty, stand naked in a row, talons clutching the seaward end of the pier, crying shrill as gulls. A thirteenth boy—Peter—with a light skin covered by blue and green bruises, tries to join them, but he is driven away by a boy he cannot see; so he must remain just out of reach of the others. Ignored by them, he performs wonderful acrobatics, keeping up a witty patter all the while; then he does a naughty little dance, sacrificing all dignity. They are impervious to his charm. One by one, with the spacing of automatons, the brown boys, morose and purposeful, hunch their shoulders, lean forward in space, and plunge headfirst into the water. In the refracted depths their limbs scrabble in squat frenzy. They ascend the ladder to stand once more in a row along the pier, crying shrill as gulls. They shiver, dance, hug themselves, flick each other's contracted buttocks with their fingernails, their teeth chatter with cold, but they do not laugh. Only Peter laughs—he is standing on tiptoe, making faces. With sudden, practiced blows, the unseen one among them again drives him away. Peter dodges and remains just out of reach. Although he is not without courage, he deserves the blows, for he is maddeningly impudent, immoral, pushing, as if he hoped to distract attention from his guilty color. Nobody really cares enough to darken him all over with bruises—nobody except that one fellow, and he is not very quick. Hard to get a good look at him.

The water darkens. Out of the midnight depths draws a vast creature without shape, her tissues joined with the currents of the water, coterminous with the ocean of which the beast's being is the veins and arteries. She is like something troubled, ominous and wise, just born out of immense age, an obscure gathering of solicitude under the skin of the waters. The formless body extends indefinitely under the sea, but the head surfaces like oil, and the flat orbs fix themselves in a kind of nestling gaze upon all the boys, even the impudent one, the white-skinned one with the bruises green and blue. Slowly her mouth opens into a well of antennae.

One by one, with the spacing of automatons, the brown boys hunch their shoulders, no longer morose, lean forward in space, and crying shrill as gulls, plunge headfirst into the mouth. Still she waits. As Peter approaches hesitantly, hardly able to believe his good fortune, a boy—like William, like Ananda—cuts in ahead of him, and, in his eagerness to follow the others, lands a cruel blow on Peter's nose, smashing it. For a moment they are locked in fierce struggle, then the other boy breaks Peter's grip and dives. There is a stirring in the depths as the ocean closes.

A deep eddy remains on the surface. The sea birds skim the water here as if Ino had sunk down in that pool. And the light-skinned boy, the impudent one with bruises green and blue, laments and strokes the air and flies out over the water, crying shrill as a gull. Overhead an electrical storm emanates in quivering waves of light from the sun, sweeps him up and bears him in mighty rhythms across the landscape. His strength has no effect on the itinerary. Like the folding of a joint, without pain or noise, his will breaks and he lies back on the journeying wind. . . .

Drifting down, he takes his place in an open-air classroom in a ravine enclosed by steep cliffs. A gentle rain is falling. Seated at his desk among the other pupils—they are pale, fair-haired, full of innocent intelligence—Peter is attempting to read a book of sermons. It is too deep for him, since it is not only his body that is dark. Furtively he tears out several pages and plasters them on his wet body to conceal his nakedness. It is not easy. Still he pores zealously over what is left of the book. More and more the rain dims his vision. First with one hand, then with both, he fans the water away from his eyes. Increasingly adept, exhilarated by his success, and taking advantage of his darkness, which renders him inconspicuous in this weather, he stands up, making vigorous downward strokes, cupping his hands. His feet begin to move as if he were treading water, and he ascends exulting into the sky.

When he has reached a considerable height, he lets himself drift down again over the classroom. The teacher, a woman with grave blue eyes and fair hair that aureoles out as if it has just been washed, glances up at him. Proof of her good will lies in the fact that she makes no mention either of his precarious status or of his base nature, although the sermon paper has come unpasted. As if her interest were purely technical, she catechizes him: "How does thee do that?" She is Aunt Mary, except that Aunt Mary would never ask such an obvious question.

Without hesitating, although he has forgotten the original message, Peter says three or more things at once, a message so abundant in meaning that it overwhelms speech.

"How did thee say that?" Now she is gaping up at him, open-mouthed, no longer Aunt Mary, but the Clerk of the Meeting.

"I just let myself go," says Peter, hovering over her with little, gentle, controlled movements. "Try it. God will put the syntax in thy mouth."

The teacher laughs profanely, they pivot on the laugh, and Peter is suddenly in her place, behind her desk, laughing up at her. With great difficulty she works her way upward, turning her spine sideways, dog-paddling with her hands, treading the air with her feet. Since she has short legs, she paddles fast; her glasses are steamed over; in order to see, she jerks her head from side to side as one does in playing the piano or beating eggs. However, she makes little headway, and Peter observes that her toes have spread out with the effort, bursting through the shoes and tearing at the hem of her dress. Long, soggy strips of blue and white cloth hang down in ribbons. Too late, he tries to dissuade her.

The teacher churns gradually upward, an inch at a time, and finally sits exhausted atop a dead tree. There, looking down, full of pity for him, she wipes her glasses and untangles her draperies from her pierced shoes. It is raining heavily—a consequence, a commentary. William leads everyone in prayer. Only Peter is unable to bow his head. Stricken with remorse, he approaches the base of the tree and apologizes, pleading with the teacher to come down and resume the class.

"Settle down," he urges brokenly, then, arguing with increasing vehemence: "Thee will marry me! All shall be as fair as tomorrow! A Rome knew only a decadent, self-Alexandrian Greece that had already long since been traduced by an Asia!"

The tearful face of Irene the beloved smiles down on him with perfect comprehension, untainted by forgiveness, and the angelic gaze fixes itself immovably upon the horizon, where the figure of a gigantic serpent—Old Holdfast—summoned by Peter's action, looms higher and higher, his cloudy coils darkening the earth. Led by William, all the other pupils have fled up out of the ravine. At the top they stand for a moment outlined, tiny, residual, exquisite, against the sky; then they wave their arms in a final, remote gesture, like the vanishing of a culture, and disappear toward their homes. Unable to fly, Peter begins to look about for the wet sermon papers —hard to distinguish them from the general muck on the floor— lighting none too good—but with their help he may yet escape in disguise. . . .

On the ground beside the sannyasi was a thick glass tumbler from which he had drunk tea that morning—evidently someone had brought it to him from a hut in the jungle, for there were no signs of preparations here. A dozen flies were buzzing around the tumbler; several were down inside, sponging up the sugar. The sannyasi's eyes shifted ever so slightly from Peter's eyes to the tumbler, then back again, without disturbing their rapport. Deliberately the brown hand reached out; with a sudden movement it turned the tumbler upside down, trapping several flies inside, and withdrew. The flies buzzed frantically behind the glass walls of their prison. Seeing that Peter understood, the sannyasi reached out again with the same slow, deliberate gesture, and turned the tumbler back to its original position. The flies all fled out into the wide world. The sannyasi laughed merrily, a ringing, boyish laughter, with his head thrown back—indeed at that moment he looked like a young boy. Then there was a subtle distancing, and Peter knew that he was dismissed.

Having thus opened himself to the Silence, with unexpected results, Peter descended again into the valley. It was late afternoon. Hot and thirsty, he jumped into the pool below the waterfall and swam around under the surface, drinking as he swam. When he came up, he had Liliu's knife which he had thrust into the sand the day before—he did not know what impulse had made him find it again, as he had fully intended to leave it hidden there forever. Climbing out, he lay where Jim Chen had scuffled with Chanchal, and prepared to relax. The rock was still warm, although it lay now in shadow. At first he felt drowsy; then it was as if the sun had moved backward, for he was no longer in shadow. A slight change in the interlacing branches—a wind passing through them, perhaps —could have accounted for it; and yet his heart began to pound furiously. He could have slowed it down to its normal rate by a simple technique of yoga—indeed, he knew how to stop it altogether for a few seconds—but now he obstinately refrained from interfering. Slowly he sat up, his nostrils distended, and looked around. Just as on the day when the other men had been here, he began to shake; this time he controlled it, although his heart continued to race.

Clutching the knife in his right hand, stooping a little, the fingers of his left claw spread out, he slid into the jungle. Silently he crept around the semicircle that bordered the pool, through fern trees and plantains and siris, bound together by parasitic creepers. In a dark place a heavy spider web met his face, but his recoil was so precise and instantaneous that the web escaped undamaged. A dun-and-orange spider four inches long ran out, took one look and retreated. There were no birds or animals, no wind, no sound but the muffled roar of the river down below.

Back at the pool again he paused only long enough to get his clothes. It was a foolhardy thing he had done. One did not hunt pythons with knives; not that flight would have helped, on the other hand, if Kaliya had really wanted him. But it was not time yet— surely it was not time! As he dressed he glanced fearfully into the pool. Pythons were water lovers. Often they lay coiled at the bottom of a pool, and if a buck or some other creature came to drink, seized it by the nose, pulled it in and swallowed it under water after shaping it up. Well, if there was a python in that pool, it was no man-eater, because he, Peter, was still alive.

Swiftly passing the krishnachura tree, Peter made a slight ironic gesture of greeting to the stone image; but the gaze of Krishna fluting dwelt on him with the unfathomable interest of God the Lover, that does not in the slightest preclude violent death to the Beloved. In his imagination the shadowed visage was one with the massive and sinuous roots of the tree, with the legendary python, with the sannyasi on the cliff above. Lest it suddenly become one with his individuated, hence imperiled, self, he bolted down the trail as fast as he could.

Where the trail formed a Y, with the shaft going up the mountain, the two sides to the Ashram and the krishnachura tree, he stopped to rest and lighten his ballast. The sun, dropping down into a more distant valley, gave him a historical shadow. Throwing back his head—exactly as the sannyasi had done—he laughed to see the active fork of him repeated in the trail, in the trees, in the valleys, in tributary streams, in the veins and branches of the world. The water from the pool rained down in a noble cascade.

It was time he did some reconnoitering, to acquaint himself in some detail with the places where a giant python would be most likely to sleep between meals. Pythons fed at regular intervals; but the bigger the python, the shorter the interval if the meal was not commensurate with his size; more accurately, the duration of the interval could be calculated from the ratio of the size of the python to the size of his habitual meal. In this instance the habit was not established. As is commonly the case where human beings compose the game preserve of a nonhuman hunter, the true size of the man-eater was unknown. The few who had actually caught a glimpse of Kaliya before they fled naturally had lost perspective, either at the time or immediately afterward. Their reports were more mythological than any Peter could remember having heard, including those of the Naga people in Upper Assam—there they had paced off seventy, eighty, ninety feet to show him the length of a python that turned out to be only thirty-nine feet six and one-half inches long, although the skin, when stretched, without the head, was over forty-four feet long. That python had fasted for exactly fourteen days between meals. A thirty-one-foot python which he killed earlier by mistake was known to have fed every thirteen days. It contained the skeletons of two small leopards which must have weighed about forty-five and fifty-five pounds. These and several other experiences of a similar nature showed that, other things being equal—season, climate, health—the rate of metabolism remained constant among individual pythons. In general they chose the prey best suited for their size. What happened when even a full-grown human being was not big enough to last for two weeks, Peter was not sure, as he had not encountered that problem till now. The logical answer would be a bigger prey. Unfortunately, man-eaters do not change their diet. Assuming, then, that Kaliya was unusually large, it was just possible that the hundred-and-twenty-pound cook in his stomach would not be sufficient to detain him for more than, say, twelve days. That would be four days from now.

Peter sat down on a boulder by the river, which he had got used to as one gets used to deafness, and sailed flat stones out across the water—they would not skip because of the turbulence. Had he thought more clearly, he might have timed his arrival at Tashiling a little better. Today would have been a good day to have arrived. Then he could have kept very busy during the several days required for the job. . . . As it was, he felt shaky and uneven in regard to such a relatively simple thing as the hunt: from over-confidence, through carelessness, he found himself in a state of un-certainty that could easily become fear; not that he was ever quite devoid of fear when he hunted—perhaps because he had hunted only man-eaters in India—but this fear was different. The complications he had found in this region of the Himalayas affected his balance, and consequently, as he knew—hence the fear—the risk of making a false move when he was actually face to face with Kaliya, that most problematical quarry.

In his distraction he had come away from Tashiling without considering what day it was: the day, the evening, the night on which he meant to familiarize himself, in various lights, with the general area which Kaliya seemed to have marked off for his own. Peter had forgotten his gun, and he now had no intention of venturing into the jungle unarmed. If he walked briskly he could get his rifle from Tino's and return here in three-quarters of an hour; but it was not likely that he would do it. Liliu would be waiting for him. Even if he succeeded in not going to her, he would arrive here in a depleted condition—and when? The prediction was a sly one. . . . Or he could return to the Ashram, borrow Jim's rifle—and there again it would be like returning to the scene of his crime, not less great, this one, for being a crime of omission, of failure. . . . Petulantly he raised his arm to hurl a rock into the water, and suddenly froze in that position. Something was behind him, quite close, although he could neither see it nor hear it. With an instantaneous movement he scooted down the river side of the boulder, turning at the same time to face—Indira!

"Sorry!" she shouted, laughing—her voice was barely audible over the roar of the water. "I called to you but you didn't hear. See, I brought you this. Take it, please; it is very heavy." With some effort she extended his own rifle toward him; then she gave him his ammunition belt which she carried looped over her shoulder.

"Where did you get this?" He led her away from the river to a spot near the jungle, where they sat on the bone-white carcass of a tree that had come down by way of some tributary stream higher up. Against the white tree trunk her dark red sari made a dramatic splash of color. He felt his ears tingling again.

"I called on you in Tashiling," she said, "but you were not there. I wanted to know if you are suffering qualms."

"What about?"

"Oh—perhaps religious, like Dr. Bhattacharya, so that you decide after all that you cannot help us if it involves taking life—or losing life."

"I'm not religious," said Peter.

"But today is late, and you did not have your gun, did you?"

"As a matter of fact, I was thinking about going after it."

"Fortunately," she said, "that is just the sort of thing I have no difficulty in believing." It was impossible to tell, from her enigmatic expression—serious though it was—whether she was being cynical or truthful or both.

"How did you know I was here?" he demanded, a little piqued, a little amused, and extraordinarily gratified by her presence even though she made him feel foolish.

"I don't know. I did not know. I thought: Approximately here is where he should be at this time, and he has forgotten his gun. Alternatively I thought: He is suffering qualms and he is elsewhere, and in that case he has no need of his gun, so I shall use it myself. My gun is not very good," she said apologetically. "I can't hit anything with it."

"And you thought you might hit something with mine!"

"I often walk by the river, and now I go armed. . . . However, I am glad you are not suffering qualms. Perhaps I could not hit anything with your gun either."

"You didn't trust me," he said sadly, "even though I told you you could."

"I trust, but I do not rely—there is a difference, is there not? How can I teach children to rely upon themselves, if I do not rely upon myself? Have you not read Emerson?"

"I have read some of Emerson," he said. "He does not speak to my condition."

"Ah, perhaps that is because you do not need him. Americans are already self-reliant, isn't it? We Indians rely too much upon one another. It is we who need Emerson. When I began to learn English, my brother gave me the essay on Self-Reliance to memorize. If you would care to hear it, I can recite it to you some evening."

"That will be charming," said Peter. "I like it when you pull my leg."

For a second she glanced in bewilderment at his long, bare legs, then she remembered the idiom. Quickly she stood up to go, embarrassed more by the reference to his body than by her momentary lapse.

"Then I shall leave the arrangements to you," she said formally. "I shall be at the Ashram if you require anything. Do not hesitate. I shall continue to practice shooting with my rifle. You may count upon me—only, remember my deficiency. There are also Mr. Chen, Mr. Kashani and Mr. Chanchal—and two of our men are good with Kukri knives and spears. . . . Is it your opinion that I should be reassured?"

My God! he thought. What self-possession, what self-assurance she must have, this slim, ivory-colored Brahmaness in the shadowy folds of a red sari, this sister of Ananda Mahadev, soft and subtle, who walked alone by the river, carrying a heavy rifle, challenging Kaliya! —to say nothing of Peter. Even as she looked at him, waiting for a response to her question, she seemed to enter another dimension. Actually she was not looking at him, but beyond him, at the fringe of jungle, black against the green, twilight sky. A pallor was on her face, her mouth opened in a silent cry, and her eyes were enormous with dread and fear and pity.

Whirling around, Peter saw a sinuous form, flowing down out of the upper branches of a tree, pause in silhouette like a long, muscular arm with fist clenched and bent back at right angles to the wrist so that the palm would be parallel with the ground if the fingers were to open; they did not, because there were no fingers, no fist, no arm. At the base of the tree, some twelve feet below the sudden form, a sloth-like creature as big as a pye-dog sat upright squealing in terror, long, rhythmical squeals, one after another. Then, with incredible swiftness and accuracy the "arm" flowed on down, lowered twelve feet more of itself out of the branches, a black, rippling length—how much of it remained aloft?—seized the screaming creature and whisked it back into the upper foliage. The whole tragedy took about six seconds. The victim—now quite silent—had made no attempt to escape. The two human witnesses had remained motionless.

"Why didn't you—" Indira stammered—released from the spell, she tottered away a few paces.

"It wasn't Kaliya," he said quietly.

"Couldn't you have frightened him? Those cries!"

"Perhaps," said Peter, "and then he would have been all the hungrier, and perhaps he would find something with more courage than that one, or with more beauty—"

Suddenly Indira went limp. Peter's cat-reflex made him clutch instantaneously at the escaping form. Before her knees had touched the ground, he caught her up lightly, gently, and held her in his arms as if she were a child. Losing consciousness, she lost the intensity that contracted her into a small, slim, nun-like elegance, not in black but ringed by irresistible flames, the sacerdotal scarlet. Completely vulnerable under his astonished gaze, she seemed to expand, to extend upon him until she filled his horizon, until she lay on him like a dark and light cloud on a dark mountain, volcanic or when the sun reddens a young night. Helplessly he kissed her, not on the mouth, but on the cheekbone, near her eye. The long, dark lashes fluttered against his cheek; she opened her eyes, looked at him vaguely, steadily, then less vaguely, then she lifted her head from his shoulder. After a moment she detached herself from him and stood by herself—she would not sit down.

"Thank you," she said. "That has never happened to me before. . . . I think it was because I forgot to eat lunch, then I missed tea, then, just now—I felt too much distress—unexpectedly."

"Next time you go hunting for Kaliya," said Peter, hovering, still solicitous, half-encircling but not touching her, "it would be well to eat a chapatti first."

"Yes"—she withdrew further from him, gave him a wan smile— "but it is also important to eat a chapatti afterward. Therefore, please do not hunt alone—take some men with you." Wordlessly there passed between them the names of the other hunters. "I shall continue to practice shooting," she said. "I can be very firm when I have had a chapatti."

As Peter escorted her back nearly to the Ashram, he blurted out: "I do things I don't mean to—I kissed you—just on the cheek, near your eye—"

"You have an affectionate nature," she observed coolly. "Do not grieve too much. It is already forgotten."

Watching her depart—how marvelously she walked, flowing, flying, coasting, a moving ripple in a line that was without beginning or ending, emerging and submerging in time, forming a mysterious continuity, a oneness with all other lines, lives. . . . Nonsense! It was only a beautiful woman walking as beautiful women should but seldom do. . . . At the precise point where her eyelashes had fluttered against his cheek, he felt the hair-like tongue of a hummingbird touching one rose only. . . .

About a quarter of a mile north-northeast of the krishnachura tree, Peter stopped and prepared to return by a different set of trails, as far as the Ashram. The other side of the river would not concern him yet, for several reasons: a python would not consider swimming a sizable river in spate unless it were desperate for game; Kaliya had never been seen on the other side of the river; pythons did not stray far from their birthplace; they never migrated. The region south of the Ashram did not much interest Peter either. In his opinion, Kaliya had grown up in the jungle along the east side of the valley, between the river and and the mountain wall; there, undetected by hunters, he had reached a good size, perhaps a considerable age, and only recently had begun to prey on human beings.

It was nearly dark now, and the moon was not up yet. Peter brooded at the black, forbidding tangle before him, and changed his mind about returning through it. Just as he started for the long, open stretch that paralleled the river, he heard a steaming of suppressed laughter, and turned to see a bunch of naked children skittering along in the underbrush beside him, wanting to be discovered.

"Hey, there!" he called out in Nepali. "Where do you live?"

"There! There!" They pointed up a dark valley a little farther on, which he had chosen to ignore.

"If I were Kaliya," he said, "a brace of brown babies would be my heart's desire." They shrieked and fluted with joy and darted up to examine him as closely as possible—their glistening eyes strove to penetrate the mysteries of his person. "Aren't you afraid?" he demanded.

"No, no, no! *You* are here! Nothing will hurt us, because *you* are here!" They elved round him, touching him shyly as if he were some wonderful, friendly beast; and indeed, a god with so much hair on his legs—they themselves were of a hair-free race—could not be so very formidable. With a little encouragement, they might have stroked him.

"And who am *I*, not to be afraid?" he asked.

"You afraid? You are Pitar! Pitar, Pitar, Pitar!" they shrilled melodically at his divine wit.

That was something that he had not counted on. Natural enough that everybody in the valley should have got wind of him—a man with a gun, after Kaliya—that they should make a temporary folk hero out of him, whether he was successful or not. Ordinarily they would not have learned his name, or they would have given him a nickname of their own, or the name of some previous dragon slayer; but somewhere along the line someone had pronounced his name, and Peter had become Pitar: Dyaus Pitar, meaning Zeus Pater, Iuppiter, Jupiter, Dieu, Père, Gott der Vater, who, as everybody knows, can wind Satan around his little finger. . . . Peter hoped they would not expect too much of him. As for arguing that it was a case of mistaken identity, he would not even try. They would not believe him. Dyaus Pitar was not in the habit of showing his wile-working hand, not while he was on a job, and he was always on some job or other.

"Go back to your village," Peter told them, and rather than send them along home in the middle of the dark, he went with them, intending to leave them on the outskirts of their village. After a brisk ten minutes, during which the children flickered around him, humming and chortling with excitement, he stopped at the sight of a cluster of thatch and wattle huts. The strong smells of wood smoke and cooking food—meat—made him all at once very hungry.

"Come, come, come, Pitar!" the children cried, alternately tugging at him, caressing him and touching the tops of his feet to show respect. "Come with us, Pitar! Stay with us, Pitar!"

Within seconds, it seemed, the whole population of the village— perhaps a hundred people—had crowded around him, eager and delighted as children, and as unawed by divinity, beseeching him to accept their hospitality. They were a small, handsome people, a mixture of Nepali and Lepcha, perhaps Bhutia also, and of very low caste, if indeed they had any caste at all. The fact that Peter, glorious though he was, obviously could have no caste either, had already created a bond between them, a covenant, as it were; also, he seemed to like their children, and so did they.

Peter went with a paunchy, wizened little ancient named Kedar, the head man. Kedar wore a beaded G-string with a merry tassel over it, and had the manners of a gentleman. After he had flushed a dozen descendants and wives out of his hut, which was the largest in the village—some twenty feet long by twelve wide—he ceremoniously spread a fresh mat on the floor for Peter and sat down beside him. Three suitable males, mysteriously elected, strolled in, sat down opposite them, and were silently charming, since it is not very respectful to food to talk at mealtime.

Dinner consisted of helpings from all the dishes that were being cooked in the village that evening: curried vegetables, yams and fruits, goat meat, chicken, and mango-loving fruit bats the size of small eagles. Kedar's head wife and two head daughters ladled the food out on plates made of plantain leaves cunningly cupped on the thin end and placed on the ground before the wonderful guest, the head man and the three elected ones opposite them. Seated cross-legged, Peter leaned far forward and dipped up the food with the first two fingers of his right hand as far as the second knuckles, plus the thumb, and conveyed it gustily to his mouth—everything tastes better with oxygen—smacking his lips and casting glances. The old woman looked happy enough to throw herself into a cooking pot for him if he would just say the word. Women crouching in darkness against the walls on the outside—the door and the one small window being full of men—listened anxiously for whispered communiqués from the two head daughters on the inside: "He is eating *your* chicken, Sita—the whole back! . . . A mouthful of *your* chutney, Bhakti—he doesn't like it—yes, he does! He just belched a little —no, no, it was a good belch—he meant it! . . . He takes vegetables —*yours*, Sona, a little of your eggplant, but he lays the rest down—no, no, only for a moment, to rest his jaws. Most of all Pitar likes meat.

That is well known, and besides he is a hunter now. Meat for a hunter! Meat! Listen to him, Pratima—almost growling! Did he growl? That is *your* roast goat. Oo-oh, there went the marrow! . . . Notice, he likes roast meat better than curried meat, when it's fresh. No wonder! Curry is to enable a man, but Pitar is all vigor—see, he has virile hair even on his toes! It makes me shiver to think of it! . . . The roast bat—look at him go after it! I'm so happy for Mother— lucky she didn't curry it after all! Will he take another one? Mother's so shy about her own cooking—she keeps giving him *your* dishes. . . . If he insists on hers, what can she do? There! Mother's giving him another roast bat. He says, No! No! and spreads his hands out over his plate. You can tell he's lying—just look at his smile! White teeth like a tiger's! What beautiful manners! He's trying to keep the bat off his plate—he knows how to act, Pitar does! This side and that —what a tussle! Mother tries to force it down between his fingers, but no! Quick, now, to one side, then the other! Dodge past—oh, joy, she did it! It's on his plate; he's picking it up as if he would swallow it whole. . . ."

After dinner, guest and host stepped outside, washed their hands and faces, rinsed their mouths noisily, and ducked back inside. Kedar grinned a happy, toothless grin and personally poured liquor from a jug into earthenware cups. Ceremoniously he passed them, first to the great visitor, then to the élite, then to himself. It was a sort of brandy made out of amloki fruit, of a clear, jacaranda-violet color with gold flecks swirling in it—mica from a stream, perhaps. Peter was sure they had never got just this color before and that they would never achieve it again, because they did not make things twice in precisely the same way. Inside, it was like fire. One swallow, and Peter considered himself fortunate to have a firm foundation of food in his stomach for that liquor to land on. If he expected to accomplish anything next day—and the day would begin, unfortunately, at three in the morning—he must manage somehow to seem to drink more than he actually would, and to get a couple of hours' sleep, perhaps right here in the hut.

Now it was time to talk, and talk they did. Of the three elect villagers, one—Kedar's brother-in-law—was old and wise, one— Kedar's son—was middle-aged and lively, and one—Kedar's great-grandson—was young and responsive, pleasing alike to eye and ego; but Kedar was older, freer, and more charming than any of them. Peter had been adroit enough to start asking them questions before they could start asking him questions, and so the pattern was set for them to do most of the talking. Had they seen Kaliya? Yes and no, chiefly no; he had not been this far north as yet, although he was expected momentarily to visit one of his queens—no, they had not seen her either, but it was common knowledge that she lived not far from here. Did there happen to be any firearms in the village? At the moment, no, there just did not happen to be any at the moment. A few years ago Kedar had had a very suitable gun, but one of his great-grandsons—that little bugger there, in fact—had carried it off and left it in the jungle, and when they found it again it was nothing but a peculiar bundle of rust and mold. Kedar still wore the ammunition from it as an amulet around his elbow—he showed Peter a .22-caliber bullet.

Just before dinner Peter had heard three fine, sonorous blasts from a conch shell, indispensable for driving away evil spirits so that people can eat in peace after nightfall. Every village had at least one conch shell for this purpose. They could be heard evenings from one end of the valley to the other. Peter now requested that the conch shell be blown only if Kaliya appeared in this vicinity. As for the other evil spirits, Peter gave Kedar his personal guarantee that they would not trouble this village so long as Kaliya remained alive. Let it be understood that no conch shell was to be blown in this valley except as a signal to Peter that Kaliya had appeared, and Peter would come at once. To this request Kedar agreed wholeheartedly, even promising to resist the temptation to summon Peter for the pleasure of his company.

After several cups of amloki brandy, Kedar's son lost his liveliness and slowly lay down in the midst of an anecdote he was telling—it had to do with a Yeti, or Abominable Snowman, which he had once encountered—and although he continued to talk for a while, it soon became evident that he had retired for the night. The old man, Kedar's brother-in-law, spoke of anterior things, with the idea of bringing the full weight of the past to bear upon the present occasion; but gradually he became as vague as the mythological beginnings with which he had so logically begun, and there he remained immersed, united with them in sleep. Kedar's great-grandson, whom Kedar had restricted to two cups, since he was only fifteen and apt to become silly, edged closer to his two fellow survivors, his ancestor and Pitar the Great Essence, as if he could not have enough of them. The god dazzled him. Rosy and beatific, the boy swayed forward, his hand went out, one finger extended, and like the children whose age group he had so recently left, he was unable to resist touching Peter, ever so lightly, just on his lordly kneecap.

"No, no!" cried his great-grandfather, laughing and smacking the boy's hand. "Where did you learn such manners, you baby? You must ask his permission first!"

"Such formality!" Peter uttered the formal Indian complaint and laid one hand on Kedar's hand and one on the boy's hand. "People should touch each other when there is no objection."

"Pay attention," Kedar whispered to his great-grandson. "Pitar is teaching."

"I am not teaching," said Peter.

"He is not teaching," Kedar murmured sadly, then more hopefully: "Perhaps he will teach you someday, boy, so that you will stop being a nothing. Sit up and pay attention so that he will remember you, can you understand?"

"I can understand, Great-Grandfather." The boy tried to look melted with gratitude, as was proper, but there was something essentially self-respecting, rebellious, and humorous in his tribal spirit that made him incapable of abasing himself in the high-flown manner of a plainsman, as more or less recommended by his ancestor just now—the godless old lecher who was probably really his father.

Peter yawned and announced that he was going to sleep for a few hours, right where he was, then leave without waking anyone up, since he would be back—he "must" come back, *nischoi*—to visit them. One mat was about as good as another, except that Peter was already sitting on the new one, so Kedar simply moved over, and Peter lay down; but Kedar had no intention of letting him go to sleep immediately. Lying down beside Peter, with his rump turned to his great-grandson, he continued in a cheerful, confidential tone:

"I have lived for two hundred and thirty-seven years, and if you care to live that long in this incarnation—keeping both your beauty and your virility—I will tell you my secret."

"I would love to know your secret," Peter murmured, closing his eyes and giving a good snoof through his nostrils so that he would not have to come out of a doze to stop a buzzing he might otherwise have in the bridge of his nose—the result of an adolescent fistfight in Swarthmore Woods. . . . So innocent, those woods, and every tree was free—not a single parasitic creeper. Today he had seen a black larch bent over, embraced by a thick, putty-colored vine that had mashed itself around the tree like a Bosch succubus around a slim, straight, black woman, so that its legs, its paws, its roots, met on the other side of the larch, and the tail went down into the ground, and the mouth was at the branches, and the whole body of the thing was sucking the life out. Tomorrow he must find that tree, and he would have his hunting knife in case he could not pull the creeper away. . . .

"Perhaps you do not really want to know," Kedar parried—he was being coy. "You need sleep. After all, what is this life?"

"I really want to know—*please* tell me." Peter turned his head toward Kedar, casting his eyes down, however, in hopes of palming off his sleepiness as docility.

"You already know the secret," said Kedar.

"No, I don't."

"Yes, you do. You are Pitar—but perhaps, like Krishna, you like to forget from time to time? Ah, yes. I, too . . ."

"I implore you."

"Well, then," said Kedar, getting more comfortable, "this is it: Copulate every day of your life."

"Oh," Peter said, and his face twitched a little.

"Woman is a pool of water," Kedar continued, "and man is a water snake. The snake that does not swim dries up. Does the snake put into the pool more than he takes out?" He drew a fingertip lightly across Peter's pectoral to wake him up with a happy sensation in case he was asleep. Peter opened both eyes, was reassured at Kedar's expression of kindly zeal, smiled and closed his eyes again.

"No," he answered, "he does not."

"And have you copulated today?"

"No—no, I haven't."

"That is why you are so tired!" Kedar exclaimed triumphantly. "As soon as I saw you, I said to myself: 'There is one who has not copulated today—and why? Because he is giving his strength to *us*, to protect us in this village; he drives himself constantly, he does not stop long enough to renew his strength, which thirsts from every hair. Now he has come to visit us—and can I be called a host if I do not provide him with everything he requires for his strength?'"

"No, no," Peter demurred, "I beg you not to worry about me—all I require is two hours' sleep."

"So I began looking about me, and I find that I have four very beautiful descendants, one of them only twelve years old, and I am going to call them in—"

"Then I am going," said Peter, sitting up. "Don't think I don't appreciate it, but—"

"I understand," Kedar said soothingly, pressing him down by degrees. "One can have too many women at once, or even one after the other in too rapid succession. Already more children have sprung from the loins of Pitar in three years of this incarnation than from Kedar's in two hundred and eighty-three years." There was a note of sadness in his voice.

"The Ashram! You mean the children at the Ashram? They're not mine, Kedar; they're not mine—they're orphans—other men's children—Englishmen, planters!"

"You are the planter, Pitar," Kedar nodded sagely, ignoring Peter's laughter, "but of course one must deny, otherwise, even I—" His voice trailed off as he looked meditatively around him at the perhaps-sleeping forms—a dozen or so people had crept in inconspicuously to lie down in their accustomed places, children, mothers, fathers, maidens, sons with young wives. Kedar resumed with more confidence, as if he were on safer ground: "There is such a thing as having too many children, Pitar, and I am the first to recognize that, although I am as fond of children as you are. I will tell you frankly, I should much prefer that you live with us here if you have a child in this village. You cannot, of course—I see it in your face. You want to stay with your other children. That is only natural. I saw them from a distance. They are very pretty. . . . We, on the other hand, would not want one of our children to leave us, even to go with you—because of the caste people. He will be happier here."

"Kedar, I am not going to have a child in this village," Peter said, trying hard to conceal his exasperation. "I am not—"

"Exactly," said Kedar. "That is why I suggest that you at least have a look at one of my granddaughters, who is not only beautiful —she is barren."

"No, God damn it, no! I don't want to!"

"I give you my personal guarantee that she is barren," Kedar pursued patiently, studying Peter's face from a few inches away.

"No women for me, thanks." Peter smiled drowsily, turned on his side, and made snoring sounds.

"I know what you mean." Kedar laid his patriarchal baldness on the mat, drifting more and more into the orbit of Peter's somnolence. "There are times . . . some things women cannot get through their heads, true. . . . My great-grandson here—no? A change now and then . . . works wonders . . . appreciate women more."

Peter snored until Kedar began to snore, then he stopped, turned quietly on his back, and gazed unthinkingly up into the thatch, smiling a little. In the distance he could hear the river. Starting in the high Himalayas, he flowed down a thousand valleys, past the place where he now was, into the Ganges—farther—into the Bay of Bengal, thence into the Outer Ocean.

It was still quite dark, although the moon had not set. This was the morning Peter was to take them to a certain pass he knew, to point out, just at dawn, the distant peak of Everest, which Tino had never seen, nor had Chanchal either, for that matter. A Tibetan woman had come to the house, dragging three nags, at 3:00 A.M., the time agreed on for the departure. Astride the shaggy little beasts that were yet somehow more horse than pony, they climbed slowly up and around the mountain of Tashiling, toward the pass. Wisps of fog drifted about them in the moonlight. Tall spires of sal trees stood silent, motionless at first, until a breeze began to blow up from the valleys of Nepal. They descended for some time, then began to climb again. The trail rounded a kind of promontory which jutted out into the gray darkness toward Tibet. A cold wind was blowing now. On the south side of the pass they tethered the horses to some bushes in the lee of a big rock. A little farther down they found an outcropping of rocks and sat down to wait for dawn.

From the time of their departure they had said very little to one another. After a few tentative remarks, Peter had given up, ascribing the gloomy dignity of Tino and Chanchal to the fact that he had been noncommittal about joining forces with them in hunting the big snake. It crossed his mind, too, that Tino's jealousy, or envy —so misplaced—might have possessed him again, although it should have been exorcised by the manful confessions they had made. Tino's cigarette lighter clicked several times, caught at last. The flame revealed his face white and drawn, and Chanchal, his hands helping to shield the flame, popeyed with sympathy.

"What is it?" Peter exclaimed.

"Not a goddamn thing." They did not speak again for several minutes. Tino's cigarette glowed fiercely, then he said, "I must have strained my shoulders."

"Weight-lifting?"

"Yes." The reply was hardly audible.

"His shoulders began to give him bloody hell yestereve," Chanchal babbled as if released from a vow of silence. "Oh, it was *such* pain! He could not restrain from crying out. I went in unto him. 'Let me summon the doctor!' 'No!' 'Then?' 'Nothing!' Nothing. He must endure it."

"I did not cry out," Tino rasped.

"No, no, he did not cry out physically," Chanchal amended hastily. "I was dreaming spiritually that he suffered, and so perturbed was I that I peeped. He was writhing in agony! You, Mr. Peter," accusingly, "you were in the arms of Morpheus, snoozing!"

"I was not writhing in agony," Tino said.

"I was not in my room," said Peter. "Does it hurt very much?"

Tino did not reply, and after a moment Chanchal said that it hurt very much indeed, more than Mr. Peter could ever know.

"I do not think," Peter reflected, "that you should have come out in this cold wind, and the dampness—"

"If you coddle a thing, it gets worse," Tino said. "It's a matter of exercise. Keep it exercised. It got stiff during the night, that's all. Now let's change the subject, O.K.?" The alternative was not another subject, but silence, during which Peter felt little empathies running through his own carcass.

"How long before dawn?" Tino asked hoarsely, lighting another cigarette with Chanchal's help.

"Less than thirty minutes," said Peter, and expanded a little. "Everest is sixty miles west-northwest of us. The sun's rays will pass over us to strike the top of it while we're still in the dark, even though we're closer to the sun—because it's the highest thing in the world. If we're lucky, we'll see the peak of it for a minute or two —a cone of snow on fire with gold—like an idea—then the clouds will close over it, and everything will be gray, and you won't be in a position to prove that you've seen it."

" 'Like an idea,' " Tino echoed jerkily as if he were forcing himself to talk. "Scotus Eriugena says man is an idea in the Divine Mind. You say Everest is an idea in the human mind. Man is much smaller than Everest. *Ergo?*"

"Everest may be God," Peter said. "Lots of people who live around it say it is."

"Mount Everest redounds to the credit of India, as well as to the universe!" Chanchal cried, his voice quivering. "She is a veracious entity endued by the Creator!"

The stirring of the wind over the tops of the trees made a sighing sound. The edge of the jungle was only a little way down the hill, tall tangles of tree and vine, orchid and fern, all in a fading black and white of moonlight. The three men huddled close together, drinking hot coffee out of a Thermos.

"How long now?" Tino asked.

"Ten minutes."

"Ten minutes—everything is ten minutes in this country. Yes, yes, Sahib, you shall have it in ten minutes. In ten minutes the mail will come, but not for you, Sahib. I shall be back in ten minutes. In ten minutes, Everest. In ten minutes, no Everest. Life is ten minutes, death is ten minutes."

"And so it will be in the next life, and the next," said Chanchal gently, "until we are released from time altogether."

"I don't like life," Tino fumed, "but I'd as soon be dead as in Nirvana."

In the obscurity to which their eyes had become accustomed —the limbo light between moonset and sunrise—Chanchal and Peter thought they saw each other amused, and for the first time they felt an affinity, but neither knew for certain whether the other felt it or not. The idea was quickly clouded over as Tino's increasing bitterness called forth in them conflicting loyalties and hostilities. A man who is standing in a bear trap of the spirit can hardly be expected not to bite, Peter thought. A guilty bystander, a well-wisher—even one who could strike the hard balance between withdrawal and involvement—must resign himself to letting his hand be chewed a little. Job's buddies—

"There was a little bastard down on the plains," Tino said with sudden vindictiveness, "near Bharat University, in a jungle. I happened on him by accident once, in the heat of the day. My brain was addled. He took me in completely. One of those wandering sadhus. Millions of 'em in India—just bums."

"A disgrace to India," Chanchal murmured soothingly, "but what to do?"

"What to do—yeah. He was sitting under a banyan tree, naked as a rock, and quite needlessly. I can't get used to that sort of thing. But in those days I was an idealist—Bridge Between East and West, all that sort of trash."

"What did he do?" Peter asked, squinting at his wrist watch—he was not sure when dawn would come, but he wished it would hurry.

"Oh, he had a stock in trade, like all of the shrewd ones. Made me sit down, eyed me for a while, grinning as if he had a secret. There was a dirty glass beside him, a tumbler, some slop he'd been drinking—drugs, no doubt. It was all full of flies. He turned the glass upside down and caught a lot of flies inside—he must have done it thousands of times." Tino paused, and there was a slight clacking of his chops, as of distaste.

"And then?"

"Then he let 'em out, of course—grinning like an idol all the while. As I said, I was taken in completely."

"Did you give him anything in return?"

"How the hell should I remember? I paid him, don't worry. . . . You think I owed him something, eh?"

"I don't know," said Peter.

"How long now—ten minutes?"

"Maybe ten minutes. Do you want to wait?"

"Of course," Tino said. "What is time?" And after a moment: "Did you ever try to climb Everest, Peter?"

Peter was quiet, meditative. "Not in reality—or, if you like, only in reality."

"Every day is a mountain, eh? The same goddamn mountain."

"The same and not the same. Can't climb the same mountain twice —'For roads are moved when you have passed.' "

"From your epic, judging by the throb in your voice! Your Everest. Every day you've got to tackle it. Some days the weather is good, your supplies and organization are adequate, you get higher. Some days you have to retreat downward without victory, eh?"

"Most days," Peter replied. "You can never rest in your defeat, and victory is always beyond, like perfection."

"I know." Tino sounded grieved, as if he were thinking of a lost beloved. "Your Everest, your epic, what do you call it? Titles are important."

"The *Krishnayana*."

"When will it be finished? In ten Indian minutes, I suppose?"

Peter smiled in the darkness, not comfortably. "I don't know. Something like that. Five years. Ten years. Fifty years."

"Goethe spent forty years on *Faust*, you know."

"And look at it." Now Peter was on his own ground, amid his own working passions and prejudices. "He didn't take it seriously enough. He had too many civic duties. Dante and the Sage Vyasa —*they* are my guides."

"Dante finished off the *Divine Comedy* in ten or fifteen years."

"And the Sage Vyasa took a thousand years for the *Ramayana!*"

"So the myth goes," said Tino coldly. These sudden, easy shifts from Measure to Maya, pretending they were the same, seemed to him an insidious Oriental trick to which Peter's mind, already unstable, was becoming more and more prone, making him an unreliable conversationalist. "There is also the legend of the Tower of Babel. It's like your mountain."

"Those are naughty symbols!" Peter grinned, impudent as the boy in the dream, then quickly bowed his head as he remembered Tino's impotence.

"Sex is trivial!" Tino snorted. "Well—it's not as important for some people—as it is for others. *Pride* is your demon. You might call him Satan, if you—"

"Yes." Peter was submissive now, determined to endure extravagantly rather than increase Tino's distress by giving him serious opposition during the vigil. "Satan likes beauty and nobility and self-sufficiency, whereas God, as is well known, likes humility and contriteness and self-sacrifice. That's why Quakers have always been against art. Catholics, being more sophisticated, have learned to respect the Enemy. They allow him his role. Someday they will convert him, as they have converted God. Yes, the Worm is my patron!" Peter burbled at himself in a frenzy of modest invention, then stopped as he caught the dim outline of Tino hunched up in pain—perhaps he had tried to laugh, and cracked something. Impulsively, forgetting that Tino did not like to be touched and did not permit it except on formal occasions, Peter put his arm around him, very lightly to keep from hurting him.

"Don't!" Tino swayed a little, but the pain of moving was too great for him to slough off the unwelcome embrace. Sitting quite still, he snarled, "Quit it!" Chanchal shifted uneasily.

"Sorry," Peter said, dropping his arm, although he felt grievously that it would help matters to do a little natural hugging. Poor Chanchal, adoring Tino as he did! How it must go against his affectionate Indian grain to have to refrain from the usual hand holding and lolling over one's friend—that slow, thin dribble of romance between males where women are set apart, which forestalls, as a rule, the pressures that lead to more drastic encounters. Surely Tino was one who needed to touch and be touched—unless it was too late and there was danger, the kind that makes men bite the hand that strokes them, for fear of melting away and being absorbed. Peter could sympathize with that; still, for Tino—

"There is a certain man I know," Tino said icily, ignoring his pain, ignoring the incident, "who is generally well informed, with some understanding of human character, and, I should say, with a degree of self-control. People imagine him to be quite sane. But I happen to know that, although he does not write poetry, he has never ceased regarding himself as the World's Greatest Poet."

"It's a passing phase, the not writing. There's something I have to do—a thing or two—then I'll get back to the poem."

"Really? After the python—then what? A giant bandicoot, or a man-eating woman? Never mind—don't answer. Let me tell you a true story," Tino said, and stopped.

"Tell it."

Still Tino did not speak. With difficulty he lit another cigarette, this time refusing Chanchal's help. When he spoke, his voice was charged with passion, although at first Peter was not sure what kind —there seemed to be both malice and self-mockery in it:

"Once upon a time there was a precocious child whose ambition was to write the greatest epic poem of all the ages. (God damn it, don't interrupt me!) In preparation for his task, he took all knowledge as his field, naturally; and naturally, in order to pursue his studies uninterruptedly, he shut himself off from the vulgar pleasures of his contemporaries. By the time he was fifteen, he had studied all the epics, most of them in the original, and he had already begun his own lifework, an epic poem, which he called *The Will of God*.

"After ten years' work on it, he began to realize that something was wrong: It was hopelessly complicated, because every time he changed his outlook on the world—and it happened every year or so, for he had a restless mind—he had to rewrite *The Will of God* around it, plot on plot, climax on climax, philosophy on philosophy, epic on epic, adding to it, unable to delete one single precious word.

He was, as they say, a bleeder—each word was agony. In time he could not bear to look at *The Will of God,* but he could not bear *not* to look at it either. It was his life and his soul. And he could write no more. The effort required for him merely to comprehend what he had already written nearly cost him his reason.

"Finally he was not pleased. His pastoral psychiatrist told him with admirable candor, that he—well, he told him a number of things that are none of your business. The poet, who had never condescended to publish a line in his life, objected to everything. His religion forbade suicide, so he went to India. There he tried reading for pleasure, but found only bitter reminders of the Idea for which he had vainly sacrificed his happiness. Other pleasures—except tobacco and liquor—so lacking in definition—were equally abortive. How to convert to ordinary uses an elaborate moon rocket that has fallen back to earth intact after having failed to reach its destination because of some trifling defect in its mechanism—a defect that is nevertheless inherent?

"One morning this deranged and monkish poet, whom the poor Indians considered to be a sane scholar, was seated in his bungalow, imagining that he was working on his epic poem. By this time, you see, it had become worse than a fixation: it had become a habit. The rusting rocket dreaming of the moon, eh? What else could it do? I say he imagined he was working. Actually, he was grieving and grieving. For two years he had done nothing but make notes about the process of working on the epic poem, and he was beginning to think of publishing the notes. That is true madness—communication at all costs. But wait. That was later.

"As I say, he was sitting there grieving over the crabbed pages of *The Will of God,* when he looked up—he was always looking up through the doorway at two young cows with underdeveloped humps, who lived under a mango tree forty feet away because they were tied there. Now he saw a stranger approaching in a leisurely manner. There was something familiar about his gait—a slight limp added strangely to his dignity. Neither of the men appeared surprised, although it must be admitted at once that the circumstances were not usual. The stranger was a gray sort of sahib with a red mouth. His eyes were heavy-lidded, half-closed, and his manners were impeccable—natural, elegant, without ostentation, as we say, eh?

"Names of human beings did not immediately register on the poet, so it was as if the polite stranger had not introduced himself at all; besides, there was a kind of assumption that they had already met somewhere. It did not occur to the poet to wonder how this urbane gentleman, this familiar stranger, came to be taking his morning stroll so far from any city. Anyway the young man gave him a cup of tea, and they sat and talked; or, rather, the poet talked, for it had been some time since he had conversed with anyone in his native dialect, which was that of San Francisco. After a few words the stranger knew all about the poet, although his interest must have been purely formal. The poet knew nothing about the stranger, except that he was 'a part-time lecturer and traveler,' and that he had mentioned New York and Hollywood and various other capitals of the world.

"After an indeterminate time—ten minutes, say—the urbane gentleman got ready to go, and without seeming to go, went, and was gone. The poet sat down to his 'work' again, but found himself unable to concentrate. In fact, he was shaking with terror. Why? Then he remembered the bland business phrases he had discounted —no, phrases he had blocked out of his consciousness, had not even heard, but now their echo came to him out of his own darkness. Veiled in cigarette smoke, leaning back in the wicker chair —which usually complained, but had not done so this time—the familiar stranger had said, in a discreet sort of drawl, like a connoisseur of antiquities, who found it necessary to protect life from too much wisdom, that he had known 'ever so many epic poets.' Some of them, he had said, had seen fit to mention him in their epics, probably not out of gratitude, but because they associated him with an important event in their lives, the decision to go ahead with their work at all costs, in fact, 'to go all the way'—he was speaking of the successful ones, who had not been above taking advice. To begin with, he had said, he was rather good at titles, and if the young poet would consider changing the present title of his epic to something else—say, *The Games at Worldsend*—he, the familiar stranger, guaranteed that things would speedily 'begin to move toward a successful conclusion.' In fact, he would be 'immediately available' when the poet had made up his mind. And, if the poet liked, he would bring him Dante's original notes!

"That night the poet was not in good condition. You may say, he stood on the thin edge of Nothing. There was no priest to help him, no psychiatrist, and he was not on speaking terms with God. Seizing his epic poem, he crossed out *The Will of God* and was about to write over it *The Games at Worldsend,* when there was a knock at the door. He thought it would be the stranger, but it was not. It was a lady—a lady he knew, come to bring him a book on Buddhism and to wish him good night. She would not come in. She just stood in the doorway for a minute, then she left. The poet smiled, and it was like a key turning in a rusty lock. Within ten minutes he had burned his epic poem—burned his life behind him. . . .

" 'Now at last,' you say, 'he will fling himself into the life of this world, he will make up for lost time, and the ironic wisdom which he acquired through failure will be a source of irresistible attraction to all creatures who do not have it. Vulgarity will become for him a precious and almost unattainable ideal.' I am sorry to disillusion you. His long discipline as an epic poet made him so fastidious that his virginal soul is chained for all eternity to the rock of perfection, while the vultures tear at his—why they should confine themselves to his liver I do not know, and I doubt that they did in the original version of the myth, with which you are undoubtedly familiar.

"His fate? He became a scholar, a professor, a critic. He desires to integrate his personality. His name? Scott, Dante Aretino Scott —he dropped the Dante in his twelfth year because he feared it might tend to limit him psychologically to a performance merely comparable to that of the other Dante, if you know what I mean."

During Tino's second confession, the wind had stopped, a moldy gray light had gradually suffused the darkness, and the three figures had become visible: Chanchal fidgeting and glancing apprehensively into the jungle; the once-handsome Tino like a sinister hunchback, clutching himself, outraged and outrageous; and Peter sitting stiff and pale as a corpse frozen upright, with its mouth square, stricken in the act of calling "Christ!" Peter was not wholly dead, only betrayed to the shards of his beginnings—houses over city gates, wherein the watcher sits and under him the fleeing figures of un-comprehending love pass, then, beckoned, pass again, patterned angles of doors, pause to kiss, and poise a needle at the eye of love; laughing withdrawals to a witty Hell.

For a while they were silent as men are when they are cast up on a shore. Peter alone saw the movement of a shadow, a rippling deliberation among the upper branches of the trees, black against a sky that was now dark green. There was no wind, but the boughs swayed as with the passage of a kingly demiurge. "Krishna, if it is time, let him choose—*now!*" He passed, if indeed it was he, it being not yet time.

"It is possible to wait too long in one place," Peter said in the voice of a man who has not spoken for years. "We shall not see Everest this morning." He was right. Climbing painfully again to the wind-scoured pass, they gazed out upon a sea of gray clouds in the distance. Nothing else.

Chanchal had only the vaguest notion of what Tino had been saying. To him, poetry was primarily something that a Brahman gave off, as flowers give off perfume, an unquestionable caste duty. Geniuses were inspired by God and wrote it, like Tagore. In order to pass examinations, one memorized it. He himself could recite any or all of the English poets, especially Shakespeare, at full speed for half a day without stopping except for a sip of tea now and then, and there was no occasion which he could not ornament with absolutely appropriate verses. That was a talent of his. . . . What he grasped darkly now was that his best friend, Tino, who had somehow bullied him out of an inferiority complex so that he was no longer anti-Western, was himself writhing in a distress of spirit as well as of body; and, still worse, as if possessed by a *rakshi*, Tino had undermined Peter Bruff's dharma in a way that he, Chanchal, could not accept. It was un-Aryan. Besides—but this was a distant, submerged land—Chanchal was jealous. Peter was, in a way, his rival for the friendship of Tino, his fellow celibate, whom he loved as the odd one must always love the foreigner as himself. On this lower level, then—although he had as many levels as multifarious Bengal—he felt intuitively that Peter's dharma, Peter's work, was a resource, the possession of which differentiated him from Tino and sustained him in a life separate from that of his friend. Without that resource, he would be bankrupt and lost, like Tino—like Chanchal—in the same boat, as it were. Chanchal did not, on this inevitable lower level, want Peter in the same boat with him and Tino.

"In India," Chanchal announced with magnificent feeling, "everything is possible. It is the land of the poem. I was suckled on the *Mahabharata* at my mother's knee. The *Ramayana,* whose sublime flights of fancy are the despair of scholars, is the common property of every poor, decent, illiterate cottager, for he can scarcely speak three words without quoting the sacred love of Rama for Sita and of Sita for Rama. Here shall be composed without difficulty *The Will of God, The Games at Worldsend,* and also the *Krishnayana!*"

The pain had grown worse. As Chanchal and Peter brought up the horses, Tino crouched, shuddering, his mouth shut like a trap. He could not move his arms. Chanchal waited—he had learned easily not to touch him, for in crowded India there are many people whom one must not touch, and for many reasons, as there are many people whom one must touch for many reasons. Then a preposterous thing happened: Tino suddenly placed his forehead on Peter's shoulder, leaned there like a limbless creature, and barked out:

"Will you accept my notes—will you?"

"Yes," Peter said, and unclamping his jaws, kissed him somewhere on the upper part of the side of the neck.

They got him on the horse, and Chanchal sidelong gave Peter that look of intimate union which Westerners, in their ignorance and too much subtlety, find needlessly passionate and disconcerting.

"Achilles' heel," Tino muttered, and one did not know whether the bumps in his voice came from the pain or the desire to laugh or weep, or merely from the badly governed horse beneath him.

"What?" said Peter.

"You can always tell it by the spur."

eleven

Irene started out very briskly, then stopped, looked around, smiling apologetically. In her giddiness—for she knew that Mary Nayler was now talking about her to Peter—she had forgotten Mr. Kashani's difficulty in keeping up with her. Just as she looked, he popped something into his mouth. As he offered no explanation, she thought it best not to mention it, although she was a little apprehensive. People often took drugs in this country, for all sorts of purposes, or so she had read. Perhaps it was an opiate for pains in the feet. Of course, he was not an Indian, but a Persian, small and gentle and polite—unlike the stereotype that lingered from her childhood, of the Mohammedan, the Saracen: gigantic, in translucent bloomers and a red vest that wouldn't shut, with a scimitar, and with a certain—well, spontaneity. Or intensity. That was an image she would like very much to demolish.

Mr. Kashani took her arm. Of course, she should have taken his, to show that she trusted him; but how kind of him! That was the Oriental, thoughtful, quick to make up for our lapses in courtesy —manners, after all, are based on kindness. In sympathy, in gratitude, to compensate, she laid her other hand on his arm for just a moment. Sedately they walked along Upper Mazumdar Lane. The ebony cane flickered out at every other step—tiny steps, for she was diminishing hers to keep down with him. By the time they had reached the head of the wooden stairs by which they must descend to find a taxi, Mr. Kashani was breathing hard. They started down. Mr. Kashani's nimble little fingers began to travel up and down her arm. As his whiskers brushed her shoulder she caught the scent of cloves. . . . Odors bothered her—they entered her body through

161

an inferior sense, one that was least amenable to intellect, so that she felt vaguely compromised, especially by pleasant ones. Cloves, of course, were quite without consequences, unless—she tightened inside—unless he had mixed the cloves with something else. One of the books she had read about the East—a quaint sort of book she had just plowed through, with the hope of understanding more about Peter—mentioned cloves. One mixed cloves with other ingredients which were called aphrodisiacs. Irene began to grow weak. . . . Possibly she had made a mistake in suggesting that Mary employ him to shoot the python. Still, with care, one might induce him to stick to the business for which he had been brought here.

At the first crosspath that intersected the stairs, Monica Dutton beamed out at them from a flower garden. Irene greeted her with relief, and approached, towing Mr. Kashani along. Reluctantly he released her arm, to bow stiffly to his landlady. They chatted aimlessly about the weather, the flowers, the view, took issue over India's deterioration since the British had left—Monica's attack on Indian character was almost absent-minded today, perfunctory, as if she were fulfilling a caste duty. Irene braced herself to move on, on into the problem of cultural conflict in the person of Mr. Kashani, who was chafing to resume his escort. If only she had had some warning —or, rather, had she heeded the warning that had really been there all the time—she could have taken it before the Lord in silent meditation, to pray, then to wait, and perhaps there would be a leading. There would certainly be a leading, in a case like this. She put her trust in the Lord. Well. Aphrodisiac or no aphrodisiac, Mr. Kashani would soon understand the difference between Eros and Agapé. Not that she had any intention of undertaking his conversion to Christianity, unless he requested it; and as for the Society of Friends —well, it was a misconception to suppose that one could just enter it except in a formal way. It was like Hinduism in that respect: one had to be born into it; a deplorable thing, a cause for endless humility. The Wider Quaker Fellowship was another thing, designed, in fact, to ease precisely such cultural difficulties. Mohammedanism was one of the principal religions, and as such ought not to be tampered with. She would begin by pointing out certain truths upon which all religions agree—and even communism agreed to some of them—by which World Peace ought to be furthered. And yet—oh dear!—she had discussed all that with him on the train.

Just as she was turning to go, and Mr. Kashani was reaching for her arm, she heard Monica Dutton say, "There's a lady who wants to meet you."

Eagerly Irene turned to greet the divine intervention for which she had wished. For a moment she was uncertain. Monica was inspecting a rose. It was as if she had spoken inadvertently, or merely to prolong the conversation.

"I'll be glad to meet her," Irene stammered. "Right now."

Monica looked confused. "I doubt if she's home."

"That's all right. We can try, can't we?"

"I hope you won't mind going through the native quarter," Monica said as she daintily picked her way through the lower town.

"It's a native country, isn't it?" Irene observed stoutly. Although she disliked subterfuges, as a rule, she felt almost lighthearted at having postponed the accounting with Mr. Kashani. She had sent him on to the Ashram to explain that she might be a little late. Mary, she was sure, would have no difficulty with him. And perhaps Peter would be there. . . .

"Nasty country, if you ask me," said Monica—she looked quite pleased.

"Perhaps they haven't the facilities for bathing that we have." As she spoke, she became aware of a patina on the back of Monica's neck, where the heavy, dark hair swung aside, and she added: "At this altitude, it would be quite understandable if people didn't bathe —regularly." After all, English people were people, too, even if they did oppress other people—not that Americans had any right to criticize, what with the South and Puerto Rico and— What else? Honolulu, Alaska, the Philippines, and Little Rock. . . . Education was the answer, education and love. Educate the oppressor. Love him. The hardest thing would be to love the oppressor of somebody else. Love him, heap coals of fire on his head—or rather—she must have got that wrong. . . .

"Not like it was when we British had control," Monica crowed estatically for thousands to hear—she was reviewing her troops before Buckingham Palace, thanks to the faith this American had in her. In an access of gratitude, she turned suddenly to Irene and whispered, "Can you keep a secret, dear?"

"Yes," Irene said, "but is it a *necessary secret?*"

Monica sniggered, marched on a few steps. "No, it isn't necessary. But if I don't tell you, you might die, and if you tell anyone I told you—why then I won't have much time to cut me own throat, will I?"

"What—What are you talking about?" Irene went pale, instinctively cast an eye over her unpromising surroundings in case she had to have help, either against the danger of which Monica spoke, or against Monica herself, for the woman must be quite—confused. That awful swagger, the brazen voice, and now the too intense, too intimate whisper! Why had she gone with her, and who was this Lulu person—or did she exist? Dear God!—Irene reeled. What if— She shut from her mind the dreadful vision of herself held captive in a house of—

"We white people have got to stick together, you know." Monica was indeed adhering to her very closely, almost embracing her as they walked—out of step—and there was something as it were glutinous in her gaze as she studied the clear, open countenance with which she longed to identify herself.

A bunch of rosy, shouting little Tibetan girls, with stiff dresses that reached down to their bare toes, came bowling down the alley, stopped as instantaneously as if they had hit an invisible wall, corked their thumbs into their mouths, and stared at Irene.

Irene also stopped. Drawing a little away from Monica, she said: "Did you want to tell me something?"

Monica could not look directly into those steady, grave eyes, but glanced down, retreated back into the secret, cunning maze where she alone lived for herself alone—but not all the way back. A wild hope, a vision of love, of acceptance, of noble camaraderie, brought her out again. She tossed her head.

"We're plucky, you and I." Monica's voice was shaking and she was breathing fast. She did not mean that they were intrepid; she meant they were vulnerable, not very sharp, without strong sur-

vival instincts, and therefore of a superior race—because the world
belonged to them and they must act as if it did, not descend to base
precautions: only people of low birth—Indians, "junglies"—did that,
people who inhabited the world only on sufferance. "Plucky," the
noblewoman repeated, and to make the fantasy true she risked her
life in an almost casual gesture. "Never trust a native," she said
with shining eyes. "Trust your own kind—*our* kind—but never
trust a native, not any of 'em. America's a nice country, no natives
there, except for the niggers and you keep them in their place—
that's right! They say it's almost like home—England. U.K. That's
where we ought to be now—*home*. India is really ghastly—ugh!
Indians stick knives in you if they don't like you—murder you in
your bed, you know. But Tibetans—ah, those are the ones, my dear.
Poisoners. You never know when they're going to poison you. I make
my Nepali boy taste everything before I allow it to pass my lips,
because you never know with Tibetans. They'll bribe your servants,
they'll—don't eat anything they give you, these Tibetans. Don't
drink anything they give you. They'll poison you, Mrs. Nayler, as
easy as you'd lick a postage stamp!" And, as Irene turned in dismay
from these sad revelations, Monica added, "Liliu Acquileia is a
Tibetan."

"Why did you bring me here?" Irene asked in a tone that, for
her, was fretful; then, regaining her calm: "Tibetans are people,"
she said. "I'm sure your fears are groundless. Mrs. Acquileia just
wants to be friendly, and I shall be happy for the opportunity of
visiting a Tibetan home. . . . Gracious!" observing Monica's satur-
nine smile, "she doesn't even know me. How could she have anything against me, unless—of course—I must prove to her that not
everyone in the West is intent upon colonizing Tibet. Why, the
Chinese Government—"

"It isn't Tibet," Monica said, snuffling preciously into her shawl,
for her nose was getting a bit runny—later she would blow vigorously to one side, then the other, using her thumbs alternately. "It's
you, a lovely young white woman, and she's just a sort of nigger."

"Mrs. Dutton!" Irene was scarlet with embarrassment and un-
Quakerly rage. "Has thee—have you—thought that it might be—
unkind—?" As a protest, and to calm herself, she sought to lay

her hand on the head of one of the little girl urchins, who dodged cleverly with a whirling motion.

"It's Mr. Bruff, you see. He's white and you're white, and naturally—"

"Mr.—Mr. Bruff?" Irene stammered. "What does he have to do with it?"

"Oh, you know what gentlemen are like, Mrs. Nayler. It don't mean anything to them. They're not always particular, if you know what I mean. Not like *us*." The race of men, even of white men, was a little below Monica's station at this moment. That she owed her own existence to the momentary exuberance of a British Tommy and a Madrassi street girl was of the lowest substructure of her consciousness. "My husband was an Irishman," she said with a trace of seemly humility, for he was not absolute English, "an Irishman from Dublin, God rest his bones. He was a good man and a devil with the ladies. He left me all those houses." It was true, he had been a good-hearted old man, grateful to her for nursing him through the last year of his life, during which he had suffered much from tropical leukemia.

"I see," said Irene, and she stood there looking up over the roofs, translucently pale, as if her earthly body were half transmuted into a metaphysical object by a sudden incandescence of the spirit. Monica thought she had never seen anyone so beautiful through-and-through as Irene, whose very name was blonde—oh, she had the blondness of the Virgin Christ and the angels, the inconceivably pure blondness of God the Father when He was very young and feminine and had a full head of hair!

"Let's go back now," said Monica. "I made a mistake. This isn't a fit place for ladies. Come, dear," and her arm made a gallant curve around Irene, sheltering her from the brown squalor.

"You might just show me where she lives," Irene said. "Or if you'd rather not, I can find my way. You really mustn't worry about me any more, you see."

"I'll take you there." Slowly Monica retreated again into the less vulnerable self, the secret maze where she might yet survive; but as she receded she could not help calling out—in her ordinary speaking voice: "Remember what I said. If you ever need me—

any time—send a boy for me." The ghost of the lady scorned to whine, even for discretion that might save her life.

Gori Govinda opened the door, his face swollen from weeping and perhaps from blows, his fox-red hair unkempt as usual. He did not invite them in. She was not there, he said. When would she be back? He did not know. Where had she gone? "Down there," he muttered darkly, and tended to shut the door. Not the Ashram? His head jerked in the Bengali way signifying assent.

"Don't go," Monica told her.

"It's where I was going all the time."

Irene got out of the jeep-taxi at a little distance from the school, to walk the rest of the way. That would be more in keeping with the manner she felt one should adopt in a country where even the possession of a bicycle set one off from the common people. Even a hat, worn by a white person, made him still more the unforgivable sahib of despotic authority, to be feared and distrusted. Last month she had got sunstroke from not wearing a hat. She was not wearing one now, although the sun was powerful overhead—before that despot she remained uncovered, as a Testimony, as other Quakers had remained obstinately covered before kings. Better death— which, as Mary said, was not definitive—than lukewarmness in the Lord.

Seated on mats, in semicircles, under the mango trees, the children were at their lessons. There was Mlle. de Rosière in a violet sari, making them recite in French. There was a graybeard pundit —a famous one from Benares, Irene had heard—who would be teaching Sanskrit or Indian History to his group. And there was Dr. Bhattacharya, whose class appeared to be very excited about something. Irene hoped it was not political. She could not see Mary or Jim Chen or Indira or—Mr. Kashani. Perhaps they were all off together someplace. Soon Mary would come, and perhaps Peter. It might be possible to tell, from looking at them, what the outcome of their talk had been—although Peter had certainly changed, was more elusive. . . . The woman—Liliu Acquileia—fantastic name, not Tibetan at all, surely. . . . Irene's heart began to beat heavily, her temples throbbed, as she walked slowly around the mango grove toward the bungalow which she could not see for the brightness. She did not believe that Peter *loved* Liliu Acquileia. He loved her, Irene, as he always had. If it had been otherwise, he would have told her this morning on the mountain. To be sure—she grew hot with shame and unwilling pride to think of it—there had been something almost impersonal in the manner of his—protestations. There might be some sort of liaison with that woman, as Monica had said. Men were different from women, she had said. What an odd thought! But of course, they had to be. A *good* thing. William had not been representative. That was God's will. If she could forgive William for not being representative, it shouldn't be too difficult to forgive Peter for trying to reconcile his difference with another woman. If there were any guilt involved, it was hers. She had driven him to it, if there was an it. She might have been more demonstrative this morning—oh, and long ago. . . . How hot the sun was! Languorously she lifted her hands, undid the great knot of hair at the back of her head, and twisted it up on top for a protection from the sun —that was what the sadhus did. The back of her neck felt naked. She had never done that except when taking a shower, and once she had seen herself that way in a mirror, and had been struck by the thought that such a hair-do might be very misleading. She had looked like—well, perhaps an actress. But that was their vocation. From *vocare*, to call. Why hadn't she thought of this before? A practical, sensible solution. It made her head feel all steamy; but it would cool off, then she would feel better.

Not far from the bungalow, she shaded her eyes and peered through the heat waves at a group of people on the veranda. Some minute and subtle impulse caused her to seek out for one instant an unbearable effect of light—some red fabric with violet in it—that seemed to pierce her retina. She shut her eyes hard, then opened them, and, feeling a bit dizzy, sat down on a large stone, usurping the spot where a lizard had been sunning itself. The lizard darted away and perched on a smaller stone, where it observed her, pushing itself up and down on its short forelegs, as if in a last-minute attempt to build up muscle for a possible assault on her; but it did not appear to be very muscular, for all its exercising, she thought. Wiry but not muscular. There was something she didn't like about

that lizard—the persistent up-and-down movement, the fixed look.
. . . It was like an obscene little man. Nonsense! It was one of
God's creatures. A reptilian vertebrate. Firmly she counted thirty
push-ups, then got to her feet and continued her walk to the bungalow.

The little group on the veranda was dispersing. Two servants
were carrying Lady Edith in a wicker chair, into the house. Indira,
in a dark red sari, was supervising them so closely that her back
was turned on the departing guest, who was coming down the stairs
—it was a Tibetan woman wearing cosmetics. Around her greenish-
blue robe was tied the rainbow apron, one stripe of which was a
kind of electric red with violet in it. That would be Liliu Acquileia,
Irene decided, and went to meet her; as Liliu turned to go up the
valley, she followed her.

Liliu Acquileia allowed herself to be overtaken in the shade of
some trees. For a moment the rivals looked at each other with intense curiosity while they groped a little for a common language.
Liliu saw at first a stately, exotic blonde, a rich superwoman from
America—almost certainly a witch—who would inevitably take
Peter from her; then, looking deeper, she saw an ignorant foreigner
who could be duped, defeated, killed if need be, although the power
of her magic had yet to be tested.

Irene saw at first a beautiful Asian, sensual and exotic as she,
Irene—could never be—though she thought she might try leaving
her hair up like this; then, looking at her in another dimension, she
saw one of God's creatures whom she must befriend and help until
that strange, secret smile—of contempt?—was replaced by one of
trust; and as for Peter—God would guide them. They would work
out something.

"Speak English," said Liliu Acquileia, testing her with a command.
"You understand Hindi?"

"I do—I do. I studied it on phonograph—on gramophone records
before I came to India, and then—"

"Then speak English. I shall speak Hindi." Liliu led her through
a sparse thicket to a place where the shade was deeper and there
was a recently fallen tree on which they could sit. Behind it was a
low place in the riverbank, a kind of estuary or swamp, flooded

every year, always wet. A hundred yards away the river roared, muted, sullen, invisible. Growing in a semicircle around the edge of the swamp were willow trees, some of them forty feet high, nearly two feet in diameter. The older trees were not straight, but lumpy and misshapen; their soft, pulpy wood could not bear the weight of the branches, and they leaned into one another's arms like very old, death-haunted sisters. Of late years when the monsoons came and the sap was heavy in the boughs, one or more of these trees would sink with a mysterious lethargy down into the water; and from the rotting trunks new branches would ascend, to stand for a while as proxies for the fallen, and then, growing larger, would emerge as representative trees, forgetting the relativity of their origins and destinies.

Six white herons stood in the water, unafraid where all was dying and being born, perfectly mirrored against the reflections of fern trees and bamboos and willows, the deceptively mauve mountain on the east, the rose-white clouds that coiled over a pure, blue-green sky. The herons, common as chickens in this land, were not so to Irene the bird watcher: They were crisp, self-contained, proud, yet they seemed autonomous rather than independent. Their sleek necks were curved, their heads bowed, as if in esoteric humility— as if they were being stroked by a hand which they alone could see, and which alone they would permit to approach their immaculateness.

"I want to thank you for inviting me," Irene said, sitting on the rotten log beside Liliu Acquileia. "I went to your house today, but the boy said you had gone to the Ashram."

"That was my son, Arjuna Bruff."

"Oh," said Irene. The boy must have been twelve years old, and Peter had not been gone nearly that long. Irene did not mention this discrepancy, although it was so obvious as to be almost straightforward. Well, she had read that Tibetans were the least Oriental of all Asiatics—happy extroverts and very hospitable. It was a relief. She had been afraid Liliu would be inscrutable. Irene would not make moral judgments anyway; she would not make the mistake of assuming that Liliu Acquileia was ever being deliberately inexact; for Asia was an Aesthetic Continuum—she had read it in *The Meeting of East and West*—and there was often an unconscious blending of literal with imaginative truth. In Liliu's aesthetic continuum Peter was the father of her son.

"Beautiful lady," Liliu exclaimed, holding up both hands in an exquisite gesture that described a nimbus around Irene, "shall we not be friends?"

"Yes—oh, yes!" Irene cried hungrily.

"Then let us exchange gifts." With a smile of childlike candor, Liliu gave her a little honey cake wrapped in silver foil.

"But I have nothing—nothing here," Irene faltered.

"You have such beautiful hair! Give me a little lock of that—then we shall be friends."

"My hair—oh, yes! Thank you so much—but I have nothing to cut it with."

Still smiling, Liliu drew a little razor-sharp knife out of her robe, and skillfully severed a strand of Irene's hair. Then, with clasped hands, she watched while Irene dutifully ate the honey cake. "No, no, you must eat it all!" she told her when Irene offered half of it to her. When the cake was gone, Liliu's manner changed again. "Why did you come here?" she asked. It was not necessarily an impolite question. People in this part of the world thought it quite correct to begin a conversation with some such question, the more intimate, the better. Irene had often been asked: Where are you going and what will you do when you get there? Do you practice free love in America? Is it true that you use a brush instead of a neem stick to clean your teeth? Do you relieve yourself in the house, as people say, or outdoors? It is not true, is it, that you clean yourself with paper instead of water? Irene always answered calmly and objectively.

"I came to help with the Friends' Service Committee. We have what we call a village project, down in Bihar—"

"You are lying," Liliu Acquileia said, still with her little smile, although her eyes were glowing behind their narrow, stylized yet eloquent apertures—except for the eyes and the rapidly rising-and-falling bosom, she seemed quite composed. Delicately she plucked a piece of bark from the log and began to roll it between her fingers.

Irene turned very pale. No one had ever said that to her before. "I am *not* lying!" she cried hotly, then compressed her lips as if she would never speak again; she closed her eyes; she clenched her hands; she tried to open her spirit to God, to pray that she might be made humble and loving, for she had felt something pretty close to hatred. In a moment all would be well, she would make it up—

"Yes, you are lying," said Liliu Acquileia with almost tranquil assurance. She did not make moral judgments either. Had it been necessary in order to hate, then she would have made moral judgments; for she was never so alive as when she hated. And now she loved also. The quality of her hatred might even have been impaired by the making of moral judgments, however inaccurate they might have been. Truth? One never reported anything about the state of his—or her—affairs except in order to advance them; and in this life survival was always at the expense of others, it could not be avoided, even if it were desirable to avoid it. One had enemies, rivals, competitors, and one disposed of them successfully and was glad. That was perfectly natural. In a world of illusion lies and truths were mere devices one employed to gain the desired effect. Survive and thrive, that was the universal law, simple *Realpolitik*. It held true of spirits after death—for she was of the Bon Po—in rocks and trees and herbs and philters and in the air, and elsewhere. In this lore she felt confident. "Yes, you are lying," she said. "You came from a land of water and little hills, crossing rivers and valleys and countries lousy with Bengalis—all to feed the hunger in your womb! The men on that side, they are like women, all of them, except *him*, whose mother was a mountain princess and his father was a lord who raped her and dragged her to your Land of Sick Ghosts, to die! Yes, I wanted to look at you, but not for long, lest I fall ill. . . . That one who fled from you too late, he feared *me*, a mere woman, although I offered myself to him, believing that he was the one mentioned in my horoscope—but no, he came only to announce, to bring the true one. Because of you, he feared women; so that he loved the dry bones of a Nepali man-priest, and this annoyed me until he died. Does *he* know"—she used the Hindi form denoting extreme respect, meaning Peter—"that you are a Tooth-

Wombed Witch who will nip off his penis and make a woman of him too?"

Some of the words Liliu used were not in Irene's Hindi-English/English-Hindi Dictionary. She did not know the significance, either, of the *vagina dentata* in Himalayan witchcraft. She did not even know that she had been complimented on her power. What she understood was that she was fighting for Peter, and she, as much as any other Friend, had a Testimony against fighting. Tenderly she smiled at Liliu Acquileia.

"I do so want to be friends," Irene said. "I still think we can be. We have a problem, haven't we? A problem in common. I think we might work on it in a spirit of—of mutual consideration."

"You want to share him with me?" Liliu asked suspiciously.

Irene took it as an offer and considered it without prejudice. Polyandry and polygamy were said to be practiced with some success in Tibet. A modified version of it in other parts of the world would not be unthinkable to the liberal mind. It could be a unifying factor. For a second she had a fantasy of nations united in love with Peter: herself, Liliu, a Chinese woman, an African. . . . As she leaned back, her hair, loosely tied up in an ancient coiffure, tumbled down over her shoulders. Smiling slowly, she gathered it up on top again and tied it there with a bit of vine that had little blue flowers on it and violet-green leaves with red veins.

"We would have to make sacrifices," she murmured reflectively. That was to be expected, perhaps even welcomed—it would be like relinquishing national sovereignty to the United Nations. Jealousy? She thought she had never been jealous in her life. It would be unconventional, but she was not afraid of that. She would follow the dictates of her conscience. Arch Street Meeting might conceivably support her position, she thought, although the discussions might be a bit lengthy. A complicated picture, though, in view of the legal barrier. "Do you love him *very* much?" she asked.

"Yes."

"So do I. Would you consider giving him up?"

"No." There was no qualification, no attempt to distribute the shock of the statement by broadening its surface.

"Neither would I," Irene said, to her own surprise. "On the other hand, I have been thinking about your kind offer. At first it seemed to me that the Christian thing to do would be to share him; but then—"

"I made no such offer," said Liliu Acquileia, a little puzzled. "I am not a Christian."

"Oh, I must have misunderstood. . . . But you invited me to your house. Perhaps you have some other constructive suggestion?"

"Only this: It will be much better for you if you go back to your country. That is what I wanted to say to you. He has run away from you before it was too late, and he has come to me. Do not try to get him back again."

"Of his own will," Irene said softly, "of his own free will he has already come back to me. I was thinking of your welfare."

"You are lying again," Liliu said contemptuously, and stood up to go. "You must lie, because you are dead. Already you are so corrupt that you dare not miss brushing your teeth for one single morning."

Irene leaped to her feet, her eyes blazing. "Don't say that to me!" The voice came from her, but she had never heard it before. It sounded horrid, thunderous, grating as the noise of the river. Trembling with rage and disgust, she fought the demon in her that fought Liliu, and succeeded in contracting its throat, but it hissed out anyway: "What do you want—money?"

This was more what Liliu had expected. In this she excelled. She stepped back, her hand in the loose sleeve of her robe. If necessary she would slip a knife between the ribs of the Tooth-Wombed One, on the chance that she might be killable in this way—but even if she were, Liliu preferred less conspicuous means. "Go back to your country right away," she said. "There, if you find a live man, you can buy him—as I would, if I were you. In this miserable land you will turn to dust in a few days at most, even if you stay in the shadows. Take my advice and go—this very day! It is I who tell you, do you understand? I!"

Standing tall as an angel, Irene looked down on her without fear. Her lips moved as if they were about to speak words of love; then they formed a hard square, showing the upper and lower teeth.

She began to quake with laughter, low at first, between clenched teeth, then shrill and violent.

Liliu Acquileia stared at her with respect, then turned and went quickly up the trail. She felt shaken. Never had she encountered such contempt in a human face—not even in her own! It was something to reckon with. That laughter! Such triumph, such disdain! The Tooth-Wombed One was mad—that was not unusual among witches. What rattled Liliu Acquileia was the deceptiveness of this one: She had not shown her hand until the very last, and then—the laughter conveyed the threat of hideous revenge. It could mean only one thing: Her magic was more potent than Liliu had anticipated, or she would not have eaten the honey cake! The strategy required to defeat it must be bold, and very shrewd, and quick—quicker than the sickness with which the White Witch had attacked her by means of the eyes.

Slowly, one by one, the herons left their vertical poses and became horizontal in the air, trailing their legs after them like mooring ropes. It was a solemn departure, as of certain superior beings who had chosen to come to the estuary for a token meal, a consequence of their voluntary incarnation. With them went Irene's strength, but she did not fall— Where to begin, where to end? She walked in the ripe and dazzling sun, not knowing, not caring where she went. . . .

Mr. Kashani was with her again, offering his arm this time, instead of taking hers. Once, leaning heavily on him, she gazed down into his face—it looked strangely blurred, but very friendly. She was grateful to him for helping her back to her room, where Mary would put a cold towel over her face, and she would sleep. . . . But it was not her room; it was a sort of barn. Of course, they were still at the Ashram, weren't they? On a tour of inspection. Perhaps that was what he had asked her, in his low, sympathetic voice, and she had not fully understood, but she had agreed. "Yes, yes, yes," she had said; all she wanted to do now was to agree and to agree. Walking was so easy, almost like floating, she could walk on and on without getting tired; there was something deep within that never got tired. . . . In here it was cool and dark and she was sitting on a pile of hay, and Mr. Kashani was embracing her. That had to be

objected to, of course—he had misunderstood, or she had, rather.
And now everything was blurry, she felt suddenly weak, her movements to defend herself were so dream-heavy, so slothful. And he
was quick and wiry, but not muscular—like that lizard! The black
whiskers, heavily scented, nuzzled her neck and breasts, bore her
back into the hay. He was crying out something passionate in French
and pressing his instinctive little thimble against her hip. One of
God's creatures. For an instant there flashed across her mind the
test conducted by some psychologist or other: male rats always
crossed red-hot griddles to get at the females on the other side and
transfer the plasm. That was cruel. . . . But she was not a female
rat; she was Irene Clifford Nayler, and this was dreadful, simply
dreadful! Gathering herself, she seized him by the whiskers with
both hands, and tried to lift him off her, but she did not have the
strength. The pain must have been considerable, for his eyes rolled
in a frightening way and he shook his head from side to side; but
he would not get off. Instead he pulled up her dress and his deft
little knee forced her legs apart. Irene had never screamed in her
life, but now her "No!" rang out like the grief of a giantess, and
a moment later she stood up.

Someone had jumped down from the loft—it must have been
fifteen feet—landing on the hay beside them, yanked Mr. Kashani
off her, and bent him over in a hammerlock. They were about the
same size, but one was stronger. Jim Chen, barefoot, wearing nothing but a pair of blue jeans, twisted the arm a little more, and Mr.
Kashani shrieked. Both tiny men, tortured and torturer, looked at
Irene. Standing there, calm and authoritative, she extended her
hand in a gesture of concern, of peace, that included them both.
The physical violence had brought her somehow into focus, freeing
her momentarily from the inner violence that had been feeding upon
her.

"Please let him go," she said. "It was my fault—a cultural conflict
—a misunderstanding."

Released, Mr. Kashani sprang away and glared at them both. "Oh,
I am *humilié!*" he sobbed. "*Toujours—humilié!*" Snatching up his
cane, he considered attacking Jim, but Jim circled around him in
such a professional crouch that he retreated to the doorway.

"I don't at all want you to be humiliated," Irene said. "Let's sit down right now and discuss the whole problem in a friendly spirit. I'm sure we can—"

"*Prostituée!*" Mr. Kashani blurted, pointing a trembling finger at her, and ran away weeping.

Jim made as if to follow, but stopped at the door, then came back in, slumping as if he were very, very tired. He seemed unable to lift his head to look at Irene, or even to speak.

"Thank you," she said, and held out her hand, which he touched briefly. Then with a sick, twisted half-smile which barely included her, he looked upward in a way that made her look upward too. A rope dangled from a rafter beside the loft. Involuntarily she put her hand to her throat.

"Just rope climbing," Jim said. "It develops the shoulders, you see." Raising his arms, he set bunches of muscles to chasing each other over his torso; then he leaped into the air, caught the end of the rope and flowed up it to the loft; came down again with his shirt and boots on. "I wasn't eavesdropping when you came in —I merely wanted to spare you the sight of so much yellow skin. . . ." He stopped, shamed by her inarticulate cry for mercy. "That was unfair of me!" he exclaimed in surprise—he had never thought to make such an apology before; but it was not enough. How could one—how could he comfort such a tall woman? And yet there was something about her that did not offend him: a prisoner in her, to whom the prisoner in him might rap out messages. . . .

twelve

"Will you not mind taking the life of this python?"

To Indira's typical Indian question Peter replied in the ancient tongue: "How shall life slay, or who shall slay it?"

It was still early morning. On their return from the pass, Tino had been in such pain that Peter had gone for the local doctor, a Bengali. The doctor had gone on horseback to a village down the valley, but would be at the Ashram within an hour, to see Lady Edith. Peter was waiting for him on the veranda, drinking tea which Indira had brought him. Classes had not yet begun.

The valley had an aquatic look, with mists and translucent arms of cloud hovering close aloft, fingering the tops of the taller trees, relinquishing them in humid farewells. A violet haze, bending the wavering light, blurred and magnified the distances. High up, on another level of air, between unfallen clouds, kites floated like sting rays in the shallows. From time to time, watching keenly, mercilessly, they called out in the piteous voices of very young chickens that have strayed from their mothers. On the terraced mountain slope, between rows of tea bushes, the sea-green grass was of an incomparable subtlety, for it had had its youth ages ago and now, in May, was only apparently young.

"The villagers believe that he was here before," Indira said, testing him. "They believe that he lives in the river. They call him Kaliya."

"I know," said Peter. "It is in the *Srimad Bhagavatam*." In his demeanor was exactly the right trace of self-deprecation; in Indira's, exactly the right trace of skepticism; in both of them a secret recognition and respect for that which endures, good or evil, for the sake

179

of that which is beyond good and evil. In modesty Peter could say no more; for he himself was cast by inference in the role of Krishna in the scriptural story: Kaliya, the Serpent King, lived in the depths of a fierce river, whence he issued from time to time in order to kill people and lay waste the crops. The boy Krishna leaped into the river to hunt him out. After a violent battle, Krishna subdued his adversary. Dancing on the head of the Serpent King, Krishna prepared to slay him. Then the Serpent Queens drew near and, bowing low, begged Krishna to spare their Lord. Kaliya himself spoke from under the heel of Krishna: "Lord of the Universe, who made all creatures, did you not also create me? Have I not obeyed the Universal Law which you yourself laid down—that every creature act according to the nature which you gave it? Is it not my duty to destroy, or have I misunderstood? Ignorance of the Law is no excuse. If I have broken the Law, slay me and take back into yourself that which you have created, for another act of creation!" Then Krishna smiled and stepped away, saying: "Again you have remembered, Kaliya. You have broken no Law. Neither have I, the Lawgiver; for it is one of the innumerable functions of the whole to mediate among the parts by intervening, as it is another of my functions to precipitate excess by not intervening." Solemnly he banished Kaliya and the Serpent Queens to an island in the Outer Ocean for another cycle of time.

"I think you are not disinterested," Indira said—how beautiful the young Brahmaness allowed herself to be at this moment!—morning light in her eyes, her black hair hanging loose down her back, vivid on the red silk of her sari, one bare foot visible, long and small-boned, very delicate. She smiled at him—her red, perfect lips were always curled upward at the corners in a little fine line—and the heart spoke in him: "It is you again! Again it is you I love!" But barely moving, she veiled herself again in subtle, immemorial hauteur. She said: "Did not the oracle accrue to Apollo when he killed the python at Delphi? You in the West—"

"I am East and West, half-caste, out-caste—" Too late, Peter realized that he had used Jim Chen's trick.

"A condition to evoke rhetoric," she agreed—he should not have her sympathies so cheaply as all that! "Probably you should not aspire to the wisdom of the serpent—or to the completion of the *Krishnayana*."

"How do you know about my work?" he asked in astonishment.

"Is it not based on the Sanskrit notes of my brother?"

"It is. The notes, the prose fragments, incomplete—I had to stop last year, because Ananda's accounts of the old folk epic broke off, and I didn't want to proceed on my own. I searched for other versions of it all through Kashmir and in Ladakh, but no one had ever heard of it. No manuscripts ever referred to it, no pundits knew about it, although some pretended to. . . ."

"It was not entrusted to writing," Indira said serenely; then, with a touch of scorn: "The pundits considered it apocryphal. It was so old that they suspected it to be pre-Aryan, of Dravidian origin. Perhaps they were right—they have always suspected Krishna because he is one of the old gods—before Mohenjodaro, before Harappa —the oldest. He glows with youth. Long ago there was—what do you call it?—a schism. The pundits of my clan held the *Krishnayana* to be sacred, but all the other pundits cast it out. Only my clan, then only my family kept it, generation after generation, never writing it, only singing it, night after night, through our long winters. It is longer than the *Divine Comedy*, yet we had no trouble in memorizing it because it was our secret and our delight. One day, after the death of our uncle, Ananda said to me: 'The *Krishnayana* is not completely fresh in my memory. Is it in yours?' I thought for a moment, then I said that it was fresh enough. He said to me: 'Fresh enough is not fresh enough. No one knows it better than we. And if we have no children? Shall the *Krishnayana* pass out of existence with us?' At first I said 'Yes,' for I was very young and conservative. Then we had a great quarrel—no, a discussion—and he convinced me. 'Let it be written down, then,' I said. That day he went back to Benares, and I never saw him again. When I received the news of his death, I went to my room and began to write down the *Krishnayana*."

"*You* wrote it down?"

"What else would I do with my—my pique? I knew that he would not have had time to complete the writing. It took me one year, for I had to sing as I wrote, and singing was not easy for me that year. I also came here. My clan has always been noted for excess."

"So it is with my clans," Peter said. "Singing was not easy for me that year either." He locked his fingers in his lap, with the palms up, and gazed down at them, unaware that he looked like a humble suppliant.

Indira regarded him intently. After a moment she said: "The *Krishnayana* is a crude folk epic, full of superstitions and bloodshed and—and silliness. Besides, it is all lopsided. Please—what have you to do with it?"

"If I am a true poet"—Peter looked up at her, wide-eyed, like a child, earnest and vulnerable—"then I would do as Homer did with the ancient ballads of his world; as Dante did with the materials of his worlds. Into the spacious myths of the *Krishnayana* will enter the range and prism of our Consciousness—complexities of East and West, North and South, from the beginnings to the ends—in the compass of one work. That is what I would do." The poet gazed at the girl in such a way that she, softening, trembled a little, feeling his energy coil round her, and she could only receive—but not yet.

"Will you bring me what you have done?" She spoke in her role of priestess, guardian of the scroll There was only one copy of his work. If it were lost, all would be lost, for he did not have the memory of the ancients—or of Indira. This he told her, simply. Then with that slight, self-negating motion of the head, eyes lowered, he made the gesture of submission, of delivering oneself into the hands of another.

"I will bring it," he said.

How bland they looked, as if nothing were at stake—how almost complacent!—as one must on remembering one's part; but only long enough to be glimpsed: longer would mean uncertainty, disproportion, a vulgar lack of confidence in one's antagonist, in his or her preparation.

"Peter Bruff." She let her head fall back and gazed at him through her eyelashes—her eyes seemed to slope up, enormously long—and she smiled at him without seeming to smile. "Why did my brother call you Arjuna?"

"That is one of my names," he said, shocked and delighted at the familiarity she allowed herself. "My mother named me Arjuna. I told Ananda—"

"It is better either to have many names or no name at all—otherwise one may not do justice to one's true position. I wish to speak to you, but not to call you anything. Is that possible?"

"I am listening."

"My brother spoke of you constantly. Naturally I was jealous of him—of you—I do not know how to use that word, but I think I must have been jealous. I was not absolutely satisfied with your character, you know." There was a rich inflection in her tone, as of a smile. "I thought it was very important. Now that I have talked with you, I do not think it is so important."

"My character?"

"What I think of it."

"It is important to me, Indira."

"I can see how it would be important to you," she said gravely. "You must speak the language of those whom you address, and you thought that I spoke the language of morality. I do, but it is not my mother tongue." She could not help laughing at the gratitude of his laughter, but from the ardor she turned her face away as if too close to a flame, and remained looking away from him. She said: "I am in great trouble, and I am neither a pundit nor a yogini. I do not know how to get out of it. My brother had confidence in you, but he was a man, and very mysterious. Can I—should I have confidence in you?"

"If you ask, then you can not, should not."

"Yes." Her voice was soft, contrite; in her turn, unconsciously, just as he had done, she interlaced her fingers, palms up, in her lap, and looked down into them as if they were a mind or a will or a womb or a bowl or a boat, whose function in season is to be empty, for how can the full be newly filled? "It may be that I am beginning to understand my brother—but how can a woman understand a man, or the living the dead? How can anyone understand the next province?"

"There is a way," said Peter, "but it is not easy."

She did not ask him what it was. That would come, too, if she did not ask. "We Indians have a taste for monuments," she said. "We make gods out of the dead, even out of the living—do we not?"

"We do," said Peter. "Who else is there?"

After a moment she said: "I must not speak of difficulties any longer with Lady Edith, because she is very ill—and yesterday something bad happened to her. I am afraid, yet I must not be. She has entrusted the Ashram to me—I shall never know why. And she also has confidence in you. . . . One difficulty no longer exists, but there are others." A quick, furtive glance met his eyes to make sure, though she was cheating, that he knew what she was referring to in passing—Mary Nayler's check for fifty thousand dollars which had been turned over to Lady Edith yesterday afternoon—in India one does not refer to such things overtly, and under no circumstances must one say "Thank you." Gratitude is far too grave a matter to be disposed of by any thinkable demonstration. Silence, impassivity, loyalty, unobtrusive service, death if the opportunity presents itself, these are permissible ways—not of proof, certainly not of reciprocity—that were presumptuous—but of initiating a new and free action of love, a fresh caress, as it were, from a new beginning. For Indira, the cup of tea she had brought to Peter was a beginning; asking his advice, a continuation. It was to take part in a timeless ritual, one of the forms reality selects for itself, a play, but serious, not earnest—for reality is too sure of its inevitability, to be earnest. This seriousness, she now assured herelf, he recognized.

"What was the bad thing that happened?"

"Then let me begin to tell you," she said, and turned to him openly in the way that says, You are my brother. "There was a woman yesterday—two women—and you—oh, it is not easy! Liliu Acquileia has tried to blackmail us. The boy she calls her half-brother—Gori Govinda—she says he has been corrupted at the Ashram, and that she has proof. She will denounce us, and she will cause others to denounce us—then the Central Government will step in and the Ashram will be closed or changed into some narrow nationalist school—and what will happen to *our* children, who do not fit anywhere except—"

"Except in the wide world, except in tomorrow," Peter said softly.

"I do not think that Liliu Acquileia will do this thing." She would not if he could help it, and it was only he who could help it, as Liliu had planned—that moral indignation of hers would not be so funny in a law court. A real setup. Unless, of course, Peter married her. . . .

"The teacher she accused has already left. And his going? I did not question him. He suffers."

"You sympathize, Indira?"

"*Nischoi*—I must. It is of the nature of men to seize upon beauty as though it were edible. It is not edible. How to convince them? And there is so much beauty, it is not possible to hide all of it— though sometimes it is our duty to try, out of respect for their feelings, to save them from futility. And *our* children," she said with pride, "are *so* beautiful that I sometimes weep. Is that not also excessive? Is it not a little mad?"

"It is well to think so just now," he bowed his head, with a little shrug, acknowledging her chivalry as well as the mysterious propensity of which she had spoken. "But tell me what it was that Liliu Acquileia wanted from you."

"First she wanted to frighten us badly, to make us cower before her, then—"

"Then what?"

"She will give us time to lose heart, then she will tell us what it is she wants. You will think it strange, but I do not believe it is money she wants. And it is not revenge, for she was not really indignant— but pleased. Why?"

"I will speak to her at some length," Peter said with an attempt at robustness, but inside he shrank from those dark, luminous eyes —so like Ananda's—which seemed to be reading his secrets. To counter her, or to explain all, he cried out inwardly, with silent brashness: "Indira, I love you!" But if she heard, or saw, or felt, she gave no sign, but merely averted her eyes, for they had gazed steadily into his for a moment, and that is barely permissible, except when one wishes to be rude.

"There is another trouble," Indira said. "The younger Mrs. Nayler —Irene, I am to call her. She is a very noble person."

"Very noble," Peter agreed. "What is the trouble?"

"I do not know, but I am sure that something is wrong."

"With her?"

"Perhaps—yes, she is not well. I am afraid for her. What has she to do with Liliu Acquileia?"

"She should have nothing to do with her," Peter said.

"But she does. Yesterday Irene arrived to visit with us, but we could not greet her immediately. She followed Liliu Acquileia up the valley. I searched for her, but could not find her. I took the rifle and went out again—I thought perhaps Kaliya— When I returned to the bungalow, she was coming from the other direction. Her hair was down, her dress torn, she looked untidy, very ill, and she would not say where she had been. Irene"—again Indira was looking into his eyes, but as it were naïvely now, unselfconscious, wondering—"Irene is very beautiful, very intelligent, very good. Why do you not marry her?"

"Because—I don't love her," he stammered, himself wondering at the truth which he had not spoken before, had not quite known until now.

Indira nodded, accepting the revelation as a matter of course. "You do not love Liliu Acquileia either."

"No."

"I can understand that," she said, "but it might be that I could also understand if you did love her—or perhaps I am boasting."

"Perhaps you are boasting, Indira; perhaps you could not understand."

Now she was pale and shy—it was as if she did not want to speak any more about this, but was carried on in spite of herself, with the feeblest of defenses. She spoke in a funny little creaking voice because all at once her throat was dry and constricted: "It is the fate of men to love those who have beauty of any kind—what is so hard to understand about that? Just as it is the fate of women to love those who have prowess of any kind. It is not unnatural for those two to love you as they do. But you—do you love no one? Are you a stony-heart?"

"I am not a stony-heart," said Peter. "I myself understand a thing or two, and my dharma is my dharma. Now I am going to tell you."

"No." Her hands clutched the arms of the wicker chair in which

she was sitting—how stricken she looked, without a ready sub-
terfuge, Indian or feminine—as if she were waiting for the knife.
"It is you I love." The words were spoken quietly, almost dispassionately.

The color came back into her face. She stood up with dignity,
and replied in a low voice, in which was both sadness and fulfillment: "Ananda showed me your photograph when I was very young.
He told me that he showed you mine. They were only reminders. We
have broken no Law. Now I am going in." Slowly she went toward
the door.

"Indira!"

"Think, and you will understand," she said. "I have always loved
you, and it will make no difference. We shall not speak of this
again." The bamboo pattern of the door closed behind her like all
the complexities of the worlds between them and within them.

The bamboo laths forming the roof of the greenhouse, where half
a dozen rose-colored linnets were courting, cast a pattern in alternate
stripes of shadow and light over the young tea plants; and the same
bird-haunted bars, crossing the children as they moved about,
made them appear continuous with the soil and the plants, as creatures in a jungle seem to be active nuclei of their medium, extending
in effect to its limits, but having no proper existence outside it. Dr.
Bhattacharya, spectacles glittering with zeal, bent over the raised
earthen beds; his brown fingers, delicate and unexpectedly precise,
formed an intimacy with the plants.

"They are vigorous!" he cried out thrillingly, and all the children
pressed around him; then, with dark drama: "But I perceive an
aphis mali here and there! Also there are depredations of the green
ladybird—an impostor: do not confuse him with the true, benign
ladybird, *Ceratomegilla fuscilabris!*"

"No, no, we shall not!" the children clamored. "Show them to us!"
And they followed the teacher in a vain search for the wicked
aphid and the green impersonator of red ladybirds, until the teacher
remembered that he had demonstrated to the previous class the
use of nicotine dust as an insect repellent for plants. It had been his
considered opinion that none of the insects would take an overdose

of the repellent unless their karma made them do it; now he thought it best not to labor the point. . . .

Peter watched and listened decorously, gleefully, scared, from the far end of the greenhouse, offering himself to the rhythm of the children; for he had never taught a class before and he was about to do it. Mlle. de Rosière had been so upset on hearing of Tino's condition, that Peter had put her into the jeep with the doctor so that she might visit the invalid. She had taken Peter's place; he would take hers. He glanced at the textbook, stuffed it into his pocket. What did it matter if he was a bit shaky in the idioms? His French, when he spoke it—and he did not speak it lightly—was entirely convincing because it was not confined to the cranium. If he spoke French, he became French; if German, German; if Nepali, Nepali. Whatever he spoke, he became. The problem was to remain himself amid all his emanations, and not to be drawn into the heady glibness that comes with linguistic ability. Today he would tell the children a story, or perhaps two stories, or three, watching their faces to see if they understood and if he understood. All would be well, and all manner of things would be well, because he would not really be teaching them anything anyway, but merely celebrating with them the vastness in which they already shared—which Indira's declaration of love told him again that he possessed.

"It is a great honor to have been visited by the Prince of Darkness" —Tino sounded as if he were in a trance—"even though I could not stay. I wonder if anything will come of it?"

"It was a bad dream, a *cauchemar*," said Mlle. de Rosière. Tenderly she stroked the auburn hair back from the pale, sweating forehead.

In spite of the sedatives which the doctor had given him he lay there rigidly in his bed, his arms at his sides, in the worst physical agony he had ever known in his life, worse even than the time he had had out those four wisdom teeth with a totally inadequate local anesthetic. Bursitis in both shoulders, the doctor had said. Inflammation of what-we-call *bursas*, meaning purses, in the shoulder joints. The patient must lie there, quite still, and take sedatives, until he felt that he could move. After that he would go to Calcutta, where there was an X-ray machine, just the thing for bursitis. Meanwhile, he should cut down on the weight-lifting.

"I understand now why so many people die peacefully in their sleep," said Tino. "They die of horror. Nobody ever knows what killed them, but I know. They are not innocent."

"My poor one!" She was sitting beside him on the bed. Very carefully, in order not to increase his anguish—for every movement made him wince with pain—she leaned over and kissed him on the cheek; and, fearful of losing her balance, she braced herself lightly by placing one hand on his chest, inadvertently touching his left nipple, which swelled—no one had thought to button his pajamas after the doctor's visit, and Tino had not cared until now.

Chanchal, watching furiously through the half-open door, turned on his heel and went out for the day. The principles of *brahmacharya* had been outraged. Only men should be permitted to kiss men openly; that was not only manners, that was scriptural. And as for the pectorals! With women there was always the danger of what-we-call *sex*, harmless to women but extremely deleterious to men. Western biology books were necessary to Progress, no doubt, but they were wrong in certain fundamentals. Every Brahman knew that it took forty days and forty drops of blood to make one drop of semen, which was stored in a smallish tank located in the cranium. Chanchal himself was haunted by the fear of nocturnal emissions, and when they happened, he always woke up in time to catch the precious juice in his hand, pop it quickly into his mouth—disagreeable though that was, even with a water chaser—and hope that none was lost. It was loss of semen that was the cause of the Decline of the West—although one always had to beat about the bush in speaking of such things. Tino was chaste, one could tell that by looking at him: lofty, austere, and chaste, though a bit short-tempered—in many ways he was like a high-caste Brahman—but he did not yet know how to guard that chastity against all eventualities, the way Brahmans did. Tomorrow he, Chanchal, would make certain discreet remarks about the instability of France. Tino would understand, but he would give no sign of having understood, since he came of a deceptive race—the Americans—distinguished from all other races by their shadowy purpose: internationalism, in which they alone really believed. He, Chanchal, was on the side of theory; still, he loved Tino Scott, and he would not see him wither away for want of an appropriate quotation. Chanchal began to churn through his extensive repertory of English and Bengali poetry. Beyond that he would not venture, for Tino, like the Brahmans of Hindustan, was pained at the impure Bengali pronunciation of Sanskrit—the result of eating fish, said the spiteful vegetarian pundits of Madhya Pravesh, who knew the Vedic regulations backward and forward. . . .

"I dozed off," Tino said in a shaking voice. "It couldn't have lasted more than five seconds, but in those five seconds—the most terrifying visitation—"

"*N'en parle pas*—do not excite yourself." Gently hovering, she continued to caress him, as she would have never dared to do had he been vertical; for he had always intimidated her professional mind with his professorial mind, with a certain rigidity of expression, an aloofness of posture that negated life. As he lay here now, wrecked, a shambles, she felt in her body, from her fingertips to her depths, the awakening of her physical intelligence—not mere compassion—which she had not been allowed to remember for a long season. Now she was his superior, safe from his icy mind, warm and strong in herself, charitable as a flower now that the bee was crippled.

"I'm not excited, Marie, I'm disturbed—I'm *scared!* My mind—" he was actually whimpering, his pupils dilated with terror and pain if not with the sedative. "I opened the door, you see, and there was a beast lying against it, waiting for me. I thought he was small, but he was big—big! He drew back, recoiled, then he—he came at me. I screamed, you know. I screamed awfully, like a damned soul—then I woke up. My hair was standing on end—actually. He was so dreadful, something in me refused, still refuses, to remember what he looked like or just how he came at me. It's blocked off. As if I might die if I remembered."

"Banish it forever," she murmured soothingly, leaning over him and not quite thinking. "Remember only that I am with you."

"Yes. . . . Maybe I won't be afraid to remember what he looked like. I—I *must* remember. If I don't—" The paralytic was shivering, his face twisted in pain because of the movements which he could not control.

Impulsively she got up, closed the door and locked it; then she came back and lay down beside him on the bed, smooth as a cloud, cradling him in her arms.

"Remember then," she said. "Remember everything."

Only a part of Tino was aware of her body against him, and this part sighed deeply—"Home at last!"—but another part of him babbled aloud from the protection of her, like a man in a confessional, or the Cave Hypnos:

"He was all gray, cat-gray, with red lips—unmasked! And the eyes, pale, plantlike—*they looked at me!*—lusting to rip and rape and chomp up my soul and drag me down into Hell! The Familiar Stranger, not Peter, not you, not the women . . . 'Immediately available,' he said, and I summoned him—almost without thinking! My own pride, my own contempt, my own fear—called on the Evil One—and he stepped out of my mirror, and he has hold of me!"

"It is only I, Marie, and I do not depart from you."

"It *is* you, isn't it—just as before." Forgetting shame then, having hit bottom, Tino wept.

She also wept and lay on the bottom of the sea with him, clinging and comforting, herself in pain, absorbing his pain with the gratitude of a woman allowed to be a woman. Intelligence of the mind, concentrated and immobilized by pain, lay far above them, like the dim, pale threat of the ocean's surface seen perhaps, perhaps not, by sea monsters in the deepest, blackest chasms of the sloshing planet. They huddled together, he and she, moaning witlessly in a clutch of anguish. They did not know when the other intelligence took over, because it worked in silence from the center, while their weeping and sighing scarcely ceased, but rather fell into another kind of rhythm, yet keeping a continuity, a kind of unconscious hypocrisy under which something quite other than grief masqueraded as grief, lest the spell be broken and daylight strike again.

All along the night-bound coves and promontories of his body, her body lapped, rising by imperceptible degrees, unknown to either.

The more-than-pity that woman has for man began to lead her hands everywhere over him—since he could not move, and life must move and be moved in the darkness that cannot know itself—not with the futile flutterings, the exasperating, birdlike brushes of one who has reservations about the adorable body, but lovingly, suicidally, with mystic certainty of the unknown, embracing at every point of contact. . . . Such was the remarkable intelligence of her body; and such was the intelligence of his, freed by pain from the prison-tower of his other intelligence, that he knew how at once both to open to her and to enter, even as the god gives himself to his own female emanation, his shakti, wherein roles are reversed at will, and the Wheel of Life turns without a hitch. Pain and joy and pride of manhood—wherein humility is endless—merged in the return of Tino when he had come into his own and knew that he was changed.

"Bring me some wine and some grapes, and a panther."

"But the grape leaves are in your hair, my friend!"

"How did you know? How did you?"

"*C'était nécessaire.* We only know what we are compelled to remember—so that we love, one to the other."

"What can have happened, Marie? What happened?"

"You."

"And you too."

"I too, Tino, I too!"

thirteen

Irene had gone with Mary Nayler to visit the sick, only to find
Mlle. de Rosière already there, gay and lovely, and the sufferer himself, as Mary had remarked dourly, bright-eyed and bushy-tailed.
Whatever that meant. Mary was very old. . . . During the past two
or three days Irene had found herself, for the first time in her life,
increasingly unable to sit still or to remain for more than a few
minutes in one place. In the soft, lagging, indeterminate way
achieved by Indian courtesy—by which she had been influenced at
first on principle, but now unconsciously—she had wandered from
Tino's bedside into the other rooms of that bachelor establishment.
In the kitchen she had surprised Balu sitting on the floor, grinding
spices on a stone slab with another stone—he had jumped to his
feet, grinning and wild-eyed, bowing, clasping his spicy hands.
"*Namaskar, Memsahib!*"
"*Namaskar.*" With the courtliness of an ambassador greeting a
maharaja, Irene had clasped her hands and had bowed to him.
"*Apni ki chan, Memsahib?*" Quite simply, What do you want?
No rudeness intended; merely an unfortunate baldness of idiom that
always comes as a shock to the subtle Western mind—a Rhadaman-
thine challenge.
"Thank you, nothing. *Kichu-na.*" And she had backed out of the
kitchen, leaving him to wag the confusion out of his head and get
down to essentials again. Why had the memsahib looked as if she
were going to cry?
Slowly then, in a sense aimlessly, she had gone to Peter's room
and out through his other door into the garden, barely aware that
she had recognized the room as his. On the narrowing margin of her

193

existence there was not even space to tell Mary where she was going or what was wrong—she herself did not really know what was wrong, for there were no forthright words telling her that Peter did not love her. Something of the dark system of necessities that guides the blind led her now toward Jim Chen as a possible resource, although she had meant only to visit the sick, then comfort the distressed of spirit. For Jim had told her, down in the barn; as if he had nothing more to lose, or feeling in her the disinterestedness of depletion, so close to wisdom, which cannot or will not summon the energy to judge, he had laid bare his distress.

The door of his little house, his hideaway, was locked this morning; as always, the blinds were drawn, just as on the night when Peter had battered his way in. This time Jim came to the door less sullenly, managing a wan smile. Irene had arrived at exactly the time she had said she would.

"I must apologize." He meant the littered room. "I'm packing, you know—the train leaves this afternoon. I have all these things. You won't mind—" He kept up a monologue, excited and unhappy, spiced with pointless references and generalities, gesturing with his small, strong hands as if seizing, inspecting, and placing back on an invisible conveyor belt the contents of his consciousness. It was as if he were afraid Irene would say something true if given the opportunity to reply.

Irene said nothing, sat down on the sofa, got up again, wandered through the disorder, clutched at tags of words that felt genuine, that she might work into being for herself.

"Have you got anything to drink?" she asked wearily; and as Jim, uncertain which way to rally, merely stared at her, she said: "Whisky, for instance."

Silently Jim brought bottles and glasses—Scotch and soda—from a cupboard. "I could do with one myself," he muttered, subsiding, grateful that all was surprisingly not as it seemed, even with others. They drank in silence.

"Now let's get out of here," Irene said, moving toward the door, the glass still in her hand.

"Out—where do you mean? Where could we go? There are people—"

"Oh, who cares!" She made a gesture of impatience, as if she were fanning away mosquitoes, and her mouth made the little square of Bryn Mawr. "Let's just get the hell out of here. I want to talk to you."

"Well," Jim said, his mouth twitching, "I don't know. My train—"

"To hell with the train," she said. "Let's go somewhere—anywhere. And bring the bottle." In her movement, in her tone, was a quality not of command that imposed her will on his, but of prophecy, of identification at a level of elemental certainty, like the common will of a flight of birds who follow no ostensible leader, yet all swerve as one, this way and that—voyage wherein to participate is to have arrived.

"I know a place," Jim said.

They went down the mountain. Four miles aloft, the cumulus rain seeds guided long, fretful lines of crows with hollow voices (and the last ragged crow had the most hollow voice) toward the rice paddies of Nepal. The great stones crouched in the hills toward Sikkim, like camels bedded until earth's incandescence. Rhododendrons beckoned among them, and the grim, ranting hawk impaled his prey on thorns well out of reach of earthbound predators. Down in the swales thick-growing clumps of hydrangea shone silver and mauve and gray where pools of fog drained into indefinite depths, and the colors were indirect and subtle—even the sky was violet-blue—flowing and passive and baffling. The mountains alone seemed not to partake. Brooding in darknesses, exalted in whitenesses, they stood more like creators than like created things. They annoyed Irene, in her restlessness, by blocking a more distant vision —ultimate vision—but at the same time, with the ambivalence of symbols, they teased her, beckoned secretly to her to travel beyond them, beyond the illusions and the sly contingencies of time and place. The rebellion which every landscape incited in her became more pure as she descended; yet she went gladly as if to put an end to the attritions of a duel too long postponed. . . . Once when they stopped to rest, Jim cocked his head to one side at the sound of goat bells.

"There were goats on the island where I grew up," he said softly. "One night I lay down among them, and they didn't object at all

—you know what I mean? Goats are fair-minded. Their judgment is always suspended. They wouldn't have objected to me even if I'd been purple and shaped like an octopus, as long as I didn't make abrupt movements."

Irene threw back her head and laughed without a sound, then she said: "I know exactly how they feel."

They went down and down and down, through geological ages, to the river, over the trail to the right, to the krishnachura tree, where they sat by the pool. Something in the atmosphere, or in their mood, or perhaps only in the slight echo over the water, against the rocks, made their voices ghostly. They talked alike.

"We used to swim here," wistfully, as if he no longer had a body.

"Did Peter come here?" wistfully, as if she had never had a body.

"Once he was here. . . ." Jim set out the bottles, the Scotch and the soda, and a pair of little whisky glasses. Irene poured them full of Scotch.

"If you go—"

"I have to go," Jim said.

"Who will help him kill the python? Tino can't move. Mr. Kashani's gone to Calcutta—I understand he has an infected foot."

"Chanchal will help him. That's what he's here for."

"I dreamed of that python," Irene said. "I dreamed he chose me out of all the others. They all escaped but me. I was glad for them."

"I dreamed of him too," Jim said. "I dreamed I shot him, but he kept coming, and I shot all around him. I couldn't hit him in the right place. So I woke up. He was like the dragons they have in parades on Chinese New Year—paper, with boys inside, walking. I did that once. . . ."

"I wonder if pythons dream?" Irene paused, looked slowly up at the cliff. As he watched her motionless figure, which seemed to endure itself like a monolith, full of the violent molecular stress of the inorganic, there came to Jim a moment of confidence such as he had never before felt with anyone, least of all a woman; he had had intimations of it down there in the barn, during that unpremeditated confession; perhaps it had to do with something authoritative in her face, in her slight smile now, something large and as it were majestic—as if she had indeed kept herself simple from birth, declining the luxury of personality—the grains of self-seeking, of necessity entailed, being reliable and easily identified. "My head is foggy," Irene said, "but it's a relief to be with you. I don't think you'll mind if I'm not very logical. That's because you're my friend."

"I am," Jim said wonderingly. She had told him a little about her husband: it was as if her marriage to William had prepared her for anything—or for nothing.

"I don't have any other friends. Not really."

"Neither do I—not really. But you—"

A horde of crows approached overhead, wheeled about suddenly, tormenting the air with their demoralized shouting, disappeared over the treetops. The glistening of their wings was like a moonlit pool in a strong wind. Irene, the bird watcher, followed them with her eyes, out of habit, through the heavy glass of character which obscured her vision of objects and their relationships—so she had come to think. Beyond that glass all things spoke their messages and *were* their meanings; but from her side, how dark they were, how subdued were the voices of those all-important strangers, the others—and how loud her blood was—or was that the river rejoicing? Perhaps this strange oppression was a prelude to death—or to revelation, the shattering of the glass, which had before now seemed very close at hand, but which never quite happened. What kind of meaning she hoped for she could not say; still she waited for "something else," outside, perhaps, to correspond with an inner inspiration merited by a construction of logic: an explosion or a subtle melting of the glass, and then—a pure and absolute vision of the Signature of All Things!

"I can't quite hear myself exist," she said.

"You have Peter," Jim pursued. "There's a solidarity between you."

Sadly she shook her head and spoke unguardedly, as a man might speak to a stranger in a bar, or a woman to her sister:

"I know now I'll never have him. . . . Once I held a head of wheat in my hand. Every fiber of it was made to move in one direction. It worked forward with every movement of my pulse—with every breath of wind. I couldn't make it go backward, without breaking the whole structure. . . . They call that karma, don't they?"

A mask of jealousy and self-pity suggested itself to him, but something else won out: relief from any possible expectations of gallantry she might ever have where he, Jim, was concerned; and this freed him to greater and warmer loyalty. Shyly he held out his hand, not touching hers, but offering. They sat there then, holding hands, not as lovers but as waifs made temporarily sexless by emotional disasters.

"You've helped me," Jim said. "We should help each other. We're both kind of—precarious, kind of lost—aren't we? But you believe in God. I don't."

"I don't know if I do or not." There was a little double furrow between her eyes as she stared into the pool. "It would serve Him right if I didn't. I used to think suffering always worked out to some unexpected advantage. Can you imagine anybody being so naïve? How can He endure what He does to us? Or do you think it's enough for us to exist as edifying spectacles for the others? Is that our purpose?"

"No!" Jim cried, exalted by the indignation that blazed in her eyes, that made her cheeks turn pink and her hand clutch his as strongly as a man's. "No, I don't. We're somebody too!"

"I've lived such a careful life—careful to serve people, careful not to hurt them, careful not to thrive too much, careful almost not to survive, for fear it would be at someone else's expense! We call that spiritual poverty, Jim."

"But you *are* alive, and people *want* to pay; they want you to cost them something of themselves—otherwise, what are *they* good for?" Jim spoke impulsively, dimly, but accurately to her rebellion, spoke unknowingly of his need to be used.

"You know," she said, with a slow, daring smile, "I think I need something horrible at this time of my life. I think I need—I want to do something—despicable! I want the jewel from the toad's head, the tongue from the nightingale, the golden egg from the goose, I want to see Nemesis—because I do not agree with God."

"Neither do I," Jim said loyally, and their hands lifted together between them as if they were making a compact. Their other hands held glasses.

"And what if it is evil? How could I expect to be free from it suddenly? All my life, it's accumulated within me. I've been crawling blind through darkness, like a spider, spinning traps for reality—bridges, always bridges. They fall, I'm buried alive in air! The things of my life, the principles I believe in—they suffocate me! I must do something—I don't know what—but *something*—"

"Then listen," Jim said intensely—disarmed by the liquor, they were sitting so close together that their knees were touching, yet the alliance of their spirits was such that they felt at least as safe as a couple of ingenuous adolescents of the same sex. "You can count on me, Irene, and if you really meant that— If I were you . . ."

Already the nighthawks were tracing their hieroglyphics in the brown sky, and all the day birds were gone, except the shifty-eyed brown towhees with their rodent squeaks. A mole in a panic struggled senselessly along the path. With a serious look on his face, Peter pinched it up by the skin of its neckless neck, supporting it with his left hand, shoved its nose into soft, promising ground such as he would have liked if he were a mole, and watched it disappear. There were perils for that one, he thought. Peter went down to the river a few paces away; for the mole, finding itself unable to nip, had instantly polluted the hand of its benefactor.

A boulder went by under water. Unslinging his rifle and laying it carefully aside, Peter washed his hands, stood up and shook them and gave an easy, keening sort of shriek, perhaps to hear himself, to assert his existence against the grinding, overwhelming roar of the river, perhaps only to relieve his eardrums from the pressure of the noise. The shriek vibrated in his head and body like a challenge—not a challenge, more a promise or, as it were, a love call, which cannot be retracted. One moment he stood with pants on, handsome and dignified in the twilight; the next, naked as a rock, he was thrashing for all he was worth in the brown flood, hanging on to a root that came out of the riverbank. If the root broke, it was quite possible that he would be finished; but it was a tolerably good root, and he had a well-developed grip.

Panting and heaving, he lay on his back for a few minutes on a warm boulder by the jungle edge. "*Mon Dieu!*" he said, shuddering a little, "*Je suis fou!*" A dark bundle of feathers seized the top of a tree nearby, exclaimed softly, and, with eyes like burning coals, began to speculate upon the pale body floating on the stone. Doubtless the owl was furious with him for having interrupted its tryst with the mole. Where would the mole be now? Peter wondered. How far had it got? Could it have been a mad mole, to travel thus unguardedly on the surface of the ground, where the whole animal world, and part of the plant world, would tumble over itself in order to seize it? Perhaps it had been driven to a momentary perversity by an unbearable tension in its relation with other moles? No. Periodically there would be a mole whose dharma it was to offer itself to the powers of the upper world. No getting around it, no honorable escape. "Doomed to a short life," that one, like Achilles, whether he fought or not. Achilles in the *Iliad*, Arjuna in the *Gita*: both warriors who refused to fight, to turn the Wheel of Life, until the gods stepped in. Peter sighed and began to dress. He would be hunting alone, probably. At least he was glad he would be hunting something he respected as much as he did Kaliya. The river had been good, too. . . . But to die before he had finished the *Krishnayana*—even though he died while loving—would merit rebirth as a mole without aspirations. . . .

Entering his room very quietly, in order not to disturb Tino, he removed his clothes in the darkness and prepared to lie down for a few minutes to rest and collect himself. All day he had been wildly exhilarated, confused, tormented. . . . As he sat down on the edge of the bed, his pulse began to race. Someone was in his bed! His eyes, a little more accustomed to the darkness, made out the form of a woman—Liliu! Peter clenched his teeth in anger, in compunction. He had not come to her, so she— Rattlebrain that he was, he had not found it necessary—or had not had the courage—to tell her outright. Perhaps he had not really wanted to until today—until this morning. No, no, her love or passion or whatever it was, was not to be taken lightly. That attempt of hers at blackmail, he thought he knew what it meant, through all the complications of her devious mind: It meant only that she intended to keep him at all costs. That was a compliment he would have found impossible to resist, if he were not in love, if he did not love Indira. Still, he must have an understanding with her. Because they were finished. Hard to convince her now, of course; or with words ever; one must act. That he knew. And anyway, during the argument, if they fought—and of course they would fight—there was the possibility, no, the likelihood—that they would reconcile their violence in bed, and it would all have to be done over again. It would be best to effect the reconciliation first, then talk. For that, there was scriptural authority. But was it possible—went the Debate of the Body and the Soul—for a man greatly in love with one woman to lie down with another? Of course not, said the body, and stood gravely at attention for the final salute.

As his farewell mouth neared hers, the odor of whisky filled his nostrils; at the same moment, in the darkness, unexpected contours and textures and passive resistances met his touch.

"Oh, Peter, Peter! Thank God—at last!" Tears and sobs burst forth like monsoon rains after a terrible summer.

Peter went limp. All at once he wanted to tear himself from her embrace, to rush out of the trap. Instead he controlled himself, although his head was whirling; he cradled her in his arms as he would an invalid child, kissed her on the forehead, that being the least sensitive part of the face, the most formal, paternal, fraternal kiss, which never, never would descend to damned incest, other things being equal.

"Poor, poor dear," he murmured, stroking her hair and rocking her gently back and forth. "It's all right, it's all right. I understand." Although he did not. He stayed her, comforted her, cozened her with disingenuous innocence and bloodless pieties, saying the same banal things over and over again, until her sobbing subsided into whimpering—best of all for her, he thought without much thinking, because she had probably never whimpered before, never sniveled, never tapped the great fund of pusillanimity, so liberally endowed by Adam, with which every educated person ought to be familiar. "It's all right, all right, all right, it's—"

Irene hiccuped, drew a long breath, sighed deeply, laid her face in the swale of his neck and shoulder. From time to time she quivered violently all over, and Peter squeezed her carefully to give her a sense of limits; but he was automatically restored, feeling her virgin splendors against him, and partially backed away. It was like wanting to pray, yet being unable, on principle, to bow one's head in Meeting.

"Baby," he whispered, "thee's confused, does thee know that? Thee got sunstroke, and thee's been drinking, and thee's jumped into the wrong bed."

"I know I'm confused," said Irene. "I got sunstroke and I've been drinking, but I'm not in the wrong bed. I couldn't sleep if I were in the wrong bed, and I was dreaming when thee lay down beside me, so I know it's all right. Thee said it was all right."

"It's—It's all right—"

"I dreamed I was in a car, driving very fast, toward a great city— I could see the outline of it, all jumbled and big and black, like Philadelphia, and everything was twilight, and I wasn't sure of the way. I stopped at a filling station, and there was an attendant and he started putting gas in the tank. I unfolded a large map—very detailed. I said: 'This map and that city are two different things.' And the attendant said: 'Oh, no. You just keep going till you reach the center, where the cross is. Then you take any direction.' He laughed, and I laughed too, because it was so obvious. Wasn't that a happy dream? It's all right, Peter!" Laughing softly, as if she were still in the dream, she turned toward him.

Peter felt now that he must, at all costs, substitute thought for action, and make her do the same. It would be hard enough—and dangerous, perhaps—to tell Liliu Acquileia that he did not love her and that he would never marry her. With Irene it would be far more complicated, far more dangerous to her in her present condition. Later, when she was stronger—perhaps tomorrow, when she would at least be sober—he would tell her; but now he must manage to be a cerebral hypocrite while his manhood strained to do her a service that might destroy her as well as himself.

"Let's just lie here awhile," he said, again kissing her on the forehead, embracing her with his arms, but trailing the rest of him away, a merman conscious of his frightful nethers. "Let's not lose our sense of proportion."

"I have nothing to lose," she said, a trace of impatience in her voice.

"We always have something to lose," he argued for the sake of cerebration, "or to be wrested from us in exchange for something else."

With a sigh she sank back on the pillow. "Must we fight even for our sorrows?"

"Yes," said Peter gently, "especially for our sorrows."

"It may well be that happiness is bad for our adjustment." The dryness of her irony, as she acceded to the mind, to habit, seemed worse to him than her tears, for now she was impersonal, fatalistic in her loneliness, not blaming him, therefore more isolated than ever—and this pierced him somehow most of all. He put his head down between her breasts, and murmured in a choking voice that he was sorry. It was she who comforted him now, stroking his head. "Thee can't help it," she said. "Neither could William. Neither can I."

"I can't marry thee," he blurted.

"I knew that when I came here," she said quietly. "If thee had loved me, I wouldn't have come. What I want of thee is a life—a life in me that I can love—not thy life, but a life *from* thee. *Sahaja,* that's what it's called, isn't it? A friend of mine told me—very sensible custom—a woman can go to a holy man and ask him to give her a child, and it's considered right and decent for him to do it—"

"*Sahaja*—but I'm not a holy man!"

"Thee doesn't have to be. Hasn't thee ever seen a nun with a begging bowl? Whatever she receives is made holy in Christ or in Buddha—"

"There are certain things that she does not receive if she can possibly help herself, Irene. If thee had a child of mine, how could I ever be free again?"

"Thee would be—but we do not know how presumptuous we are, Liliu and I. We go against God, Who has decreed that the rich shall get richer and the poor shall get poorer, and everything shall be more and more itself and then die."

Outside the window a contralto owl shuddered down the scale, then dived into the moonlight with a cry of triumph, as if avenged.

"I'm afraid for *thee,* Irene!"

"Thy fear is my danger. I'm being punished in kind, aren't I? For not knowing that people want you to cost them something of themselves"—unwittingly she repeated Jim's phrases—"so they can feel the loss—a pearl of great price—giving all, ye shall receive all —unto life everlasting!" She began to shake with mirthless laughter, weeping without tears, desolation of the sybil fated for a long and bitter ice age.

Appalled and giddy, he covered her mouth with his, to hush her. Through the whisky fog he tasted the acridness of her grief. There he arrived at a tentative decision; indeed, he had begun to fulfill what he had suddenly conceived to be his moral responsibility, and might have done so at once in his nervousness, had she not writhed with an unexpected resurgence of spirit, nearly fatal in its inconsistency.

"In Christ, pierced for our sins!" she cried, tossing her head from side to side on the pillow.

Slowly Peter sat up and remained sitting even after her religious fervor had subsided. Disaffected to begin with, his forces had fled the joyless field of dharma and sequestered themselves in the higher centers, so that in certain respects he was indeed like the holy men who, in *sahaja,* granted their seed—if any remained to them after their terrible austerities—to childless women, provided that no pleasure was involved.

"Thee tried," she said in a dead voice. "God knows, thee also tried in thy turn. . . . There is a river I shall never enter. . . . They have big religious festivals at the place where the Jumma flows into the Ganges. Eight hundred people were trampled to death there one year, trying to immerse themselves. They burned their bodies and cast their ashes into the water. I wish I had been there. . . . Thee needn't lie down again, Peter. I'm going—if thee'll get out of my way. . . . Has thee got a chill?" At first she did not know what to do; then clumsily, like Veronica with her napkin, she blotted his face with a corner of the sheet, because he was covered with cold sweat. Strangely, it was this sweat that was more repugnant to her than anything else. It was wet and sticky, and in the darkness it was like blood.

It was quite dark under the sal trees on the mountainside. Peter's body itched violently under the skin, as if devil grass had begun to sprout in it. Quickly he thrust himself into a low-hanging branch, writhing on the acid twigs like a fly-tormented horse. The irritation under the skin became unbearable—how he would have liked to shed it! He flung himself down and rolled in the humid earth. Sitting up, he ran an exploring finger over his teeth, for he had slapped himself on the jaw much more vigorously than he had intended. It was such a generalized sensation, that he could not be sure whether it was a nervous breakdown caused by the violation of him—or merely some stupid love potion administered through Balu, who, judging from his shifty looks, could easily be in the pay of Liliu herself. Belladonna, a first-class aphrodisiac whose only drawback, aside from the reduction of one's humanity, was its fatal side effect, grew abundantly hereabouts, a thousand feet lower down. Liliu, an inveterate herb collector, would not be likely to pass it by; not at this juncture of her life, anyway. Gritting his teeth—he was generous, but he was not always a dupe—he determined to have an accounting with Liliu; then he would leave this place forever. If karma was character as the sum total of all one's past decisions, through many lifetimes, now was the time to exert the crushing force of freedom in one life, which was also his heritage. An accounting with Liliu, though. . . . The best thing for him would be to leave as soon as possible—to kill Kaliya and go; yet he felt an obscure dread of going, as if because of him a doom hung over everyone he knew here, that would descend on them all the sooner at his departure, and on him too if he stayed. Certainly this foreboding had to do with Liliu, whose horoscope contained, for her at least, a conjunction of planetary tombs, himself the center and dark sun, and her his shakti-consort the moon goddess. Anyone who crossed Liliu had to have good reasons—meaning resources: quickness, mobility, strength, and an unscrupulousness comparable to hers. Yet she was seldom cruel merely for the sake of cruelty, perhaps because her inner economy was really quite shaky: once lost, her balance might be irrecoverable; but she was not yet mad, he thought. Peter did not agree with her in the matter of the disposition of other people's lives, particularly his own—in fact, it was more than possible that he hated her, as he hated most things that threatened him with servitudes he himself did not choose; but although he was not deficient in resources to combat her—except that he was not very unscrupulous—he suffered under a great disadvantage, perhaps because he did hate her: When he was with her, he was not dominated by reason, or even by imagination, but by sex and death; for there was that in her, in him also, that made him want to kill her, and that desire was as inevitable as the desire of a caged thing to destroy its cage. The lust was strong now, even though he was not with her. In his present mood he must not go near her, lest the nature of his "accounting" be wholly destructive, a triumph of the fragmentary, the partial, the special power of Liliu.

Back in his room Peter smoothed out the bed and sat on it cross-legged, trying to think, but his thoughts would not come clearly. Neither would his feelings. After a few minutes he poured himself a tumbler of whisky straight. Things lost their rigidity, tumbled into a kind of sequence, not as thoughts, not logically: pictorially, rather, a series of flashes of himself dominating events, masterful, moving with alacrity toward freedom and greatness and love. First, without delay, he must see the sannyasi—he did not know why, but that was the way it began—and he must invite Kaliya daily without fail, and nightly, till Kaliya agreed. . . .

At midnight he was in the jungle, drunk. Halfway up the cliff where the sannyasi had been, he had dropped his rifle and had had to go down after it. When he had finally reached the top of the cliff, the sannyasi was not there. Swaying perilously on the high ledge, Peter had finished the bottle of whisky and had flung it into space; then he had slid down the cliff, scraping his legs, tearing his shirt nearly off and losing the seat of his shorts. His elation was also gone. It was a descent into gloom; from this he tried to rescue himself by bravado, staggering along trails he could not remember, calling aloud: "Kaliya! Kaliya!" the braver because he felt it was not time. . . . Sometimes he could see, sometimes not. The moon in its clouds was like a strained white face lost in a mob of dark people, running and rioting, their long, black hair streaming out behind them.

Above the Ashram he crouched like a beast in the tea bushes for a long time, spying on the darkened bungalow where Indira slept; then he slunk away. Not there—he must not go there! Kedar, perhaps, and the descendant, barren or otherwise, who would ease Pitar of his blackness. . . . Somewhere between the Ashram and the krishnachura tree, on his way to Kedar's village, he stopped on the riverbank and stared down into the black, swirling flood. Ganga Mata had looked like this when the darkness of it had called to the darkness in Ananda Mahadev and he had returned by that route to the Outer Ocean. . . . Something interrupted Peter—the feeling of a presence in the jungle behind him. With a sense of relief, he walked slowly toward it, away from the river that had tempted him, though it was too male in its violence to seduce him easily at this season. The moon chose that moment to go behind clouds. Whatever it was—Kaliya or the sannyasi or some other creature—it merely watched while he stalked it noisily and blindly. On and on he went, through savage woods, groping, sometimes crawling. . . . All at once, not more than fifty feet away from him, the death cries of a sambar rang out, with the growls of the leopard that was twisting its neck—a quick job for a tiger, but apt to be a long-drawn-out affair for a leopard if the sambar happens to be a big buck or one that whirls at the crucial moment and is awkwardly taken. The blood-curdling noises receded. The leopard was having a long ride. The terror struck that had been coiled under Peter's alcoholic courage, and he went crashing down an animal trail, as if the death he fled was his own. . . . Then there was an open space. The moon mocked him with unendurable brightness for a moment, and turned away from him. He was on the main trail to Tashiling.

Once again he stood outside Liliu Acquileia's house, but he could not quite go in yet. On the way he had stumbled into a Tibetan all-night wedding party and had drunk things that grew beards on contact with the whisky in his stomach. It was a tossup whether he was going to vomit now or later. If he did it within the next ten minutes, as he thought he might, he wanted it to be outside with no one watching.

A creature darting down from the low roof, brushing his cheek, lit on the ground, ran across his feet. At first he thought it was a bird, but as it disappeared into a pile of rubble by the gutter, he realized that it was a rat. Wiping his face with the back of his hand, Peter stared dully at the moon as it scuttled behind dark clouds. Tashiling swam like Venice, that ship, under the night sky. Eerily off balance, it staggered, so that he barked his elbow against a wall, and sat down abruptly on the pile of rubble. Something crept up to him out of the darkness and the filth, huddled against him, trembling. It was a white mongrel, a sort of bulldog with a huge, misshapen head. It took his wrist very gently in its jaws, slobbering, and looked up at him fixedly out of great dark eyes. The beast could have crushed his arm, but Peter in his drunkenness knew from the beginning that it would not.

"Artow a bitch?" he muttered.

The dog opened its powerful jaws, loosed his wrist, licked away the slobber, gazed and gazed with eyes that became for him miraculous, starlight in their depths, like those of a Mater Dolorosa.

"I am glad you have come," Peter sighed.

The beast crouched close beside him, trembling as if her fate and his lay in the balance. Peter spread his torn shirt over her; then, while she pretended to sleep, he supported himself on his elbow beside her, stroking her. The door of Liliu Acquileia's house opened and someone came out. In a voice heavy with antiquity Peter said to the animal: "I must go, else it would appear that I am dead." Discreetly, as if the meeting were fulfilled, she went away.

The male figure coming out of the house started back on seeing Peter, stood for a fretful moment against the closed door, as if considering whether to go back in or perhaps flee elsewhere.

"Gori?" Peter mumbled—it had been impossible to keep the boy from spying on them from the very first: houses here were not made for privacy, no one believed in privacy, people usually knew what other people were doing, took a friendly interest, watched whenever they could. Gradually Peter's futile attempts to preserve the ignorance of the young, according to Western standards, had given way to fatalism and perhaps complaisance, for there was in him also a strain of sociability. What he felt now, though, in his deepest degradation, was guilt. It was because of him that the boy was even now going out to some futureless encounter. . . . "Gori," he repeated brokenly, his head sunk on his chest.

"Yes." It was Jim Chen standing over him.

Peter lolled his head back and stared up at him, open-mouthed.

"You want me to lie to you?" Jim hissed, and raised his arm as if he were going to strike Peter in the face. "You waited for me, didn't you!"

"Lo!" said Peter. He meant No, but his mouth muscles were slack.

"You're drunk," Jim said in sudden commiseration, and he began to wrestle with Peter to get him to his feet. They stood dancing in the narrow alley, the little man supporting the big man whose limbs lurched out in spastic abandon in the direction of Liliu Acquileia's door. "Not in there," Jim pleaded, still whispering. "I'm sorry I said what I did. Don't go in there."

"I'm expected!"

"Not now—they're not expecting you. They've gone to bed, to sleep. Come home with me. I'll take you to Tino's house. You'll be all right there. O.K.?"

"No, in *there.*"

"Not in there." The little man had him exactly about the waist, like one who knows. With one hand he grasped Peter's rifle. "You're too drunk, Pete. Drunk and dirty and filthy—but they'll make you worse, see? *She* will, not— It isn't just the body—but you don't understand at all, do you? You do not."

"Not? Hoh!" Peter began to be vaguely aware that he was gruesome.

"Not. Not very much. Not at all. Let me take you home."

"No, not *home,* for Chrissake!"

"Am I your friend?" The honor of his friendship was evident from the firm propriety of his embrace. "Maybe you don't trust me?"

"I truss you," said Peter, hanging his arm, heavy as a cross, over Jim's shoulders. "I truss you."

Laboriously, intricately they walked away, on up the mountain, until they stood before Tino's house. Peter stopped, refused to go in. "Not there," he said. "Stranger in my own bed—too familiar. I'm going back."

"No, no, go on in. I'll help you get to bed. There's no stranger. It'll be all right—if you trust me?"

"I truss you fine," Peter affirmed. "I toll you, I truss you!"

"Then go on in."

"No. Tino's sick, and I'm gonna *puke.*"

"Oh," said Jim, "then come to my place."

Just inside the front door of Jim's house, Peter turned green, sank to his knees, lunged forward on his hands, and prepared to render an account of his folly with *chang,* wine, and adulterated whisky. Jim snatched up an unread newspaper, placed it on the floor before Peter, who glanced at the headlines and arched his back. Quickly Jim turned the page, offering a broader surface to the cataclysm. Peter responded passionately. Supporting his forehead to keep him from going downstream, Jim turned the pages neatly, adeptly, systematically, until Peter had progressed as far as the obituary notices. Then Jim helped him into a chair and wiped his foul face with a handkerchief, tenderly as a mother.

"Do you want to sleep?" Jim asked.

"No," said Peter. "Gotta settle things."

There was a pot of water on the coals, in the kitchen. Jim made coffee, the powdered kind with lumps. Peter blistered his tongue.

"Regarding your question at the time we met," Peter said with dignity, and smiled a little and was lost in the rotund beauty of the phrase.

"What question? Don't worry—I was—I was confused."

Frowning into the coffee and running his tongue over the scorched rim of his mouth, Peter sought to recover the train of his thought. "I noticed an article—" He grinned wanly at the place on the floor where the paper had lain, and Jim sniggered. " 'Professor Chakrabarty, Professor of Pathology, Calcutta Central Universary, *says:'* "

"Says what?"

"Um." Peter downed the coffee, meditated heavily for a moment. "Very profound. Gotta think about it. Could I have a bath?"

"There's no hot water. Just cold."

"Just cold is what I need."

As Peter's movements were still uncertain, he leaned massively against the bathroom wall while Jim, in a prim white apron, threw mugs of cold water over him. With his head bowed in thought, Peter looked like a persecuted philosopher. Once he muttered: "Am I doing you a disservice?" And Jim replied: "Don't think about that. Am I doing you one?" Splash. "How the hell would you do that?" Dash. "I don't know. . . ."

"Professor Chakrabarty, Professor of Pathology, Calcutta Central Universary, *says:*" Peter tried unsuccessfully to dry himself, nearly fell, relinquished the towel to Jim.

"Says what?"

"We never master our p-pathology. If we do, we master nothing else. Nothing." Peter made a large, negative gesture.

"You're a lightning reader?"

"I am."

"Typical Indian statement." Jim sounded tolerant. "His, and yours too."

"Extremely true," Peter agreed, beginning to shiver with cold, and he accepted Jim's formal ministrations with a second towel. "Illustrated in *Faust*, Tibetan version: Man deals with Mephisto, tries to back out. Flees through the world, doing good. Mephisto follows in differing disguises, sick with fun. Man enters rugged country, hides, flees again, falls over cliff—just in time. Feels himself escaping as he hurtles through the air. W-Wakes up. Pale, antiseptic men with yellow gloves, scalpels—Chakrabarty Hospital for Tropical Exuberances. Swimming vision of room. Serious call for volunteers—special blood—Omega-type. Little old lady comes in. Mother! Tube from her Omega arm to his. Ah, that's better! With her free hand she moves aside her v-veil. M-Mephisto! Grins down with devilish cheer. Man gives a lost cry and falls back, completely recovered."

Jim laughed carefully, strove to contain himself, burst into a series of short, vigorous chortles, and turned away to keep from showing teeth which he had never shown except to a dentist. His

own face working spasmodically, Peter gave a whoop and laid his
head against the wall, hiding his face in the crook of his skinned
elbow.

"Chakrabarty said that?" Jim's voice soared out of control.

"Cer'nly, Chakrabarty." Peter looked up, into a mirror that hung
on the wall, shuddered and averted his gaze from the sight of his
own eyes. They were like spoiled almonds with edges rendered indefinite by a kind of foggy mold. The mirror was dirty and the light
none too good, but he did not think of that. "I think I better lie
down," Peter said.

"You take my bed. I'll take the sofa."

"Beds are bad. I'll take the sofa—rest for an hour, then go. I
recup'rate fast."

"You read fast. Do you do everything fast?"

"N-N-N-No!"

Jim put him to bed—it was a short, broad bed and Peter had to
lie with his legs hooped out like a harbor, which made him think of
hospitality.

"You can come in," Peter muttered brokenly. "Everybody else is.
'I am large, I contain multitudes.'"

"No offense," Jim said gently. "Good night," and, turning off the
lights, he went and lay down on the sofa, curled up like a cat.

It is dark in Peter's dream, but there is a lurid glow on the
mountainside, up out of the jungle, an inflammation of light. Trees
of fungus grow between the buildings. Tawny shapes—panthers
—stalk silently through the town. Here he faces the laughter of
blond uniforms, repetitious, worse than the squall of the springing
panther; blond laughter, cunning to widen dark weaknesses. Now
he is the object of their curiosity; he is insulted, tricks are played
on him; but he dares not kill, and to defend himself is to kill. He
must act the clown, the poet, get himself tolerated, exonerated, win
allies. Craftily he watches the red, gnomish faces, gauges their
moods to see what will make them split into laughter. It is not so
difficult, although he can never be certain of his techniques. They
laugh at his anxiety, at the wittiness of his size—he is small, indeed he looks very much like Jim Chen—at the way he tortures

himself to suppress his rage, even more than at the self-mockery which he expounds so badly to their jaded ears. He begins to perform acrobatics. To his relief, they get up and begin a Russian sailors' dance, which he joins. A sluggish uniformity is the main thing. They are dressed in rusty iron jock straps and greenish celluloid visors, which he had not noticed before. They look like misers, scholars, gouty athletes. Still shuffling from one foot to the other, on the outer edges of their feet—perhaps the floor is syphilitic—they lean over a brass rail with a green curtain on it, drink whisky, and gaze out through a plate-glass shop window. Outside, people are running down the dark street. They are naked and they have flowing black hair; their pale arms grow straight up in terror, rigid and jointless like white oaks struck by lightning; they have no traces of sex; there is a clean, unbroken, concave sweep from thighs to belly; no nipples or breasts, no navels. Their crying mouths are round as knotholes, but there is silence in the street, except for the faint rustling of their hair as they flee from the pursuer. They disappear in the darkness, and for a moment there is nothing to be seen. Then Kaliya appears. The blond planters fall to their knees. Peter rushes out—he has earned the responsibility—and harangues him in order to divert him from his victims. What Peter has not noticed until now is that Kaliya's coils have preceded all the dark people who fled, and are slowly bringing them back, along with the blond planters, toward the great, smiling jaws, unopened as yet, but capable of unlimited distension. Peter stares boldly into those eyes—enormous, like his own, but dark where his are light—clasps his hands, bows formally in the *namaskar*, and asks Kaliya's permission to slay him. The python's expression does not change. Fixedly he gazes at Peter. From the groove in front of the jaws a long, forked tongue licks forth, soft and sensitive and dark. The jaws open, advance toward Peter. . . .

Jim Chen was rocking him back and forth. "You're having a bad dream. Wake up and turn over, then you won't have the same dream again."

"What time is it?" Peter sat up and stared at the desolate room, the suitcases packed but gaping open, at Jim Chen fully dressed.

"Three-ten. You might as well go back to sleep."

"You haven't slept?"

"I never sleep. You should sleep, though. Your eyes are sunken."

"No, I'm all right now. Are they very sunken?" Peter swung his legs over the edge of the bed.

"Not so very."

"Sunken eyes bulge inward." Peter pulled on his torn, dirty pants as far as they would go without his standing up. "Ever think of that?"

"Never," said Jim, helping him.

"You don't sleep either, eh? What do you do?"

"I lift weights, I write long letters, take long walks, sometimes I read. . . . Shouldn't you go back to bed?"

"I can't sleep, not yet. Do you ever make coffee when you can't sleep?"

With a happy, contented expression, Jim flew into the kitchen. Peter finished dressing, avoiding the sight of himself in the mirror until he had to comb his hair. What a beast! Sour blurs for eyes— but not as bad as he had thought at first. It was just the taste of them inside. . . .

They sat in the other room to drink the coffee. A naked light bulb —very bright because the other lights in town were out—hung down from the ceiling. Not a reader's light, Peter thought miserably, hiding his eyes with his coarse, black lashes. Fortunately his eyelids were rather thicker than most people's.

"Time to go," he said, noisily vacuuming at the surface of his coffee, like an Indian.

"Where to? What for? Wait a while." Jim made him another cup so quickly, he might have been saying: Endure me, *this* is what I need to do.

"Tino's got something wrong with him. I haven't seen him today —since yesterday morning. He couldn't move. I don't know whether Chanchal—"

"Chanchal is gone," said Jim. "He got mad at Tino."

"God damn!"

"Tino's all right now," Jim said.

"How do you know? How could he be all right?"

"I just know. He has a nurse. That's why Chanchal left."

Peter drank his coffee more slowly.

"So he's all right, eh?"

"Quite all right," Jim said with an unhappy leer.

"Well, that's nice," Peter quirked his mouth a little, but quickly stopped because his head felt like granite cracking.

"I thought you'd be all right too—now."

Something in Jim's expression, in the intonation of his voice, enraged Peter. Suddenly gripping Jim's jumpy knees in his talons, he shouted at him:

"I trusted you—now what have you done to me? What have you done to *her?*"

Falling back in his chair, Jim laughed nervously, wincing, without daring to disengage those fingers—tomorrow he would have dark bruises to inspect. "Don't, don't!" he moaned. "I didn't know—a person has to try, doesn't he? I did my best! Honest to God, I did my best! Don't hate me!"

"Then you made an error," Peter muttered, releasing him. "Did you make an error, or are you playing games with me?"

"I would not play games with you," Jim said with dignity, "not *any* kind—for a reason you would not want to hear."

"You wish me well," Peter ventured reluctantly.

"I do—didn't you know it?"

Briefly he read Jim's face, which concealed little at that moment; then, as if to atone for his limitations, he looked straight up into the light bulb overhead, into the inner filaments, until his vision was wiped out by illumination.

"So be it," Peter said humbly, and turned on Jim a blind gaze that saw only the fiery aura of a Person.

"You're used to love."

"Never! I never get used to it—not to loving, not to being loved. God help me if I ever do!"

For a moment Jim sat and considered his lostness; then he said:

"I sent her to you because I also love *her*—and I'm no good for *her* either, you understand? The greatest thing I could think of for her was you, and for you, her—*not* Liliu Acquileia! Pete—you don't know—Liliu—I tell you—understand?"

Peter bowed his head; he knew that the true value of the advice of the damned lay not in the possibility of applying it, but in the fact that the advice was given at all—that love and freedom should exist even in Hell. Dante had noticed that.

"Short of love, it doesn't work," Peter said, "not with Irene, not with me. There has been a case of mistaken identity. I am not Jesus Christ. I am not even a latter-day saint."

"You don't understand her." Sadly Jim shook his head at Peter's willful obtuseness.

"Help her," said Peter. "She listens to you."

"What? I—?"

"I think so. Don't walk out on her—not after what you did to her."

Jim stared at him with something akin to horror, then slowly, slowly the grin of the Olympic Champion—embarrassed, modest, pleased—spread across his face.

"Why—if you say so—I never thought of it that way," he stammered, "but I guess maybe in a way you're right—aren't you?"

"Yes, I am," said Peter. "And another thing: I'm afraid of snakes. Don't walk out on me either, will you?"

"I'll do anything you say!" It came almost as a groan, it was so heartfelt. As if unable to endure any more, Jim jumped up and bustled joyfully about—more coffee and some strawberry jam and some scones from a little English bakery that had changed hands and was now not quite English. The scones were more like chapattis.

"How could the world have anticipated this?" Tino exclaimed from his pillow, observing the dawn over the icy mountains of Tibet.

"It couldn't have," said Peter calmly. "Thanks to my insomnia, I saw it develop, the dawn. I heard it being circulated by all the cocks of the world, from east to west, but even I could not have anticipated it." He had come in as silently as a burglar, only after watching Mlle. de Rosière depart a little before dawn.

"If anyone could have anticipated it, you would have done so," Tino said in a conciliatory tone. "How complex it is! What organization! The purple is risky. Rouge, rose, mauve. Dare I mention green?"

"It is green."

"Beginning with jade. Best not to mention colors. . . . But the gold fires on that distant ice—could that possibly be Everest?"

"That is Everest," said Peter reverently, hoping Tino would not want to put on his glasses. "You are very lucky. It is almost never seen from here."

"The presence of a second person is needed to establish some proof of the existence of Everest, isn't it?"

"I believe it is."

"It's not credible in itself."

"No."

"You're an innocent fellow, Peter!"

"Yes, I am."

"And simple! I never realized before how simple you are!"

"So are you." Peter laughed, standing over him.

"You *know*, don't you!" Tino beamed, rosy with more than the dawn—how red his lips were! "You *know*—oh, you bastard! *Maestro di color che sanno!* To begin with, how shall we— Here, you can rub my shoulders—here, where they don't hurt so much. Oh! Ah! Not too much, not too long—you are not so gentle. . . . For the first time in my life, I feel discovered, almost ordinary, like you. We understand each other, eh? Of the same quality, different uses. You know Brunetto Latini, Dante's teacher? No, no more questions, not now. Later. O.K., *caro*, that's enough." Tino grinned a new grin, a happy one—he would have laughed, but he feared the pain. Then, suddenly grave: "But you are you, after all, and you are not happy—except now in a special way, for me. . . . You understand that I am loyal?"

Peter considered for a moment. "How high can you lift your arms?" he asked.

"Not very high. About as high as the hips."

"It's too painful to lift them higher?"

"Impossible, not just painful," Tino said cheerfully. "If it were desirable?"

Still smiling a little, relaxed from the massage he had given Tino, Peter tucked the covers up around his friend's neck. It would hardly be practicable, he reflected, to attempt to shoot from the hip at a charging python, the swiftest of all wingless creatures—even if one had good eyesight and were an experienced hunter.

"Peter," said Tino, "do you remember the holy man I told you about—the one who caught flies in a glass and gave me a deep look, then let 'em go?"

"I remember."

"Well, I gave him a champak flower. Was that right?"

"That was right," said Peter.

fourteen

"I beg thy pardon!" Peter cried, stopping the Land-Rover and helping his aunt to right herself. "My mind was roving. I forgot I had passengers."

The Land-Rover had gyred steeply down a road that looked from a distance like a careless scrawl on the mountainside, although it was the laborious creation of seasons of men and women and children. Fortunately the road was used chiefly by vehicles that came to and from the Asham, and they were few; for in that four-thousand-foot descent there were no more than five places where one vehicle could pass another. To Peter, the road curled as inevitably as the coils of Kaliya, upon whom he was thinking, measured and sedate as the rhythms of the Silent Meeting to which he and his passengers were going. At a certain hairpin turn Mary Nayler had slammed into his side like a wardrobe trunk on a pitching ship.

"Some people still prefer to walk to Meeting," she replied ponderously, getting out. "However, don't let me impede thy progress." She started off with a hard, capable stride. The Land-Rover coasted along beside her, ignition off.

"It's two thousand feet down," Tino called out from the back seat, where he sat braced between Irene and Mlle. de Rosière. "Peter will be more careful—won't he?"

"Yes," said Peter, "I'll be more careful."

"It might be more dangerous on foot," Tino remarked silkily. "Listen to those drums." As Mary glanced at him, he nodded toward the jungle below.

Sometime during the night, casual, almost inaudible fumblings

219

of sound, without beginning, developed: the summonings of hand on hide, of finger, thumb, and palm on beast skins stretched tightly over hollow wood or clay pots. By dawn the incessant, thrumming boom had the nerves of all the people of the valley—perhaps of the beasts also—mysteriously encircled, stretched, excited, responding helplessly to a rhythm both powerful and elusive. Now the sun was well up, the drums more compulsive than ever, the rhythms more complicated, more unexpected, addressing the most ancient denizens of personality, guardians of uncouth origins, the leaping horde, whose strength is in its obscurity wherein body is mind and mind is body and both emerge from the molecular strife of earth and air, fire and water. It was the time for the invocation of the power of Lord Krishna. Passionately the valley besought him to give victory over the python—to allow the triumph of one emanation of himself over another, Kaliya slain again.

"It's not a very good time for the Silent Meeting," Irene said, leaning forward nervously to address Mary who was marching along beside the Land-Rover. "Maybe we should postpone it. There's too much competition."

"There's no competition in the Spirit," Mary said grimly. "Friends have met under much worse circumstances—Indian attack, for instance. It's just a matter of centering down."

"It isn't First Day, though! It's only Fourth Day!"

"First Day or no First Day, Lady Edith asked us to hold this Silent Meeting, and I really think we ought to. It might be her Last Day."

"Oh," said Irene, and, looking at the others, she found no reassurance in their faces. They had known, and she, so involved in herself, had not known—had not really known with her heart—that Lady Edith was dying. "Please get in, Mary," she said quietly. "It takes too long to get there this way."

After a moment Mary did get in, feeling that she had punished Peter enough; and indeed his driving was subdued and conscientious. With more confidence, now that she need not watch the road so closely, Mary half turned in the seat, to address Tino behind her.

"Are you quite comfortable?" she asked. "Do these ladies brace you sufficiently?"

"They brace me very well," said Tino.

"And do your shoulders hurt you very much?"

"They hurt me very much indeed," Tino said. "The pain is exquisite."

"That has always struck me as a curious expression. . . . The early Christian martyrs were often cheerful under surprisingly adverse circumstances. I am cognizant of the effort you have made, and I am personally grateful to you for coming—as I think we all are. Does it hurt you to speak?"

"Not at all," Tino said. "I am in constant pain, the worst I have ever felt in my life. It makes no difference. It's much better now, thanks." Under a light blanket he was in much contact with Mlle. de Rosière. The skin-tight Roman trousers which he was wearing at last, having lost some weight, were almost more than he had bargained for—he felt like some naughty Protestant image being carried in procession. When the time came to get out of the car, he must manage to keep hold of that blanket. . . .

"Then if it's all the same," Mary drawled, "would you mind telling me what danger you were referring to a moment ago? Or was it merely a supposition? I have heard drums before, and I feel in a position to suggest that people in underprivileged areas do not always *attack* after drumming."

"Oh, that isn't what I had in mind. I was just thinking—all those drums might be effective after all. They might drive the python out. He might come this way—see what I mean?" Tino's head languished to one side, beatific—St. Sebastian fulfilled with arrows.

"They all have to participate," Peter said, cautiously maneuvering the Land-Rover around a casually engineered turn.

"I'm a tough old woman. He wouldn't like me."

"The python's choice is like Divine Grace," Peter said, aware that the comparison would stir Mary to the depths—he saw her lips compress. "It is essentially enigmatic. No heart is too hard, no will is too tough. Pythons have a wonderful flow of digestive juices."

"I daresay they recognize certain limits—unlike the Deity," Mary said dryly. "I have observed large reptiles in the zoo, and not one of them looked big enough to swallow me. Is this one so exceptional?"

"It is." Peter glanced at her obliquely, hesitated, then, careful of his words: "One becomes quite malleable just before one is—ingested."

"I see." Mary turned a bit pale, and sat silently for a time. The drums were audible over the sound of the motor. It was as if the sky were a skin stretched over the valley, and the valley itself were a gigantic drum beaten by hands invisible to those within.

"It is forcible," said Mlle. de Rosière. When she spoke English her words carried something of the bottomless metaphysical style of certain arcane books through which she had attempted to learn the language while pursuing her Buddhist studies. Only her voice made it credible—it had a dark, crooning yet hesitant quality, as if she were half-creating, half-recalling poetry. To Tino, whatever she said was an original donation to the world of musical meaning. "The tambours—"

"Drums," Tino the pedagogue crooned back tenderly.

"The drums—are a danger esoteric to the soul. What unknown primitives in the forest have usurped partial control of my autonomic nervous system? What will they do, the tenebrous ones?"

"They are asking the god who sent the serpent to take him away, now they have been chastened."

"The tambours invade one with an excitation mysterious and inconsolable."

"You shivered! Are you cold? Don't be afraid. I—"

"You have named the emotion of once upon a time. In my heart I am not cold. I feel—Kaliya will not make an error."

Irene sat cold and stiff against Tino's other side, afraid to move lest the idea of the python take possession of her; for fear of adding to Tino's pain; for fear of bursting into tears. She should have been in the front seat with Peter. Instead she had taken Mary's place beside the invalid. How they all took one another's places! Mlle. de Rosière was taking Chanchal's place with Tino. Peter was taking Mlle. de Rosière's place at the Ashram—his belongings were strapped to the back of the Land-Rover; he was moving down there. Jim Chen was moving into Peter's room at Tino's house until Tino felt better. Only she, Irene, did not change places, because she had no place to exchange—like the Son of Man, no place to lay her head.

There were no drums at the Ashram itself; they would begin later that night when the students, the servants, and the nearer villagers celebrated the Krishna Puja; but from more distant villages reverberations of drums against the valley walls set up rhythms and counter-rhythms to create a sound as steady as that of the river itself. Perhaps the open doors and windows of the bungalow absorbed the shock of sound, for it was oddly quiet on the veranda. There a few people sat in wicker chairs, facing each other, or nothing, or everything, in silence, "after the manner of Friends." Although it was customary to speak during a Silent Meeting if one was convinced it was the Spirit that moved one, it sometimes took courage to overcome that doubt, to break that Silence.

With his eyes nearly closed, Peter sat and was aware. Whether his awareness was of the controversial kind that is designated by the term "clairvoyant," or the traveling kind ascribed to yogis, or merely the kind explained as common empathy that internalizes, as it were, the supposed thoughts and feelings of others, perhaps suggested by their movements and appearances, to say nothing of one's personal absorption in their histories, it did not at that moment occur to him to consider. Special indeed was the urgency that made him leave in abeyance his consciousness of himself as Peter the Separate, and identify with the psyches of others present, almost as if they were points of view in a multiple personality, his own. What he experienced was "true," in the sense that imaginative reality affects character more than does objective reality, so that to be at all real, one must use one's imagination to the full.

Lady Edith was in her big chair, her face highly rouged, her hair very white, gay bolsters around her to counter the aggressions of her skeleton. At first her hand clawed a bit at the arm of the chair, as if responding to the drums; then her head sank back and she smiled faintly. Although her face was too raddled, stretched over the false teeth that had not shrunk with the flesh, to tell the factual observer what went on within, Peter knew: By one device or another, such as the ruse of the Silent Meeting, she had got them all there, drawing her resources together for a final effort, to pray for the victory of the hunter over the python, of Krishna's godhood over Krishna's demonhood, cosmos over chaos, Ashram over jungle, quality over quantity, great over petty, Self over self. Thus—her last act—she in her turn seduced Peter who was nothing if not frail, nothing at all. With a shudder, he gave up. "The important thing," he felt her saying, "is the work—'not for the fruit of the action, but for the action itself.' Of course, there's only one thing to do with ripe fruit, that's to eat it, if you have any appetite by then—when the fruit and the action are one. . . . Now it can go on just as well without me. You form like clouds, not to take my place —nobody takes anybody else's place—but to come next, then next and next, like the rhythms of those drums. . . . I am not afraid. Do not be afraid. Not all griefs declare themselves. Not all joys are recognizable. Survive and thrive, Peter! Victory in the hunt!"

Sitting firmly upright, hands folded in her lap, Mary Nayler drew a deep breath, and Peter knew she was composing her mind and her body, accomplished Quakeress that she was, attempting to "center down," to withdraw further inward, contemplative, to wait upon the Inner Light; and he knew that she could not. Like the servants, like the children who watched discreetly from a distance, she was not yogini enough to shut out the bombardment of a violent world of sensations: the drums, the excitement of the puja with its confusing image of God as both python and python slayer —festive, incongruous as Death in a flamboyant shawl. Without intending to speak—a good test for Spirit—she spoke aloud in the Silent Meeting; and the Spirit assumed in the others present her own need for order, balance, symmetry, for "a sense of proportion."

She mentioned the three centuries in which Friends had met peacefully during various disturbances, such as History, to still the voices of self-will, to wait upon the Lord, which was to say, to listen for the voices of Truth—since Friends did not claim that Truth had only one voice; so that people of every faith and of no faith often meditated with Friends, without fear that their prejudices would be tampered with or held against them, Truth being, as it were, the opening of doors, not the closing. She spoke of the world as composed of many warring groups, each zealously dedicated to its own goals. If they could but meet, she said, as this group was meeting today, they might realize that their goals were similar, or if they were not quite similar, then at least they could be reconciled in the spirit of mutual tolerance, and wars would become a thing of the past. She spoke of brotherly love, of international understanding, of cultural exchange, of the meeting of East and West. Finally she spoke of the Ashram and of her concern to bring it to the attention of Arch Street Meeting when she returned to Philadelphia. The Spirit did not move her to recognize in words the existence of the python. Anything so immediate and so novel (to say nothing of its quasi-idolatrous character) could scarcely fail to have a disturbing effect upon the Meeting.

As Peter listened to the staid eloquence that he knew so well, he resolved anew that no Group would ever again enter the Republic of his individuality. To him, all groups were majorities whose sole function was to oppress him, not by excluding him necessarily, but by withholding individuals from him. Yet, feeling Indira's rest-lessness—she sat watchfully beside Lady Edith—he was suddenly apprehensive lest she miss the elusive greatness of his father's peo-ple, that was capable of referring obliquely to the Revolutionary War as "the prevailing commotion," and of ignoring not just the op-position between python and python slayer, but their unity also—there being only one immediacy, one emergency: the Eternal Now, to be dealt with by lifelong principles, not Maya images. Solitary introspection was so much the medium of Indira's race, he thought, that she must find herself unable immediately to grasp the principle of corporate meditation by which a type of Western people manage to utilize one another's presences as an aid to introversion.

As she looked out now through her long black lashes at the world of temporarily individuated spirits through which she must stride, she had a sense of the unseriousness of those opposites; which would not do at all; not in practice. Though one were nonattached, one must act as if one were attached, as if one's interests were de-pendent upon the slaying of Kaliya. That was the ancient difficulty; but without it, would the Wheel of Life turn? Probably it would after all. The concept itself was an act of thought, to which most Hindus were obstinately attached. . . . She smiled a little, a very little, unwillingly, for it was unseemly to betray a sense of uncom-municable realities, to luxuriate in comfortable perspectives which one could not share at will, even though they were there for everyone to actualize. . . . The old Quakeress, Mrs. Nayler—Mary Nayler— (One must not use titles with Quakers and Quakeresses. If one said Quakeress, why not say Directress? No, that was like Duchess. Quakeress and Duchess, but not Directress) —appeared to have adumbrations of a possible point of view, on account of her relativism; but there was so much that she did not understand about cultural variation. For instance, the Tibetan woman (apparently a shamanist) had absolutely no interest in reconciling her differences with anyone except Peter, but secretly scorned and hated them all—all except Peter; for she was a prisoner of *tamas*, obsessed by the senses, the body, her own and Peter's. Being without philosophy, she supposed him to be reducible to *tamas*. By what shameless methods would she go about reducing him? Women like that one, though unenlightened, were undoubtedly well versed in the lore which taught one how to deal with a man in such a way that he lost interest in freedom. Then he would no longer be a man, but only a mechanism.

Quietly, deliberately, Indira bit the inside of her cheek until she felt pain, then she stopped. Although she, who had embraced no man (except her brother, according to a custom so tender and delicate that only the honorable and purifiable in heart may understand it), had read the *Kama Sutra*—the Book of Love—in Sanskrit at the age of twelve, it was only now that she thought of applying it in her own interest. Almost immediately she rejected the idea, with the curious feeling that it had been somehow placed in her mind by Liliu Acquileia. It might be that Peter loved her, Indira, out of all the women in the world, but a fairly representative cross section of these appeared to love him also—if one could call it love—for a variety of reasons.

Feeling his presence again, she blushed at her own dishonesty and acknowledged that she was very jealous—so jealous that she would rather lose him to Kaliya than to Liliu Acquileia. Or so she felt at that moment. As he was aware? What was she, that he should be mindful of her? With great difficulty she fought down the desire to meet his gaze, for then her love would be known to all who saw, and that would be not only dangerous, but cruel. Inexpedient. There was not only Liliu Acquileia, who would know somehow, there was Irene Nayler—how beautiful she was, how splendid, and how unhappy! Even now Irene sat there, so very pale, her consciousness centered upon the Divine Atman, a look of ecstasy on her face. That was good, but when she returned—? Selfish interests—Peter —should not come between them. They would become friends. If Peter survived in spite of everything, perhaps Irene would be better for him. . . . So difficult to know other people, even people of one's own province, village, caste! How could one know people from other lands, with languages barely related to Sanskrit, with other ways of being? Yet there were ways (for Westerners this séance would be such a way) to break through the limits of place and time and zone in which one happened to have been born—so Peter had said—ways to transcend the conditions that determine those who are determined to be determined, ways to cut across Process at any point, regardless of other people and their karmas, meaning one's environment; for people were as tricky and magical as their thoughts, and in a split second could flicker into their opposites. Man might be an idea in the Divine Mind, but he was not a fixed idea. The Lord Krishna, ultimately inscrutable, was also capable of changing his mind without notice, without giving a reason, and ideas that seemed good and worthy to men—ideas such as the Ashram—might be turned under like rice stubble beneath the bullock plow, along with those who thought they were doing his work—so many—Ananda Mahadev, Lady Edith, Indira herself.

Involuntarily she looked out at the jungle. What leisurely choice was being made there even now? Peter! Her eyes sought his, and they exchanged the unguarded look. Only for a moment, then gently—for she had invited him—she withdrew from the outer marches of the soul and her expression became vestigial like a haiku note that might have suggested, without seeming to suggest, that she had gone, at dawn on the previous day, to the place of the Reclining Buddha, but would probably return before sunset on the following day. At that place she found Peter waiting for her.

Although Jim Chen had the habit of spinning on his own axis rather exclusively, and had a one-way communication system, Peter could scarcely avoid his orbit in that cramped space, time, and

zone; in any case Peter would have involved himself, out of dumb
respect for affliction, even if he had not assumed that whatever
was truly useful to his understanding would be good for the Ashram.
Furthermore, having persuaded Jim to connive at his own integra-
tion—thus, step by step, with growing fatalism, Peter grudgingly
accepted the role of Universal Father (the consequence of having
been a Cosmic Lover)—he was bound to see Jim through to the
end of this particular line. To his knowledge—so he had told Indira
—the question of the corruption of Gori Govinda was not so simple
as Liliu had represented it. Thanks to the varied uses to which Liliu
had put him, the boy was probably already more experienced than
Jim, certainly in more ways. It seemed likely that Liliu had used
him to gain power over Jim, indirectly over the Ashram, and over
Peter. . . .

It had taken courage for Jim to accept the invitation to return to
the Ashram, even for a visit on the present occasion; but as nobody
had yet made any formal charges against him, to stay away would
be to admit guilt. Moreover, to his grateful surprise, people were
standing by him like friends. They even regarded him as a victim,
and this rôle he could not resist. Peter had said to him, rather too
forcefully: "Either you are alive or you are dead. Anyone who tries
halfway measures can only lose face. Furthermore, you have contracted obligations to me which a dead man cannot fulfill." Upon
this, Jim had capitulated—so few people had cared enough about
him to compel his presence by bullying him in a personal way. It
gave him a gratifying sense of limitations, something approaching
orderliness. . . .

Jim began to pay attention to the Silent Meeting in which he was
sitting, without knowing how to participate, without quite caring to.
The Chinese never could get into a trance, he thought cheerfully.
Hullo, Peter. Hullo, Irene, you poor fertile white thing. What did
we do to you, Peter and I? Wish I'd been both of you. No overlap-
ping of function, no duplication of structure. I'd miss that, I think.
Maybe I'm conservative. I wonder? I condescend to lie all spread
out in my Peter-self so the goddess Irene, my female emanation,
can worship my gorgeousness. I am really worshiping myself. I

get tired of that. I give her free will. My shakti is overawed. I am
too much for her. I feel sorry for her, but there's only one thing
to do—sacrifice her: drive this noble beast into the cage God
made for it. Ugh! What an arrangement! Can't see! No, wait.
God has carefully reversed a man so that he will fit another man
and be worthy of his masculine splendor, and this man who has
been chosen for his virtues to suffer the reversal of his apparatus
—to receive the one who has been allowed, for his kingliness, to
remain kingly—the man chosen to bear the consequences of this
perilous poking, is called *woman*—perhaps because of the reversal,
more than the poking and the bearing, the man suffers woe, hence
woe-man, or wo-man; but it is such a great honor to be turned thus
outside—in and drawn and blown up a trifle this way and that, that
he—or "she," as he is now called—ceases feeling shame at the
indignity as soon as he is well and truly poked: he knows now that
he, and he alone, can solace the Alone One—that he (or "she")
is needed for the perfection of the godhood. . . . "I don't deserve
it!" she cries with incredulous gratitude at this gesture of restora-
tion. "But it is yours," I reply with Oriental magnanimity, and
again I give it to her, for a god must give and give and give, must
put cosmos where there was chaos, something where there was
nothing. . . .

Thus Jim Chen, who had lived to one side, felt toward Irene,
who had lived to another side, something more than the conde-
scension he needed to feel, something more than sympathy; a movement of mysterious ease such as he had not felt before, and the
illogical beginning of—not joy but perhaps confidence. It was immediate to him; that is, it was mystical, in the sense that he was
not aware of mediation, say, of Peter in the unsounded wisdom of
his hindsight, to say nothing of another possible intruder. . . .

Irene listened, without hearing, to the well-worn ideals of Mary
Nayler, which she shared on principle, as she shared the same
blood, but could no longer feel. The drums of Krishna broke through
the silent niche in which she sat. Perfumes followed, the odors of
Indian flowers, lurking suggestively—at night they were scandalous.

It had been a mistake to train her attention in this direction; but she had read and observed that the sense of smell was very important in the East, and she knew that one had to bridge the gap in cultural minutiae as well as in the larger differences between East and West. To her, smell had always been the lowest sense because it was dissociated from form and from metaphysical content. She could no more yield to it than she could to a snake. One had little control over it. She did not like *any* odors at all. Liking them less and less, in fact, she had become increasingly sensitive to them. For instance, there had been a tree, the odor of which had nearly made her faint: a tree with a thick, smooth trunk and gigantic limbs, covered with flame-red flowers that were very big and perfect—circlets—not coarse but pure, like big shy maidens. At least she associated the smell with what had made her giddy, which was the sun again, or rather that and the blow of guilt (which she could ill afford at that moment) at having unwittingly trespassed, with her shoes on, at the shrine of a little dancing idol, and there was the priest himself sitting right there. Coming suddenly out of the sun into the shade, she had not seen him at first. In her confusion she had done something she blushed to think of, even though she had subsequently brought it before the Savior: Not content with taking her shoes off, she had knelt down before that graven image, not really to pray, but to apologize, to show that she respected other people's religions, they being all essentially the same. Only in kneeling had she noticed that the priest was quite naked, young and beautiful—something feminine about him that made him all the more seductive, because it was so disarming! He had smiled at her out of enormously large, wide-set eyes, as great age might smile at an infant sprawling there. Irene had run away. That was—when and where? How foolish! She could not remember at the moment. The more she tried to remember, the more dreamlike it seemed. The line between reality and illusion was wavering, serpentine—not a comforting experience. If it persisted, she would have to discuss the matter with Dr. Hoskins, a Friend who was generally conceded to have had some success in dealing with cases of confusion. . . .

It would only be later that she would know whether she had

actually got up and left the Meeting and wandered off by herself in physical space, or whether, in her murky condition, she had accidentally fallen through the barrier of individuated consciousness, to move about in the landscape of another, infinitely composite, not-specifically-Anglo-Saxon mind. . . . As if obsessed by a fatal tryst with the sun, she stumbled interminably down terraces of identical small tea trees, flat-topped ones (or perhaps they were bushes) interlacing at the top, whereon appeared, this being the monsoon month, the first succulent pale shoots with tiny, curled hairs on the tips. She who had been so sure-footed, lost her footing and fell, crushing tiny blue flowers, which she attempted vainly to smooth out, to straighten up. . . . Out of the ferment of leaves, a flock of brown and violet titmice, the size of thimbles, observed her activities. It might have been thought that they were compassionate, if they had not had gimlet eyes. Like sentries they swarmed around a young child in the tea bushes: a half-caste idiot, so lovely that he was malformed, holding up a white champak flower as if inviting Irene to study it in order that she might become like himself. The hands were like crumpled pale brown orchids; the eyes were as those of one who is loath to look away from a horizon. Encountered by a white rock in Pennsylvania; by a river where there were boys swimming, and they brought up a white snake; on a ship torpedoed at midnight or a little thereafter; on a certain day among Huguenots; or one quiet First Day in a delirium—somewhere, sometime, this meeting had already happened. . . . The used flower dropped to the ground, as it would have anyway, but the hand remained up as in the mudra of teaching.

"Child, what is it that you know?" Her voice trembled with the ritual secret of the departing herons.

"*You know*," the echoing child, his voice deep as a well.

"Tell me what it is you know!"

"*It is. You know.*" As if unaccustomed to the force of gravity, he staggered to his feet, his arms jerked upward, he began to leap, this side and that, without leaving the ground. And all through the spastic dance, his eyes remained fixed on hers in smiling recognition. The movements, clumsy and wooden at first, became more flowing, sinuous, like the dancing of Manipur. So the boy moved

away, looking back at her half-listlessly, and she followed. . . .
On and on, down the long lane of bird-filled trees whose shadows
were beginning to merge, she went stumbling and slipping, after
the tarantist. The passive leaves, stirred by no wind, brooded over
the darkening ground. The air was filled with the murmuring of
birds and the sound of their wings. All manner of birds, they went
seeking one another everywhere. Never had she seen so many
—thousands upon thousands rising about her, rising, winnowing
up in relays, whirling and settling in broken patterns over the tea
bushes, on trees and ground, on one another, resting for seconds
on one another's wings. . . . There below them she crouched, her
hands hanging like the idiot's hands, and she glimpsed her body
walking through the pit Chaos, coals underfoot and swords, light
years of limbless striving with that armless multitude that gangs
in and out of the soul; fighting, falling, slimed over; and her intellect
was only a whirling fever, minuscule threads of fire pursued by
ashes, racing mad into carbon blackness, as when a crumpled cloth
is burned: all dark but for the sullen and improvident fibers. "Lord,
the time is at hand when I shall have no conduit for my life, and
the shadows shall claim me, impure and unperformed and unde-
livered of soul. *I cannot live unless Thou are there!*"

"I am here as well as there." He whom she had seen darkly under
a flowering tree, stood now on the mountainside, between the sun
and her; and all the birds had risen up into the air and were wheel-
ing about in a dense and rapid circle, the sound of their wings and
their songs increasingly intense and as it were luminous.

"I cannot look upon Thee!"

"There is no need. I look upon thee."

"Art Thou the power of the sun, or the Inner Light? Art Thou
Christ?"

"I am sun and moon; I am the Inner Light and the Inner Darkness that knoweth it well, Christ and Krishna, Ananta the Endless
One, Bhrigu the Sage, Yama, the Idiot, Pitar the Lover. Wilt thou
have me?"

"Lord—have Thee?"

"Didst thou not call Me through the bitter seed of *sahaja*, through
Pitar's loins?"

"Lord, I am not worthy!"

"Thou hast the perfection of the unopened eye, and thou didst call out to me from Hell, so that I could not resist thee. Thou shalt be my birthplace."

"What shall I do, Lord?"

"Thou wilt forget like the others, since I am only God. It is much better that way, my mother."

From the jungle edge nearest the bungalow, in a thick clump of plantain trees, Liliu watched intently. Of the quiet group on the veranda, only two persons interested her: Peter and—the woman. It was not Irene—the pale sorceress sat there in a trance, her mouth open, showing the whites of her eyes: a woman who could do that did not need a man. No, it was the Kashmiri woman who had exchanged a look with Peter that had been sufficiently informative. . . . Then that was the way it was. It was as if Liliu Acquileia had had prior knowledge of it, and was merely reluctant to recognize it. She was slow to respond, tenacious once she had committed herself, not because she was essentially dull, but because she had an underlying contempt for the persons involved, and was loath to consider the issues that arose from them, did not care enough for their souls to torture them. Now she was particularly piqued because she had not done justice to Indira. For one instant she had seen her through Peter's eyes, and she saw that Indira was very powerful by reason of her beauty, her wit, her scope—all of them greater than Liliu's, greater also than Irene's. And courage! By taking the Chinese back—for there was Chen seated in the midst of them—Indira had defied Liliu, flouted her, declared war. Why had Liliu so underestimated that slim, fiery girl? An error, wishful perhaps. She had believed Peter and Indira to be enemies. Her informant, Gori Govinda, had strengthened this belief from the first. Deliberately the brat had misled her because of his sullen, secret hatred of her. He would be punished suitably. She knew, for instance, of a certain boy brothel—and yet, that might not be completely repugnant to him. . . . In any case, Indira would have to be dissuaded in some definitive way—the simpler, the better—and that was somehow more troublesome than all that had gone before, because of the energy Liliu had already expended on secondary objectives: not wasted, exactly, but diffused. Where would it end? How could she be sure? There might be other women. And there was a scroll, a sacred scroll, which she felt she must destroy. . . . Sometimes, when closing in upon a dangerous quarry, a hunter, even an experienced one, tends to be impetuous. Increasingly desensitized, tired out by the long, nerve-racking effort required in stalking, he is at his most vulnerable. Liliu knew this, in her way; but it was hard, very hard, to make a new plan now, to encounter a fresh adversary at the moment when victory had seemed almost certain. . . . The knife she carried was suitable for surprise attack, but only on certain types of animal, at the right time and the right place. It would not do to stay in the jungle after nightfall, either, the python being a nocturnal creature. . . .

snake shoot at tashiling

"And likerous folk, after that they ben dede,
Shul whirle aboute the erthe alwey in peyne,
Tyl many a world be passed, out of drede."
                              —*The Parlement of Fowles*

fifteen

Lanterns hanging in the mango grove dimly illumined a circle a hundred feet across. Students and villagers sat cross-legged on mats, facing one edge of the circle where the light was brightest. The ground, packed hard and swept clean of dust, was the stage. The drums of the valley were focused on the drums here, on tablas, drone, tambura. Three boys played them, and played them well, for their music teacher during the winter had been the great Ostad Ala-uddin, master of the sarodh, who had promised Ananda Mahadev that he would come to the Ashram for a few months each year. A blond boy played the tablas, beginning with a slow, muffled beat, passing into occasional sallies of vibrant, ringing slaps, bare hand on hide, overt, daring the strict limits of the medium—the round drum and the long drum. He wore only the white ceremonial dhoti, like the other boys. As he worked away at the tablas, his pale, slender body, still half in childhood, arched and bucked, his green eyes languished or glowed "dangerously," all in the ancient convention handed down to him by the great court musician. . . . Mary Nayler, on a little wicker stool at the edge of the circle, observed these writhings with unshakable, unseeing tolerance, while Irene, seated beside her, gazed fixedly into the dark branches of the mango trees overhead. The villagers, illiterate but not innocent, smirked approvingly; theirs was not the cultural standard which prescribes asceticism for the young.

An unsmiling girl, seated cross-legged, swaying back and forth in unpredictable sympathies with the drum rhythms, was singing in a pure, keening, brazen voice, sliding into quarter-notes and out again, free from any vibrato. It had begun inaudibly, one did not know

237

quite when or where: perhaps, one thought, in the murmurings of
the audience or in the distant, muffled drums, or in the jungle itself,
and then one was hearing it and seeing the singer. The words were
from the Sanskrit drama Śakuntala, in which the king "feels long-
ings that are illogical," since kings weep only to beautify their eyes
—then he remembers friendships of another birth, "which remain
clinging to the soul, and are of the soul." Under or over the mind
of listeners trained in oblique approaches, there was a reference,
purposely obscure and doubtful, to the present occasion, and spe-
cifically—the king being, among other things, a hunter with a
troubled dharma—to Pitar.

The song stopped or was abandoned, as if it had been interrupted by some thought of the singer, who would now turn to other
enterprises, equally indeterminate, which had been going on all
along, to which she could now refer the attention of the audience
as to equally important parts of the same endless undertaking.
And the other aspect of this activity, so almost languidly differentiated as a gesture toward human limitations, was a dance or a
dancing that was even then being performed by five girls in saris.
Little silver bells on their ankles tinkled with exact rhythms as they
moved. It was a decorative, sinuous dance of Manipur. Their arms
and hands seemed to flow like water and snakes, their saris rippling
around them, their bare feet gliding. All their movements were variations upon the horizontal, but they could almost as well have been
variations upon the vertical, both being curves whose logic is the
circle and therefore all-embracing. So the dance transpired, as it
were, like the music, without an introduction, without a climax even
in the accompaniment of the drums and strings—tablas, sitar, sarodh.
It was as if everything, by the curious faculty of seeming peripheral,
gracefully negative—neti, neti, not this, not that, not here, not there,
not I—referred to a center that must not be mentioned or even
looked at overtly, although everyone took it for granted—like the
early Buddhist paintings and sculpture in which the outward form
of the Buddha was not portrayed, but a vacant place was left, and
sometimes two footprints. . . .

Dr. Bhattacharya was playing the flute, other teachers the sitar,
the sarodh, the tambura. This would be an exacting performance,

pedagogical in nature, presented by the adults of the Ashram as their single offering. Indira herself was dancing the classical role of Krishna appearing before King Arjuna on the field of battle, as set forth in the *Bhagavad-Gita*. She wore a blouse of crimson silk. Blue silk trousers, in the Punjabi style, were gathered in at her ankles by circlets of little gold bells. Bangles, gold and jeweled, tinkled on her arms. A headdress of rubies in gold, with a flame-colored crest like that of the krishnachura flower, made her appear very tall. Between her eyebrows gleamed the jeweled caste mark. Just before she began, she gave Peter a steady, compelling look which said, before everyone: "This is for you, Pitar, hunter, guru!"

Stamping, leaping, whirling, Indira-Krishna was dancing with the controlled violence, the vertical movements of Kathakali, the masculine dance, enjoining action, determination, bravery. The hands with long, jeweled nails of silver attached to the fingers, danced like attendant spirits, narrating by means of the mudras, the hand language. The face also danced, the great dark eyes, glowing in a fullness of life, widening, narrowing, rolling or flashing supernaturally, the eyebrows soaring, writhing, according to strict rules of the dance. The head, weaving back and forth on the slender neck, affirmed the serpent principle in the god:

King Arjuna on the battlefield, "the field of dharma," in the timeless moment before the two armies clash, feels his resolve weakening. Then his charioteer reveals himself as none other than Krishna, Lord of the Universe. Restraining rather than asserting his infinite power, hypnotically urgent, yet insisting only that Arjuna follow out the logic of his own free will, Krishna restricts himself to the mode of address which is appropriate to the limitations of Arjuna: Man is god and god is man and all things else. The collective unconscious, which is really infinite self-knowledge forgotten—not a receptacle, but the universe—unites mankind as one, and yet they must forget that they are all-encompassing, must rebel and strive, must fight, unfolding life in the midst of death, intensifying life for the sake of life. To the hero's objections Krishna replies with a vision of universal destiny in which all are involved, some to a greater extent, others to a smaller, but each "supremely with respect to him-

self," and each according to his lights. Each is a free prisoner of
himself, for the only bars are the bars of his self-will. It is more important that he exercise his franchise than that he be "right." Why?
Most people fight without being aware that it is against themselves
that they are fighting. The human race may be in love with itself,
Arjuna admits, but wars—are they mere lovers' quarrels? And why
should he fight against the opposing army when it is only a projec-
tion of himself? Again the vision of creation, of destiny, the life
principle unfolding itself to itself by a process which involves the
exhaustion of alternatives, the strife and reconciliation of its own
seeming opposites. But knowing this, how can Arjuna fight for a completely relative "victory" in good faith, with the hot blood of a warrior? It is easy. Sooner than he now thinks possible, he will forget
that he is to act "with detachment," for philosophy is indeed as weakening to the fighter as disaffection for one's own cause, or sympathy
for the enemy. . . . At Arjuna's command, Krishna the charioteer
gathered up the reins, and they went forth into battle.

Many were the levels of understanding possible to the viewers,
the silent participants of the dance, ranging from the purely sensuous, through the erotic—young Krishna being in fact the Indian
Eros—to the most abstruse of metaphysical interpretations, and in
other directions, to lively misunderstanding, more fertile in its consequences than mere knowledge.

The dance was finished, Indira had slipped unobtrusively into the
wings—darkness—the audience was swaying and nodding, calling
out their approval: "*Sadhu! Sadhu!* Well done!" The drums and the
other instruments had paused, but it was uncertain whether they
had stopped entirely or merely subsided a little. Gradually they became audible again over the murmuring of near voices and distant
drums, and again the unsmiling girl with the keening voice was
singing something from the old play. The reference to Indira, the
new director, was more than likely in the benediction of the Spirits
of the Air upon Śakuntala: "May her path be frequently surprised
by blue lotus lakes, the sun's power disciplined by shade trees, the
dust underfoot springy and suave as pollen of lotuses—may her way
be auspicious, under the gentler breezes."

During Indira's dance, one of the spectators who sat among the villagers let the shawl fall slowly from his head, as if his reason for concealment was no longer important to him. It was Gori Govinda. All through the dance, with increasing intensity, he had stared at Indira, as absorbed in her as King Arjuna at the revelations of Lord Krishna. Now, with a little open-mouthed smile on the side of his slightly vulpine face, he gazed blindly at the place where Indira had danced. When the song was over, he went quietly out of the audience. Peter had left his seat and was standing, his arms folded, on the outskirts of the crowd, brooding over the heads of a group of villagers, when he felt in the darkness something soft brushing his bare toes. It was Gori Govinda "taking the dust" from his feet, placing it on his own head—*pranam*, the ritual abasement, gesture of the savage youth before the civilization of age: a chastening experience at best, and most pleasant for both parties, when properly done.

"Why do you do that?" Peter chid him according to the same ritual, pulling him up and rocking him gently back and forth. He stopped, seeing the boy's pallor and odd, exalted smile.

"Elder brother, come!" Gori said in a voice that ended in a creak, for his voice was changing, and he led Peter away, farther into the mango grove, where it was dark and they could hear once again the drums across the river and at the farther ends of the valley. Gori opened his mouth to speak, but no words came—only a slight choking sound, and then, quite unexpectedly, a sort of howl, not loud but eerie enough to make one's skin prickle. Peter laid hold of him to comfort him, and the boy buried his face in Peter's abdomen to muffle his howls. "Pitar!" Gori sobbed at length, and Peter thought in passing that here was the origin of his name in these parts. "You are my father!" And Peter admitted that that was so, in a sense, in the sense that he was his elder brother, which was to say, his friend and adviser, and that he felt responsible for him. "You are my mother!" That was going rather far, but, yes, he would concede that also, since everyone had a woman for a mother and a man for a father, and so was of mixed ancestry, although for practical purposes it was probably better in the long run if one chose sides.

Gori Govinda, at that vulnerable age when conversions, evil and

good, are most likely to strike, had beheld for the first time in
Indira's dance—mistakenly or not—the field of dharma and his own
role therein, so that he wept to think of all that he had done wrong,
and what he must do to make it right, even though it meant his
death; for Liliu would surely kill him, and perhaps not in a simple
way. His sister was mad, he told Pitar. No one knew it as well as he,
Gori Govinda, whose body bore old and fresh scars from her, like a
favorite tree on which a tigress sharpens her claws. Lady Edith's
cook, who was now dead—Liliu had bribed him to give Lady Edith
certain honey cakes, which Gori had to bring him, and these honey
cakes had a spell in them that had made Lady Edith summon Pitar—
but Lady Edith, whom even Gori loved as the Great *Ma*, mother
of them all—she was dying! And Liliu had forced him to go to Jim
Chen in the night, and Gori would almost rather die than betray
him—but he had done it, he and Liliu, by means of certain letters,
only not for money this time. And now it was Indira, because she was
beautiful and the god dwelt in her. Let Pitar take her away, far
away, now, this very night!

The drums had stopped, first those up the valley, then those down
the valley, then those across the river, and just now the ones at
the Ashram itself. The silence was deafening, confusing, as if life
had been defined and compressed into its various forms by that continuous noise, and then, the noise ceasing, the pressures of atmosphere and gravity had been removed and life floated free of its
formative limits, in imminent danger of explosion. Peter strained
to catch the sound of conch shells, but he heard only the muttering
of the people who had been at the entertainment. They were moving away quickly in the directions of their homes. In their sudden
dispersal there was something oddly subdued and grave. The wailing of a baby pierced the air for only a moment, then it too hushed.
As Peter went rapidly back to the lighted area, Jim Chen ran up to
him, followed at a distance by a village boy in tight-calved Nepali
trousers, a black, embroidered skullcap, and a long shirt that hung
outside the trousers.

"It's come." Jim's face was gray. He was shaking violently.

"How do you know? It's not time for him yet—it must be another
one."

"I saw him—down by the river. He was d-drinking." Jim's voice cracked with fear. "It was the most God-awful thing I've ever s-seen in my life!"

Peter hesitated for a moment. The village boy appeared less frightened than Jim, through fatalism or perhaps only through greater sophistication in the ways of the green world. Jim might have been startled, and one naturally tends to enlarge upon that which causes an unwonted loss of composure.

"There are many pythons in the woods," said Peter. "Some are bigger than others. There's only one man-eater in the valley."

"He was sixty feet long," Jim Chen said, looking him straight in the eye.

"Forty feet is a good length," said Peter. "Moonlight is deceptive, and it's only a half-moon tonight—hard to judge lengths, even by a full moon."

"Sixty feet," Jim repeated emphatically in a clipped voice which he had got under control with the help of anger. "I can judge lengths, if you can't. I tell you—it's a monster!"

"I don't doubt you. All I say is, big pythons always look endless in the moonlight."

"All right, ask *him*," Jim rapped out, indicating the village boy. "Ask him. I can't speak his language."

Peter asked the boy in Nepali, and the boy said that the snake was as long as the river, because he was Kaliya. He had seen many pythons, he said, and this one was the king of all serpents, whom Pitar had come to meet.

Then Indira was there, and Gori Govinda was suddenly at her feet. "*Ma, O Ma!*" he cried, and could say no more. The touch of her fingers lifted him up. For a second they faced each other in a relation at once formal and intimate. Both of them seemed to gather strength from his unexpected utterance of the formula—he had called her Mother, a title that cannot be merely honorific, but reminds the woman that she—she also—is Shri Lakshmi, Magna Mater, servant and protectress, forgiving all.

"*Chela,*" she said, lightly placing her hand on his head. "My son, I have waited for you." Then turning to Peter without relinquishing the boy, she said: "Kaliya has come early. We must go meet him. I have asked your aunt and Irene and the others to remain here tonight."

Peter closed his eyes for a moment, and all the elements that had been heaping up in his mind fell away into their places, because of a special faculty he had for withdrawing the arbitrary supports of things—his ideas.

"I'd like everyone to follow my instructions," he said.

"We have understood," Indira said. "Wherever Kaliya appears in the valley, conch shells will sound, and all those who have guns will go there at once."

"Now there are three guns, not five," said Peter, "and one should stay at the Ashram. Indira, I am asking you to remain. Jim will go with me."

"I must tell you," she replied earnestly, "that yesterday my shooting improved, and Kaliya will not come to the Ashram—will he?"

"The best way to find out is to sit on the veranda, and wait. Kindly do that."

"You think I would be in your way?"

"I do—sorry to be blunt, but there's no time."

"Very well." There was a note of exasperation in her voice.

"Another thing: I wish you'd stay close to Lady Edith and my aunt and Irene, and keep Gori Govinda with you. Gori thinks his sister means to harm you tonight. If you'll all stay together, there may not be any danger—but don't take risks."

"You do not believe this!"

"I don't know. Will you please do what I ask you?"

Indira shook her head in disbelief, but at the same time she made a gesture of obedience as Peter turned to go. They did not say good-bye.

All available lights would burn tonight, not only at the Ashram but also in the tiny villages along the valley. All the students, girls and boys alike, would spend the night in the boys' dormitory, for the sake of companionship and greater protection. Here, with the teachers present, they would be allowed to sit up to listen to music as late as they pleased, since no one would really sleep tonight anyway. It was hoped that fatigue would make them sleep eventually, in spite of the lights. Behind locked doors the students played and listened to music and to stories of Krishna and Radha, Rama and Sita, Nala and Damayanti, and stories of La Fontaine which, Mlle. de Rosière told them, came out of the *Dhammapada* Prakrit into Sanskrit, from Sanskrit into Persian, Persian to Arabic, Arabic to Hebrew, thence into Greek and Latin and into the vernaculars of Europe. But there were no stories of snakes that night. From time to time a hush fell over them and they cocked their ears at the windows without approaching them—the wooden bars on them were not built to withstand a really determined beast of any size.

The valley was silent as a lamasery full of scrolls, before the reading begins. Puja was over. In the three villages another kind of activity had begun, another phase of the ritual, the infinite politics of prayer: prayer to Krishna, to his effect-emanations, to his cause-emanations, such as Vishnu, his source-emanation, who sent him down to earth to protect, to punish, to moderate evil and good; to Laksmi, to Shiva, to Brahman; prayers also to Adi-Buddha, to Padmapani; prayers to Christ, to the Virgin Mary—this in the household of a little family of Untouchables—Harijan, "God's People"—who served as sweepers in the south end of the valley; in Kedar's village, at the north end of the valley, they offered prayers and bribes to a little fat Earth Mother whose fruitful, benign, yet stern visage was that of Queen Victoria—a relic from the days of the East India Company. Everywhere people preferred to remain with people, preferred, in short, anything but wandering abroad, alone.

The servants at the Ashram were armed with Kukris, hoes, spears; but their morale was not of a nature to lead them into provocative action. They huddled together under an electric light, between the dormitories and the bungalow, not so close to the edge of the jungle as to promise an immediate meal to Kaliya, but far enough from the buildings to convey the impression that they stood between the inhabitants and danger.

The sandy place by the river where Jim and the villager had seen Kaliya was smoothed as by a giant hand, in a swerving pattern, steady and deep. It came from the jungle and it went back into the jungle, and disappeared. Peter flashed his electric torch upward into the branches. It was dark and forbidding. Jim's torch wavered uncertainly through the underbrush.

"Pete"—Jim's voice was like the rattle of a dead leaf in a little breeze—"don't count on me."

Peter did not look at him, but held out his hand in back of him, toward Jim. "Feel," he said. Jim felt. The hand was icy cold and wet with sweat, and it gripped Jim's hand convulsively. "Are you as scared as that?"

"Yes."

"O.K., I won't count on you." Grimly Peter started back toward the Ashram.

"Where are you going?" Jim was nearly breathing down his neck.

"After the bait, of course. I couldn't count on the servants either."

"Shall I bring it?" Jim asked.

"Fine! The goat in the barn—remember?—with the rope."

"With the rope. Right."

"Snug, not too tight. While you're gone, I'll work on a *machan* in one of those trees."

"A *machan*. Right. . . . A goat—for Kaliya?"

"Man-eaters associate goats with people."

"People—right."

"I'm going to sit up for him," Peter said—he wished Jim would not say "right"—the fright behind it was catching.

"Right."

"Bring the goat," Peter said gruffly, turning away. "If I'm not here when you get back, wait for me there by the river—O.K.?"

"O.K.—only, what if he hears the goat?"

"You mean, while you're leading it?"

"Yes."

"Shoot him. Let him get close, switch on your gun-torch, and shoot him. Remember, the bigger he is, the more accurately you have to shoot to kill him, not merely to wound him."

"Pete! I—I forgot what you told me! What shall I aim at?"

"The head," said Peter. "Aim at the head, or the backbone just behind the head. That part will be steady. Hit him there and you'll stop him."

"What if it doesn't stop him?"

Peter laid his hand on Jim's double-barrel rifle, which was like his own. A bullet weighing 480 grams, with 85 grams of cordite behind it, would leave the barrel at a muzzle velocity of 2,200 feet a second, developing 5,170 pounds of energy—of this he reminded Jim. Two of these bullets could be fired in very rapid succession, the gun being in effect a double rifle, coming up to the shoulder like a shotgun for short-range snap shooting. "This will stop or kill any creature known to me," said Peter. "This"—he indicated the electric torch attached to the barrels—"is considered unsporting. I can never be a sport, because I have night vision. Also, I expect to use my torch. Use yours."

Jim faded away down the river, and Peter entered the jungle. Silently, very slowly, he proceeded up an animal trail, stooping under interlacings of sodden foliage in darkness so deep that that night vision, which depended on ever so little light, was not of much use. Unknowingly the hunter adapted himself to the character of the hunted. In the movement of Peter's body, as he put himself in the other's place, there was a very slight change, a fluency, a graceful slow steadiness and purposefulness such as he imagined, or rather felt, to be the same as that of Kaliya upon leaving the river.

Overhead there was a stirring of the branches as a breeze wandered fitfully over the forest, swirled up by the seething of the river. Mostly it was silent; for when Kaliya hunts, all other creatures make themselves very inconspicuous. When the breeze had passed there was only a faint rustling, the soft dripping of the trees, the compassionate, rooted ones, *lacrimae rerum*, for the precarious destinies of those who move over the face of the earth. The moonlight pierced through the tangle of vegetation into a little clearing. Without moving his head very much this way and that—peripheral vision being more valuable at night than in the daytime—Peter continued to survey the dark branches above him: junipers, screw pines, larches, virile tufts of moss hanging from the underside of every branch, trailing creepers binding the trees together—thick cables which he could easily mistake for Kaliya; worse, he could mistake Kaliya for one of them. It had happened often: a great "vine" dropped on a man, whipped itself about him, and began to prepare him. . . .

On the edge of the clearing three junipers stood choked together by coils of vines in which orchids had sprouted, forming a heavy mass about fifteen feet from the ground. This would be the place for the *machan,* provided it was not already inhabited. Peter considered for a long moment, listening and studying the surrounding branches as well as the terrain. Removing his shirt, he folded it over his gun, which he leaned against the base of one of the three trees he had elected to climb. The shirt would keep moisture from dripping down the gun barrel. Again he paused and listened; then, kicking off his sandals and making sure the hunting knife in his belt came freely out of its sheath, he worked his way slowly up the tree, using a vine as a rope. Orchids brushed his face. Parting these and the latas, he inspected the inside of the dense clump of foliage. Nothing attacked him or warned him off, so he pulled himself in and looked about him. Only a little work would be required to make the hunter's nest. As silently as possible, he cut off foliage from above, which obstructed the rays of the moon, and arranged it around and under him, it being more important to have light on the sights than on the target, but also necessary to conceal the hunter. Pulling small branches together, he secured them by a rough weaving of vines. This would do well enough for a seat, provided Kaliya did not delay too long in coming to investigate the goat, which would be visible in the clearing, from the *machan.* Swiftly Peter slid down the tree, put on his damp shirt, and went back along the animal trail toward the river, feeling his way where he could not see, by something of the blind man's subtle intelligence of proximities, to whom space is palpable. . . .

Perched on a rock by the river, Jim Chen cuddled his rifle. The goat was tethered to another rock by a twenty-foot rope. It bleated unhappily. Peter untied it.

"I'll be up a tree over there, if you want me," Peter said leading the reluctant goat toward the jungle. "Don't come, though. Call, if you have to, and I'll come to you."

"Shall I stay here?"

"Suit yourself," said Peter. "I think you should know, I don't really have much of a plan, except for myself."

"No plan!"

"Not really. I didn't want to upset anybody, but there is no standard technique for hunting pythons at night. They feed so infrequently, you never know where they'll be, and they don't come back to a kill the way a tiger does. On the other hand, they don't travel far between kills."

"But the goat—the *machan!*"

"The goat's supposed to attract Kaliya to me. You see, if I make noises myself, I won't be able to concentrate on my surroundings. My problem will be to watch and listen to everything at once. He could come through the underbrush, or he could come through the upper branches, behind me."

"Good God!"

"You see," said Peter, "there's an element of uncertainty, both for him and for me. I believe in giving myself a chance. You, the other night—you were conservative, weren't you? Killing yourself! That's taking no chances whatsoever, playing it absolutely safe!"

"I'm not here to discuss that," Jim said brusquely. "Any objection if I join you?"

"That was our agreement. . . . You know that narrow strip of jungle between the river and the little swamp, down toward the Ashram? You'll find a fallen tree there. If you take cover behind it, you might intercept him if he goes down the valley."

"I'll be there."

"Keep an eye on the swamp, too," Peter called after him. "Good luck!"

"I know what you mean," Jim replied softly. "So long, Dad."

The goat set up a considerable resistance to entering the jungle. Bleating horribly, it kept trying to bolt. Grimly Peter dragged it along, then he picked it up in his arms and carried it until he came once again to the *machan*. In the middle of the little clearing he tethered the goat to a stout root. Slinging his gun and sandals over his shoulder by means of a strap, he climbed up the tree into the *machan*, and prepared to sit up for Kaliya. First he made sure that he had a clear view of the goat through the leaves and that the moonlight fell directly on his sights; then he became motionless—or nearly so, since he had to watch behind him. Kaliya could approach quite noiselessly through the branches and seize him as if he were a monkey, the favorite food of most pythons. Perhaps Kaliya, because of his greater size, had simply graduated from monkeys to men, seeing their close kinship and the correspondingly greater nutriment in the latter. . . .

The piteous bleating of the goat penetrated deep into the listening jungle, as Peter had intended it should; unknowingly it was calling to Kaliya: "Come, get your man!" Those cries would be hard for Peter to bear for any great length of time. The poor scapegoat felt grossly abused, abandoned and betrayed by those who had pretended to be his friends. Were it only possible to explain to him the service he was rendering, Peter thought, the tether might not be necessary, would indeed be unworthy of his station. In that case, though, his bleating would have a rhetorical or specious quality at which Kaliya might be justifiably suspicious.

Before long Peter was able to distinguish clearly between two levels of sound: the racket made by the goat, and the noises of the jungle. Although he could not shut out the former, he heard it with a separate part of his consciousness, which held it up, as it were, like a canopy, while the rest of him listened and watched and felt for the announcement of Kaliya. At every unaccountable sound, every movement of leaves or branches, his senses strained to know what it was. From time to time he wiped his palms on his shorts. The gun barrel, which easily became slippery with sweat, he wiped with a handkerchief. With his legs half crossed, half bent, loosely gripping a branch, he waited. After fifteen minutes he wished he had devoted a little more time to the shaping of the *machan*. The branches and vines made an inexorable cross on his fundament, regardless of which way he sat. Insects also he endured, of which the worst were a few tiny gnats that were obsessed by the possibility of getting at his brain through his ears. One of them went into his eye, thereby reducing his fractional vision by half, for some time.

An hour went by, then another hour. The moon was nearing the mountain behind which it would soon disappear, leaving the valley in almost total darkness. Peter squirmed and swore silently. On the back of his neck was a knot of nerves that seemed to be trying to form itself into a large eye, and like all changes it was painful. The bleating of the goat had taken on a mechanical, shattering tone.

Too much time was passing. What was holding Kaliya back? Merely
the fact that he was a man-eater, and had absolutely no interest in
goats? Either Peter had overestimated Kaliya's judgment in assuming that he would associate the bleating goat with a human attendant, or he had underestimated it. In a short while now it would
be so dark that his chances of sighting the python before the python
sighted him would be much reduced. Instead of continuing to secrete
himself in silence, he must give some evidence of his presence—not
out in the open where the goat was, certainly, but here in the
machan, so that he would have some chance; that is, he would half-
reveal himself. After that, if Kaliya did not come, he would have to
go find Kaliya. Unless he could lure this doubtful quarry by some
means, it was a mistake to remain stationary while it roved freely,
to choose at leisure—perhaps at the Ashram itself.

Peter had a rough, dark voice for singing, but he could chant a
mantra, and that he proceeded to do. When he had chanted a while,
he stopped to listen, for he could hear nothing while his skull was
vibrating. The syllables of the Vedic hymns tumbled forth like grand
supernatural personages, passed invisibly through the forest, with
a deliberate emphasis of wings, seeking though they had no need
to seek for themselves, being fulfilled, like a pageant of bodhisattvas.
The goat bleated with relief. Even though the moon was down, Pitar
was with him.

After some twenty minutes of chanting and listening in the dark,
Peter had about made up his mind to climb down from the *machan,*
when a slight noise froze him to his perch. It did not come again
at once, but stopped. Dry-throated, he listened for a while, then
risked more chanting—only a little, in a soft voice, but during it he
heard the noise again. This time he thought he could tell the direction of it, but he could not be sure; nor did he move as yet. Again
he chanted a few syllables, and again he heard the noise—a very
slight rustling. With relief now he knew that it was approaching
along the ground, not behind him through the branches, but roughly
in the direction of the animal trail along which he had come. It
was too dark down there for him to see. All at once he felt very
cold. The creature moved only while Peter was chanting, as if
fully aware that its approach would be less likely to be detected

then. A lesser python would not have to use its intelligence in this way; its weight being less, it could move more silently. This time Peter moved while he was chanting, aware that Kaliya would also be moving, and so would be less likely to notice the movement of the hunter whom he was hunting. Peter's gun was now pointed in the direction from which the thing was coming; but he was undecided whether to snap on his electric torch, for that would mean that he would have to fire almost instantly, before Kaliya struck. The torch would give the human quarry away. Yet there might be a tree or two between them, through which Kaliya could glide like a bolt of lightning, but through which Peter could not shoot. On the other hand, if he delayed, it might be too late. Kaliya, with real nocturnal vision, might have spotted him, might indeed be already reared silently twenty feet in the air, gathering himself to strike. . . . Peter steeled himself. Not yet! Wait for a sign, another noise, only a little noise to tell him that Kaliya had entered the clearing; then Peter would snap on the beam of the electric torch and fire— once, twice. Those shots had better be good. Not the swirling, massive coils, but the head, the steady head, mathematically directed toward him. . . .

Then it was in the clearing, close to the bait—the goat was bleating in a kind of ecstasy, as if recognizing its doom or deliverer; then softly, softly, as if it were yielding. Peter took aim, pressed the button on the electric torch—and nearly fell out of the tree. Standing there, outlined in the sights of his rifle, was Indira. Shielding her eyes from the glaring light, "Hello, Peter," she said mildly, and, laying down her rifle, with the muzzle in the dirt, began to untie the goat.

Furiously Peter slid down the tree and stood over her.

"Do you want to die?"

"Never!" she laughed softly, then cried out, because he had laid hands on her—rough only in their suddenness and only for a moment, for although she was quite tangible, she was not very big and she did not resist at all, and it was as if he had taken his own life in his hands.

"Forgive me," he muttered, and meant to let go of her, but his arms bent in spite of him, and he hugged her close as if she were indeed his life. "I will not let you go!"

"There is no need, then." And she held him also.

So deeply absorbed were they toward that Center, the same for Eros as for Art, Strife, and the Mystic, though variously apprehended, wherein pleasure and distress, security and peril are appreciable but secondary to the venture—that they might not have been aware immediately of Kaliya, had he entered the clearing at that moment and encircled them with his coils. The goat, however, tugged at its halter which Indira still held—although it had no intention of leaving her company—and bleated its sense of the awkwardness of their present circumstances.

"You shouldn't have come here," Peter said.

"I felt that I should."

"In the dark?"

"My torch went out, but I was already close—I heard you chanting the mantra. I heard the goat, too."

"Both were to attract Kaliya. I hope we failed." He snapped on his torch, picked up Indira's rifle, and led her quickly back along the trail toward the river. The goat pressed so closely behind her that it kept nudging her calves with its nose, as if urging her to move faster. At the edge of the jungle, where the sandy desolation of the river began, Indira stopped.

"I am not afraid," she said.

"Your post is at the Ashram."

"I knew why you were chanting, Peter, but your accent is not quite perfect in certain respects."

"What a time to tell me this!"

He reached for her hand, but she caught his fingers with the tips of hers, so that he could not pull her with him.

"Try to understand," she said. "Kaliya is very critical. Let us choose a suitable spot within the jungle, and I shall chant in the tradition of Guru Vikramaditya. That will make a difference. You will see."

"Absolutely not," said Peter.

"The resonance is like that of the flute. It has been proved—"

"No."

"You are selfish! If you die, what would I be?"

"Director of the Ashram—that is for you."

"It is for you, Peter! Without you I am not large enough—and you are determined to die! No?"

"I'm determined to live," said Peter, and he picked her up quickly, lightly, and carried her down to the river path. There he set her down. With his arm around her, he walked her toward the Ashram, kicking the too companionable goat, which now preceded them, at every other step. "Now listen," he said, "I want you to stay at the Ashram. Be on your guard, as I told you, because I don't know what might happen there. Maybe nothing, but don't take chances. To-morrow I'll be with you."

As she left, with the goat leaning against her like a cat, she turned on him a glance eloquent with love and forboding. He did not look in Jim Chen's direction as he returned toward the area where he believed he would find Kaliya or Kaliya would find him. Jim had let Indira get past him without a warning.

In the bungalow Lady Edith slept fitfully within the big square box of the mosquito curtain. At a window in the same room Irene sat keeping vigil—a post entrusted to her by Indira, who usually slept on a little wooden bed nearby in order to be on hand in case Lady Edith wanted anything during the night. Irene would not lie down on Indira's bed. The harsh electric lights shone in from the veranda. It was too hot to close the shutters. Deeply, gently, Mary Nayler snored in the next room. Tino's room was at the other end of the bungalow—he was under sedation as a result of the day's activities. . . . Irene got up and leaned out through the window to see if there was any cool air to be had. Just under the window, in the full glare of the lights, lay Gori Govinda asleep on a straw mat, wearing only a *gamcha*, orange-colored, loosely knotted about his waist. At the far end of the veranda two villagers squatted apathetically with Kukri knives beside them and waited for dawn, which was not very far off.

Indira had been sitting in a wicker chair on the veranda, from which she could see most of the Ashram grounds. From time to time, ludicrously carrying a gun that was almost as big as she was, she would walk out on the playground, survey the mango grove, then return after a few minutes to her post. Irene was glad she was gone now—she did not like to be guarded in this way, not by a woman, especially not by Indira. The two women embarrassed each other. Indira's native quickness of speech had given Irene the idea that she, Indira, needed to talk, and so Irene refrained from talking in order to give her the chance. Indira, finding Irene gauche and tongue-tied in her presence, always talked too volubly in a misguided attempt to balance matters. Also, Indira did not know that Irene required increasingly frequent pauses for reflection—not reflection, really; mulling, rather, the same things over and over, like Tibetan prayer beads, *om mani padme hum.* Yes, she would have to have help. Dr. Hoskins, perhaps. What a comedown that would be! Better to humble one's spirit before a graven image than before a human authority. Neither could give her what she needed in order to live; namely, life. . . . There was a second-best thing, of which Jim had reminded her—but killing herself had always been against her principles. Of course, she was always doing it in her mind nowadays, and perhaps, like that other thing Christ spoke of, it was as bad to think about it as to do it. . . . If death would only come as the result of a day's work well done! Probably one ought not to plan on it. Unless, of course, it were for someone else's benefit, and one refused on principle to be intimidated, and just went ahead and did what the situation required—without thought for one's own convenience. She would not wish it to be noted of her some day in the Friends Journal that unsatisfactory personal relations appeared to have determined her demise.

Something still more questionable might have been noted of her at this moment—something that both impeded the swift progress of her doom, and was at the same time more painful to think of than that doom: It was the hope of success—the possibility that she might yet "win" at the expense of others. The boy who lay there so innocently asleep—he was actually sucking his thumb, like a much younger child—had told Indira that Liliu Acquileia meant to kill her tonight. Of course, Indira had not believed it, had intimated to Irene, who was present, that the boy had an overheated

imagination as the result of certain experiences. Swayed by her confidence, Irene had not believed it either. Violence was so abhorrent
to her that she could scarcely credit anyone with wanting to initiate
it, especially someone with whom she was acquainted; but now,
during this dark night of the soul, wherein the self was python to
the self, she thought increasingly, even cunningly, of the death of
Indira. Yet it did not come into the dwindled foreground of her
consciousness until now, now that she saw the empty chair on the
veranda, and all around, the jungle, where death in many forms
—even the form of herself, Irene—could strike with impunity, according to its need, then give itself to life awhile, then to another
and greater death. . . . In her exhaustion she felt little emotion at
this submerged half-revelation of her depravity, except perhaps a
vague satisfaction in coming up against limits, in being able to
document the theoretical guilt which she had, up to now, maintained
largely as an act of faith.

Gori Govinda moved restlessly in his sleep, the loose *gamcha*
came untied and fell away from him, exposing him naked under
Irene's startled gaze. How hemmed in she was, like a somnambulist
surrounded by wonderful sleepers whom she must not awaken upon
pain of death! The boy lay gracefully half-turned on his back, one
arm flung out in a gesture of giving, the other extending down, the
slender fingers cupping his loins, as if they were the source of his
gifts. Where was the red fox, the venal and furtive one, the *Lust-
knabe*? On the sleeper's face was the look of the stone Krishna, of
the holy man, of the boy with the white flower. . . . Irene did not
turn away, but gazed on him long and earnestly, as at the secret of
the herons unfolded before her, that had only to be deciphered.

Had he seen her face at first, looking out of the window over him,
he might have been frightened back into the red-fox incarnation; but
what he saw upon waking was the reflection of his own sleeping
expression, that of a love-dream, which had passed into the face
of Irene. Kneeling beside him, she had stroked his cheek very lightly.
Quickly he covered his nakedness; but he continued to see himself
in her gentle face, so that he did not entirely awaken to the world
of traps and hares.

"Listen," Irene said to him in a very low voice, almost whispering,

"I have to go out now. Will you do something? Sit in here, in Lady Edith's room, in this chair. If she wants anything—water, perhaps —give it to her. Will you, please?"

"I—in there?" Wonderingly he gazed through the window at the white curtains that shrouded the woman he had helped to poison; but still attached, as in sleep, to the self revealed to him in Indira's dance, he knew what he must do. There was no irony in his temperament; he did not know what irony was. In his duty now was no contradiction but an acknowledgment and a rectification and a newness of spirit, smooth-flowing, endless, without a break. "I will come in," he said, "and I will give her water when she needs it, and while I watch, no one will disturb her—no one."

Irene walked out into the middle of the schoolground and stopped, awkward, as if many eyes were focused on her, awaiting the words of a soliloquy that she had forgotten. It was eerie, with all those lights in the surrounding buildings—how flimsy they looked against the solid darkness of the jungle! It was like a theater that has been suddenly abandoned by audience and actors because of some catastrophe not in the play itself. The unseen eyes were not awaiting her soliloquy, perhaps not even her action—crime or fumbling virtue or fall. . . . There she stood, not like herself but like another person, in the middle of nowhere, in an impermanent light, at no time at all, not knowing herself or exactly what she was going to do. How warm and moist it was, even now, in this early morning—or was it still evening? The light cotton dress she wore compromised her limbs with its clinging dampness. She would have liked to strip it off and swim in the river—forever.

Quickly she passed the boys' dormitory, where all the students were, boys and girls alike, and all the teachers. At this late-early hour they were listening to music—Tipperah flute and drums, very spirited, alternative, receptacle for other excitements. The girls' dormitory, some distance away, was brightly lighted; it was supposed to be empty, but Irene distinctly saw shadows moving there, through the wooden bars; then she remembered that Indira's study was in a corner of that building. With no clear purpose, she ran into the building toward the sound of voices, just audible over the music, and flung open a door.

The scene that confronted her made her turn at once to run away, but she could not. Two women were struggling physically in the most execrable taste! Liliu Acquileia, with the ecstatic look sometimes produced by hashish, was circling around Indira, trying to stab her with a knife. Indira was warding off the blows with Peter's portfolio containing the *Krishnayana,* which she held in both hands, using it as a shield. The big rifle lay on the floor.

"Get help!" Indira called, glancing desperately at Irene. "I cannot use this gun!"

Irene stood in the doorway, unable to move from the spot, so profound was her embarrassment. It was what she had come to see, what she had wanted to see, what she had even wanted to do! Profiting from Liliu's momentary distraction, Indira tried to rush past her to the doorway, but the Tibetan woman was too quick for her. The knife shot out. Indira fell, her head striking the edge of a desk with a final sound, and lay still. A dark purple stain began to spread on the blue sari.

The portfolio had fallen at Irene's feet. Automatically she crouched, picked it up, and suddenly raised it in a defense reflex. The knife glanced off the leather case instead of entering her body; only the sharp point passed across three fingers of her right hand, gashing them to the bone.

"God forgive us!" she cried, staring at the scandalous color she had kept hidden inside her. "Oh, God forgive us!" Now she was in Indira's place, fighting for her life, warding off the knife time after time with the portfolio. As she was taller than Indira, and had longer arms, she had rather better success in getting to the doorway. Just as she whirled to run, she saw, in the periphery of her vision, a slight movement from the girl on the floor. Liliu saw it too, and turned to finish the job, crouching over Indira. Almost at the same instant Irene sprang after her. "God forgive us!" she breathed, and brought the portfolio down hard on Liliu's head, spilling papers in all directions. Then her hands were in Liliu's hair, dragging her backward over the floor. The hand with the dagger flashed out blindly, wounding Irene on the forearm. Catlike, Liliu writhed free and jumped to her feet, her face distorted with hatred. With the knife out, she advanced upon Irene, crouching so low that she seemed like some kind of animal gathering itself to spring at the throat of its adversary.

All at once Irene grinned that square, mirthless grin—excessive now, going back beyond Bryn Mawr and Quakerdom and Christ, back to its origin, the baring of fangs. With a quick gesture she pulled off her "plain" walking shoe. As Liliu sprang at her, she threw it in her face, then pulled off the other shoe. Liliu staggered back, spitting. A shoe! A most beastly thing in the hands of one's enemy! A most unclean thing, an abomination that could scarcely be wiped out with blood, although she would try. If she died, she would take this mocking bitch with her, and the other one too!

As Liliu came at her again, Irene stepped back, turned and ran, clutching a shoe in her bloody hand; but in her confusion she went out the back way, along a shrub-lined path, away from the buildings. A plan half formed itself in her mind, to lead Liliu away from Indira. Perhaps Indira would be able to get help. And then Peter was in the jungle somewhere, and it was quiet there—he would hear her when she called. He would save her. . . .

It was nearly dawn. Irene could just make out the path that went along by the river toward the krishnachura tree. As she fled barefoot up this path, followed by Liliu, she felt wonderfully released, exhilarated by the courtship of external death. At last she was outside herself! Afraid of dying, yes, but almost coyly, as of a first kiss —afraid of *dying*, not of living! And there were all sorts of possibilities. She could outrun Liliu; she could hide from her in the jungle; she could even try swimming the river. Sooner or later she would find Peter or Peter would find her, or Jim Chen would. If she stopped, she might manage to get the knife away from Liliu. Perhaps she could reason with her, persuade her to abandon this dangerous game. Glancing back, she saw Liliu stop abruptly, the long, black hair streaming loose over her shoulders, the oil in it making it cling together in snaky strands. Then Liliu was going back—to finish off Indira!

Irene hesitated for a moment, then she called out, "Catch me if you can!" The noise of the river drowned her voice.

Desperately she ran after Liliu; then, after a few paces, she hurled the other shoe after her. Irene had always been able to throw a ball rather better than other girls, but she had never in her life tried to hit anyone, until a moment before, when she had thrown the first shoe in Liliu's face. She did not mean to hit her this time; had she thrown a dozen more times with the intention of hitting her, the chances were that subconscientious objections would have prevented her from being accurate. She meant only to attract Liliu's attention now. The shoe caught Liliu in the middle of the back.

With a cry of pain and rage, Liliu whirled around. There was no mistaking her resolve as she again went toward Irene, this time with measured steps, as if conserving her energy for a final struggle.

"Now you will die!" she muttered through clenched teeth—she looked both ugly and beautiful at that moment, like certain dangerous beasts.

"Catch me and you can kill me!" Irene called out almost gaily, and as the fear of death took hold of her, her lips parted again in that disdainful grin that so infuriated Liliu Acquileia. Again Irene ran up the trail toward the krishnachura tree, ran with that long-legged stride that soon outdistanced her pursuer.

It did not last long, that race for life. Irene was not in good condition, and she had lost blood. Her limbs grew heavier and heavier, as if she were running in a dream, swimming, flying, crawling, all at once. She was gasping for breath. In vain now she glanced about as she ran along the jungle edge. If there were stones here, the jungle had claimed them. Not even a stick—they all looked decomposed, or else they would be rooted, the way things were here. If she paused to make sure, and made a mistake, that would be the end, because Liliu was quite close.

It was light now, although the sun had not yet hurdled the mountain to shine down into the valley. Irene stopped where the trail ended between the river and the krishnachura tree. Her breath came in painful sobs; her side ached as if the knife had already entered. She could go no farther. If only she could get to the river, she would throw herself in and float away to some place downstream where she would be safe. Perhaps she could return to the Ashram that way. She turned in that direction, dragging her bruised feet, and saw her path cut off: Liliu had anticipated this move, and was coming toward her from the river, heading her off, leisurely, sure of herself; but now she was approaching cautiously, as if expecting Irene to show sudden strength and treachery at the end. Irene had no more strength, and no ideas except to plead with her attacker; but one look at Liliu's face convinced her that that would be worse than futile. She did not want to die this way—but this was the way it would be.

"Peter!" Her voice was so feeble, so like a little girl's voice, that Liliu's red lips writhed back in a mocking smile as she approached, prolonging the moment. Weakly Irene lifted her hands to ward off the blow. "'Our Father which art in Heaven,'" she whispered, shrinking back toward the krishnachura tree, "hallowed be Thy name. . . .'"

Liliu stopped, stood there like a bright, cruel bird in the dawn.

"'Thy kingdom come, Thy will be done. . . .'" Irene continued to move backward; but her enemy was not following. Liliu was gazing fixedly, not at Irene but beyond her, with an expression of abject terror. An inchoate cry burst from her throat, and she turned to run. Then Irene saw, behind her, what Liliu had seen.

Out of the grotto, above the pool, beyond the krishnachura tree, emerged a long and sinuous form, extending high into the air, above the plantain trees—a slenderness like the neck of a black swan, but endless, endless and vast. As it moved, the dawn light celebrated it with mines and harmonies of color, iridescences of pigeon's breast, and grace, endless grace. For a moment it hung there in the air, a listening, curving line, a tallness, a Presence summoned by a mudra-gesture of the smiling, dancing, Fluting One.

Swiftly the great Kaliya glided toward Irene. She neither moved nor cried out, but stood there to receive him, like a priestess in a trance. Majestic and beautiful, his head soaring along over his massive coils as serenely as an eagle flying down a river, he towered for a timeless moment over her, seeming to stay forever, but never pausing; then he was gone, and the vast river of him was gone, flowing past Irene without touching her, although he had been so close that she might have touched him.

With effortless ease he coasted down upon Liliu, forestalling her, turning this way and that as she made frantic efforts to run to the right or the left. How was it that he was so slow and yet so fast, and she so fast, yet so slow! So graceful, so measured, so leisurely was he, that it was like some courtly ritual or an ancient temple choreography, in which the movements were so inevitable that the consent of the victim surely had been obtained since the beginning of time. Liliu stood cornered on the promontory, her back to the torrent—perhaps she hoped for a last-minute rescue, or that Kaliya would not risk the water; but she paused, and in that pause, with deceptive speed, Kaliya was upon her. Lightly, tenderly, delicately as a lover he enveloped her. Within seconds she was hidden in those sparkling coils which tightened with her every breath, her every heartbeat. Subtly the body of the lover kept her upright as he had found her—otherwise she would have fallen. The knife struck once or twice at the coils, glanced off harmlessly; the arm holding it was pressed out straight, unable to bend. Slowly the knife dropped to the ground near the edge of the riverbank where it had been undermined by the torrent. The agonized face of Liliu Acquileia looked momentarily at Irene—the mouth parted in a cry for help, but no sound came. Closer and closer to her face came the gigantic face of Kaliya, with its perpetual, curling, stony smile.

Irene found herself approaching, although she did not know what she would do. There were no stones—only the knife which lay to one side of Them, and Liliu had been powerless with it. Helplessly Irene glanced about her as she went toward them, and found only a brittle, forked branch, about three feet long, that had fallen from the krishnachura tree. Liliu's face was no longer visible. The protruding arm hung limp over coils as thick as a man's waist. For a moment the regal head of the lover turned, and as he looked down upon Irene and her little forked stick, one might have imagined that there was tolerance in that formal, half-human smile; then, forgetting her in the rapture of the act, he gazed again upon his chosen one.

There was the loud explosion of a rifle fired at close range. Irene caught a glimpse of Peter preparing to fire again, of Indira behind him, of Jim rushing up. Then Kaliya's tail lashed out, carried her violently forward with him as he fell. The cliff crumbled under them. Irene fell free, slid down the embankment into the water, unresisting, clutching the forked stick. Kaliya disappeared with

Liliu still in his embrace, sinking slowly, gracefully into the torrent. For some time the great head, crowned with red, remained visible above the water, then it too sank, under the weight of the ceremonial wound Pitar had given it.

At first Irene fought to stay afloat, but the water pulled her down and over and over. Great rumbling stones bruised her body as she struck against them or they against her. Just before she went unconscious she became vaguely aware that something had her by the hair and was dragging her somewhere. With a peevish gesture she tried to push off the would-be rescuer; for she was about to enter a wonderful cavern at the heart of the world, where a smiling boy held up a flower that she had only to touch. . . .

Seven Tibetan coolie women squatted by the roadside in Tash-iling, smoking rolled-up bidi leaves. Their eyes, already popping with gossip, glistened as the sannyasi approached with his effort-less, dreamy walk, headed this time in the direction of the plains. A bit of yellow silk, like a lady's scarf, covered his shapely loins.

"Do you come from the valley, then?" they cried, crowding around him.

"Is there only one valley?" he replied with gentle irony. "I come from many places, my mothers."

"You know what we mean, Sannyasi! We have heard—we have heard of Liliu's death. Her horoscope did not say that she would be chosen by Kaliya, Sannyasi! How do you explain that, you who know everything?"

"Did I cast her horoscope upon the day of her birth?"

"We do not accuse you, Sannyasi—"

"Well, perhaps I did."

"No, no, you are too young, as young as she—younger! Forgive us!"

"You have committed no impieties, my mothers. I am indeed very young. Who, then, made her horoscope?"

"Some priest in Lhasa."

"Was it his dharma to work with the will of God or against the will of God?"

"With it, Sannyasi, with it!"

"Then would he cast a horoscope which would warn her of God's intentions so that she might escape?"

"No, Sannyasi," they sighed, fumbling uncomfortably with the
265

amulets containing their own horoscopes, "no, of course not. It was necessary to lie to her, because she had a will of her own, that one. God's will is very great. It must have been difficult to get Pitar away from her and give him to Indira-devi!"

"You may say so, my mothers."

"And the unhappy memsahib—how many children will the China-man give her? Is it true that she died in the river, and he brought her to life again? What of her soul, in that case? Must she always do his bidding?"

"Peace," said the sannyasi, and peace shone forth timelessly from his eyes as he held out the begging bowl.

"Do not leave just yet!"

"How can we leave each other, who have never met? How can we meet each other, who have never been parted since the beginning of time?"

They nodded their heads sagely, and proceeded to disregard his wisdom.

"Did Liliu die with much agony, Sannyasi?"

"No more than necessary."

"Where did she go then, Sannyasi? And is Kaliya really dead?"

"Both of them went down the river to Ganga Mata, thence to the Outer Ocean where all things are reconciled. Peace! All that which I know you also know. Nothing is withheld from you, save what you withhold from yourselves, that you may ask questions of me, and the Truth may become manifest upon the screen of illusion. Thus do you turn the Wheel of Life; thus do I turn it. Peace," he said, "the peace that is. May your burdens be lighter, even though it be by no more than the tiniest coins that will you drop into my begging bowl by way of salutation. . . . Peace!"